REMEMBRANCE OF THINGS PAST

" When to the sessions of sweet silent thought
I summon up remembrance of things past . . ."

VOLUME V

THE
GUERMANTES WAY

PART ONE

Marcel Proust's continuous novel *À la Recherche du Temps Perdu* (REMEMBRANCE OF THINGS PAST) was originally published in eight parts, the titles and dates of which were: I. *Du Côté de Chez Swann* (1913); II. *À l'Ombre des Jeunes Filles en Fleurs* (1918), awarded the Prix Goncourt in 1919; III. *Le Côté de Guermantes* I (1920); IV. *Le Côté de Guermantes* II, *Sodome et Gomorrhe* I (1921); V. *Sodome et Gomorrhe* II (1922); VI. *La Prisonnière* (1923); VII. *Albertine Disparue* (1925); VIII. *Le Temps Retrouvé* (1927).

Du Côté de Chez Swann has been published in English as SWANN'S WAY: *À l'Ombre des Jeunes Filles en Fleurs* as WITHIN A BUDDING GROVE: *Le Côté de Guermantes* as THE GUERMANTES WAY: *Sodome et Gomorrhe* as CITIES OF THE PLAIN: *La Prisonnière* as THE CAPTIVE: *Albertine Disparue* as THE SWEET CHEAT GONE: and *Le Temps Retrouvé* as TIME REGAINED. The first seven parts were translated by C. K. Scott Moncrieff; the eighth was first translated by Stephen Hudson but is now reissued in a new translation by Andreas Mayor.

In the present uniform edition the volumes are as follows:—

THE GUERMANTES AT THE THEATRE

MARCEL PROUST

THE
GUERMANTES WAY

PART ONE

Translated by
C. K. Scott Moncrieff

ILLUSTRATED BY
PHILIPPE JULLIAN

1978
CHATTO & WINDUS
LONDON

First published in English (cr. 8vo) 1925
First issued in the Phoenix Library 1930
First issued in the Uniform Edition
(12 vols.) 1941
Reprinted 1943, 1949, 1952
Illustrated Edition 1957
Reprinted 1960, 1966, 1971, 1972 and 1978

ISBN 0 7011 1056 2

Printed in Great Britain by
Redwood Burn Limited
Trowbridge, Esher

A

LÉON DAUDET

A l'auteur

du VOYAGE DE SHAKESPEARE,
du PARTAGE DE L'ENFANT,
de L'ASTRE NOIR,
de FANTOMES ET VIVANTS,
du MONDE DES IMAGES,
de tant de chefs-d'œuvre,
A l'incomparable ami

en témoignage
de reconnaissance et d'admiration

M. P.

To
MRS. H——,
on her Birthday

OBERON, *in the* ATHENIAN *glade,*
Reduced by deft TITANIA'S *power,*
Invented arts for NATURE'S *aid*
And from a snowflake shaped a flower:
NATURE, *to outdo him, wrought of human clay*
A fairy blossom, which we acclaim to-day.

HEBE, *to high* OLYMPUS *borne,*
Undoomed to death, by age uncurst,
XERES *and* PORTO, *night and morn,*
Let flow, to appease celestial thirst:
Ev'n so, untouched by years that envious pass
YOUTH *greets the guests to-night and fills the glass.*

HESIONE, *for monstrous feast,*
Against a rock was chained, to die;
Young HERCLES *came, he slew the beast,*
Nor won the award of chivalry:
E. S. P. H., *whom monsters hold in awe,*
Shield thee from injury, and enforce the law!

C. K. S. M.

CONTENTS

✳

The French text of Le Côté de Guermantes
being extremely inaccurate, every care has been
taken to correct it in the process of translation.
In three places in this volume the sequence of
paragraphs has been altered, as the reader may
discover by comparing the French and English
texts.

ILLUSTRATIONS

*

THE GUERMANTES WAY

CHAPTER ONE

THE twittering of the birds at daybreak sounded insipid to Françoise. Every word uttered by the maids upstairs made her jump; disturbed by all their running about, she kept asking herself what they could be doing. In other words, we had moved. Certainly the servants had made no less noise in the attics of our old home; but she knew them, she had made of their comings and goings familiar events. Now she faced even silence with a strained attention. And as our new neighbourhood appeared to be as quiet as the boulevard on to which we had hitherto looked had been noisy, the song (distinct at a distance, when it was still quite faint, like an orchestral *motif*) of a passer-by brought tears to the eyes of a Françoise in exile. And so if I had been tempted to laugh at her in her misery at having to leave a house in which she was " so well respected on all sides " and had packed her trunks with tears, according to the Use of Combray, declaring superior to all possible houses that which had been ours, on the other hand I, who found it as hard to assimilate new as I found it easy to abandon old conditions, I felt myself drawn towards our old servant when I saw that this installation of herself in a building where she had not received from the hall-porter, who did not yet know us, the marks of respect necessary to her moral wellbeing, had brought her positively to the verge of dissolution. She alone could understand what I was feeling ; certainly her young footman was not the person to do so ; for him, who was as unlike the Combray type as it was possible to conceive, packing up, moving, living in another district, were all like taking a holiday in which the novelty of one's surroundings gave one the same sense of refreshment as if one had actually travelled; he thought he was in the country ; and a cold in the head afforded him, as though he had been sitting in a draughty railway carriage, the delicious sensation of having seen the world ; at each fresh sneeze he rejoiced that he had found so smart a place, having always longed to be with people who travelled a lot. And so, without giving him a thought, I went straight to Françoise, who, in return for my having laughed at her tears over a removal which had left me cold, now shewed an icy indifference to my sorrow, but because she shared it. The "sensibility" claimed by neurotic people is matched by their egotism; they cannot abide the flaunting by others of the sufferings to which they pay an ever increasing attention in themselves. Françoise, who would not allow the least of her own ailments to pass unnoticed, if I were in pain would turn her head from me so that I should not have the satisfaction of seeing my sufferings pitied, or so much as observed. It was the same as soon as I tried to speak to her about our new house. Moreover, having been obliged, a day or two later, to return to the house we had just left, to retrieve some clothes which had been overlooked in our removal, while I, as a result of it, had still a "temperature", and like a boa constrictor that has just swallowed an ox felt myself painfully distended by the sight of a long trunk which my eyes had still to digest,

Françoise, with true feminine inconstancy, came back saying that she had really thought she would stifle on our old boulevard, it was so stuffy, that she had found it quite a day's journey to get there, that never had she seen such stairs, that she would not go back to live there for a king's ransom, not if you were to offer her millions—a pure hypothesis—and that everything (everything, that is to say, to do with the kitchen and " usual offices ") was much better fitted up in the new house. Which, it is high time now that the reader should be told—and told also that we had moved into it because my grandmother, not having been at all well (though we took care to keep this reason from her), was in need of better air—was a flat forming part of the Hôtel de Guermantes.

At the age when a Name, offering us an image of the unknowable which we have poured into its mould, while at the same moment it connotes for us also an existing place, forces us accordingly to identify one with the other to such a point that we set out to seek in a city for a soul which it cannot embody but which we have no longer the power to expel from the sound of its name, it is not only to towns and rivers that names give an individuality, as do allegorical paintings, it is not only the physical universe which they pattern with differences, people with marvels, there is the social universe also; and so every historic house, in town or country, has its lady or its fairy, as every forest has its spirit, as there is a nymph for every stream. Sometimes, hidden in the heart of its name, the fairy is transformed to suit the life of our imagination by which she lives; thus it was that the atmosphere in which Mme. de Guermantes existed in me, after having been for years no more than the shadow cast by a magic lantern slide or the light falling through a painted window, began to let its colours fade when quite other dreams impregnated it with the bubbling coolness of her flowing streams.

And yet the fairy must perish if we come in contact with the real person to whom her name corresponds, for that person the name then begins to reflect, and she has in her nothing of the fairy; the fairy may revive if we remove ourself from the person, but if we remain in her presence the fairy definitely dies and with her the name, as happened to the family of Lusignan, which was fated to become extinct on the day when the fairy Mélusine should disappear. Then the Name, beneath our successive " restorations " of which we may end by finding, as their original, the beautiful portrait of a strange lady whom we are never to meet, is nothing more than the mere photograph, for identification, to which we refer in order to decide whether we know, whether or not we ought to bow to a person who passes us in the street. But let a sensation from a bygone year—like those recording instruments which preserve the sound and the manner of the various artists who have sung or played into them— enable our memory to make us hear that name with the particular ring with which it then sounded in our ears, then, while the name itself has apparently not changed, we feel the distance that separates the dreams which at different times its same syllables have meant to us. For a moment, from the clear echo of its warbling in some distant spring, we can extract, as from the little tubes which we use in painting, the exact, forgotten, mysterious, fresh tint of the days which we had believed ourself to be recalling, when, like a bad painter, we were giving to the whole of our past, spread out on the same canvas, the tones, conventional and all alike, of our unprompted memory. Whereas on the contrary, each of the moments that composed it employed, for an original creation, in a matchless harmony, the colour of those days which we no longer know, and which, for that matter, will still suddenly enrapture me if by any chance the name "Guermantes", resuming for a moment, after all these years, the sound, so different from its sound to-day, which it had for me on the day of Mlle. Percepied's marriage, brings back to me that mauve—so delicate, almost too bright, too new —with which the billowy scarf of the young Duchess glowed, and, like two periwinkle flowers, growing beyond reach and blossoming now again, her two eyes, sunlit with an azure smile. And the name Guermantes of those days is also like one of those little balloons which have been filled with oxygen, or some such gas; when I come to explode it, to make it emit what it contains, I breathe the air of the Combray of that year, of that day, mingled with a fragrance of hawthorn blossom blown by the wind from the corner of the square, harbinger of rain, which now sent the sun packing, now let him spread himself over the red woollen carpet to the sacristy, steeping it in a bright geranium scarlet, with that, so to speak, Wagnerian harmony in its gaiety which makes the wedding service always impressive. But even apart from rare moments such as these, in which suddenly we feel the original entity quiver and resume its form, carve itself out of the syllables now soundless, dead; if, in the giddy rush of daily life, in which they serve only the most practical purposes, names have lost all their colour, like a prismatic top that spins too quickly and seems only grey, when, on the other hand, in our musings we reflect, we seek, so as to return to the past, to slacken, to suspend the perpetual motion by which we are borne along, gradually we see once more appear, side by side, but entirely distinct from one another, the tints which in the course of our existence have been successively presented to us by a single name.

What form was assumed in my mind by this name Guermantes when my first nurse—knowing no more, probably, than I know to-day in whose honour it had been composed—sang me to sleep with that old ditty, *Gloire à la Marquise de Guermantes*, or when, some years later, the veteran Maréchal de Guermantes, making my nursery-maid's bosom swell with pride, stopped in the Champs-Elysées to remark: "A fine child, that!" and gave me a chocolate drop from his comfit-box, I cannot, of course, now say. Those years of my earliest childhood are no longer a part of myself; they are external to me; I can learn nothing of them save—as we learn things that happened before we were born—from the accounts given me by other people. But more recently I find in the period of that name's occupation of me seven or eight different shapes which it has successively assumed; the earliest were the most beautiful; gradually my musings, forced by reality to abandon a position that was no longer tenable, established themselves anew in one slightly less advanced until they were obliged to retire still farther. And, with Mme. de Guermantes, was transformed simultaneously her dwelling, itself also the offspring of that name, fertilised from year to year by some word or other that came to my ears and modulated the tone of my musings; that dwelling of hers reflected them in its very stones, which had turned to mirrors, like the surface of a cloud or of a lake. A dungeon keep without mass, no more indeed than

6

a band of orange light from the summit of which the lord and his lady dealt out life and death to their vassals, had given place—right at the end of that "Guermantes way" along which, on so many summer afternoons, I retraced with my parents the course of the Vivonne—to that land of bubbling streams where the Duchess taught me to fish for trout and to know the names of the flowers whose red and purple clusters adorned the walls of the neighbouring gardens; then it had been the ancient heritage, famous in song and story, from which the proud race of Guermantes, like a carved and mellow tower that traverses the ages, had risen already over France when the sky was still empty at those points where, later, were to rise Notre Dame of Paris and Notre Dame of Chartres, when on the summit of the hill of Laon the nave of its cathedral had not yet been poised, like the Ark of the Deluge on the summit of Mount Ararat, crowded with Patriarchs and Judges anxiously leaning from its windows to see whether the wrath of God were yet appeased, carrying with it the types of the vegetation that was to multiply on the earth, brimming over with animals which have escaped even by the towers, where oxen grazing calmly upon the roof look down over the plains of Champagne; when the traveller who left Beauvais at the close of day did not yet see, following him and turning with his road, outspread against the gilded screen of the western sky, the black, ribbed wings of the cathedral. It was, this "Guermantes", like the scene of a novel, an imaginary landscape which I could with difficulty picture to myself and longed all the more to discover, set in the midst of real lands and roads which all of a sudden would become alive with heraldic details, within a few miles of a railway station; I recalled the names of the places round it as if they had been situated at the foot of Parnassus or of Helicon, and they seemed precious to me, as the physical conditions—in the realm of topographical science—required for the production of an unaccountable phenomenon. I saw again the escutcheons blazoned beneath the windows of Combray church; their quarters filled, century after century, with all the lordships which, by marriage or conquest, this illustrious house had brought flying to it from all the corners of Germany, Italy and France; vast territories in the North, strong cities in the South, assembled there to group themselves in Guermantes, and, losing their material quality, to inscribe allegorically their dungeon vert, or castle triple-towered argent upon its azure field. I had heard of the famous tapestries of Guermantes, I could see them, mediaeval and blue, a trifle coarse, detach themselves like a floating cloud from the legendary, amaranthine name at the foot of the ancient forest in which Childebert went so often hunting; and this delicate, mysterious background of their lands, this vista of the ages, it seemed to me that, as effectively as by journeying to see them, I might penetrate all their secrets simply by coming in contact for a moment in Paris with Mme. de Guermantes, the princess paramount of the place and lady of the lake, as if her face, her speech must possess the local charm of forest groves and streams, and the same secular peculiarities as the old customs recorded in her archives. But then I had met Saint-Loup; he had told me that the castle had borne the name of Guermantes only since the seventeenth century, when that family had acquired it. They had lived, until then, in the neighbourhood, but their title was not taken from

8

those parts. The village of Guermantes had received its name from the castle round which it had been built, and so that it should not destroy the view from the castle, a servitude, still in force, traced the line of its streets and limited the height of its houses. As for the tapestries, they were by Boucher, bought in the nineteenth century by a Guermantes with a taste for the arts, and hung, interspersed with a number of sporting pictures of no merit which he himself had painted, in a hideous drawing-room upholstered in " adrianople " and plush. By these revelations Saint-Loup had introduced into the castle ele-ments foreign to the name of Guermantes which made it impossible for me to continue to extract solely from the resonance of the syllables the stone and mortar of its walls. And so, in the heart of the name, was effaced the castle mirrored in its lake, and what now became apparent to me, surrounding Mme. de Guermantes as her dwelling, had been her house in Paris, the Hôtel de Guermantes, limpid like its name, for no material and opaque element intervened to interrupt and blind its transparence. As the word church signifies not only the temple but the assembly of the faithful also, this Hôtel de Guermantes comprised all those who shared the life of the Duchess, but these intimates on whom I had never set eyes were for me only famous and poetic names, and knowing exclusively per-sons who themselves also were names only, did but en-hance and protect the mystery of the Duchess by extend-ing all round her a vast halo which at the most declined in brilliance as its circumference increased.

In the parties which she gave, since I could not imagine the guests as having any bodies, any moustaches, any boots, as making any utterances that were commonplace, or even original in a human and rational way, this whirl-pool of names, introducing less material substance than would a phantom banquet or a spectral ball, round that statuette in Dresden china which was Madame de Guermantes, kept for her palace of glass the transparence of a showcase. Then, after Saint-Loup had told me various anecdotes about his cousin's chaplain, her gardener, and the rest, the Hôtel de Guermantes had become—as the Louvre might have been in days gone by—a kind of castle, surrounded, in the very heart of Paris, by its own domains, acquired by inheritance, by virtue of an ancient right that had quaintly survived, over which she still enjoyed feudal privileges. But this last dwelling itself vanished when we had come to live beside Mme. de Villeparisis in one of the flats adjoining that occupied by Mme. de Guermantes in a wing of the Hôtel. It was one of those old town houses, a few of which are perhaps still to be found, in which the court of honour—whether they were alluvial deposits washed there by the rising tide of democracy, or a legacy from a more primitive time when the different trades were clustered round the overlord—is flanked by little shops and workrooms, a shoemaker's, for instance, or a tailor's, such as we see nestling between the buttresses of those cathedrals which the aesthetic zeal of the restorer has not swept clear of such accretions; a porter who also does cobbling, keeps hens, grows flowers, and, at the far end, in the main building, a " Comtesse " who, when she drives out in her old carriage and pair, flaunting on her hat a few nasturtiums which seem to have escaped from the plot by the porter's lodge (with, by the coachman's side on the box, a footman who gets down to leave cards at every aristocratic mansion in the neighbourhood), scat-

ters vague little smiles and waves her hand in greeting
to the porter's children and to such of her respectable
fellow-tenants as may happen to be passing, who, to her
contemptuous affability and levelling pride, seem all the
same.

In the house in which we had now come to live, the
great lady at the end of the courtyard was a Duchess,
smart and still quite young. She was, in fact, Mme. de
Guermantes and, thanks to Françoise, I soon came to
know all about her household. For the Guermantes (to
whom Françoise regularly alluded as the people " below ",
or "downstairs") were her constant preoccupation from
the first thing in the morning when, as she did Mamma's
hair, casting a forbidden, irresistible, furtive glance down
into the courtyard, she would say: "Look at that, now;
a pair of holy Sisters; that'll be for downstairs, surely; "
or, "Oh! just look at the fine pheasants in the kitchen
window; no need to ask where they came from, the
Duke will have been out with his gun!"—until the last
thing at night when, if her ear, while she was putting out
my night-things, caught a few notes of a song, she would
conclude: "They're having company down below; gay
doings, I'll be bound; " whereupon, in her symmetrical
face, beneath the arch of her now snow-white hair, a
smile from her young days, sprightly but proper, would
for a moment set each of her features in its place, arranging them in an intricate and special order, as though for
a country-dance.

But the moment in the life of the Guermantes which
excited the keenest interest in Françoise, gave her the
most complete satisfaction and at the same time the
sharpest annoyance was that at which, the two halves of

the great gate having been thrust apart, the Duchess stepped into her carriage. It was generally a little while after our servants had finished the celebration of that sort of solemn passover which none might disturb, called their midday dinner, during which they were so far taboo that my father himself was not allowed to ring for them, knowing moreover that none of them would have paid any more attention to the fifth peal than to the first, and that the discourtesy would therefore have been a pure waste of time and trouble, though not without trouble in store for himself. For Françoise (who, in her old age, lost no opportunity of standing upon her dignity) would without fail have presented him, for the rest of the day, with a face covered with the tiny red cuneiform hieroglyphs by which she made visible—though by no means legible—to the outer world the long tale of her griefs and the profound reasons for her dissatisfactions. She would enlarge upon them, too, in a running "aside", but not so that we could catch her words. She called this practice—which, she imagined, must be infuriating, "mortifying" as she herself put it, "vexing" to us—"saying low masses all the blessed day."

The last rites accomplished, Françoise, who was at one and the same time, as in the primitive church, the celebrant and one of the faithful, helped herself to a final glass, undid the napkin from her throat, folded it after wiping from her lips a stain of watered wine and coffee, slipped it into its ring, turned a doleful eye to thank " her " young footman who, to shew his zeal in her service, was saying: "Come, ma'am, a drop more of the grape; it's d'licious to-day," and went straight across to the window, which she flung open, protesting that it was too hot to breathe in "this wretched kitchen". Dexterously casting, as she turned the latch and let in the fresh air, a glance of studied indifference into the courtyard below, she furtively elicited the conclusion that the Duchess was not ready yet to start, brooded for a moment with contemptuous, impassioned eyes over the waiting carriage, and, this meed of attention once paid to the things of the earth, raised them towards the heavens, whose purity she had already divined from the sweetness of the air and the warmth of the sun; and let them rest on a corner of the roof, at the place where, every spring, there came and built, immediately over the chimney of my bedroom, a pair of pigeons like those she used to hear cooing from her kitchen at Combray.

"Ah! Combray, Combray!" she cried. And the almost singing tone in which she declaimed this invocation might, taken with the Arlesian purity of her features, have made the onlooker suspect her of a Southern origin and that the lost land which she was lamenting was no more, really, than a land of adoption. If so, he would have been wrong, for it seems that there is no province that has not its own South-country; do we not indeed constantly meet Savoyards and Bretons in whose speech we find all those pleasing transpositions of longs and shorts that are characteristic of the Southerner? "Ah, Combray, when shall I look on thee again, poor land! When shall I pass the blessed day among thy hawthorns, under our own poor lily-oaks, hearing the grasshoppers sing, and the Vivonne making a little noise like someone whispering, instead of that wretched bell from our young master, who can never stay still for half an hour on end without having me run the length of that wicked corridor. And even then he

makes out I don't come quick enough; you'ld need to
hear the bell ring before he has pulled it, and if you're a
minute late, away he flies into the most towering rage.
Alas, poor Combray; maybe I shall see thee only in death,
when they drop me like a stone into the hollow of the
tomb. And so, nevermore shall I smell thy lovely hawthorns, so white and all. But in the sleep of death I dare
say I shall still hear those three peals of the bell which
will have driven me to damnation in this world."

Her soliloquy was interrupted by the voice of the waistcoat-maker downstairs, the same who had so delighted
my grandmother once, long ago, when she had gone to
pay a call on Mme. de Villeparisis, and now occupied no
less exalted a place in Françoise's affections. Having raised
his head when he heard our window open, he had already
been trying for some time to attract his neighbour's attention, in order to bid her good day. The coquetry of the
young girl that Françoise had once been softened and
refined for M. Jupien the querulous face of our old cook,
dulled by age, ill-temper and the heat of the kitchen fire,
and it was with a charming blend of reserve, familiarity
and modesty that she bestowed a gracious salutation on
the waistcoat-maker, but without making any audible response, for if she did infringe Mamma's orders by looking into the courtyard, she would never have dared to go
the length of talking from the window, which would have
been quite enough (according to her) to bring down on
her " a whole chapter " from the Mistress. She pointed
to the waiting carriage, as who should say: " A fine pair,
eh! " though what she actually muttered was: " What
an old rattle-trap! " but principally because she knew
that he would be bound to answer, putting his hand

to his lips so as to be audible without having to shout:
" *You* could have one too if you liked, as good as they
have and better, I dare say, only you don't care for that
sort of thing."

And Françoise, after a modest, evasive signal of delight,
the meaning of which was, more or less: " Tastes differ,
you know; simplicity's the rule in this house," shut the
window again in case Mamma should come in. These
" you " who might have had more horses than the Guermantes were ourselves, but Jupien was right in saying
" you " since, except for a few purely personal gratifi-
cations, such as, when she coughed all day long without
ceasing and everyone in the house was afraid of catching
her cold, that of pretending, with an irritating little titter,
that she had not got a cold, like those plants that an
animal to which they are wholly attached keeps alive with
food which it catches, eats and digests for them and of
which it offers them the ultimate and easily assimilable
residue, Françoise lived with us in full community; it
was we who, with our virtues, our wealth, our style of
living, must take on ourselves the task of concocting
those little sops to her vanity out of which was formed
—with the addition of the recognised rights of freely practising the cult of the midday dinner according to the traditional custom, which included a mouthful of air at the
window when the meal was finished, a certain amount of
loitering in the street when she went out to do her market-
ing, and a holiday on Sundays when she paid a visit to
her niece—the portion of happiness indispensable to her
existence. And so it can be understood that Françoise
might well have succumbed in those first days of our
migration, a victim, in a house where my father's claims

to distinction were not yet known, to a malady which she herself called "wearying", wearying in the active sense in which the word *ennui* is employed by Corneille, or in the last letters of soldiers who end by taking their own lives because they are wearying for their girls or for their native villages. Françoise's wearying had soon been cured by none other than Jupien, for he at once procured her a pleasure no less keen, indeed more refined than she would have felt if we had decided to keep a carriage. "Very good class, those Juliens," (for Françoise readily assimilated new names to those with which she was already familiar) "very worthy people; you can see it written on their faces." Jupien was in fact able to understand, and to inform the world that if we did not keep a carriage it was because we had no wish for one. This new friend of Françoise was very little at home, having obtained a post in one of the Government offices. A waistcoat-maker first of all, with the "chit of a girl" whom my grandmother had taken for his daughter, he had lost all interest in the exercise of that calling after his assistant (who, when still little more than a child, had shewn great skill in darning a torn skirt, that day when my grandmother had gone to call on Mme. de Villeparisis) had turned to ladies' fashions and become a seamstress. A prentice hand, to begin with, in a dressmaker's workroom, set to stitch a seam, to fasten a flounce, to sew on a button or to press a crease, to fix a waistband with hooks and eyes, she had quickly risen to be second and then chief assistant, and having formed a connexion of her own among ladies of fashion now worked at home, that is to say in our courtyard, generally with one or two of her young friends from the workroom, whom she had taken on as apprentices. After this, Jupien's presence in the place had ceased to matter. No doubt the little girl (a big girl by this time) had often to cut out waistcoats still. But with her friends to assist her she needed no one besides. And so Jupien, her uncle, had sought employment outside. He was free at first to return home at midday, then, when he had definitely succeeded the man whose substitute only he had begun by being, not before dinner-time. His appointment to the "regular establishment" was, fortunately, not announced until some weeks after our arrival, so that his courtesy could be brought to bear on her long enough to help Françoise to pass through the first, most difficult phase without undue suffering. At the same time, and without underrating his value to Françoise as, so to speak, a sedative during the period of transition, I am bound to say that my first impression of Jupien had been far from favourable. At a little distance, entirely ruining the effect that his plump cheeks and vivid colouring would otherwise have produced, his eyes, brimming with a compassionate, mournful, dreamy gaze, led one to suppose that he was seriously ill or had just suffered a great bereavement. Not only was he nothing of the sort, but as soon as he opened his mouth (and his speech, by the way, was perfect) he was quite markedly cynical and cold. There resulted from this discord between eyes and lips a certain falsity which was not attractive, and by which he had himself the air of being made as uncomfortable as a guest who arrives in morning dress at a party where everyone else is in evening dress, or as a commoner who having to speak to a Royal Personage does not know exactly how he ought to address him and gets round the difficulty by cutting down his remarks to almost nothing.

Jupien's (here the comparison ends) were, on the contrary, charming. Indeed, corresponding possibly to this overflowing of his face by his eyes (which one ceased to notice when one came to know him), I soon discerned in him a rare intellect, and one of the most spontaneously literary that it has been my privilege to come across, in the sense that, probably without education, he possessed or had assimilated, with the help only of a few books skimmed in early life, the most ingenious turns of speech. The most gifted people that I had known had died young. And so I was convinced that Jupien's life would soon be cut short. Kindness was among his qualities, and pity, the most delicate and the most generous feelings for others. But his part in the life of Françoise had soon ceased to be indispensable. She had learned to put up with understudies.

Indeed, when a tradesman or servant came to our door with a parcel or message, while seeming to pay no attention and merely pointing vaguely to an empty chair, Françoise so skilfully put to the best advantage the few seconds that he spent in the kitchen, while he waited for Mamma's answer, that it was very seldom that the stranger went away without having ineradicably engraved upon his memory the conviction that, if we " did not have " any particular thing, it was because we had " no wish " for it. If she made such a point of other people's knowing that we " had money " (for she knew nothing of what Saint-Loup used to call partitive articles, and said simply " have money ", " fetch water "), of their realising that we were rich, it was not because riches with nothing else besides, riches without virtue, were in her eyes the supreme good in life; but virtue without riches was not her ideal either.

Riches were for her, so to speak, a necessary condition of virtue, failing which virtue itself would lack both merit and charm. She distinguished so little between them that she had come in time to invest each with the other's attributes, to expect some material comfort from virtue, to discover something edifying in riches.

As soon as she had shut the window again, which she did quickly—otherwise Mamma would, it appeared, have heaped on her " every conceivable insult "—Françoise began with many groans and sighs to put straight the kitchen table.

" There are some Guermantes who stay in the Rue de la Chaise," began my father's valet; " I had a friend who used to be with them; he was their second coachman. And I know a fellow, not my old pal, but his brother-in-law, who did his time in the Army with one of the Baron de Guermantes's stud grooms. Does your mother know you're out? " added the valet, who was in the habit, just as he used to hum the popular airs of the season, of peppering his conversation with all the latest witticisms. Françoise, with the tired eyes of an ageing woman, eyes which moreover saw everything from Combray, in a hazy distance, made out not the witticism that underlay the words, but that there must be something witty in them since they bore no relation to the rest of his speech and had been uttered with considerable emphasis by one whom she knew to be a joker. She smiled at him, therefore, with an air of benevolent bewilderment, as who should say: "Always the same, that Victor!" And she was genuinely pleased, knowing that listening to smart sayings of this sort was akin—if remotely—to those reputable social pleasures for which, in every class of society, people make haste to dress themselves in their best and run the risk of catching cold. Furthermore, she believed the valet to be a friend after her own heart, for he never left off denouncing, with fierce indignation, the appalling measures which the Republic was about to enforce against the clergy. Françoise had not yet learned that our cruellest adversaries are not those who contradict and try to convince us, but those who magnify or invent reports which may make us unhappy, taking care not to include any appearance of justification, which might lessen our discomfort, and perhaps give us some slight regard for a party which they make a point of displaying to us, to complete our torment, as being at once terrible and triumphant.

" The Duchess must be connected with all that lot," said Françoise, bringing the conversation back to the Guermantes of the Rue de la Chaise, as one plays a piece over again from the andante. "I can't recall who it was told me that one of them had married a cousin of the Duke. It's the same kindred, anyway. Ay, they're a great family, the Guermantes! " she added, in a tone of respect, founding the greatness of the family at once on the number of its branches and the brilliance of its connexions, as Pascal founds the truth of Religion on Reason and on the Authority of the Scriptures. For since there was but the single word " great " to express both meanings, it seemed to her that they formed a single idea, her vocabulary, like cut stones sometimes, shewing thus on certain of its facets a flaw which projected a ray of darkness into the recesses of her mind. " I wonder now if it wouldn't be them that have their castle at Guermantes, not a score of miles from Combray; then they must be kin to their

cousin at Algiers, too." My mother and I long asked ourselves who this cousin at Algiers could be until finally we
discovered that Françoise meant by the name "Algiers"
the town of Angers. What is far off may be more familiar
to us than what is quite near. Françoise, who knew the
name "Algiers" from some particularly unpleasant dates
that used to be given us at the New Year, had never heard
of Angers. Her language, like the French language itself,
and especially that of place-names, was thickly strewn
with errors. "I meant to talk to their butler about it.
What is it again you call him?" she interrupted herself
as though putting a formal question as to the correct procedure, which she went on to answer with: "Oh, of
course, it's Antoine you call him!" as though Antoine had
been a title. "He's the one who could tell me, but he's
quite the gentleman, he is, a great scholar, you'ld say
they'd cut his tongue out, or that he'd forgotten to learn
to speak. He makes no response when you talk to him,"
went on Françoise, who used "make response" in the
same sense as Mme. de Sévigné. "But," she added, quite
untruthfully, "so long as I know what's boiling in my
pot, I don't bother my head about what's in other people's.
Whatever he is, he's not a Catholic. Besides, he's not a
courageous man." (This criticism might have led one to
suppose that Françoise had changed her mind about physical bravery which, according to her, in Combray days,
lowered men to the level of wild beasts. But it was not
so. "Courageous" meant simply a hard worker.) "They
do say, too, that he's thievish as a magpie, but it doesn't
do to believe all one hears. The servants never stay long
there because of the lodge; the porters are jealous and
set the Duchess against them. But it's safe to say that

he's a real twister, that Antoine, and his Antoinesse is no better," concluded Françoise, who, in furnishing the name " Antoine " with a feminine ending that would designate the butler's wife, was inspired, no doubt, in her act of word-formation by an unconscious memory of the words *chanoine* and *chanoinesse*. If so, she was not far wrong. There is still a street near Notre-Dame called Rue Chanoinesse, a name which must have been given to it (since it was never inhabited by any but male Canons) by those Frenchmen of olden days of whom Françoise was, properly speaking, the contemporary. She proceeded, moreover, at once to furnish another example of this way of forming feminine endings, for she went on: " But one thing sure and certain is that it's the Duchess that has Guermantes Castle. And it's she that is the Lady Mayoress down in those parts. That's always something."

" I can well believe that it is something," came with conviction from the footman, who had not detected the irony.

" You think so, do you, my boy, you think it's something? Why, for folk like them to be Mayor and Mayoress, it's just thank you for nothing. Ah, if it was mine, that Guermantes Castle, you wouldn't see me setting foot in Paris, I can tell you. I'm sure a family who've got something to go on with, like Monsieur and Madame here, must have queer ideas to stay on in this wretched town rather than get away down to Combray the moment they're free to start, and no one hindering them. Why do they put off retiring? They've got everything they want. Why wait till they're dead? Ah, if I had only a crust of dry bread to eat and a faggot to keep me warm in winter, a fine time I'ld have of it at home in my brother's poor old house at Combray. Down there you do feel you're

alive; you haven't all these houses stuck up in front of
you, there is so little noise at night-time, you can hear the
frogs singing five miles off and more."

"That must indeed be fine!" exclaimed the young footman with enthusiasm, as though this last attraction had
been as peculiar to Combray as the gondola is to Venice.
A more recent arrival in the household than my father's
valet, he used to talk to Françoise about things which
might interest not himself so much as her. And Françoise, whose face wrinkled up in disgust when she was
treated as a mere cook, had for the young footman, who
referred to her always as the " housekeeper ", that peculiar tenderness which Princes not of the blood royal
feel towards the well-meaning young men who dignify
them with a " Highness ".

" At any rate one knows what one's about, there, and
what time of year it is. It isn't like here where you won't
find one wretched buttercup flowering at holy Easter any
more than you would at Christmas, and I can't hear so
much as the tiniest angelus ring when I lift my old bones
out of bed in the morning. Down there, you can hear
every hour; there's only the one poor bell, but you say
to yourself: ' My brother will be coming in from the field
now,' and you watch the daylight fade, and the bell rings
to bless the fruits of the earth, and you have time to take
a turn before you light the lamp. But here it's day time
and it's night time, and you go to bed, and you can't say
any more than the dumb beasts what you've been about
all day."

" I gather Méséglise is a fine place, too, Madame,"
broke in the young footman, who found that the conversation was becoming a little too abstract for his liking,

and happened to remember having heard us, at table, mention Méséglise.

"Oh! Méséglise, is it?" said Françoise with the broad smile which one could always bring to her lips by uttering any of those names—Méséglise, Combray, Tansonville. They were so intimate a part of her life that she felt, on meeting them outside it, on hearing them uséd in conversation, a hilarity more or less akin to that which a professor excites in his class by making an allusion to some contemporary personage whose name the students had never supposed could possibly greet their ears from the height of the academic chair. Her pleasure arose also from the feeling that these places were something to her which they were not for the rest of the world, old companions with whom one has shared many delights; and she smiled at them as if she found in them something witty, because she did find there a great part of herself.

"Yes, you may well say so, son, it is a pretty enough place is Méséglise;" she went on with a tinkling laugh, "but how did you ever come to hear tell of Méséglise?"

"How did I hear of Méséglise? But it's a well-known place; people have told me about it—yes, over and over again," he assured her with that criminal inexactitude of the informer who, whenever we attempt to form an impartial estimate of the importance that a thing which matters to us may have for other people, makes it impossible for us to succeed.

"I can tell you, it's better down there, under the cherry trees, than standing before the fire all day."

She spoke to them even of Eulalie as a good person. For since Eulalie's death Françoise had completely forgotten that she had loved her as little in her life time

as she loved every one whose cupboard was bare, who
was dying of hunger, and after that came, like a good
for nothing, thanks to the bounty of the rich, to " put
on airs ". It no longer pained her that Eulalie had so
skilfully managed, Sunday after Sunday, to secure her
" trifle " from my aunt. As for the latter, Françoise never
left off singing her praises.

" But it was at Combray, surely, that you used to be,
with a cousin of Madame? " asked the young footman.

" Yes, with Mme. Octave—oh, a dear, good, holy
woman, my poor friends, and a house where there was
always enough and to spare, and all of the very best, a
good woman, you may well say, who had no pity on the
partridges, or the pheasants, or anything; you might turn
up five to dinner or six, it was never the meat that
was lacking, and of the first quality too, and white wine,
and red wine, and everything you could wish." (Françoise
used the word " pity " in the sense given it by La
Bruyère.) " It was she that paid the damages, always,
even if the family stayed for months and years." (This
reflexion was not really a slur upon us, for Françoise belonged to an epoch when the word " damages " was not
restricted to a legal use and meant simply expense.) " Ah,
I can tell you, people didn't go empty away from that
house. As his reverence the Curé has told us, many's the
time, if there ever was a woman who could count on going
straight before the Throne of God, it was she. Poor
Madame, I can hear her saying now, in the little voice she
had: ' You know, Françoise, I can eat nothing myself,
but I want it all to be just as nice for the others as if I
could.' They weren't for her, the victuals, you may be
quite sure. If you'd only seen her, she weighed no more

than a bag of cherries; there wasn't that much of her. She would never listen to a word I said, she would never send for the doctor. Ah, it wasn't in that house that you'ld have to gobble down your dinner. She liked her servants to be fed properly. Here, it's been just the same again to-day; we haven't had time for so much as to break a crust of bread; everything goes like ducks and drakes."

What annoyed her more than anything were the rusks of pulled bread that my father used to eat. She was convinced that he had them simply to give himself airs and to keep her "dancing". "I can tell you frankly," the young footman assured her, "that I never saw the like." He said it as if he had seen everything, and as if in him the range of a millennial experience extended over all countries and their customs, among which was not anywhere to be found a custom of eating pulled bread. "Yes, yes," the butler muttered, "but that will all be changed; the men are going on strike in Canada, and the Minister told Monsieur the other evening that he's clearing two hundred thousand francs out of it." There was no note of censure in his tone, not that he was not himself entirely honest, but since he regarded all politicians as unsound the crime of peculation seemed to him less serious than the pettiest larceny. He did not even stop to ask himself whether he had heard this historic utterance aright, and was not struck by the improbability that such a thing would have been admitted by the guilty party himself to my father without my father's immediately turning him out of the house. But the philosophy of Combray made it impossible for Françoise to expect that the strikes in Canada could have any repercussion on the use of pulled bread. " So long as the world goes round, look, there'll be masters to keep us on the trot, and servants to do their bidding." In disproof of this theory of perpetual motion, for the last quarter of an hour my mother (who probably did not employ the same measures of time as Françoise in reckoning the duration of the latter's dinner) had been saying:

" What on earth can they be doing? They've been at least two hours at their dinner."

And she rang timidly three or four times. Françoise, " her " footman, the butler heard the bell ring, not as a summons to themselves, and with no thought of answering it, but rather like the first sounds of the instruments being tuned when the next part of a concert is just going to begin, and one knows that there will be only a few minutes more of interval. And so, when the peals were repeated and became more urgent, our servants began to pay attention, and, judging that they had not much time left and that the resumption of work was at hand, at a peal somewhat louder than the rest gave a collective sigh and went their several ways, the footman slipping downstairs to smoke a cigarette outside the door, Françoise, after a string of reflexions on ourselves, such as: " They've got the jumps to-day, surely," going up to put her things tidy in her attic, while the butler, having supplied himself first with note-paper from my bedroom, polished off the arrears of his private correspondence.

Despite the apparent stiffness of their butler, Françoise had been in a position, from the first, to inform me that the Guermantes occupied their mansion by virtue not of an immemorial right but of a quite recent tenancy, and that the garden over which it looked on the side that I did not know was quite small and just like all the gardens along the street; and I realised at length that there were not to be seen there pit and gallows or fortified mill, secret chamber, pillared dovecot, manorial bakehouse or tithe-barn, dungeon or drawbridge, or fixed bridge either for that matter, any more than toll-houses or pinnacles, charters, muniments, ramparts or commemorative mounds. But just as Elstir, when the bay of Balbec, losing its mystery, had become for me simply a portion, interchangeable with any other, of the total quantity of salt water distributed over the earth's surface, had suddenly restored to it a personality of its own by telling me that it was the gulf of opal painted by Whistler in his " Harmonies in Blue and Silver ", so the name Guermantes had seen perish under the strokes of Françoise's hammer the last of the dwellings that had issued from its syllables when one day an old friend of my father said to us, speaking of the Duchess: " She is the first lady in the Faubourg Saint-Germain; hers is the leading house in the Faubourg Saint-German." No doubt the most exclusive drawing-room, the leading house in the Faubourg Saint-Germain was little or nothing after all those other mansions of which in turn I had dreamed. And yet in this one too, (and it was to be the last of the series) there was something, however humble, quite apart from its material components, a secret differentiation.

And it became all the more essential that I should be able to explore in the drawing-room of Mme. de Guermantes, among her friends, the mystery of her name, since I did not find it in her person when I saw her leave the house in the morning on foot, or in the afternoon in her carriage. Once before, indeed, in the church at Combray, she had appeared to me in the blinding flash of a transfiguration, with cheeks irreducible to, impenetrable by the colour of the name Guermantes and of afternoons on the banks of the Vivonne, taking the place of my shattered dream like a swan or willow into which has been changed a god or nymph, and which henceforward, subjected to natural laws, will glide over the water or be shaken by the wind. And yet, when that radiance had vanished, hardly had I lost sight of it before it formed itself again, like the green and rosy afterglow of sunset after the sweep of the oar that has broken it, and in the solitude of my thoughts the name had quickly appropriated to itself my impression of the face. But now, frequently, I saw her at her window, in the courtyard, in the street, and for myself at least if I did not succeed in integrating in her the name Guermantes, I cast the blame on the impotence of my mind to accomplish the whole act that I demanded of it; but she, our neighbour, she seemed to make the same error, nay more to make it without discomfiture, without any of my scruples, without even suspecting that it was an error. Thus Mme. de Guermantes shewed in her dresses the same anxiety to follow the fashions as if, believing herself to have become simply a woman like all the rest, she had aspired to that elegance in her attire in which other ordinary women might equal and perhaps surpass her; I had seen her in the street gaze admiringly at a well-dressed actress; and in the morning, before she sallied forth on foot, as if the opinion of the passers-by, whose vulgarity she accentuated by parading familiarly through their midst her inaccessible life, could be a tribunal competent to judge her, I would see her before the glass playing, with a conviction free from all pretence or irony, with passion, with ill-humour, with conceit, like a queen who has consented to appear as a servant-girl in theatricals at court, this part, so unworthy of her, of a fashionable woman; and in this mythological oblivion of her natural grandeur, she looked to see whether her veil was hanging properly, smoothed her cuffs, straightened her cloak, as the celestial swan performs all the movements natural to his animal species, keeps his eyes painted on either side of his beak without putting into them any glint of life, and darts suddenly after a bud or an umbrella, as a swan would, without remembering that he is a god. But as the traveller, disappointed by the first appearance of a strange town, reminds himself that he will doubtless succeed in penetrating its charm if he visits its museums and galleries, so I assured myself that, had I been given the right of entry into Mme. de Guermantes's house, were I one of her friends, were I to penetrate into her life, I should then know what, within its glowing orange-tawny envelope, her name did really, objectively enclose for other people, since, after all, my father's friend had said that the Guermantes set was something quite by itself in the Faubourg Saint-Germain.

The life which I supposed them to lead there flowed from a source so different from anything in my experience, and must, I felt, be so indissolubly associated with that particular house that I could not have imagined the presence, at the Duchess's parties, of people in whose company I myself had already been, of people who really existed. For not being able suddenly to change their nature, they would have carried on conversations there of the sort that I knew; their partners would perhaps have stooped to reply to them in the same human speech; and, in the course of an evening spent in the leading house in the Faubourg Saint-Germain, there would have been moments identical with moments that I had already lived. Which was impossible. It was thus that my mind was embarrassed by certain difficulties, and the Presence of Our Lord's Body in the Host seemed to me no more obscure a mystery than this leading house in the Faubourg, situated here, on the right bank of the river, and so near that from my bed, in the morning, I could hear its carpets being beaten. But the line of demarcation that separated me from the Faubourg Saint-Germain seemed to me all the more real because it was purely ideal. I felt clearly that it was already part of the Faubourg, when I saw the Guermantes doormat, spread out beyond that intangible Equator, of which my mother had made bold to say, having like myself caught a glimpse of it one day when their door stood open, that it was in a shocking state. For the rest, how could their dining-room, their dim gallery upholstered in red plush, into which I could see sometimes from our kitchen window, have failed to possess in my eyes the mysterious charm of the Faubourg Saint-Germain, to form part of it in an essential fashion, to be geographically situated within it, since to have been entertained to dinner in that room was to have gone into the Faubourg Saint-Germain, to have breathed its atmosphere, since the people who, before going to table, sat down by the side of Mme. de Guermantes on the leather-covered sofa in that gallery were all of the Faubourg Saint-Germain. No doubt elsewhere than in the Faubourg, at certain parties, one might see now and then, majestically enthroned amid the vulgar herd of fashion, one of those men who were mere names and varyingly assumed, when one tried to form a picture of them, the aspect of a tournament or of a royal forest. But here, in the leading house in the Faubourg Saint-Germain, in the drawing-room, in the dim gallery, there were only they. They were, wrought of precious materials, the columns that upheld the temple. Indeed for quiet family parties it was from among them only that Mme. de Guermantes might select her guests, and in the dinners for twelve, gathered around the dazzling napery and plate, they were like the golden statues of the Apostles in the Sainte-Chapelle, symbolic, consecrative pillars before the Holy Table. As for the tiny strip of garden that stretched between high walls at the back of the house, where on summer evenings Mme. de Guermantes had liqueurs and orangeade brought out after dinner, how could I not have felt that to sit there of an evening, between nine and eleven, on its iron chairs—endowed with a magic as potent as the leathern sofa—without inhaling the breezes peculiar to the Faubourg Saint-Germain was as impossible as to take a siesta in the oasis of Figuig without thereby being necessarily in Africa. Only imagination and belief can differentiate from the rest certain objects, certain people, and can create an atmosphere. Alas, those picturesque sites, those natural accidents, those local curiosities, those works of art of the Faubourg Saint-Germain, never probably should I be permitted to set my feet among them. And I must content myself with a shiver of excitement as I sighted, from the deep sea (and without the least hope of ever landing there) like an outstanding minaret, like the first palm, like the first signs of some exotic industry or vegetation, the well-trodden doormat of its shore.

But if the Hôtel de Guermantes began for me at its

hall-door, its dependencies must be regarded as extending a long way farther, according to the Duke, who, looking on all the other tenants as farmers, peasants, purchasers of forfeited estates, whose opinion was of no account, shaved himself every morning in his nightshirt at the window, came down into the courtyard, according to the warmth or coldness of the day, in his shirt-sleeves, in pyjamas, in a plaid coat of startling colours, with a shaggy nap, in little light-coloured covert coats shorter than the jackets beneath, and made one of his grooms lead past him at a trot some horse that he had just been buying. More than once, indeed, the horse broke the window of Jupien's shop, whereupon Jupien, to the Duke's indignation, demanded compensation. "If it were only in consideration of all the good that Madame la Duchesse does in the house, here, and in the parish," said M. de Guermantes, "it is an outrage on this fellow's part to claim a penny from us." But Jupien had stuck to his point, apparently not having the faintest idea what "good" the Duchess had ever done. And yet she did do good, but— since one cannot do good to everybody at once—the memory of the benefits that we have heaped on one person is a valid reason for our abstaining from helping another, whose discontent we thereby make all the stronger. From other points of view than that of charity the quarter appeared to the Duke—and this over a considerable area— to be only an extension of his courtyard, a longer track for his horses. After seeing how a new acquisition trotted by itself he would have it harnessed and taken through all the neighbouring streets, the groom running beside the carriage holding the reins, making it pass to and fro before the Duke who stood on the pavement, erect, gigantic, enormous in his vivid clothes, a cigar between his teeth, his head in the air, his eyeglass scrutinous, until the moment when he sprang on to the box, drove the horse up and down for a little to try it, then set off with his new turn-out to pick up his mistress in the Champs-Elysées. M. de Guermantes bade good day, before leaving the courtyard, to two couples who belonged more or less to his world; the first, some cousins of his who, like working-class parents, were never at home to look after their children, since every morning the wife went off to the Schola to study counterpoint and fugue, and the husband to his studio to carve wood and beat leather; and after them the Baron and Baronne de Norpois, always dressed in black, she like a pew-opener and he like a mute at a funeral, who emerged several times daily on their way to church. They were the nephew and niece of the old Ambassador who was our friend, and whom my father had, in fact, met at the foot of the staircase without realising from where he came; for my father supposed that so important a personage, one who had come in contact with the most eminent men in Europe and was probably quite indifferent to the empty distinctions of rank, was hardly likely to frequent the society of these obscure, clerical and narrow-minded nobles. They had not been long in the place; Jupien, who had come out into the courtyard to say a word to the husband just as he was greeting M. de Guermantes, called him " M. Norpois," not being certain of his name.

"Monsieur Norpois, indeed! Oh, that really is good! Just wait a little! This individual will be calling you Comrade Norpois next!" exclaimed M. de Guermantes, turning to the Baron. He was at last able to vent his spleen against Jupien who addressed him as "Monsieur," instead of "Monsieur le Duc."

One day when M. de Guermantes required some information upon a matter of which my father had professional knowledge, he had introduced himself to him with great courtesy. After that, he had often some neighbourly service to ask of my father and, as soon as he saw him begin to come downstairs, his mind occupied with his work and anxious to avoid any interruption, the Duke, leaving his stable-boys, would come up to him in the courtyard, straighten the collar of his great-coat, with the serviceable deftness inherited from a line of royal body-servants in days gone by, take him by the hand, and, holding it in his own, patting it even to prove to my father, with a courtesan's or courtier's shamelessness, that he, the Duc de Guermantes, made no bargain about my father's right to the privilege of contact with the ducal flesh, lead him, so to speak, on leash, extremely annoyed and thinking only how he might escape, through the carriage entrance out into the street. He had given us a sweeping bow one day when we had come in just as he was going out in the carriage with his wife; he was bound to have told her my name; but what likelihood was there of her remembering it, or my face either? And besides, what a feeble recommendation to be pointed out simply as being one of her tenants! Another, more valuable, would have been my meeting the Duchess in the drawing-room of Mme. de Villeparisis, who, as it happened, had just sent word by my grandmother that I was to go and see her, and, remembering that I had been intending to go in for literature, had added that I should meet several authors there. But my father felt that I was still a little young to go into society, and as the state of my health continued to give him uneasiness he did not see the use of establishing precedents that would do me no good.

As one of Mme. de Guermantes's footmen was in the habit of talking to Françoise, I picked up the names of several of the houses which she frequented, but formed no impression of any of them; from the moment in which they were a part of her life, of that life which I saw only through the veil of her name, were they not inconceivable?

" To-night there's a big party with a Chinese shadow show at the Princesse de Parme's," said the footman, " but we shan't be going, because at five o'clock Madame is taking the train to Chantilly, to spend a few days with the Duc d'Aumale; but it'll be the lady's maid and valet that are going with her. I'm to stay here. She won't be at all pleased, the Princesse de Parme won't, that's four times already she's written to Madame la Duchesse."

" Then you won't be going down to Guermantes Castle this year? "

" It's the first time we shan't be going there: it's be- cause of the Duke's rheumatics, the doctor says he's not to go there till the hot pipes are in, but we've been there every year till now, right on to January. If the hot pipes aren't ready, perhaps Madame will go for a few days to Cannes, to the Duchesse de Guise, but nothing's settled yet."

" And to the theatre, do you go, sometimes? "

" We go now and then to the Opéra, usually on the evenings when the Princesse de Parme has her box, that's once a week; it seems it's a fine show they give there, plays, operas, everything. Madame refused to subscribe to it herself, but we go all the same to the boxes Madame's

friends take, one one night, another another, often with
the Princesse de Guermantes, the Duke's cousin's lady.
She's sister to the Duke of Bavaria. And so you've got to
run upstairs again now, have you?" went on the footman,
who, albeit identified with the Guermantes, looked upon
masters in general as a political estate, a view which allowed him to treat Françoise with as much respect as if
she too were in service with a duchess. "You enjoy good
health, ma'am."

"Oh, if it wasn't for these cursed legs of mine! On the
plain I can still get along" ("on the plain" meant in the
courtyard or in the streets, where Françoise had no objection to walking, in other words "on a plane surface")
"but it's these stairs that do me in, devil take them.
Good day to you, sir, see you again, perhaps, this evening."

She was all the more anxious to continue her conversations with the footman after he mentioned to her that the
sons of dukes often bore a princely title which they retained until their fathers were dead. Evidently the cult
of the nobility, blended with and accommodating itself to
a certain spirit of revolt against it, must, springing heredi-
tarily from the soil of France, be very strongly implanted
still in her people. For Françoise, to whom you might
speak of the genius of Napoleon or of wireless telegraphy
without succeeding in attracting her attention, and without her slackening for an instant the movements with
which she was scraping the ashes from the grate or laying the table, if she were simply to be told these idiosyncrasies of nomenclature, and that the younger son of the
Duc de Guermantes was generally called Prince d'Oléron,
would at once exclaim: "That's fine, that is!" and stand
there dazed, as though in contemplation of a stained win-

dow in church.

Françoise learned also from the Prince d'Agrigente's valet, who had become friends with her by coming often to the house with notes for the Duchess, that he had been hearing a great deal of talk in society about the marriage of the Marquis de Saint-Loup to Mlle. d'Ambresac, and that it was practically settled.

That villa, that opera-box, into which Mme. de Guermantes transfused the current of her life, must, it seemed to me, be places no less fairylike than her home. The names of Guise, of Parme, of Guermantes-Bavière, differentiated from all possible others the holiday places to which the Duchess resorted, the daily festivities which the track of her bowling wheels bound, as with ribbons, to her mansion. If they told me that in those holidays, in those festivities, consisted serially the life of Mme. de Guermantes, they brought no further light to bear on it. Each of them gave to the life of the Duchess a different determination, but succeeded only in changing the mystery of it, without allowing to escape any of its own mystery which simply floated, protected by a covering, enclosed in a bell, through the tide of the life of all the world. The Duchess might take her luncheon on the shore of the Mediterranean at Carnival time, but, in the villa of Mme. de Guise, where the queen of Parisian society was nothing more, in her white linen dress, among numberless princesses, than a guest like any of the rest, and on that account more moving still to me, more herself by being thus made new, like a star of the ballet who in the fantastic course of a figure takes the place of each of her humbler sisters in succession; she might look at Chinese shadow shows, but at a party given by the Princesse de

Parme, listen to tragedy or opera, but from the box of the Princesse de Guermantes.

As we localise in the body of a person all the potentialities of that person's life, our recollections of the people he knows and has just left or is on his way to meet, if, having learned from Françoise that Mme. de Guermantes was going on foot to luncheon with the Princesse de Parme, I saw her, about midday, emerge from her house in a gown of flesh coloured satin over which her face was of the same shade, like a cloud that rises above the setting sun, it was all the pleasures of the Faubourg Saint-Germain that I saw before me, contained in that small compass, as in a shell, between its twin valves that glowed with roseate nacre.

My father had a friend at the Ministry, one A. J. Moreau, who, to distinguish him from the other Moreaus, took care always to prefix both initials to his name, with the result that people called him, for short, " A. J." Well, somehow or other, this A. J. found himself entitled to a stall at the Opéra-Comique on a gala night; he sent the ticket to my father, and as Berma, whom I had not been again to see since my first disappointment, was to give an act of *Phèdre,* my grandmother persuaded my father to pass it on to me.

To tell the truth, I attached no importance to this possibility of hearing Berma which, a few years earlier, had plunged me in such a state of agitation. And it was not without a sense of melancholy that I realised the fact of my indifference to what at one time I had put before health, comfort, everything. It was not that there had been any slackening of my desire for an opportunity to contemplate close at hand the precious particles of reality of which my imagination caught a broken glimpse. But my imagination no longer placed these in the diction of a great actress; since my visits to Elstir, it was on certain tapestries, certain modern paintings that I had brought to bear the inner faith I had once had in this acting, in this tragic art of Berma; my faith, my desire, no longer coming forward to pay incessant worship to the diction, the attitudes of Berma, the counterpart that I possessed of them in my heart had gradually perished, like those other counterparts of the dead in ancient Egypt which had to be fed continually in order to maintain their originals in eternal life. This art had become a feeble, tawdry thing. No deep-lying soul inhabited it any more.

That evening, as, armed with the ticket my father had received from his friend, I was climbing the grand staircase of the Opera, I saw in front of me a man whom I took at first for M. de Charlus, whose bearing he had; when he turned his head to ask some question of one of the staff I saw that I had been mistaken, but I had no hesitation in placing the stranger in the same class of society, from the way not only in which he was dressed but in which he spoke to the man who took the tickets and to the box-openers who were keeping him waiting. For, apart from personal details of similarity, there was still at this period between any smart and wealthy man of that section of the nobility and any smart and wealthy man of the world of finance or " big business " a strongly marked difference. Where one of the latter would have thought he was giving proof of his exclusiveness by adopting a sharp, haughty tone in speaking to an inferior, the great gentleman, affable, pleasant, smiling, had the air of considering, practising an affection of humility and patience, a pretence of being just one of the audience, as a privilege of his good breeding. It is quite likely that, on seeing him thus dissemble behind a smile overflowing with good nature the barred threshold of the little world apart which he carried in his person, more than one wealthy banker's son, entering the theatre at that moment, would have taken this great gentleman for a person of no importance if he had not remarked in him an astonishing resemblance to the portrait that had recently appeared in the illustrated papers of a nephew of the Austrian Emperor, the Prince of Saxony, who happened to be in Paris at the time. I knew him to be a great friend of the Guermantes. As I reached the attendant I heard the Prince of Saxony (or his double) say with a smile: " I don't know the number; it was my cousin who told me I had only to ask for her box."

He may well have been the Prince of Saxony; it was perhaps of the Duchesse de Guermantes (whom, in that event, I should be able to watch in the process of living one of those moments of her unimaginable life in her cousin's box) that his eyes formed a mental picture when he referred to " my cousin who told me I had only to ask for her box," so much so that that smiling gaze peculiar to himself, those so simple words caressed my heart (far more gently than would any abstract meditation) with the alternative feelers of a possible happiness and a vague distinction. Whatever he was, in uttering this sentence to the attendant he grafted upon a commonplace evening in my everyday life a potential outlet into a new world; the passage to which he was directed after mentioning the word " box " and along which he now proceeded was moist and mildewed and seemed to lead to subaqueous grottoes, to the mythical kingdom of the water-nymphs. I had before me a gentleman in evening dress who was walking away from me, but I kept playing upon and round him, as with a badly fitting reflector on a lamp, and without ever succeeding in making it actually coincide with him, the idea that he was the Prince of Saxony and was on his way to join the Duchesse de Guermantes. And, for all that he was alone, that idea, external to himself, impalpable, immense, unstable as the shadow projected by a magic lantern, seemed to precede and guide him like that deity, invisible to the rest of mankind, who stands beside the Greek warrior in the hour of battle.

I took my seat, striving all the time to recapture a line from *Phèdre* which I could not quite remember. In the form in which I repeated it to myself it had not the right number of feet, but as I made no attempt to count them, between its unwieldiness and a classical line of poetry it seemed as though no common measure could exist. It would not have surprised me to learn that I must subtract at least half a dozen syllables from that portentous phrase to reduce it to alexandrine dimensions. But suddenly I remembered it, the irremediable asperities of an inhuman world vanished as if by magic; the syllables of the line at once filled up the requisite measure, what there was in excess floated off with the ease, the dexterity of a bubble of air that rises to burst on the water's brink. And, after all, this excrescence with which I had been struggling consisted of but a single foot.

A certain number of orchestra stalls had been offered for sale at the box office and bought, out of snobbishness or curiosity, by such as wished to study the appearance of people whom they might not have another opportunity of seeing at close quarters. And it was indeed a fragment of their true social life, ordinarily kept secret, that one could examine here in public, for, the Princesse de Parme having herself distributed among her friends the seats in stalls, balconies and boxes, the house was like a drawing-room in which everyone changed his place, went to sit here or there wherever he caught sight of a woman whom he knew.

Next to me were some common people who, not knowing the regular subscribers, were anxious to shew that they were capable of identifying them and named them aloud. They went on to remark that these subscribers behaved there as though they were in their own drawing-rooms, meaning that they paid no attention to what was being played. Which was the exact opposite of what did happen. A budding genius who has taken a stall in order to hear Berma thinks only of not soiling his gloves, of not disturbing, of making friends with the neighbour whom chance has put beside him, of pursuing with an intermittent smile the fugitive—avoiding with apparent want of politeness the intercepted gaze of a person of his acquaintance whom he has discovered in the audience and to whom, after a thousand indecisions, he makes up his mind to go and talk just as the three hammer-blows from the stage, sounding before he has had time to reach his friend, force him to take flight, like the Hebrews in the Red Sea, through a heaving tide of spectators and spectatresses whom he has obliged to rise and whose dresses he tears as he passes, or tramples on their boots. On the other hand it was because the society people sat in their boxes (behind the general terrace of the balcony, as in so many little drawing-rooms, the fourth walls of which had been removed, or in so many little cafés, to which one might go for refreshment, without letting oneself be intimidated by the mirrors in gilt frames or the red plush seats, in the Neapolitan style, of the establishment), it was because they rested an indifferent hand on the gilded shafts of the columns which upheld this temple of the lyric art, it was because they remained unmoved by the extravagant honours which seemed to be being paid them by a pair of carved figures which held out towards the boxes branches of palm and laurel, that they and they only would have had minds free to listen to the play, if only they had had minds.

At first there was nothing visible but vague shadows, in which one suddenly struck—like the gleam of a precious stone which one cannot see—the phosphorescence of a pair of famous eyes, or, like a medallion of Henri IV on a dark background, the bent profile of the Duc d'Aumale, to whom an invisible lady was exclaiming " Monseigneur must allow me to take his coat, " to which the Prince replied, " Oh, come, come! Really, Madame d'Ambresac, " She took it, in spite of this vague prohibition, and was envied by all the rest her being thus honoured.

But in the other boxes, everywhere almost, the white deities who inhabited those sombre abodes had flown for shelter against their shadowy walls and remained invisible. Gradually, however, as the performance went on, their vaguely human forms detached themselves, one by one, from the shades of night which they patterned, and, raising themselves towards the light, allowed their semi-nude bodies to emerge, and rose, and stopped at the limit of their course, at the luminous, shaded surface on which their brilliant faces appeared behind the gaily breaking foam of the feather fans they unfurled and lightly waved, beneath their hyacinthine locks begemmed with pearls, which the flow of the tide seemed to have caught and drawn with it; this side of them, began the orchestra stalls, abode of mortals for ever separated from the transparent, shadowy realm to which, at points here and there, served as boundaries, on its brimming surface, the limpid, mirroring eyes of the water-nymphs. For the folding seats on its shore, the forms of the monsters in the stalls were painted upon the surface of those eyes in simple obedience to the laws of optics and according to their angle of incidence, as happens with those two sections of external reality to which, knowing that they do not possess any soul, however rudimentary, that can be considered as analogous to our own, we should think ourselves mad if we addressed a smile or a glance of recognition: namely, minerals and people to whom we have not been introduced. Beyond this boundary, withdrawing from the limit of their domain, the radiant daughters of the sea kept turning at every moment to smile up at the bearded tritons who clung to the anfractuosities of the cliff, or towards some aquatic demi-god, whose head was a polished stone to which the tides had borne a smooth covering of seaweed, and his gaze a disc of rock crystal. They leaned towards these creatures, offering them sweetmeats; sometimes the flood parted to admit a fresh Nereid who, belated, smiling, apologetic, had just floated into blossom out of the shadowy depths; then, the act ended, having no further hope of hearing the melodious sounds of earth which had drawn them to the surface, plunging back all in a moment the several sisters vanished into the night. But of all these retreats, to the thresholds of which

45

their mild desire to behold the works of man brought the curious goddesses who let none approach them, the most famous was the cube of semi-darkness known to the world as the stage box of the Princesse de Guermantes.

Like a mighty goddess who presides from far aloft over the sports of lesser deities, the Princess had deliberately remained a little way back on a sofa placed sideways in the box, red as a reef of coral, beside a big, glassy splash of reflexion which was probably a mirror and made one think of the section cut by a ray of sunlight, vertical, clear, liquid, through the flashing crystal of the sea. At once plume and blossom, like certain subaqueous growths, a great white flower, downy as the wing of a bird, fell from the brow of the Princess along one of her cheeks, the curve of which it followed with a pliancy, coquettish, amorous, alive, and seemed almost to enfold it like a rosy egg in the softness of a halcyon's nest. Over her hair, reaching in front to her eyebrows and caught back lower down at the level of her throat, was spread a net upon which those little white shells which are gathered on some shore of the South Seas alternated with pearls, a marine mosaic barely emerging from the waves and at every moment plunged back again into a darkness in the depths of which even then a human presence was revealed by the ubiquitous flashing of the Princess's eyes. The beauty which set her far above all the other fabulous daughters of the dusk was not altogether materially and comprehensively inscribed on her neck, her shoulders, her arms, her figure. But the exquisite, unfinished line of the last was the exact starting point, the inevitable focus of invisible lines which the eye could not help prolonging, marvellous lines, springing into life round the woman like the spectrum of an ideal form projected upon the screen of darkness.

"That's the Princesse de Guermantes," said my neighbour to the gentleman beside her, taking care to begin the word "Princesse" with a string of 'P's, to shew that a title like that was absurd. "She hasn't been sparing with her pearls. I'm sure, if I had as many as that, I wouldn't make such a display of them; it doesn't look at all well, not to my mind."

And yet, when they caught sight of the Princess, all those who were looking round to see who was in the audience felt springing up for her in their hearts the rightful throne of beauty. Indeed, with the Duchesse de Luxembourg, with Mme. de Morienval, with Mme. de Sainte-Euverte, and any number of others, what enabled one to identify their faces would be the juxtaposition of a big red nose to a hare-lip, or of a pair of wrinkled cheeks to a faint moustache. These features were nevertheless sufficient in themselves to attract the eye, since having merely the conventional value of a written document they gave one to read a famous and impressive name; but also they gave one, cumulatively, the idea that ugliness had about it something aristocratic, and that it was unnecessary that the face of a great lady, provided it was distinguished, should be beautiful as well. But like certain artists who, instead of the letters of their names, set at the foot of their canvas a form that is beautiful in itself, a butterfly, a lizard, a flower, so it was the form of a delicious face and figure that the Princess had put in the corner of her box, thereby shewing that beauty can be the noblest of signatures; for the presence there of Mme. de Guermantes-Bavière, who brought to the theatre only such persons as at other times formed part of her intimate circle, was in the eyes of specialists in aristocracy the best possible certificate of the authenticity of the picture which her box presented, a sort of evocation of a scene in the ordinary private life of the Princess in her palaces in Munich and in Paris.

Our imagination being like a barrel organ out of order, which always plays some other tune than that shewn on its card, every time that I had heard any mention of the Princesse de Guermantes-Bavière, a recollection of certain sixteenth century masterpieces had begun singing in my brain. I was obliged to rid myself quickly of this association, now that I saw her engaged in offering crystallised fruit to a stout gentleman in a swallowtail coat. Certainly I was very far from the conclusion that she and her guests were mere human beings like the rest of the audience. I understood that what they were doing there was all only a game, and that as a prelude to the acts of their real life (of which, presumably, this was not where they spent the important part) they had arranged, in obedience to a ritual unknown to me, they were feigning to offer and decline sweetmeats, a gesture robbed of its ordinary significance and regulated beforehand like the step of a dancer who alternately raises herself on her toes and circles about an upheld scarf. For all I knew, perhaps at the moment of offering him her sweetmeats the goddess was saying, with that note of irony in her voice (for I saw her smile): "Do have one, won't you?" What mattered that to me? I should have found a delicious refinement in the deliberate dryness, in the style of Mérimée or Meilhac, of such words addressed by a goddess to a demi-god who, conscious himself what were the sublime thoughts which they both had in their minds, in reserve, doubtless, until the moment when they would begin again to live their true life, consenting to join in the game, was answering with the same mysterious bitterness: "Thanks; I should like a cherry." And I should have listened to this dialogue with the same avidity as to a scene from *Le Mari de la Débutante,* where the absence of poetry, of lofty thoughts, things so familiar to me which, I suppose, Meilhac could easily, had he chosen, have put into it a thousand times over, seemed to me in itself a refinement, a conventional refinement and therefore all the more mysterious and instructive.

"That fat fellow is the Marquis de Ganançay," came in a knowing tone from the man next to me, who had not quite caught the name whispered in the row behind.

The Marquis de Palancy, his face bent downwards at the end of his long neck, his round bulging eye glued to the glass of his monocle, was moving with a leisurely displacement through the transparent shade and appeared no more to see the public in the stalls than a fish that drifts past, unconscious of the press of curious gazers, behind the glass wall of an aquarium. Now and again he paused, a venerable, wheezing monument, and the audience could not have told whether he was in pain, asleep, swimming, about to spawn, or merely taking breath. No one else aroused in me so much envy as he, on account of his apparent familiarity with this box and the indifference with which he allowed the Princess to hold out to him her box of sweetmeats; throwing him, at the same time, a glance from her fine eyes, cut in a pair of diamonds which at such moments wit and friendliness seemed to liquefy, whereas, when they were at rest, reduced to their purely material beauty, to their mineral brilliance alone, if the least reflected flash disturbed them ever so slightly, they set the darkness ablaze with inhuman horizontal splendid fires. But now, because the act of *Phèdre* in which Berma was playing was due to start, the Princess came to the front of the box; whereupon, as if she herself were a theatrical production, in the zone of light which she traversed, I saw not only the colour but the material of her adornments change. And in the box, dry now, emerging, a part no longer of the watery realm, the Princess, ceasing to be a Nereid, appeared turbanned in white and blue like some marvellous tragic actress dressed for the part of Zaïre, or perhaps of Orosmane; finally, when she had taken her place in the front row I saw that the soft halcyon's nest which tenderly shielded the rosy nacre of her cheeks was—downy, dazzling, velvety, an immense bird of paradise.

But now my gaze was diverted from the Princesse de Guermantes's box by a little woman who came in, ill-dressed, plain, her eyes ablaze with indignation, followed by two young men, and sat down a few places from me. At length the curtain went up. I could not help being saddened by the reflexion that there remained now no trace of my old disposition, at the period when, so as to miss nothing of the extraordinary phenomenon which I would have gone to the ends of the earth to see, I kept my mind prepared, like the sensitive plates which astronomers take out to Africa, to the West Indies, to make and record an exact observation of a comet or an eclipse; when I trembled for fear lest some cloud (a fit of ill humour on the artist's part or an incident in the audience) should prevent the spectacle from presenting itself with the maximum of intensity; when I should not have believed that I was watching it in the most perfect conditions had I not gone to the very theatre which was consecrated to it like an altar, in which I then felt to be still a part of it, though an accessory part only, the officials with their white carnations, appointed by her, the vaulted balcony covering a pit filled with a shabbily dressed crowd, the women selling programmes that had her photograph, the chestnut trees in the square outside, all those companions, those confidants of my impressions of those days which seemed to me to be inseparable from them. *Phèdre*, the " Declaration Scene ", Berma, had had then for me a sort of absolute existence. Standing aloof from the world of current experience they existed by themselves, I must go to meet them, I should penetrate what I could of them, and if I opened my eyes and soul to their fullest extent I should still absorb but a very little of them. But how pleasant life seemed to me: the triviality of the form of it that I myself was leading mattered nothing, no more than the time we spend on dressing, on getting ready to go out, since, transcending it, there existed in an absolute form, good and difficult to approach, impossible to possess in their entirety, those more solid realities, *Phèdre* and the way in which Berma spoke her part. Steeped in these dreams of perfection in the dramatic art (a strong dose of which anyone who had at that time subjected my mind to analysis at any moment of the day or even the night would have been able to prepare from it), I was like a battery that accumulates and stores up electricity. And a time had come when, ill as I was, even if I had believed that I should die of it, I should still have been compelled to go and hear Berma. But now, like a hill which from a distance seems a patch of azure sky, but, as we draw nearer, returns to its place in our ordinary field of vision, all this had left the world of the absolute and was no more than a thing like other things, of which I took cognisance because I was there, the actors were people of the same substance as the people I knew, trying to speak in the best possible way these lines of *Phèdre,* which themselves no longer formed a sublime and individual essence, distinct from everything else, but were simply more or less effective lines ready to slip back into the vast corpus of French poetry, of which they were merely a part. I felt a discouragement that was all the more profound in that, if the object of my headstrong and active desire no longer existed, the same tendencies, on the other hand, to indulge in a perpetual dream, which varied from year to year but led me always to sudden impulses, regardless of danger, still persisted. The day on which I rose from my bed of sickness and set out to see, in some country house or other, a picture by Elstir or a mediaeval tapestry, was so like the day on which I ought to have started for Venice, or that on which I did go to hear Berma, or start for Balbec, that I felt before going that the immediate object of my sacrifice would, after a little while, leave me cold, that then I might pass close by the place without stopping even to look at that picture, those tapestries for which I would at this moment risk so many sleepless nights, so many hours of pain. I discerned in the instability of its object the vanity of my effort, and at the same time its vastness, which I had not before noticed, like a neurasthenic whose exhaustion we double by pointing out to him that he is exhausted. In the mean time my musings gave a distinction to everything that had any connexion with them. And even in my most carnal desires, magnetised always in a certain direction, concentrated about a single dream, I might have recognised as their primary motive an idea, an idea for which I would have laid down my life, at the innermost core of which, as in my day dreams while I sat reading all afternoon in the garden at Combray, lay the thought of perfection.

I no longer felt the same indulgence as on the former occasion towards the deliberate expressions of affection or anger which I had then remarked in the delivery and gestures of Aricie, Ismène and Hippolyte. It was not that the players—they were the same, by the way—did not still seek, with the same intelligent application, to impart now a caressing inflexion, or a calculated ambiguity to their voices, now a tragic amplitude, or a suppliant meekness to their movements. Their intonations bade the voice: "Be gentle, sing like a nightingale, caress and woo"; or else, "now wax furious," and then hurled themselves upon it, trying to carry it off with them in their frenzied rush. But it, mutinous, independent of their diction, remained unalterably their natural voice with its material defects or charms, its everyday vulgarity or affectation, and thus presented a sum-total of acoustic or social phenomena which the sentiment contained in the lines they were repeating was powerless to alter.

Similarly the gestures of the players said to their arms, to their garments: "Be majestic." But each of these unsubmissive members allowed to flaunt itself between shoulder and elbow a biceps which knew nothing of the part; they continued to express the triviality of everyday

life and to bring into prominence, instead of fine shades
of Racinian meaning, mere muscular attachments; and the
draperies which they held up fell back again along vertical
lines in which the natural law that governs falling bodies
was challenged only by an insipid textile pliancy. At this
point the little woman who was sitting near me exclaimed:

" Not a hand! Did you ever see such a get-up? She's
too old; she can't play the part; she ought to have retired
ages ago. "

Amid a sibilant protest from their neighbours the two
young men with her succeeded in making her keep quiet
and her fury raged now only in her eyes. This fury could,
moreover, be prompted only by the thought of success,
of fame, for Berma, who had earned so much money, was
overwhelmed with debts. Since she was always making
business or social appointments which she was prevented
from keeping, she had messengers flying with apologies
along every street in Paris, and what with rooms in hotels
which she would never occupy engaged in advance, oceans
of scent to bathe her dogs, heavy penalties for breaches
of contract with all her managers, failing any more serious
expense and being not so voluptuous as Cleopatra, she
would have found the means of squandering on telegrams
and jobmasters provinces and kingdoms. But the little
woman was an actress who had never tasted success, and
had vowed a deadly hatred against Berma. The latter had
just come on to the stage. And then—oh, the miracle—
like those lessons which we laboured in vain to learn
overnight, and find intact, got by heart, on waking up
next morning, like, too, those faces of dead friends which
the impassioned efforts of our memory pursue without
recapturing them, and which, when we are no longer

thinking of them, are there before our eyes just as they were in life—the talent of Berma, which had evaded me when I sought so greedily to seize its essential quality, now, after these years of oblivion, in this hour of indifference, imposed itself, with all the force of a thing directly seen, on my admiration. Formerly, in my attempts to isolate the talent, I deducted, so to speak, from what I heard the part itself, a part common to all the actresses who appeared as Phèdre, which I had myself studied beforehand so that I might be capable of subtracting it, of receiving in the strained residue only the talent of Mme. Berma. But this talent which I sought to discover outside the part itself was indissolubly one with it. So with a great musician (it appears that this was the case with Vinteuil when he played the piano), his playing is that of so fine a pianist that one cannot even be certain whether the performer is a pianist at all, since (not interposing all that mechanism of muscular effort, crowned here and there with brilliant effects, all that spattering shower of notes in which at least the listener who does not quite know where he is thinks that he can discern talent in its material, tangible objectivity) his playing is become so transparent, so full of what he is interpreting, that himself one no longer sees and he is nothing now but a window opening upon a great work of art. The intentions which surrounded, like a majestic or delicate border, the voice and mimicry of Aricie, Ismène or Hippolyte I had been able to distinguish, but Phèdre had taken hers into herself, and my mind had not succeeded in wresting from her diction and attitudes, in apprehending in the miserly simplicity of their unbroken surfaces those treasures, those effects of which no sign emerged, so completely had they been absorbed. Berma's voice, in which not one atom of lifeless matter refractory to the mind remained undissolved, did not allow any sign to be discernible around it of that overflow of tears which one could feel, because they had not been able to absorb it in themselves, trickling over the marble voice of Aricie or Ismène, but had been brought to an exquisite perfection in each of its tiniest cells like the instrument of a master violinist, in whom one means, when one says that his music has a fine sound, to praise not a physical peculiarity but a superiority of soul; and, as in the classical landscape where in the place of a vanished nymph there is an inanimate waterspring, a clear and concrete intention had been transformed into a certain quality of tone, strangely, appropriately, coldly limpid. Berma's arms, which the lines themselves, by the same dynamic force that made the words issue from her lips, seemed to raise on to her bosom like leaves disturbed by a gush of water; her attitude, on the stage, which she had gradually built up, which she was to modify yet further, and which was based upon reasonings of a different profundity from those of which traces might be seen in the gestures of her fellow-actors, but of reasonings that had lost their original deliberation, and had melted into a sort of radiance in which they sent throbbing, round the person of the heroine, elements rich and complex, but which the fascinated spectator took not as an artistic triumph but as a natural gift; those white veils themselves, which, tenuous and clinging, seemed to be of a living substance and to have been woven by the suffering, half-pagan, half-Jansenist, around which they drew close like a frail, shrinking chrysalis; all of them, voice, attitude, gestures, veils, were nothing more, round this embodiment of an idea, which a line of poetry is (an embodiment that, unlike our human bodies, covers the soul not with an opaque screen which prevents us from seeing it, but with a purified, a quickened garment through which the soul is diffused and we discover it), than additional envelopes which instead of concealing shewed up in greater splendour the soul that had assimilated them to itself and had spread itself through them, than layers of different substances, grown translucent, the interpolation of which has the effect only of causing a richer refraction of the imprisoned, central ray that pierces through them, and of making more extensive, more precious and more fair the matter purified by fire in which it is enshrined. So Berma's interpretation was, around Racine's work, a second work, quickened also by the breath of genius.

My own impression, to tell the truth, though more pleasant than on the earlier occasion, was not really different. Only, I no longer put it to the test of a pre-existent, abstract and false idea of dramatic genius, and I understood now that dramatic genius was precisely this. It had just occurred to me that if I had not derived any pleasure from my first hearing of Berma, it was because, as earlier still when I used to meet Gilberte in the Champs-Elysées, I had come to her with too strong a desire. Between my two disappointments there was perhaps not only this resemblance, but another more profound. The impression given us by a person or a work (or a rendering, for that matter) of marked individuality is peculiar to that person or work. We have brought to it the ideas of " beauty ", " breadth of style ", " pathos " and so forth which we might, failing anything better, have had the illusion of discovering in the commonplace show of a "correct" face or talent, but our critical spirit has before it the insistent challenge of a form of which it possesses no intellectual equivalent, in which it must detect and isolate the unknown element. It hears a shrill sound, an oddly interrogative intonation. It asks itself: "Is that good? Is what I am feeling just now admiration? Is that richness of colouring, nobility, strength?" And what answers it again is a shrill voice, a curiously questioning tone, the despotic impression caused by a person whom one does not know, wholly material, in which there is no room left for "breadth of interpretation". And for this reason it is the really beautiful works that, if we listen to them with sincerity, must disappoint us most keenly, because in the storehouse of our ideas there is none that corresponds to an individual impression.

This was precisely what Berma's acting shewed me. This was what was meant by nobility, by intelligence of diction. Now I could appreciate the worth of a broad, poetical, powerful interpretation, or rather it was to this that those epithets were conventionally applied, but only as we give the names of Mars, Venus, Saturn to planets which have no place in classical mythology. We feel in one world, we think, we give names to things in another; between the two we can establish a certain correspondence, but not bridge the interval. It was quite narrow, this interval, this fault that I had had to cross when, that afternoon on which I went first to hear Berma, having strained my ears to catch every word, I had found some difficulty in correlating my ideas of "nobility of interpretation", of "originality", and had broken out in applause only after a moment of unconsciousness and as if my applause sprang not from my actual impression but was connected in some way with my preconceived ideas, with the pleasure that I found in saying to myself: "At last I am listening to Berma." And the difference that there is between a person, or a work of art which is markedly individual and the idea of beauty, exists just as much between what they make us feel and the idea of love, or of admiration. Wherefore we fail to recognise them. I had found no pleasure in listening to Berma (any more than, earlier still, in seeing Gilberte). I had said to myself: "Well, I do not admire this." But then I was thinking only of mastering the secret of Berma's acting, I was preoccupied with that alone, I was trying to open my mind as wide as possible to receive all that her acting contained. I understood now that all this amounted to nothing more nor less than admiration.

This genius of which Berma's rendering of the part was only the revelation, was it indeed the genius of Racine and nothing more?

I thought so at first. I was soon to be undeceived when the curtain fell on the act from *Phèdre,* amid enthusiastic recalls from the audience, through which the old actress, beside herself with rage, drawing her little body up to its full height, turning sideways in her seat, stiffened the muscles of her face and folded her arms on her bosom to shew that she was not joining the others in their applause, and to make more noticeable a protest which to her appeared sensational though it passed unperceived. The piece that followed was one of those novelties which at one time I had expected, since they were not famous, to be inevitably trivial and of no general application, devoid as they were of any existence outside the performance that was being given of them at the moment. But I had not with them as with a classic the disappointment of seeing the infinity and eternity of a masterpiece occupy no more space or time than the width of the footlights and the length of a performance which would finish it as effectively as a piece written for the occasion. Besides, at every fresh passage which, I felt, had appealed to the audience and would one day be famous, in place of the fame which it was prevented from having won in the past I added that which it would enjoy in the future, by a mental process the converse of that which consists in imagining masterpieces on the day of their first thin performance, when it seemed inconceivable that a title which no one had ever heard before could one day be set, bathed in the same mellow light, beside those of the author's other works. And this part would be set one day in the list of her finest impersonations, next to that of Phèdre. Not that in itself it was not destitute of all literary merit. But Berma was as sublime in one as in the other. I realised then that the work of the playwright was for the actress no more than the material, the nature of which was comparatively unimportant, for the creation of her masterpiece of interpretation, just as the great painter whom I had met at Balbec, Elstir, had found the inspiration for two pictures of equal merit in a school building without any character and a cathedral which was in itself a work of art. And as the painter dissolves houses, carts, people, in some broad effect of light which makes them all alike, so Berma spread out great sheets of terror or tenderness over words that were all melted together in a common mould, lowered or raised to one level, which a lesser artist would have carefully detached from one another. No doubt each of them had an inflexion of its own, and Berma's diction did not prevent one from catching the rhythm of the verse. Is it not already a first element of ordered complexity, of beauty, when, on hearing a rhyme, that is to say something which is at once similar to and different from the preceding rhyme, which was prompted by it, but introduces the variety of a new idea, one is conscious of two systems overlapping each other, one intellectual, the other prosodic? But Berma at the same time made her words, her lines, her whole speeches even, flow into lakes of sound vaster than themselves, at the margins of which it was a joy to see them obliged to stop, to break off; thus it is that a poet takes pleasure in making hesitate for a moment at the rhyming point the word which is about to spring forth, and a composer in merging the various words of his libretto in a single rhythm which contradicts, captures and controls them. Thus into the prose sentences of the modern playwright as into the poetry of Racine Berma managed to introduce those vast images of grief, nobility, passion, which were the masterpieces of her own personal art, and in which she could be recognised as, in the portraits which he has made of different sitters, we recognise a painter.

I had no longer any desire, as on the former occasion, to be able to arrest and perpetuate Berma's attitudes, the fine colour effect which she gave for a moment only in a beam of limelight which at once faded never to re-appear, nor to make her repeat a single line a hundred times over. I realised that my original desire had been more exacting than the intentions of the poet, the actress, the great decorative artist who supervised her productions, and that that charm which floated over a line as it was spoken, those unstable poses perpetually transformed into others, those successive pictures were the transient result, the momentary object, the changing masterpiece which the art of the theatre undertook to create and which would perish were an attempt made to fix it for all time by a too much enraptured listener. I did not even make a resolution to come back another day and hear Berma again. I was satisfied with her; it was when I admired too keenly not to be disappointed by the object of my admiration, whether that object were Gilberte or Berma, that I demanded in advance, of the impression to be received on the morrow, the pleasure that yesterday's impression had refused to afford me. Without seeking to analyse the joy which I had begun now to feel, and might perhaps have been turning to some more profitable use, I said to myself, as in the old days I might have said to one of my schoolfellows: "Certainly, I put Berma first!" not without a confused feeling that Berma's genius was not, perhaps, very accurately represented by this affirmation of my preference, or this award to her of a "first" place, whatever the peace of mind that it might incidentally restore to me.

Just as the curtain was rising on this second play I looked up at Mme. de Guermantes's box. The Princess was in the act—by a movement that called into being an exquisite line which my mind pursued into the void—of turning her head towards the back of the box; her party were all standing, and also turning towards the back, and between the double hedge which they thus formed, with all the assurance, the grandeur of the goddess that she was, but with a strange meekness which so late an arrival, making every one else get up in the middle of the performance, blended with the white muslin in which she was attired, just as an adroitly compounded air of simplicity, shyness and confusion tempered her triumphant smile, the Duchesse de Guermantes, who had at that moment entered the box, came towards her cousin, made a profound obeisance to a young man with fair hair who was seated in the front row, and turning again towards the amphibian monsters who were floating in the recesses of the cavern, gave to these demi-gods of the Jockey Club—who at that moment, and among them all M. de Palancy in particular, were the men who I should most have liked to be—the familiar "good evening" of an old and intimate friend, an allusion to the daily sequence of her relations with them during the last fifteen years. I felt the mystery, but could not solve the riddle of that smiling gaze which she addressed to her friends, in the azure brilliance with which it glowed while she surrendered her hand to one and then to another, a gaze which, could I have broken up its prism, analysed its crystallisation, might perhaps have revealed to me the essential quality of the unknown form of life which became apparent in it at that moment. The Duc de Guermantes followed his wife, the flash of his monocle, the gleam of his teeth, the whiteness of his carnation or of his pleated shirt-front scattering, to make room for their light, the darkness of his eyebrows, lips and coat; with a wave of his outstretched hand which he let drop on to their shoulders, vertically, without moving his head, he commanded the inferior monsters, who were making way for him, to resume their seats, and made a profound bow to the fair young man. One would have said that the Duchess had guessed that her cousin, of whom, it was rumoured, she was inclined to make fun for what she called her "exaggerations" (a name which, from her own point of view, so typically French and restrained, would naturally be applied to the poetry and enthusiasm of the Teuton), would be wearing this evening one of those costumes in which the Duchess thought of her as "dressed up", and that she had decided to give her a lesson in good taste. Instead of the wonderful downy plumage which, from the crown of the Princess's head, fell and swept her throat, instead of her net of shells and pearls, the Duchess wore in her hair only a simple aigrette, which, rising above her arched nose and level eyes, reminded one of the crest on the head of a bird. Her neck and shoulders emerged from a drift of snow-white muslin, against which fluttered a swansdown fan, but below this her gown, the bodice of which had for its sole ornament innumerable spangles (either little sticks and beads of metal, or possibly brilliants), moulded her figure with a precision that was positively British. But different as their two costumes were, after the Princess had given her cousin the chair in which she herself had previously been sitting, they could be seen turning to gaze at one another in mutual appreciation.

Possibly a smile would curve the lips of Mme. de Guermantes when next day she referred to the headdress, a little too complicated, which the Princess had worn, but certainly she would declare that it had been, all the same, quite lovely, and marvellously arranged; and the Princess, whose own tastes found something a little cold, a little austere, a little "tailor-made" in her cousin's way of dressing, would discover in this rigid sobriety an exquisite refinement. Moreover the harmony that existed between them, the universal and pre-established gravitation exercised by their upbringing neutralised the contrasts not only in their apparel but in their attitude. By those invisible magnetic longitudes which the refinement of their manners traced between them the expansive nature of the Princess was stopped short, while on the other side the formal correctness of the Duchess allowed itself to be attracted and relaxed, turned to sweetness and charm. As, in the play which was now being performed, to realise how much personal poetry Berma extracted from it one had only to entrust the part which she was playing, which she alone could play, to no matter what other actress, so the spectator who should raise his eyes to the balcony might see in two smaller boxes there how an " arrangement " supposed to suggest that of the Princesse de Guermantes simply made the Baronne de Morienval appear eccentric, pretentious and ill-bred, while an effort, as painstaking as it must have been costly, to imitate the clothes and style of the Duchesse de Guermantes only made Mme. de Cambremer look like some provincial schoolgirl, mounted on wires, rigid, erect, dry, angular, with a plume of raven's feathers stuck vertically in her hair. Perhaps the proper place for this lady was not a theatre in which it was only with the brightest stars of the season that the boxes (even those in the highest tier, which from below seemed like great hampers brimming with human flowers and fastened to the gallery on which they stood by the red cords of their plush-covered partitions) composed a panorama which deaths, scandals, illnesses, quarrels would soon alter, but which this evening was held motionless by attention, heat, giddiness, dust, smartness or boredom, in that so to speak everlasting moment of unconscious waiting and calm torpor which, in retrospect, seems always to have preceded the explosion of a bomb or the first flicker of a fire.

The explanation of Mme. de Cambremer's presence on this occasion was that the Princesse de Parme, devoid of snobbishness as are most truly royal personages, and to make up for this devoured by a pride in and passion for charity which held an equal place in her heart with her taste for what she believed to be the Arts, had bestowed a few boxes here and there upon women like Mme. de Cambremer who were not numbered among the highest aristocratic society but with whom she was connected in various charitable undertakings. Mme. de Cambremer never took her eyes off the Duchesse and Princesse de Guermantes, which was all the simpler for her since, not being actually acquainted with either, she could not be suspected of angling for recognition. Inclusion in the visiting lists of these two great ladies was nevertheless the goal towards which she had been marching for the last ten years with untiring patience. She had calculated that she might reach it, possibly, in five years more. But having been smitten by a relentless malady, the inexorable character of which—for she prided herself upon her medical knowledge—she thought she knew, she was afraid that she might not live so long. This evening she was happy at least in the thought that all these women whom she barely knew would see in her company a man who was one of their own set, the young Marquis de Beausergent, Mme. d'Argencourt's brother, who moved impartially in both worlds and with whom the women of the second were greatly delighted to bedizen themselves before the eyes of those of the first. He was seated behind Mme. de Cambremer on a chair placed at an angle, so that he might rake the other boxes with his glasses. He knew everyone in the house, and, to greet his friends, with the irresistible charm of his beautifully curved figure, and fine fair head, he half rose from his seat, stiffening his body, a smile brightening his blue eyes, with a blend of deference and detachment, a picture delicately engraved, in its rectangular frame, and placed at an angle to the wall, like one of those old prints which portray a great nobleman in his courtly pride. He often accepted these invitations to go with Mme. de Cambremer to the play. In the theatre itself, and on their way out, in the lobby, he stood gallantly by her side in the thick of the throng of more brilliant friends whom he saw about him, and to whom he refrained from speaking, to avoid any awkwardness, just as though he had been in doubtful company. If at such moments there swept by him the Princesse de Guermantes, lightfoot and fair as Diana, letting trail behind her the folds of an incomparable cloak, turning after her every head and followed by every eye (and, most of all, by Mme. de Cambremer's), M. de Beausergent would become absorbed in conversation with his companion, acknowledging the friendly and dazzling smile of the Princess only with constraint, under compulsion, and with the well-bred reserve, the considerate coldness of a person whose friendliness might at the moment have been inconvenient.

Had not Mme. de Cambremer known already that the box belonged to the Princess, she could still have told that the Duchesse de Guermantes was the guest from the air of keener interest with which she was surveying the spectacle of stage and stalls, out of politeness to her hostess. But simultaneously with this centrifugal force,

an equal and opposite force generated by the same desire
to be sociable drew her attention back to her own attire,
her plume, her necklace, her bodice and also to that of
the Princess, whose subject, whose slave her cousin seemed
thus to proclaim herself, come thither solely to see her,
ready to follow her elsewhere should it have taken the
fancy of the official occupant of the box to rise and leave,
and regarding as composed merely of strangers, worth
looking at simply as curiosities, the rest of the house, in
which, nevertheless, she numbered many friends to whose
boxes she regularly repaired on other evenings and with
regard to whom she never failed on those occasions to
demonstrate a similar loyalism, exclusive, conditional and
hebdomadary. Mme. de Cambremer was surprised to see
her there that evening. She knew that the Duchess was
staying on very late at Guermantes, and had supposed her
to be there still. But she had been told, also, that sometimes, when there was some special function in Paris which
she considered it worth her while to attend, Mme. de Guermantes would order one of her carriages to be brought
round as soon as she had taken tea with the guns, and,
as the sun was setting, start out at a spanking pace
through the gathering darkness of the forest, then over
the high road, to join the train at Combray and so be
in Paris the same evening. "Perhaps she has come up
from Guermantes on purpose to hear Berma," thought
Mme. de Cambremer, and marvelled at the thought. And
she remembered having heard Swann say in that ambiguous jargon which he used in common with M. de
Charlus: "The Duchess is one of the noblest souls in
Paris, the cream of the most refined, the choicest society."
For myself, who derived from the names Guermantes,

Bavaria and Condé what I imagined to be the life, the thoughts of the two cousins (I could no longer so ascribe their faces, having seen them), I would rather have had their opinion of *Phèdre* than that of the greatest critic in the world. For in his I should have found merely intellect, an intellect superior to my own but similar in kind. But what the Duchesse and Princesse de Guermantes might think, an opinion which would have furnished me with an invaluable clue to the nature of these two poetic creatures, I imagined with the aid of their names, I endowed with an irrational charm, and, with the thirst, the longing of a fever-stricken wretch, what I demanded that their opinion of *Phèdre* should yield to me was the charm of the summer afternoons that I had spent in wandering along the Guermantes way.

Mme. de Cambremer was trying to make out how exactly the cousins were dressed. For my own part, I never doubted that their garments were peculiar to themselves, not merely in the sense in which the livery with red collar or blue facings had belonged once exclusively to the houses of Guermantes and Condé, but rather as is peculiar to a bird the plumage which, as well as being a heightening of its beauty, is an extension of its body. The toilet of these two ladies seemed to me like a materialisation, snow-white or patterned with colour, of their internal activity, and, like the gestures which I had seen the Princesse de Guermantes make, with no doubt in my own mind that they corresponded to some idea latent in hers, the plumes which swept downward from her brow, and her cousin's glittering spangled bodice seemed each to have a special meaning, to be to one or the other lady an attribute which was hers and hers alone, the significance of which I would eagerly have learned; the bird of paradise seemed inseparable from its wearer as her peacock is from Juno, and I did not believe that any other woman could usurp that spangled bodice, any more than the fringed and flashing aegis of Minerva. And when I turned my eyes to their box, far more than on the ceiling of the theatre, painted with cold and lifeless allegories, it was as though I had seen, thanks to a miraculous rending of the clouds that ordinarily veiled it, the Assembly of the Gods in the act of contemplating the spectacle of mankind, beneath a crimson canopy, in a clear lighted space, between two pillars of Heaven. I gazed on this brief transfiguration with a disturbance which was partly soothed by the feeling that I myself was unknown to these Immortals; the Duchess had indeed seen me once with her husband, but could surely have kept no memory of that, and it gave me no pain that she found herself, owing to the place that she occupied in the box, in a position to gaze down upon the nameless, collective madrepores of the public in the stalls, for I had the happy sense that my own personality had been dissolved in theirs, when, at the moment in which, by the force of certain optical laws, there must, I suppose, have come to paint itself on the impassive current of those blue eyes the blurred outline of the protozoon, devoid of any individual existence, which was myself, I saw a ray illumine them; the Duchess, goddess turned woman, and appearing in that moment a thousand times more lovely, raised, pointed in my direction the white-gloved hand which had been resting on the balustrade of the box, waved it at me in token of friendship; my gaze felt itself trapped in the spontaneous incandescence of the flashing eyes of the Princess, who had unconsciously set them ablaze merely by turning her head to see who it might be that her cousin was thus greeting, while the Duchess, who had remembered me, showered upon me the sparkling and celestial torrent of her smile.

And now every morning, long before the hour at which she would appear, I went by a devious course to post myself at the corner of the street along which she generally came, and, when the moment of her arrival seemed imminent, strolled homewards with an air of being absorbed in something else, looking the other way and raising my eyes to her face as I drew level with her, but as though I had not in the least expected to see her. Indeed, for the first few mornings, so as to be sure of not missing her, I waited opposite the house. And every time that the carriage gate opened (letting out one after another so many people who were none of them she for whom I was waiting) its grinding rattle continued in my heart in a series of oscillations which it took me a long time to subdue. For never was devotee of a famous actress whom he did not know, posting himself and patrolling the pavement outside the stage door, never was angry or idolatrous crowd, gathered to insult or to carry in triumph through the streets the condemned assassin or the national hero whom it believes to be on the point of coming whenever a sound is heard from the inside of the prison or the palace, never were these so stirred by their emotion as I was, awaiting the emergence of this great lady who in her simple attire was able, by the grace of her movements (quite different from the gait she affected on entering a drawing-room or a box), to make of her morning walk—and for me there was no one in the world but herself out walking—a whole poem of elegant refinement and the finest ornament, the most curious flower of the season. But after the third day, so that the porter should not discover my stratagem, I betook myself much farther afield, to some point upon the Duchess's usual route. Often before that evening at the theatre I had made similar little excursions before luncheon when the weather was fine; if it had been raining, at the first gleam of sunshine I would hasten downstairs to take a turn, and if, suddenly, coming towards me, on the still wet pavement changed by the sun into a golden lacquer, in the transformation scene of a crossroads dusty with a grey mist which the sun tanned and gilded, I caught sight of a schoolgirl followed by her governess or of a dairy-maid with her white sleeves, I stood motionless, my hand pressed to my heart which was already leaping towards an unexplored form of life; I tried to bear in mind the street, the time, the number of the door through which the girl (whom I followed sometimes) had vanished and failed to reappear. Fortunately the fleeting nature of these cherished images, which I promised myself that I would make an effort to see again, prevented them from fixing themselves with any vividness in my memory. No matter, I was less sad now at the thought of my own ill health, of my never having summoned up courage to set to work, to begin a book, the world appeared to me now a pleasanter place to live in, life a more interesting experience now that I had learned that the streets of Paris, like the roads round Balbec, were aflower with those unknown beauties whom I had so often sought to evoke from the woods of Méséglise, each one of whom aroused a sensual longing which she alone appeared capable of assuaging.

On coming home from the Opéra-Comique I had added for next morning to the list of those which for some days past I had been hoping to meet again the form of Mme. de Guermantes, tall, with her high-piled crown of silky, golden hair; with the kindness promised me in the smile which she had directed at me from her cousin's box. I would follow the course which Françoise had told me that the Duchess generally took, and I would try at the same time, in the hope of meeting two girls whom I had seen a few days earlier, not to miss the break-up of their respective class and catechism. But in the mean time, ever and again, the scintillating smile of Mme. de Guermantes, the pleasant sensation it had given me returned. And without exactly knowing what I was doing, I tried to find a place for them (as a woman studies the possible effect on her dress of some set of jewelled buttons that have just been given her) beside the romantic ideas which I had long held and which Albertine's coldness, Gisèle's premature departure, and before them my deliberate and too long sustained separation from Gilberte had set free (the idea, for instance of being loveu by a woman, of having a life in common with her); next, it had been the image of one or other of the two girls seen in the street that I brought into relation with those ideas, to which immediately afterwards I was trying to adapt my memory of the Duchess. Compared with those ideas my memory of Mme. de Guermantes at the Opéra-Comique was a very little thing, a tiny star twinkling beside the long tail of a blazing comet; moreover I had been quite familiar with the ideas long before I came to know Mme. de Guermantes; my memory of her, on the con-

trary, I possessed but imperfectly; every now and then
it escaped me; it was during the hours when, from floating vaguely in my mind in the same way as the images
of various other pretty women, it passed gradually into
a unique and definite association—exclusive of every
other feminine form—with those romantic ideas of so
much longer standing than itself, it was during those few
hours in which I remembered it most clearly that I ought
to have taken steps to find out exactly what it was; but
I did not then know the importance which it was to
assume for me; it was pleasant merely as a first private
meeting with Mme. de Guermantes inside myself, it was
the first, the only accurate sketch, the only one taken
from life, the only one that was really Mme. de Guermantes; during the few hours in which I was fortunate
enough to retain it without having the sense to pay it
any attention, it must all the same have been charming,
that memory, since it was always to it, and quite freely
moreover, to that moment, without haste, without strain,
without the slightest compulsion or anxiety, that my ideas
of love returned; then, as gradually those ideas fixed it
more definitely, it acquired from them a proportionately
greater strength but itself became more vague; presently
I could no longer recapture it; and in my dreams I probably altered it completely, for whenever I saw Mme. de
Guermantes I realised the difference—never twice, as it
happened, the same—between what I had imagined and
what I saw. And now every morning, certainly at the
moment when Mme. de Guermantes emerged from her
gateway at the top of the street I saw again her tall
figure, her face with its bright eyes and crown of silken
hair—all the things for which I was there waiting; but,

any longer, I was sorrowfully making my way homewards; and, absorbed in my own disappointment, looking
absently after and not seeing a carriage that had over-
taken me, I realised suddenly that the movement of the
head which I saw a lady make through the carriage window was meant for me, and that this lady, whose features,
relaxed and pale, or it might equally be tense and vivid,
composed, beneath a round hat which nestled at the foot
of a towering plume, the face of a stranger whom I had
supposed that I did not know, was Mme. de Guermantes,
by whom I had let myself be greeted without so much
as acknowledging her bow. And sometimes I came upon
her as I entered the gate, standing outside the lodge where
the detestable porter whose scrutinous eye I loathed and
dreaded was in the act of making her a profound obeisance
and also, no doubt, his daily report. For the entire staff
of the Guermantes household, hidden behind the window
curtains, were trembling as they watched a conversation
which they were unable to overhear, but which meant
as they very well knew that one or other of them would
certainly have his " day out " stopped by the Duchess to
whom this Cerberus was betraying him. In view of the
whole series of different faces which Mme. Guermantes
displayed thus one after another, faces that occupied a
relative and varying extent, contracted one day, vast the
next, in her person and attire as a whole, my love was
not attached to any one of those changeable and ever-
changing elements of flesh and fabric which replaced one
another as day followed day, and which she could modify,
could almost entirely reconstruct without altering my
disturbance because beneath them, beneath the new collar
and the strange cheek, I felt that it was still Mme. de

Guermantes. What I loved was the invisible person who set all this outward show in motion, her whose hostility so distressed me, whose approach set me trembling, whose life I would fain have made my own and driven out of it her friends. She might flaunt a blue feather or shew a fiery cheek without her actions' losing their importance for me.

I should not myself have felt that Mme. de Guermantes was tired of meeting me day after day, had I not learned it indirectly by reading it on the face, stiff with coldness, disapproval and pity which Françoise shewed when she was helping me to get ready for these morning walks. The moment I asked her for my outdoor things I felt a contrary wind arise in her worn and battered features. I made no attempt to win her confidence, for I knew that I should not succeed. She had, for at once discovering any unpleasant thing that might have happened to my parents or myself, a power the nature of which I have never been able to fathom. Perhaps it was not super- natural, but was to be explained by sources of informa- tion that were open to her alone: as it may happen that the news which often reaches a savage tribe several days before the post has brought it to the European colony has really been transmitted to them not by telepathy but from hill-top to hill-top by a chain of beacon fires. So, in the particular instance of my morning walks, possibly Mme. de Guermantes's servants had heard their mistress say how tired she was of running into me every day without fail wherever she went, and had repeated her remarks to Françoise. My parents might, it is true, have attached some servant other than Françoise to my person, still I should have been no better off. Françoise was in a sense less of a servant than the others. In her way of feeling things, of being kind and pitiful, hard and distant, superior and narrow, of combining a white skin with red hands she was still the village maiden whose parents had had " a place of their own " but having come to grief had been obliged to put her into service. Her presence in our household was the country air, the social life of a farm of fifty years ago wafted to us by a sort of reversal of the normal order of travel whereby it is the place that comes to visit the person. As the glass cases in a local museum are filled with specimens of the curious handiwork which the peasants still carve or embroider or whatever it may be in certain parts of the country, so our flat in Paris was decorated with the words of Françoise, inspired by a traditional local sentiment and governed by extremely ancient laws. And she could in Paris find her way back as though by clues of coloured thread to the songbirds and cherry trees of her childhood, to her mother's deathbed, which she still vividly saw. But in spite of all this wealth of background, once she had come to Paris and had entered our service she had acquired—as, obviously, anyone else coming there in her place would have acquired—the ideas, the system of interpretation used by the servants on the other floors, compensating for the respect which she was obliged to shew to us by repeating the rude words that the cook on the fourth floor had used to her mistress, with a servile gratification so intense that, for the first time in our lives, feeling a sort of solidarity between ourselves and the detestable occupant of the fourth floor flat, we said to ourselves that possibly we too were " employers " after all. This alteration in Françoise's character was perhaps inevitable. Certain forms of existence are so abnormal that they are bound to produce certain characteristic faults; such was the life led by the King at Versailles among his courtiers, a life as strange as that of a Pharaoh or a Doge—and, far more even than his, the life of his courtiers. The life led by our servants is probably of an even more monstrous abnormality, which only its familiarity can prevent us from seeing. But it was actually in details more intimate still that I should have been obliged, if I had dismissed Françoise, to keep the same servant. For various others might, in years to come, enter my service; already furnished with the defects common to all servants, they underwent nevertheless a rapid transformation with me. As, in the rules of tactics, an attack in one sector compels a counter-attack in another, so as not to be hurt by the asperities of my nature, all of them effected in their own an identical resilience, always at the same points, and to make up for this took advantage of the gaps in my line to thrust out advanced posts. Of these gaps I knew nothing, any more than of the salients to which they gave rise, precisely because they were gaps. But my servants, by gradually becoming spoiled, taught me of their existence. It was from the defects which they invariably acquired that I learned what were my own natural and invariable shortcomings; their character offered me a sort of negative plate of my own. We had always laughed, my mother and I, at Mme. Sazerat, who used, in speaking of her servants, expressions like " the lower orders " or " the servant class ". But I am bound to admit that what made it useless to think of replacing Françoise by anyone else was that her successor would inevitably have belonged just as much to the race of servants in general and to the class of my servants in particular.

To return to Françoise, I never in my life experienced any humiliation without having seen beforehand on her face a store of condolences prepared and waiting; and if then in my anger at the thought of being pitied by her I tried to pretend that on the contrary I had scored a distinct success, my lies broke feebly on the wall of her respectful but obvious unbelief and the consciousness that she enjoyed of her own infallibility. For she knew the truth. She refrained from uttering it, and made only a slight movement with her lips as if she still had her mouth full and was finishing a tasty morsel. She refrained from uttering it, or so at least I long believed, for at that time I still supposed that it was by means of words that one communicated the truth to others. Indeed the words that people used to me recorded their meaning so unalterably on the sensitive plate of my mind that I could no more believe it to be possible that anyone who had professed to love me did not love me than Françoise herself could have doubted when she had read it in a newspaper that some clergyman or gentleman was prepared, on receipt of a stamped envelope, to furnish us free of charge with an infallible remedy for every known complaint or with the means of multiplying our income an hundredfold. (If, on the other hand, our doctor were to prescribe for her the simplest ointment to cure a cold in the head, she, so stubborn to endure the keenest suffering, would complain bitterly of what she had been made to sniff, insisting that it tickled her nose and that life was not worth living.) But she was the first person to prove to me by her example (which I was not to understand until long afterwards, when it was given me afresh and to my greater discomfort, as will be found in the later volumes of this work, by a person who was dearer to me than Françoise) that the truth has no need to be uttered to be made apparent, and that one may perhaps gather it with more certainty, without waiting for words, without even bothering one's head about them, from a thousand outward signs, even from certain invisible phenomena, analogous in the sphere of human character to what in nature are atmospheric changes. I might perhaps have suspected this, since to myself at that time it frequently occurred that I said things in which there was no vestige of truth, while I made the real truth plain by all manner of involuntary confidences expressed by my body and in my actions (which were at once interpreted by Françoise); I ought perhaps to have suspected it, but to do so I should first have had to be conscious that I myself was occasionally untruthful and dishonest. Now untruthfulness and dishonesty were with me, as with most people, called into being in so immediate, so contingent a fashion, and in self-defence, by some particular interest, that my mind, fixed on some lofty ideal, allowed my character, in the darkness below, to set about those urgent, sordid tasks, and did not look down to observe them. When Françoise, in the evening, was polite to me, and asked my permission before sitting down in my room, it seemed as though her face became transparent and I could see the goodness and honesty that lay beneath. But Jupien, who had lapses into indiscretion of which I learned only later, revealed afterwards that she had told him that I was not worth the price of a rope to hang me, and that I had tried to insult her in every possible way. These

words of Jupien set up at once before my eyes, in new
and strange colours, a print of the picture of my relations
with Françoise so different from that on which I used to
like letting my eyes rest, and in which, without the least
possibility of doubt, Françoise adored me and lost no opportunity of singing my praises, that I realised that it
is not only the material world that is different from the
aspect in which we see it; that all reality is perhaps
equally dissimilar from what we think ourselves to be
directly perceiving; that the trees, the sun and the sky
would not be the same as what we see if they were
apprehended by creatures having eyes differently constituted from ours, or, better still, endowed for that purpose with organs other than eyes which would furnish
trees and sky and sun with equivalents, though not visual.
However that might be, this sudden outlet which Jupien
threw open for me upon the real world appalled me. So
far it was only Françoise that was revealed, and of her
I barely thought. Was it the same with all one's social
relations? And in what depths of despair might this not
some day plunge me, if it were the same with love? That
was the future's secret. For the present only Françoise
was concerned. Did she sincerely believe what she had
said to Jupien? Had she said it to embroil Jupien with
me, possibly so that we should not appoint Jupien's girl
as her successor? At any rate I realised the impossibility
of obtaining any direct and certain knowledge of whether
Françoise loved or lothed me. And thus it was she who
first gave me the idea that a person does not (as I had
imagined) stand motionless and clear before our eyes
with his merits, his defects, his plans, his intentions with
regard to ourself exposed on his surface, like a garden

at which, with all its borders spread out before us, we gaze through a railing, but is a shadow which we can never succeed in penetrating, of which there can be no such thing as direct knowledge, with respect to which we form countless beliefs, based upon his words and sometimes upon his actions, though neither words nor actions can give us anything but inadequate and as it proves contradictory information—a shadow behind which we can alternately imagine, with equal justification, that there burns the flame of hatred and of love.

I was genuinely in love with Mme. de Guermantes. The greatest happiness that I could have asked of God would have been that He should overwhelm her under every imaginable calamity, and that ruined, despised, stripped of all the privileges that divided her from me, having no longer any home of her own or people who would condescend to speak to her, she should come to me for refuge. I imagined her doing so. And indeed on those evenings when some change in the atmosphere or in my own condition brought to the surface of my consciousness some forgotten scroll on which were recorded impressions of other days, instead of profiting by the refreshing strength that had been generated in me, instead of employing it to decipher in my own mind thoughts which as a rule escaped me, instead of setting myself at last to work, I preferred to relate aloud, to plan out in the third person, with a flow of invention as useless as was my declamation of it, a whole novel crammed with adventure, in which the Duchess, fallen upon misfortune, came to implore assistance from me—me who had become, by a converse change of circumstances, rich and powerful. And when I had let myself thus for hours on

end imagine the circumstances, rehearse the sentences
with which I should welcome the Duchess beneath my
roof, the situation remained unaltered; I had, alas, in
reality, chosen to love the very woman who, in her own
person, combined perhaps the greatest possible number of
different advantages; in whose eyes, accordingly, I could
not hope, myself, ever to cut any figure; for she was as
rich as the richest commoner—and noble also; without
reckoning that personal charm which set her at the pin-
nacle of fashion, made her among the rest a sort of queen.

I felt that I was annoying her by crossing her path
in this way every morning; but even if I had had the
courage to refrain, for two or three days consecutively,
from doing so, perhaps that abstention, which would have
represented so great a sacrifice on my part, Mme. de
Guermantes would not have noticed, or would have set it
down to some obstacle beyond my control. And indeed
I could not have succeeded in making myself cease to
track her down except by arranging that it should be
impossible for me to do so, for the need incessantly
reviving in me to meet her, to be for a moment the object
of her attention, the person to whom her bow was addressed, was stronger than my fear of arousing her dis-
pleasure. I should have had to go away for some time;
and for that I had not the heart. I did think of it
more than once. I would then tell Françoise to pack my
boxes, and immediately afterwards to unpack them. And
as the spirit of imitation, the desire not to appear behind
the times, alters the most natural and most positive form
of oneself, Françoise, borrowing the expression from
her daughter's vocabulary, used to remark that I was
"dippy". She did not approve of this; she said that I

was always " balancing ", for she made use, when she was not aspiring to rival the moderns, of the language of Saint-Simon. It is true that she liked it still less when I spoke to her as master to servant. She knew that this was not natural to me, and did not suit me, a condition which she rendered in words as " where there isn't a will ". I should never have had the heart to leave Paris except in a direction that would bring me closer to Mme. de Guermantes. This was by no means an impossibility. Should I not indeed find myself nearer to her than I was in the morning, in the street, solitary, abashed, feeling that not a single one of the thoughts which I should have liked to convey to her ever reached her, in that weary patrolling up and down of walks which might be continued, day after day, for ever without the slightest advantage to myself, if I were to go miles away from Mme. de Guermantes, but go to some one of her acquaintance, some one whom she knew to be particular in the choice of his friends and who would appreciate my good qualities, would be able to speak to her about me, and if not to obtain it from her at least to make her know what I wanted, some one by means of whom, in any event, simply because I should discuss with him whether or not it would be possible for him to convey this or that message to her, I should give to my solitary and silent meditations a new form, spoken, active, which would seem an advance, almost a realisation. What she did during the mysterious daily life of the " Guermantes " that she was—this was the constant object of my thoughts; and to break through the mystery, even by indirect means, as with a lever, by employing the services of a person to whom were not forbidden the town house of the Duchess, her parties, unrestricted conversation with her, would not that be a contact more distant but at the same time more effective than my contemplation of her every morning in the street?

The friendship, the admiration that Saint-Loup felt for me seemed to me undeserved and had hitherto left me unmoved. All at once I attached a value to them, I would have liked him to disclose them to Mme. de Guermantes, I was quite prepared even to ask him to do so. For when we are in love, all the trifling little privileges that we enjoy we would like to be able to divulge to the woman we love, as people who have been disinherited and bores of other kinds do to us in every-day life. We are distressed by her ignorance of them; we seek consolation in the thought that just because they are never visible she has perhaps added to the opinion which she already had of us this possibility of further advantages that must remain unknown.

Saint-Loup had not for a long time been able to come to Paris, whether, as he himself explained, on account of his military duties, or, as was more likely, on account of the trouble that he was having with his mistress, with whom he had twice now been on the point of breaking off relations. He had often told me what a pleasure it would be to him if I came to visit him at that garrison town, the name of which, a couple of days after his leaving Balbec, had caused me so much joy when I had read it on the envelope of the first letter I received from my friend. It was (not so far from Balbec as its wholly inland surroundings might have led one to think) one of those little fortified towns, aristocratic and military, set in a broad expanse of country over which on fine days there floats so often into the distance a sort of intermittent haze of sound which—as a screen of poplars by its sinuosities outlines the course of a river which one cannot see—indicates the movements of a regiment on parade that the very atmosphere of its streets, avenues and squares has been gradually tuned to a sort of perpetual vibration, musical and martial, while the most ordinary note of cartwheel or tramway is prolonged in vague trumpet calls, indefinitely repeated, to the hallucinated ear, by the silence. It was not too far away from Paris for me to be able, if I took the express, to return, join my mother and grandmother and sleep in my own bed. As soon as ‘I realised this, troubled by a painful longing, I had too little will power to decide not to return to Paris but rather to stay in this town; but also too little to prevent a porter from carrying my luggage to a cab and not to adopt, as I walked behind him, the unburdened mind of a traveller who is looking after his luggage and for whom no grandmother is waiting anywhere at home, to get into the carriage with the complete detachment of a person who, having ceased to think of what it is that he wants, has the air of knowing what he wants, and to give the driver the address of the cavalry barracks. I thought that Saint-Loup might come to sleep that night at the hotel at which I should be staying, so as to make less painful for me the first shock of contact with this strange town. One of the guard went to find him, and I waited at the barrack gate, before that huge ship of stone, booming with the November wind, out of which, every moment, for it was now six o'clock, men were emerging in pairs into the street, staggering as if they were coming ashore in some foreign port in which they found themselves temporarily anchored.

Saint-Loup appeared, moving like a whirlwind, his eye-glass spinning in the air before him; I had not given my name, I was eager to enjoy his surprise and delight. " Oh! What a bore! " he exclaimed, suddenly catching sight of me, and blushing to the tips of his ears. " I have just had a week's leave, and I shan't be off duty again for another week."

And, preoccupied by the thought of my having to spend this first night alone, for he knew better than anyone my bed-time agonies, which he had often remarked and soothed at Balbec, he broke off his lamentation to turn and look at me, coax me with little smiles, with tender though unsymmetrical glances, half of them coming directly from his eye, the other half through his eyeglass, but both sorts alike an allusion to the emotion that he felt on seeing me again, an allusion also to that important matter which I did not always understand but which concerned me now vitally, our friendship.

" I say! Where are you going to sleep? Really, I can't recommend the hotel where we mess; it is next to the Exhibition ground, where there's a show just starting; you'll find it beastly crowded. No, you'ld better go to the Hôtel de Flandre; it is a little eighteenth-century palace with old tapestries. It ' makes ' quite an ' old world residence '."

Saint-Loup employed in every connexion the word " makes " for " has the air of ", because the spoken language, like the written, feels from time to time the need of these alterations in the meanings of words, these refinements of expression. And just as journalists often have not the least idea from what school of literature come the " turns of speech " that they borrow, so the vocabulary, the very diction of Saint-Loup were formed in imitation of three different aesthetes, none of whom he knew personally but whose way of speaking had been indirectly instilled into him. "Besides," he concluded, "the hotel I mean is more or less adapted to your supersensitiveness of hearing. You will have no neighbours. I quite see that it is a slender advantage, and as, after all, another visitor may arrive to-morrow, it would not be worth your while to choose that particular hotel with so precarious an object in view. No, it is for its appeal to the eye that I recommend it. The rooms are quite attractive, all the furniture is old and comfortable; there is something reassuring about that." But to me, less of an artist than Saint-Loup, the pleasure that an attractive house could give was superficial, almost non-existent, and could not calm my growing anguish, as painful as that which I used to feel long ago at Combray when my mother did not come upstairs to say good night, or that which I felt on the evening of my arrival at Balbec in the room with the unnaturally high ceiling, which smelt of flowering grasses. Saint-Loup read all this in my fixed gaze.

"A lot you care, though, about this charming palace, my poor fellow; you're quite pale; and here am I like a great brute talking to you about tapestries which you won't have the heart to look at, even. I know the room they'll put you in; personally I find it most enlivening, but I can quite understand that it won't have the same effect on you with your sensitive nature. You mustn't think I don't understand; I don't feel the same myself, but I can put myself in your place."

At that moment a serjeant who was exercising a horse on the square, entirely absorbed in making the animal jump, disregarding the salutes of passing troopers, but hurling volleys of oaths at such as got in his way, turned with a smile to Saint-Loup and, seeing that he had a friend with him, saluted us. But his horse at once reared. Saint-Loup flung himself at its head, caught it by the bridle, succeeded in quieting it and returned to my side.

" Yes," he resumed; " I assure you that I fully understand; I feel for you as keenly as you do yourself. I am wretched," he went on, laying his hand lovingly on my shoulder, " when I think that if I could have stayed with you to-night, I might have been able, if we talked till morning, to relieve you of a little of your unhappiness. I can lend you any number of books, but you won't want to read if you're feeling like that. And I shan't be able to get anyone else to take my duty here; I've been off now twice running because my girl came down to see me."

And he knitted his brows partly with vexation and also in the effort to decide, like a doctor, what remedy he might best apply to my disease.

" Run along and light the fire in my quarters," he called to a trooper who passed us. " Hurry up; get a move on! "

After which he turned once more to me, and his eyeglass and his peering, myopic gaze hinted an allusion to our great friendship.

" No! To see you here, in these barracks where I have spent so much time thinking about you, I can scarcely believe my eyes. I must be dreaming. And how are you? Better, I hope. You must tell me all about yourself presently. We'll go up to my room; we mustn't hang about too long on the square, there's the devil of a draught; I don't feel it now myself, but you aren't accustomed to it, I'm afraid of your catching cold. And what about your work;

have you started yet? No? You are a quaint fellow! If I had your talent I'm sure I should be writing morning, noon and night. It amuses you more to do nothing? What a pity it is that it's the useless fellows like me who are always ready to work, and the ones who could if they wanted to, won't. There, and I've clean forgotten to ask you how your grandmother is. Her Proudhons are in safe keeping. I never part from them."

An officer, tall, handsome, majestic, emerged with slow and solemn gait from the foot of a staircase. Saint-Loup saluted him and arrested the perpetual instability of his body for the moment occupied in holding his hand against the peak of his cap. But he had flung himself into the action with so much force, straightening himself with so sharp a movement, and, the salute ended, let his hand fall with so abrupt a relaxation, altering all the positions of shoulder, leg, and eyeglass, that this moment was one not so much of immobility as of a throbbing tension in which were neutralised the excessive movements which he had just made and those on which he was about to embark. Meanwhile the officer, without coming any nearer us, calm, benevolent, dignified, imperial, representing, in short, the direct opposite of Saint-Loup, himself also, but without haste, raised his hand to the peak of his cap.

"I must just say a word to the Captain," whispered Saint-Loup. "Be a good fellow, and go and wait for me in my room. It's the second on the right, on the third floor; I'll be with you in a minute."

And setting off at the double, preceded by his eyeglass which fluttered in every direction, he made straight for the slow and stately Captain whose horse had just been brought round and who, before preparing to mount, was giving orders with a studied nobility of gesture as in some historical painting, and as though he were setting forth to take part in some battle of the First Empire, whereas he was simply going to ride home, to the house which he had taken for the period of his service at Doncières, and which stood in a Square that was named, as though in an ironical anticipation of the arrival of this Napoleonid, Place de la République. I started to climb the staircase, nearly slipping on each of its nail-studded steps, catching glimpses of barrack-rooms, their bare walls edged with a double line of beds and kits. I was shewn Saint-Loup's room. I stood for a moment outside its closed door, for I could hear some one stirring; he moved something, let fall something else; I felt that the room was not empty, that there must be somebody there. But it was only the freshly lighted fire beginning to burn. It could not keep quiet, it kept shifting its faggots about, and very clumsily. I entered the room; it let one roll into the fender and set another smoking. And even when it was not moving, like an ill-bred person it made noises all the time, which, from the moment I saw the flames rising, revealed themselves to me as noises made by a fire, although if I had been on the other side of a wall I should have thought that they came from some one who was blowing his nose and walking about. I sat down in the room and waited. Liberty hangings and old German stuffs of the eighteenth century managed to rid it of the smell that was exhaled by the rest of the building, a coarse, insipid, mouldy smell like that of stale toast. It was here, in this charming room, that I could have dined and slept with a calm and happy mind. Saint-Loup seemed almost to be present by reason of the text-books which littered his table, between his photo-

graphs, among which I could make out my own and that
of the Duchesse de Guermantes, by the light of the fire
which had at length grown accustomed to the grate, and,
like an animal crouching in an ardent, noiseless, faithful
watchfulness, let fall only now and then a smouldering
log which crumbled into sparks, or licked with a tongue
of flame the sides of the chimney. I heard the tick of
Saint-Loup's watch, which could not be far away. This
tick changed its place every moment, for I could not see
the watch; it seemed to come from behind, from in front
of me, from my right, from my left, sometimes to die
away as though at a great distance. Suddenly I caught
sight of the watch on the table. Then I heard the tick
in a fixed place from which it did not move again. That
is to say, I thought I heard it at this place; I did not hear
it there; I saw it there, for sounds have no position in
space. Or rather we associate them with movements, and
in that way they serve the purpose of warning us of those
movements, of appearing to make them necessary and
natural. Certainly it happens commonly enough that a
sick man whose ears have been stopped with cotton-wool
ceases to hear the noise of a fire such as was crackling at
that moment in Saint-Loup's fireplace, labouring at
the formation of brands and cinders, which it then lets
fall into the fender, nor would he hear the passage of the
tramway-cars whose music took its flight, at regular intervals, over the Grand'place of Doncières. Let the sick
man then read a book, and the pages will turn silently
before him, as though they were moved by the fingers of
a god. The dull thunder of a bath which is being filled
becomes thin, faint and distant as the twittering of birds
in the sky. The withdrawal of sound, its dilution, take

from it all its power to hurt us; driven mad a moment ago by hammer-blows which seemed to be shattering the ceiling above our head, it is with a quiet delight that we now gather in their sound, light, caressing, distant, like the murmur of leaves playing by the roadside with the passing breeze. We play games of patience with cards which we do not hear, until we imagine that we have not touched them, that they are moving of their own accord, and, anticipating our desire to play with them, have begun to play with us. And in this connexion we may ask ourselves whether, in the case of love (to which indeed we may add the love of life and the love of fame, since there are, it appears, persons who are acquainted with these latter sentiments), we ought not to act like those who, when a noise disturbs them, instead of praying that it may cease, stop their ears; and, with them for our pattern, bring our attention, our defensive strength to bear on ourselves, give ourselves as an objective to capture not the " other person " with whom we are in love but our capacity for suffering at that person's hands.

To return to the problem of sounds, we have only to thicken the wads which close the aural passages, and they confine to a pianissimo the girl who has just been playing a boisterous tune overhead; if we go farther, and steep the wad in grease, at once the whole household must obey its despotic rule; its laws extend even beyond our portals. Pianissimo is not enough; the wad instantly orders the piano to be shut, and the music lesson is abruptly ended; the gentleman who was walking up and down in the room above breaks off in the middle of his beat; the movement of carriages and tramways is interrupted as though a Sovereign were expected to pass. And indeed this attenuation of sounds sometimes disturbs our slumbers instead of guarding them. Only yesterday the incessant noise in our ears, by describing to us in a continuous narrative all that was happening in the street and in the house, succeeded at length in making us sleep, like a boring book; to-night, through the sheet of silence that is spread over our sleep a shock, louder than the rest, manages to make itself heard, gentle as a sigh, unrelated to any other sound, mysterious; and the call for an explanation which it emits is sufficient to awaken us. Take away for a moment from the sick man the cotton-wool that has been stopping his ears and in a flash the full daylight, the sun of sound dawns afresh, dazzling him, is born again in his universe; in all haste return the multitude of exiled sounds; we are present, as though it were the chanting of choirs of angels, at the resurrection of the voice. The empty streets are filled for a moment with the whirr of the swift, consecutive wings of the singing tramway-cars. In the bedroom itself, the sick man has created, not, like Prometheus, fire, but the sound of fire. And when we increase or reduce the wads of cotton-wool, it is as though we were pressing alternately one and the other of the two pedals with which we have extended the resonant compass of the outer world.

Only there are also suppressions of sound which are not temporary. The man who has grown completely deaf cannot even heat a pan of milk by his bedside, but he must keep an eye open to watch, on the tilted lid, for the white, arctic reflexion, like that of a coming snow-storm, which is the warning sign which he is wise to obey, by cutting off (as Our Lord bade the waves be still) the electric current; for already the swelling, jerkily climbing

egg of boiling milk-film is reaching its climax in a series
of sidelong movements, has filled and set bellying the
drooping sails with which the cream has skimmed its surface, sends in a sudden storm a scud of pearly substance
flying overboard—sails which the cutting off of the current, if the electric storm is hushed in time, will fold back
upon themselves and let fall with the ebbing tide, changed
now to magnolia petals. But if the sick man should not be
quick enough in taking the necessary precautions, presently, when his drowned books and watch are seen barely
emerging from the milky tide, he will be obliged to call
the old nurse who, though he be himself an eminent
statesman or a famous writer, will tell him that he has
no more sense than a child of five. At other times in the
magic chamber, between us and the closed door, a person
who was not there a moment ago makes his appearance;
it is a visitor whom we did not hear coming in, and who
merely gesticulates, like a figure in one of those little puppet theatres, so restful for those who have taken a dislike
to the spoken tongue. And for this totally deaf man, since
the loss of a sense adds as much beauty to the world as
its acquisition, it is with ecstasy that he walks now upon
an earth grown almost an Eden, in which sound has not
yet been created. The highest waterfalls unfold for his
eyes alone their ribbons of crystal, stiller than the glassy
sea, like the cascades of Paradise. As sound was for him
before his deafness the perceptible form in which the cause
of a movement was draped, objects moved without sound
seemed to be being moved also without cause; deprived
of all resonant quality, they shew a spontaneous activity,
seem to be alive. They move, halt, become alight of their
own accord. Of their own accord they vanish in the air

like the winged monsters of prehistoric days. In the solitary and unneighboured home of the deaf man the service
which, before his infirmity was complete, was already
shewing an increased discretion, was being carried on in
silence, is now assured him with a sort of surreptitious
deftness, by mutes, as at the court of a fairy-tale king.
And, as upon the stage, the building on which the deaf
man looks from his window—be it barracks, church, or
town hall—is only so much scenery. If one day it should
fall to the ground, it may emit a cloud of dust and leave
visible ruins; but, less material even than a palace on the
stage, though it has not the same exiguity, it will subside
in the magic universe without letting the fall of its heavy
blocks of stone tarnish, with anything so vulgar as sound,
the chastity of the prevailing silence.

The silence, though only relative, which reigned in the
little barrack-room where I sat waiting was now broken.
The door opened and Saint-Loup, dropping his eyeglass,
dashed in.

" Ah, my dear Robert, you make yourself very comfortable here;" I said to him; " how jolly it would be if
one were allowed to dine and sleep here."

And to be sure, had it not been against the regulations,
what repose untinged by sadness I could have tasted there,
guarded by that atmosphere of tranquillity, vigilance and
gaiety which was maintained by a thousand wills controlled and free from care, a thousand heedless spirits, in
that great community called a barracks where, time having
taken the form of action, the sad bell that tolled the hours
outside was replaced by the same joyous clarion of those
martial calls, the ringing memory of which was kept perpetually alive in the paved streets of the town, like the

dust that floats in a sunbeam;—a voice sure of being heard, and musical because it was the command not only of authority to obedience but of wisdom to happiness.

" So you'ld rather stay with me and sleep here, would you, than go to the hotel by yourself? " Saint-Loup asked me, smiling.

" Oh, Robert, it is cruel of you to be sarcastic about it," I pleaded; " you know it's not possible, and you know how wretched I shall be over there."

" Good! You flatter me! " he replied. " It occurred to me just now that you would rather stay here to-night. And that is precisely what I stopped to ask the Captain."

" And he has given you leave? " I cried.

" He hadn't the slightest objection."

" Oh! I adore him! "

" No; that would be going too far. But now, let me just get hold of my batman and tell him to see about our dinner," he went on, while I turned away so as to hide my tears.

We were several times interrupted by one or other of Saint-Loup's friends' coming in. He drove them all out again.

" Get out of here. Buzz off! "

I begged him to let them stay.

" No, really; they would bore you stiff; they are absolutely uncultured; all they can talk about is racing, or stables shop. Besides, I don't want them here either; they would spoil these precious moments I've been looking forward to. But you mustn't think, when I tell you that these fellows are brainless, that everything military is devoid of intellectuality. Far from it. We have a major here who is a splendid chap. He's given us a course in which military history is treated like a demonstration, like a problem in algebra. Even from the aesthetic point of view there is a curious beauty, alternately inductive and deductive, about it which you couldn't fail to appreciate."

"That's not the officer who's given me leave to stay here to-night?"

"No; thank God! The man you 'adore' for so very trifling a service is the biggest fool that ever walked the face of the earth. He is perfect at looking after messing, and at kit inspections; he spends hours with the serjeant major and the master tailor. There you have his mentality. Apart from that he has a vast contempt, like everyone here, for the excellent major I was telling you about. No one will speak to him because he's a freemason and doesn't go to confession. The Prince de Borodino would never have an outsider like that in his house. Which is pretty fair cheek, when all's said and done, from a man whose great-grandfather was a small farmer, and who would probably be a small farmer himself if it hadn't been for the Napoleonic wars. Not that he hasn't a lurking sense of his own rather ambiguous position in society, where he's neither flesh nor fowl. He hardly ever shews his face at the Jockey, it makes him feel so deuced awkward, this so-called Prince," added Robert, who, having been led by the same spirit of imitation to adopt the social theories of his teachers and the worldly prejudices of his relatives, had unconsciously wedded the democratic love of humanity to a contempt for the nobility of the Empire.

I was looking at the photograph of his aunt, and the thought that, since Saint-Loup had this photograph in his possession, he might perhaps give it to me, made me feel all the fonder of him and hope to do him a thousand services, which seemed to me a very small exchange for it. For this photograph was like one encounter more, added to all those that I had already had, with Mme. de Guermantes; better still, a prolonged encounter, as if, by some sudden stride forward in our relations, she had stopped beside me, in a garden hat, and had allowed me for the first time to gaze at my leisure at that plump cheek, that arched neck, that tapering eyebrow (veiled from me hitherto by the swiftness of her passage, the bewilderment of my impressions, the imperfection of memory); and the contemplation of them, as well as of the bare bosom and arms of a woman whom I had never seen save in a high-necked and long-sleeved bodice, was to me a voluptuous discovery, a priceless favour. Those lines, which had seemed to me almost a forbidden spectacle, I could study there, as in a text-book of the only geometry that had any value for me. Later on, when I looked at Robert, I noticed that he too was a little like the photograph of his aunt, and by a mysterious process which I found almost as moving, since, if his face had not been directly created by hers, the two had nevertheless a common origin. The features of the Duchesse de Guermantes, which were pinned to my vision of Combray, the nose like a falcon's beak, the piercing eyes, seemed to have served also as a pattern for the cutting out—in another copy analogous and slender, with too delicate a skin—of Robert's face, which might almost be superimposed upon his aunt's. I saw in him, with a keen longing, those features characteristic of the Guermantes, of that race which had remained so individual in the midst of a world with which it was not confounded, in which it remained isolated in the glory of an ornithomorphic divinity, for it seemed to have been the issue, in the age of mythology, of the union of a goddess with a bird.

Robert, without being aware of its cause, was touched by my evident affection. This was moreover increased by the sense of comfort inspired in me by the heat of the fire and by the champagne which bedewed at the same time my brow with beads of sweat and my cheeks with tears; it washed down the partridges; I ate mine with the dumb wonder of a profane mortal of any sort when he finds in a form of life with which he is not familiar what he has supposed that form of life to exclude—the wonder, for instance, of an atheist who sits down to an exquisitely cooked dinner in a presbytery. And next morning, when I awoke, I rose and went to cast from Saint-Loup's window, which being at a great height overlooked the whole countryside, a curious scrutiny to make the acquaintance of my new neighbour, the landscape which I had not been able to distinguish the day before, having arrived too late, at an hour when it was already sleeping beneath the outspread cloak of night. And yet, early as it had awoken from its sleep, I could see the ground, when I opened the window and looked out, only as one sees it from the window of a country house, overlooking the lake, shrouded still in its soft white morning gown of mist which scarcely allowed me to make out anything at all. But I knew that, before the troopers who were busy with their horses in the square had finished grooming them, it would have cast its gown aside. In the meantime, I could see only a meagre hill, rearing close up against the side of the barracks a back already swept clear of darkness, rough and wrinkled. Through the transparent curtain of frost I could not take my eyes from this stranger who, too, was looking at me for the first time. But when I had formed the habit of coming to the barracks, my consciousness that the hill was there, more real, consequently, even when I did not see it, than the hotel at Balbec, than our house in Paris, of which I thought as of absent—or dead—friends, that is to say without any strong belief in their existence, brought it about that, even although I was not aware of it myself, its reflected shape outlined itself on the slightest impressions that I formed at Doncières, and among them, to begin with this first morning, on the pleasing impression of warmth given me by the cup of chocolate prepared by Saint-Loup's batman in this comfortable room, which had the effect of being an optical centre from which to look out at the hill—the idea of there being anything else to do but just gaze at it, the idea of actually climbing it being rendered impossible by this same mist. Imbibing the shape of the hill, associated with the taste of hot chocolate and with the whole web of my fancies at that particular time, this mist, without my having thought at all about it, succeeded in moistening all my subsequent thoughts about that period, just as a massive and un-melting lump of gold had remained allied to my impressions of Balbec, or as the proximity of the outside stairs of blackish sandstone gave a grey background to my impressions of Combray. It did not, however, persist late into the day; the sun began by hurling at it, in vain, a few darts which sprinkled it with brilliants before they finally overcame it. The hill might expose its grizzled rump to the sun's rays, which, an hour later, when I went down to the town, gave to the russet tints of the autumn leaves, to the reds and blues of the election posters pasted on the walls an exaltation which raised my spirits also and made me stamp, singing as I went, on the pavements from which I could hardly keep myself from jumping in the air for joy.

But after that first night I had to sleep at the hotel. And I knew beforehand that I was doomed to find there sorrow. It was like an unbreathable aroma which all my life long had been exhaled for me by every new bedroom, that is to say by every bedroom; in the one which I usually occupied I was not present, my mind remained elsewhere, and in its place sent only the sense of familiarity. But I could not employ this servant, less sensitive than myself, to look after things for me in a new place, where I preceded him, where I arrived by myself, where I must bring into contact with its environment that " Self " which I rediscovered only at year-long intervals, but always the same, having not grown at all since Combray, since my first arrival at Balbec, weeping, without any possibility of consolation, on the edge of an unpacked trunk.

As it happened, I was mistaken. I had no time to be sad, for I was not left alone for an instant. The fact of the matter was that there remained of the old palace a superfluous refinement of structure and decoration, out of place in a modern hotel, which, released from the service of any practical purpose, had in its long spell of leisure acquired a sort of life: passages winding about in all directions, which one was continually crossing in their aimless wanderings, lobbies as long as corridors and as ornate as drawing-rooms, which had the air rather of being dwellers there themselves than of forming part of a dwelling, which could not be induced to enter and settle down in any of the rooms but wandered about outside mine and came up at once to offer me their company—neighbours of a sort, idle but never noisy, menial ghosts of the past who had been granted the privilege of staying, provided they kept quiet, by the doors of the rooms which were let to visitors, and who, every time that I came across them, greeted me with a silent deference. In short, the idea of a lodging, of simply a case for our existence from day to day which shields us only from the cold and from being overlooked by other people, was absolutely inapplicable to this house, an assembly of rooms as real as a colony of people, living, it was true, in silence, but things which one was obliged to meet, to avoid, to appreciate, as one came in. One tried not to disturb them, and one could not look without respect at the great drawing-room which had formed, far back in the eighteenth century, the habit of stretching itself at its ease, among its hangings of old gold and beneath the clouds of its painted ceiling. And one was seized with a more personal curiosity as to the smaller rooms which, without any regard for symmetry, ran all round it, innumerable, startled, fleeing in disorder as far as the garden, to which they had so easy an access down three broken steps.

If I wished to go out or to come in without taking the lift or being seen from the main staircase, a smaller private staircase, no longer in use, offered me its steps so skilfully arranged, one close above another, that there seemed to exist in their gradation a perfect proportion of the same kind as those which, in colours, scents, savours, often arouse in us a peculiar, sensuous pleasure. But the pleasure to be found in going up and downstairs I had had to come here to learn, as once before to a health resort in the Alps to find that the act—as a rule not noticed—

of drawing breath could be a perpetual delight. I received that dispensation from effort which is granted to us only by the things to which long use has accustomed us, when I set my feet for the first time on those steps, familiar before ever I knew them, as if they possessed, deposited on them, perhaps, embodied in them by the masters of long ago whom they used to welcome every day, the prospective charm of habits which I had not yet contracted and which indeed could only grow weaker once they had become my own. I looked into a room; the double doors closed themselves behind me, the hangings let in a silence in which I felt myself invested with a sort of exhilarating royalty; a marble mantelpiece with ornaments of wrought brass—of which one would have been wrong to think that its sole idea was to represent the art of the Directory—offered me a fire, and a little easy chair on short legs helped me to warm myself as comfortably as if I had been sitting on the hearthrug. The walls held the room in a close embrace, separating it from the rest of the world and, to let in, to enclose what made it complete, parted to make way for the bookcase, reserved a place for the bed, on either side of which a column airily upheld the raised ceiling of the alcove. And the room was prolonged in depth by two closets as large as itself, the latter of which had hanging from its wall, to scent the occasion on which one had recourse to it, a voluptuous rosary of orris-roots; the doors, if I left them open when I withdrew into this innermost retreat, were not content with tripling its dimensions without its ceasing to be well-proportioned, and not only allowed my eyes to enjoy the delights of extension after those of concentration, but added further to the pleasure of my soli-

tude, which, while still inviolable, was no longer shut in,
the sense of liberty. This closet looked out upon a courtyard, a fair solitary stranger whom I was glad to have for
a neighbour when next morning my eyes fell on her, a
captive between her high walls in which no other window
opened, with nothing but two yellowing trees which were
enough to give a pinkish softness to the pure sky above.

Before going to bed I decided to leave the room in order
to explore the whole of my fairy kingdom. I walked down
a long gallery which did me homage successively with all
that it had to offer me if I could not sleep, an armchair
placed waiting in a corner, a spinet, on a table against the
wall a bowl of blue crockery filled with cinerarias, and,
in an old frame, the phantom of a lady of long ago whose
powdered hair was starred with blue flowers, holding in
her hand a bunch of carnations. When I came to the end,
the bare wall in which no door opened said to me simply:
" Now you must turn and go back, but, you see, you are
at home here, the house is yours," while the soft carpet,
not to be left out, added that if I did not sleep that night
I could easily come in barefoot, and the unshuttered windows, looking out over the open country, assured me that
they would hold a sleepless vigil and that, at whatever
hour I chose to come in, I need not be afraid of disturbing anyone. And behind a hanging curtain I surprised
only a little closet which, stopped by the wall and unable
to escape any farther, had hidden itself there with a guilty
conscience and gave me a frightened stare from its little
round window, glowing blue in the moonlight. I went to
bed, but the presence of the eiderdown quilt, of the pillars,
of the neat fireplace, by straining my attention to a pitch
beyond that of Paris, prevented me from letting myself

go upon my habitual train of fancies. And as it is this particular state of strained attention that enfolds our slumbers, acts upon them, modifies them, brings them into line with this or that series of past impressions, the images that filled my dreams that first night were borrowed from a memory entirely distinct from that on which I was in the habit of drawing. If I had been tempted while asleep to let myself be swept back upon my ordinary current of remembrance, the bed to which I was not accustomed, the comfortable attention which I was obliged to pay to the position of my various limbs when I turned over were sufficient to correct my error, to disentangle and to keep running the new thread of my dreams. It is the same with sleep as with our perception of the external world. It needs only a modification in our habits to make it poetic, it is enough that while undressing we should have dozed off unconsciously upon the bed, for the dimensions of our dream-world to be altered and its beauty felt. We awake, look at our watch, see "four o'clock"; it is only four o'clock in the morning, but we imagine that the whole day has gone by, so vividly does this nap of a few minutes, unsought by us, appear to have come down to us from the skies, by virtue of some divine right, full-bodied, vast, like an Emperor's orb of gold. In the morning, while worrying over the thought that my grandfather was ready, and was waiting for me to start on our walk along the Méséglise way, I was awakened by the blare of a regimental band which passed every day beneath my windows. But on several occasions—and I mention these because one cannot properly describe human life unless one shews it soaked in the sleep in which it plunges, which, night after night, sweeps round it as a promontory is encircled by the sea—the intervening layer of sleep was strong enough to bear the shock of the music and I heard nothing. On the other mornings it gave way for a moment; but, still velvety with the refreshment of having slept, my consciousness (like those organs by which, after a local anaesthetic, a cauterisation, not perceived at first, is felt only at the very end and then as a faint burning smart) was touched only gently by the shrill points of the fifes which caressed it with a vague, cool, matutinal warbling; and after this brief interruption in which the silence had turned to music it relapsed into my slumber before even the dragoons had finished passing, depriving me of the latest opening buds of the sparkling clangorous nosegay. And the zone of my consciousness which its springing stems had brushed was so narrow, so circumscribed with sleep that later on, when Saint-Loup asked me whether I had heard the band, I was no longer certain that the sound of its brasses had not been as imaginary as that which I heard during the day echo, after the slightest noise, from the paved streets of the town. Perhaps I had heard it only in a dream, prompted by my fear of being awakened, or else of not being awakened and so not seeing the regiment march past. For often, when I was still asleep at the moment when, on the contrary, I had supposed that the noise would awaken me, for the next hour I imagined that I was awake, while still drowsing, and I enacted to myself with tenuous shadow-shapes on the screen of my slumber the various scenes of which it deprived me but at which I had the illusion of looking on.

What one has meant to do during the day, as it turns out, sleep intervening, one accomplishes only in one's

dreams, that is to say after it has been distorted by sleep
into following another line than one would have chosen
when awake. The same story branches off and has a different ending. When all is said, the world in which we live
when we are asleep is so different that people who have
difficulty in going to sleep seek first of all to escape from
the waking world. After having desperately, for hours on
end, with shut eyes, revolved in their minds thoughts similar to those which they would have had with their eyes
open, they take heart again on noticing that the last minute
has been crawling under the weight of an argument in
formal contradiction of the laws of thought, and their
realisation of this, and the brief " absence " to which it
points, indicate that the door is now open through which
they will perhaps be able, presently, to escape from the
perception of the real, to advance to a resting-place more
or less remote on the other side, which will mean their
having a more or less " good " night. But already a great
stride has been made when we turn our back on the real,
when we reach the cave in which " auto-suggestions " prepare—like witches—the hell-broth of imaginary maladies
or of the recurrence of nervous disorders, and watch for
the hour at which the storm that has been gathering during
our unconscious sleep will break with sufficient force to
make sleep cease.

Not far thence is the secret garden in which grow like
strange flowers the kinds of sleep, so different one from
another, the sleep induced by datura, by the multiple ex-
tracts of ether, the sleep of belladonna, of opium, of
valerian, flowers whose petals remain shut until the day
when the predestined visitor shall come and, touching
them, bid them open, and for long hours inhale the aroma

of their peculiar dreams into a marvelling and bewildered being. At the end of the garden stands the convent with open windows through which we hear voices repeating the lessons learned before we went to sleep, which we shall know only at the moment of awakening; while, a presage of that moment, sounds the resonant tick of that inward alarum which our preoccupation has so effectively regulated that when our housekeeper comes in with the warning: " It is seven o'clock," she will find us awake and ready. On the dim walls of that chamber which opens upon our dreams, within which toils without ceasing that oblivion of the sorrows of love whose task, interrupted and brought to nought at times by a nightmare big with reminiscence, is ever speedily resumed, hang, even after we are awake, the memories of our dreams, but so overshadowed that often we catch sight of them for the first time only in the broad light of the afternoon when the ray of a similar idea happens by chance to strike them; some of them brilliant and harmonious while we slept, but already so distorted that, having failed to recognise them, we can but hasten to lay them in the earth like dead bodies too quickly decomposed or relics so seriously damaged, so nearly crumbling into dust that the most skilful restorer could not bring them back to their true form or make anything of them. Near the gate is the quarry to which our heavier slumbers repair in search of substances which coat the brain with so unbreakable a glaze that, to awaken the sleeper, his own will is obliged, even on a golden morning, to smite him with mighty blows, like a young Siegfried. Beyond this, again, are the nightmares of which the doctors foolishly assert that they tire us more than does insomnia, whereas on the contrary they enable the thinker to escape from the strain of thought; those nightmares with their fantastic picture-books in which our relatives who are dead are shewn meeting with a serious accident which at the same time does not preclude their speedy recovery. Until then we keep them in a little rat-cage, in which they are smaller than white mice and, covered with big red spots, out of each of which a feather sprouts, engage us in Ciceronian dialogues. Next to this picture-book is the revolving disc of awakening, by virtue of which we submit for a moment to the tedium of having to return at once to a house which was pulled down fifty years ago, the memory of which is gradually effaced as sleep grows more distant by a number of others, until we arrive at that memory which the disc presents only when it has ceased to revolve and which coincides with what we shall see with opened eyes.

Sometimes I had heard nothing, being in one of those slumbers into which we fall as into a pit from which we are heartily glad to be drawn up a little later, heavy, over-fed, digesting all that has been brought to us (as by the nymphs who fed the infant Hercules) by those agile, vegetative powers whose activity is doubled while we sleep.

That kind of sleep is called " sleeping like lead ", and it seems as though one has become, oneself, and remains for a few moments after such a sleep is ended, simply a leaden image. One is no longer a person. How then, seeking for one's mind, one's personality, as one seeks for a thing that is lost, does one recover one's own self rather than any other? Why, when one begins again to think, is it not another personality than yesterday's that is incarnate in one? One fails to see what can dictate the choice, or why, among the millions of human beings any one of whom one might be, it is on him who one was over-night that unerringly one lays one's hand? What is it that guides us, when there has been an actual interruption —whether it be that our unconsciousness has been com-plete or our dreams entirely different from ourself? There has indeed been death, as when the heart has ceased to beat and a rhythmical friction of the tongue revives us. No doubt the room, even if we have seen it only once before, awakens memories to which other, older memories cling. Or were some memories also asleep in us of which we now become conscious? The resurrection at our awakening—after that healing attack of mental alienation which is sleep—must after all be similar to what occurs when we recapture a name, a line, a refrain that we had forgotten. And perhaps the resurrection of the soul after death is to be conceived as a phenomenon of memory.

When I had finished sleeping, tempted by the sunlit sky—but discouraged by the chill—of those last autumn mornings, so luminous and so cold, in which winter begins, to get up and look at the trees on which the leaves were indicated now only by a few strokes, golden or rosy, which seemed to have been left in the air, on an invisible web, I raised my head from the pillow and stretched my neck, keeping my body still hidden beneath the bedclothes; like a chrysalis in the process of change I was a dual creature, with the different parts of which a single environment did not agree; for my eyes colour was sufficient, without warmth; my chest on the other hand was anxious for warmth and not for colour. I rose only after my fire had been lighted, and studied the picture, so delicate and transparent, of the pink and golden morning, to which I had now added by artificial means the element of warmth that it lacked, poking my fire which burned and smoked like a good pipe and gave me, as a pipe would have given me, a pleasure at once coarse because it was based upon a material comfort and delicate because beyond it was printed a pure vision. The walls of my dressing-room were covered with a paper on which a violent red background was patterned with black and white flowers, to which it seemed that I should have some difficulty in growing accustomed. But they succeeded only in striking me as novel, in forcing me to enter not into conflict but into contact with them, in modulating the gaiety, the songs of my morning toilet, they succeeded only in imprisoning me in the heart of a sort of poppy, out of which to look at a world which I saw quite differently from in Paris, from the gay screen which was this new dwelling-place, of a different aspect from the house of my parents, and into which flowed a purer air. On certain days, I was agitated by the desire to see my grandmother again, or by the fear that she might be ill, or else it was the memory of some undertaking which I had left half-finished in Paris, and which seemed to have made no progress; sometimes again it was some difficulty in which, even here, I had managed to become involved. One or other of these anxieties had kept me from sleeping, and I was without strength to face my sorrow which in a moment grew to fill the whole of my existence. Then from the hotel I sent a messenger to the barracks, with a line to Saint-Loup: I told him that, should it be materially possible—I knew that it was extremely difficult for him—I should be most grateful if he would look in for a minute.

An hour later he arrived; and on hearing his ring at the door I felt myself liberated from my obsessions. I knew that, if they were stronger than I, he was stronger than they, and my attention was diverted from them and concentrated on him who would have to settle them. He had come into the room, and already he had enveloped me in the gust of fresh air in which from before dawn he had been displaying so much activity, a vital atmosphere very different from that of my room, to which I at once adapted myself by appropriate reactions.

"I hope you weren't angry with me for bothering you; there is something that is worrying me, as you probably guessed."

"Not at all; I just supposed you wanted to see me, and I thought it very nice of you. I was delighted that you should have sent for me. But what is the trouble? Things not going well? What can I do to help?"

He listened to my explanations, and gave careful answers; but before he had uttered a word he had transformed me to his own likeness; compared with the important occupations which kept him so busy, so alert, so happy, the worries which, a moment ago, I had been unable to endure for another instant seemed to me as to him negligible; I was like a man who, not having been able to open his eyes for some days, sends for a doctor, who neatly and gently raises his eyelid, removes from beneath it and shews him a grain of sand; the sufferer is healed and comforted. All my cares resolved themselves into a telegram which Saint-Loup undertook to dispatch. Life seemed to me so different, so delightful; I was flooded with such a surfeit of strength that I longed for action.

"What are you doing now?" I asked him.

" I must leave you, I'm afraid; we're going on a route march in three quarters of an hour, and I have to be on parade."

" Then it's been a great bother to you, coming here? "

" No, no bother at all, the Captain was very good about it; he told me that if it was for you I must go at once; but you understand, I don't like to seem to be abusing the privilege."

" But if I got up and dressed quickly and went by my-self to the place where you'll be training, it would interest me immensely, and I could perhaps talk to you during the breaks."

" I shouldn't advise you to do that; you have been lying awake, racking your brains over a thing which, I assure you, is not of the slightest importance, but now that it has ceased to worry you, lay your head down on the pillow and go to sleep, which you will find an excellent antidote to the demineralisation of your nerve-cells; only you mustn't go to sleep too soon, because our band-boys will be coming along under your windows; but as soon as they've passed I think you'll be left in peace, and we shall meet again this evening, at dinner."

But soon I was constantly going to see the regiment being trained in field operations, when I began to take an interest in the military theories which Saint-Loup's friends used to expound over the dinner-table, and when it had become the chief desire of my life to see at close quarters their various leaders, just as a person who makes music his principal study and spends his life in the concert halls finds pleasure in frequenting the cafés in which one mingles with the life of the members of the orchestra. To reach the training ground I used to have to take tremendously long walks. In the evening after dinner the longing for sleep made my head drop every now and then as in a swoon. Next morning I realised that I had no more heard the band than, at Balbec, after the evenings on which Saint-Loup had taken me to dinner at Rivebelle, I used to hear the concert on the beach. And at the moment when I wished to rise I had a delicious feeling of incapacity; I felt myself fastened to a deep, invisible ground by the articulations (of which my tiredness made me conscious) of muscular and nutritious roots. I felt myself full of strength; life seemed to extend more amply before me; this was because I had reverted to the good tiredness of my childhood at Combray on the mornings following days on which we had taken the Guermantes walk. Poets make out that we recapture for a moment the self that we were long ago when we enter some house or garden in which we used to live in our youth. But these are most hazardous pilgrimages, which end as often in disappointment as in success. The fixed places, contemporary with different years, it is in ourselves that we should rather seek to find them. This is where the advantage comes in, to a certain extent, of great exhaustion followed by a good night's rest. Good nights, to make us descend into the most subterranean galleries of sleep, where no reflexion from overnight, no gleam of memory comes to lighten the inward monologue (if so be that it cease not also), turn so effectively the soil and break through the surface stone of our body that we discover there, where our muscles dive down and throw out their twisted roots and breathe the air of the new life, the garden in which as a child we used to play. There is no need to travel in order to see it again; we must dig down inwardly to discover it. What once covered the earth is no longer upon it but beneath; a mere excursion does not suffice for a visit to the dead city, excavation is necessary also. But we shall see how certain impressions, fugitive and fortuitous, carry us back even more effectively to the past, with a more delicate precision, with a flight more light-winged, more immaterial, more headlong, more unerring, more immortal than these organic dislocations.

Sometimes my exhaustion was greater still; I had, without any opportunity of going to bed, been following the operations for several days on end. How blessed then was my return to the hotel! As I got into bed I seemed to have escaped at last from the hands of enchanters, sorcerers like those who people the " romances " beloved of our forebears in the seventeenth century. My sleep that night and the lazy morning that followed it were no more than a charming fairy tale. Charming; beneficent perhaps also. I reminded myself that the keenest sufferings have their place of sanctuary, that one can always, when all else fails, find repose. These thoughts carried me far.

On days when, although there was no parade, Saint-Loup had to stay in barracks, I used often to go and visit him there. It was a long way; I had to leave the town and cross the viaduct, from either side of which I had an immense view. A strong breeze blew almost always over this high ground, and filled all the buildings erected on three sides of the barrack-square, which howled incessantly like a cave of the winds. While I waited for Robert—he being engaged on some duty or other—outside the door of his room or in the mess, talking to some of his friends to whom he had introduced me (and whom later on I came now and then to see, even when he was not to be there), looking down from the window three hundred feet to the country below, bare now except where recently sown fields, often still soaked with rain and glittering in the sun, shewed a few stripes of green, of the brilliance and translucent limpidity of enamel, I could hear him discussed by the others, and I soon learned what a popular favourite he was. Among many of the volunteers, belonging to other squadrons, sons of rich business or professional men who looked at the higher aristocratic society only from outside and without penetrating its enclosure, the attraction which they naturally felt towards what they knew of Saint-Loup's character was reinforced by the distinction that attached in their eyes to the young man whom, on Saturday evenings, when they went on pass to Paris, they had seen supping in the Café de la Paix with the Duc d'Uzès and the Prince d'Orléans. And on that account, into his handsome face, his casual way of walking and saluting officers, the perpetual dance of his eyeglass, the affectation shewn in the cut of his service dress—the caps always too high, the breeches of too fine a cloth and too pink a shade—they had introduced the idea of a "tone" which, they were positive, was lacking in the best turned-out officers in the regiment, even the majestic Captain to whom I had been indebted for the privilege of sleeping in barracks, who seemed, in comparison, too pompous and almost common.

One of them said that the Captain had bought a new horse. "He can buy as many horses as he likes. I passed Saint-Loup on Sunday morning in the Allée des Acacias; now he's got some style on a horse!" replied his companion, and knew what he was talking about, for these young fellows belonged to a class which, if it does not frequent the same houses and know the same people, yet, thanks to money and leisure, does not differ from the nobility in its experience of all those refinements of life which money can procure. At any rate their refinement had, in the matter of clothes, for instance, something about it more studied, more impeccable than that free and easy negligence which had so delighted my grandmother in Saint-Loup. It gave quite a thrill to these sons of big stockbrokers or bankers, as they sat eating oysters after the theatre, to see at an adjoining table Serjeant Saint-Loup. And what a tale there was to tell in barracks on Monday night, after a week-end leave, by one of them who was in Robert's squadron, and to whom he had said how d'ye do "most civilly", while another, who was not in the same squadron, was quite positive that, in spite of this, Saint-Loup had recognised him, for two or three times he had put up his eyeglass and stared in the speaker's direction.

"Yes, my brother saw him at the Paix," said another, who had been spending the day with his mistress; "my brother says his dress coat was cut too loose and didn't fit him."

"What was the waistcoat like?"

"He wasn't wearing a white waistcoat; it was purple, with sort of palms on it; stunning!"

To the "old soldiers" (sons of the soil who had never heard of the Jockey Club and simply put Saint-Loup in the category of ultra-rich non-commissioned officers, in which they included all those who, whether bankrupt or not, lived in a certain style, whose income or debts ran into several figures, and who were generous towards their men), the gait, the eyeglass, the breeches, the caps of Saint Loup, even if they saw in them nothing particularly aristocratic, furnished nevertheless just as much interest and meaning. They recognized in these peculiarities the character, the style which they had assigned once and for all time to this most popular of the " stripes " in the regiment, manners like no one's else, scornful indifference to what his superior officers might think, which seemed to them the natural corollary of his goodness to his subordinates. The morning cup of coffee in the canteen, the afternoon " lay-down " in the barrack-room seemed pleasanter, somehow, when some old soldier fed the hungering, lazy section with some savoury tit-bit as to a cap in which Saint-Loup had appeared on parade.

" It was the height of my pack."

" Come off it, old chap, you don't expect us to believe that; it couldn't have been the height of your pack," interrupted a young college graduate who hoped by using these slang terms not to appear a " learned beggar ", and by venturing on this contradiction to obtain confirmation of a fact the thought of which enchanted him.

" Oh, so it wasn't the height of my pack, wasn't it? You measured it, I suppose! I tell you this much, the C. O. glared at it as if he'ld have liked to put him in clink. But you needn't think the great Saint-Loup felt squashed; no, he went and he came, and down with his head and up with his head, and that blinking glass screwed in his eye all the time. We'll see what the ' Capstan ' has to say when he hears. Oh, very likely he'll say nothing, but you may be sure he won't be pleased. But there's nothing so wonderful about that cap. I hear he's got thirty of 'em and more at home, at his house in town."

"Where did you hear that, old man? From our blasted corporal-dog?" asked the young graduate, pedantically displaying the new forms of speech which he had only recently acquired and with which he took a pride in garnishing his conversation.

"Where did I hear it? From his batman; what d'you think?"

"Ah! Now you're talking. That's a chap who knows when he's well off!"

"I should say so! He's got more in his pocket than I have, certain sure! And besides he gives him all his own things, and everything. He wasn't getting his grub properly, he says. Along comes de Saint-Loup, and gives cooky hell: 'I want him to be properly fed, d'you hear,' he says, 'and I don't care what it costs.'"

The old soldier made up for the triviality of the words quoted by the emphasis of his tone, in a feeble imitation of the speaker which had an immense success.

On leaving the barracks I would take a stroll, and then, to fill up the time before I went, as I did every evening, to dine with Saint-Loup at the hotel in which he and his friends had established their mess, I made for my own, as soon as the sun had set, so as to have a couple of hours in which to rest and read. In the square, the evening light bedecked the pepper-pot turrets of the castle with little pink clouds which matched the colour of the bricks, and completed the harmony by softening the tone of the latter where it bathed them. So strong a current of vitality coursed through my nerves that no amount of movement on my part could exhaust it; each step I took, after touching a stone of the pavement, rebounded off it. I seemed to have growing on my heels the wings of Mercury. One of the fountains was filled with a ruddy glow, while in the other the moonlight had already begun to turn the water opalescent. Between them were children at play, uttering shrill cries, wheeling in circles, obeying some necessity of the hour, like swifts or bats. Next door to the hotel, the old National Courts and the Louis XVI orangery, in which were installed now the savings-bank and the Army Corps headquarters, were lighted from within by the palely gilded globes of their gas-jets which, seen in the still clear daylight outside, suited those vast, tall, eighteenth-century windows from which the last rays of the setting sun had not yet departed, as would have suited a complexion heightened with rouge a headdress of yellow tortoise-shell, and persuaded me to seek out my fireside and the lamp which, alone in the shadowy front of my hotel, was striving to resist the gathering darkness, and for the sake of which I went indoors before it was quite dark, for pleasure, as to an appetising meal. I kept, when I was in my room, the same fulness of sensation that I had felt outside. It gave such an apparent convexity of surface to things which as a rule seem flat and empty, to the yellow flame of the fire, the coarse blue paper on the ceiling, on which the setting sun had scribbled cork-screws and whirligigs, like a schoolboy with a piece of red chalk, the curiously patterned cloth on the round table, on which a ream of essay paper and an inkpot lay in readiness for me, with one of Bergotte's novels, that ever since then these things have continued to seem to me to be enriched with a whole form of existence which I feel that I should be able to extract from them if it were granted me to set eyes on them again. I thought with joy of the barracks that I had just left and of their

weather-cock turning with every wind that blew. Like a
diver breathing through a pipe which rises above the surface of the water, I felt that I was in a sense maintaining
contact with a healthy, open-air life when I kept as a bait-
ing-place those barracks, that towering observatory, domi-
nating a country-side furrowed with canals of green
enamel, into whose various buildings I esteemed as a priceless privilege, which I hoped would last, my freedom to go
whenever I chose, always certain of a welcome.

At seven o'clock I dressed myself and went out again
to dine with Saint-Loup at the hotel where he took his
meals. I liked to go there on foot. It was by now pitch
dark, and after the third day of my visit there began to
blow, as soon as night had fallen, an icy wind which
seemed a harbinger of snow. As I walked, I ought not,
strictly speaking, to have ceased for a moment to think
of Mme. de Guermantes; it was only in the attempt to
draw nearer to her that I had come to visit Robert's garrison. But a memory, a grief, are fleeting things. There are
days when they remove so far that we are barely conscious
of them, we think that they have gone for ever. Then we
pay attention to other things. And the streets of this town
had not yet become for me what streets are in the place
where one is accustomed to live, simply means of communication between one part and another. The life led
by the inhabitants of this unknown world must, it seemed
to me, be a marvellous thing, and often the lighted windows of some dwelling-house kept me standing for a long
while motionless in the darkness by laying before my eyes
the actual and mysterious scenes of an existence into which
I might not penetrate. Here the fire-spirit displayed to
me in purple colouring the booth of a chestnut seller in

which a couple of serjeants, their belts slung over the backs of chairs, were playing cards, never dreaming that a magician's wand was making them emerge from the night, like a transparency on the stage, and presenting them in their true lineaments at that very moment to the eyes of an arrested passer-by whom they could not see. In a little curiosity shop a candle, burned almost to its socket, projecting its warm glow over an engraving reprinted it in sanguine, while, battling against the darkness, the light of the big lamp tanned a scrap of leather, inlaid a dagger with fiery spangles, on pictures which were only bad copies spread a priceless film of gold like the patina of time or the varnish used by a master, made in fact of the whole hovel, in which there was nothing but pinchbeck rubbish, a marvellous composition by Rembrandt. Sometimes I lifted my gaze to some huge old dwelling-house on which the shutters had not been closed and in which amphibious men and women floated slowly to and fro in the rich liquid that after nightfall rose incessantly from the wells of the lamps to fill the rooms to the very brink of the outer walls of stone and glass, the movement of their bodies sending through it long unctuous golden ripples. I proceeded on my way, and often, in the dark alley that ran past the cathedral, as long ago on the road to Méséglise, the force of my desire caught and held me; it seemed that a woman must be on the point of appearing, to satisfy it; if, in the darkness, I felt suddenly brush past me a skirt, the violence of the pleasure which I then felt made it impossible for me to believe that the contact was accidental and I attempted to seize in my arms a terrified stranger. This gothic alley meant for me something so real that if I had been successful in raising and enjoying a woman there, it would have been impossible for me not to believe that it was the ancient charm of the place that was bringing us together, and even though she were no more than a common street-walker, stationed there every evening, still the wintry night, the strange place, the darkness, the mediaeval atmosphere would have lent her their mysterious glamour. I thought of what might be in store for me; to try to forget Mme. de Guermantes seemed to me a dreadful thing, but reasonable, and for the first time possible, easy perhaps even. In the absolute quiet of this neighbourhood I could hear ahead of me shouted words and laughter which must come from tipsy revellers staggering home. I waited to see them, I stood peering in the direction from which I had heard the sound. But I was obliged to wait for some time, for the surrounding silence was so intense that it allowed to travel with the utmost clearness and strength sounds that were still a long way off. Finally the revellers did appear; not, as I had supposed, in front of me, but ever so far behind. Whether the intersection of side-streets, the interposition of buildings had, by reverberation, brought about this acoustic error, or because it is very difficult to locate a sound when the place from which it comes is not known, I had been as far wrong over direction as over distance.

The wind grew stronger. It was thick and bristling with coming snow. I returned to the main street and jumped on board the little tramway-car on which, from its platform, an officer, without apparently seeing them, was acknowledging the salutes of the loutish soldiers who trudged past along the pavement, their faces daubed crimson by the cold, reminding me, in this little town which the sudden leap from autumn into early winter seemed to have transported farther north, of the rubicund faces which Breughel gives to his merry, junketing, frostbound peasants.

And sure enough at the hotel where I was to meet Saint-Loup and his friends and to which the fair now beginning had attracted a number of people from near and far, I found, as I hurried across the courtyard with its glimpses of glowing kitchens in which chickens were turning on spits, pigs were roasting, lobsters being flung, alive, into what the landlord called the " everlasting fire ", an influx (worthy of some *Numbering of the People before Bethlehem* such as the old Flemish masters used to paint) of new arrivals who assembled there in groups, asking the landlord or one of his staff (who, if he did not like the look of them, would recommend lodgings elsewhere in the town) whether they could have dinner and beds, while a scullion hurried past holding a struggling fowl by the neck. And similarly, in the big dining-room which I crossed the first day before coming to the smaller room in which my friend was waiting for me, it was of some feast in the Gospels portrayed with a mediaeval simplicity and an exaggeration typically Flemish that one was reminded by the quantity of fish, pullets, grouse, woodcock, pigeons, brought in dressed and garnished and piping hot by breathless waiters who slid over the polished floor to gain speed and set them down on the huge carving table where they were at once cut up but where—for most of the people had nearly finished dinner when I arrived— they accumulated untouched, as though their profusion and the haste of those who brought them in were due not so much to the requirements of the diners as to respect for the sacred text, scrupulously followed in the letter but quaintly illustrated by real details borrowed from local custom, and to an aesthetic and religious scruple for making evident to the eye the solemnity of the feast by the profusion of the victuals and the assiduity of the servers. One of these stood lost in thought at the far end of the room by a sideboard; and to find out from him, who alone appeared calm enough to be capable of answering me, in which room our table had been laid, making my way forward among the chafing-dishes that had been lighted here and there to keep the late comers' plates from growing cold (which did not, however, prevent the dessert, in the centre of the room, from being piled on the outstretched hands of a huge mannikin, sometimes supported on the wings of a duck, apparently of crystal, but really of ice, carved afresh every day with a hot iron by a sculptor-cook, quite in the Flemish manner), I went straight—at the risk of being knocked down by his colleagues—towards this servitor, in whom I felt that I recognised a character who is traditionally present in all these sacred subjects, for he reproduced with scrupulous accuracy the blunt features, fatuous and ill-drawn, the musing expression, already half aware of the miracle of a divine presence which the others have not yet begun to suspect. I should add that, in view probably of the coming fair, this presentation was strengthened by a celestial contingent, recruited in mass, of cherubim and seraphim. A young angel musician, whose fair hair enclosed a fourteen-year-old face, was not, it was true, playing on any instrument, but stood musing before a gong or a pile of plates, while other less infantile angels flew swiftly across the boundless expanse of the room, beating the air with the ceaseless fluttering of the napkins which fell along the lines of their bodies like the wings in "primitive" paintings, with pointed ends. Fleeing those ill-defined regions, screened by a hedge of palms through which the angelic servitors looked, from a distance, as though they had floated down out of the empyrean, I explored my way to the smaller room in which Saint-Loup's table was laid. I found there several of his friends who dined with him regularly, nobles except for one or two commoners in whom the young nobles had, in their school days, detected likely friends, and with whom they readily associated, proving thereby that they were not on principle hostile to the middle class, even though it were Republican, provided it had clean hands and went to mass. On the first of these evenings, before we sat down to dinner, I drew Saint-Loup into a corner and, in front of all the rest but so that they should not hear me, said to him:

"Robert, this is hardly the time or the place for what I am going to say, but I shan't be a second. I keep on forgetting to ask you when I'm in the barracks; isn't that Mme. de Guermantes's photograph that you have on your table?"

"Why, yes; my good aunt."

"Of course she is; what a fool I am; you told me before that she was; I'd forgotten all about her being your aunt. I say, your friends will be getting impatient, we must be quick, they're looking at us; another time will do; it isn't at all important."

"That's all right; go on as long as you like. They can wait."

"No, no; I do want to be polite to them; they're so nice; besides, it doesn't really matter in the least, I assure you."

" Do you know that worthy Oriane, then? "

This " worthy Oriane," as he might have said, " that good Oriane," did not imply that Saint-Loup regarded Mme. de Guermantes as especially good. In this instance the words " good ", " excellent ", " worthy " are mere reinforcements of the demonstrative " that ", indicating a person who is known to both parties and of whom the speaker does not quite know what to say to someone outside the intimate circle. The word " good " does duty as a stopgap and keeps the conversation going for a moment until the speaker has hit upon " Do you see much of her? " or " I haven't set eyes on her for months," or " I shall be seeing her on Tuesday," or " She must be getting on, now, you know."

" I can't tell you how funny it is that it should be her photograph, because we're living in her house now, in Paris, and I've been hearing the most astounding things " (I should have been hard put to it to say what) " about her, which have made me immensely interested in her, only from a literary point of view, don't you know, from a—how shall I put it—from a Balzacian point of view; but you're so clever you can see what I mean; I don't need to explain things to you; but we must hurry up; what on earth will your friends think of my manners? "

" They will think absolutely nothing; I have told them that you are sublime, and they are a great deal more alarmed than you are."

" You are too kind. But listen, what I want to say is this: I suppose Mme. de Guermantes hasn't any idea that I know you, has she? "

" I can't say; I haven't seen her since the summer, because I haven't had any leave since she's been in town."

"What I was going to say is this: I've been told that she looks on me as an absolute idiot."

"That I do not believe; Oriane is not exactly an eagle, but all the same she's by no means stupid."

"You know that, as a rule, I don't care about your advertising the good opinion you're kind enough to hold of me; I'm not conceited. That's why I'm sorry you should have said flattering things about me to your friends here (we will go back to them in two seconds). But Mme. de Guermantes is different; if you could let her know—if you would even exaggerate a trifle—what you think of me, you would give me great pleasure."

"Why, of course I will, if that's all you want me to do; it's not very difficult; but what difference can it possibly make to you what she thinks of you? I suppose you think her no end of a joke, really; anyhow, if that's all you want we can discuss it in front of the others or when we are by ourselves; I'm afraid of your tiring yourself if you stand talking, and it's so inconvenient too, when we have heaps of opportunities of being alone together."

It was precisely this inconvenience that had given me courage to approach Robert; the presence of the others was for me a pretext that justified my giving my remarks a curt and incoherent form, under cover of which I could more easily dissemble the falsehood of my saying to my friend that I had forgotten his connexion with the Duchess, and also did not give him time to frame—with regard to my reasons for wishing that Mme. de Guermantes should know that I was his friend, was clever, and so forth—questions which would have been all the more disturbing in that I should not have been able to answer them.

"Robert, I'm surprised that a man of your intelligence should fail to understand that one doesn't discuss the things that will give one's friends pleasure; one does them. Now I, if you were to ask me no matter what, and indeed I only wish you would ask me to do something for you, I can assure you I shouldn't want any explanations. I may ask you for more than I really want; I have no desire to know Mme. de Guermantes, but just to test you I ought to have said that I was anxious to dine with Mme. de Guermantes; I am sure you would never have done it."

"Not only should I have done it, I will do it."

"When?"

"Next time I'm in Paris, three weeks from now, I expect."

"We shall see; I dare say she won't want to see me, though. I can't tell you how grateful I am."

"Not at all; it's nothing."

"Don't say that; it's everything in the world, because now I can see what sort of friend you are; whether what I ask you to do is important or not, disagreeable or not, whether I am really keen about it or ask you only as a test, it makes no difference; you say you will do it, and there you shew the fineness of your mind and heart. A stupid friend would have started a discussion."

Which was exactly what he had just been doing; but perhaps I wanted to flatter his self-esteem; perhaps also I was sincere, the sole touchstone of merit seeming to me to be the extent to which a friend could be useful in respect of the one thing that seemed to me to have any importance, namely my love. Then I went on, perhaps from cunning, possibly from a genuine increase of affection inspired by gratitude, expectancy, and the copy of Mme. de Guermantes's very features which nature had made in producing her nephew Robert: "But, I say, we mustn't keep them waiting any longer, and I've mentioned only one of the two things I wanted to ask you, the less important; the other is more important to me, but I'm afraid you will never consent. Would it bore you if we were to call each other *tu*?"

"Bore me? My dear fellow! Joy! Tears of joy! Undreamed-of happiness!"

"Thank you—*tu* I mean; you begin first—ever so much. It is such a pleasure to me that you needn't do anything about Mme. de Guermantes if you'ld rather not, this is quite enough for me."

"I can do both."

"I say, Robert! Listen to me a minute," I said to him later while we were at dinner. "Oh, it's really too absurd the way our conversation is always being interrupted, I can't think why—you remember the lady I was speaking to you about just now."

"Yes."

"You're quite sure you know who' I mean?"

"Why, what do you take me for, a village idiot?"

"You wouldn't care to give me her photograph, I suppose?"

I had meant to ask him only for the loan of it. But when the time came to speak I felt shy, I decided that the request was indiscreet, and in order to hide my confusion I put the question more bluntly, and increased my demand, as if it had been quite natural.

"No; I should have to ask her permission first," was

his answer.

He blushed as he spoke. I could see that he had a reservation in his mind, that he credited me also with one, that he would give only a partial service to my love, under the restraint of certain moral principles, and for this I hated him.

At the same time I was touched to see how differently Saint-Loup behaved towards me now that I was no longer alone with him, and that his friends formed an audience. His increased affability would have left me cold had I thought that it was deliberately assumed; but I could feel that it was spontaneous and consisted only of all that he had to say about me in my absence and refrained as a rule from saying when we were together by ourselves. In our private conversations I might certainly suspect the pleasure that he found in talking to me, but that pleasure he almost always left unexpressed. Now, at the same remarks from me which, as a rule, he enjoyed without shewing it, he watched from the corner of his eye to see whether they produced on his friends the effect on which he had counted, an effect corresponding to what he had promised them beforehand. The mother of a girl in her first season could be no more unrelaxing in her attention to her daughter's responses and to the attitude of the public. If I had made some remark at which, alone in my company, he would merely have smiled, he was afraid that the others might not have seen the point, and put in a " What's that? " to make me repeat what I had said, to attract attention, and turning at once to his friends and making himself automatically, by facing them with a hearty laugh, the fugleman of their laughter, presented me for the first time with the opinion that he actually held of me and must often have expressed to them. So that I caught sight of myself suddenly from without, like a person who reads his name in a newspaper or sees himself in a mirror.

It occurred to me, one of these evenings, to tell a mildly amusing story about Mme. Blandais, but I stopped at once, remembering that Saint-Loup knew it already, and that when I had tried to tell him it on the day following my arrival he had interrupted me with: "You told me that before, at Balbec." I was surprised, therefore, to find him begging me to go on and assuring me that he did not know the story, and that it would amuse him immensely. "You've forgotten it for the moment," I said to him, "but you'll remember as I go on." "No, really; I swear you're mistaken. You've never told me. Do go on." And throughout the story he fixed a feverish and enraptured gaze alternately on myself and on his friends. I realised only after I had finished, amid general laughter, that it had struck him that this story would give his friends a good idea of my wit, and that it was for this reason that he had pretended not to know it. Such is the stuff of friendship.

On the third evening, one of his friends, to whom I had not had an opportunity before of speaking, conversed with me at great length; and I overheard him telling Saint-Loup how much he had been enjoying himself. And indeed we sat talking together almost all evening, leaving our glasses of sauterne untouched on the table before us, isolated, sheltered from the others by the sumptous curtains of one of those intuitive sympathies between man and man which, when they are not based upon any physical attraction, are the only kind that is altogether mysterious. Of such an enigmatic nature had seemed to me, at Balbec, that feeling which Saint-Loup had for me, which was not to be confused with the interest of our conversations, a feeling free from any material association, invisible, intangible, and yet a thing of the presence of which in himself, like a sort of inflammatory gas, he had been so far conscious as to refer to it with a smile. And yet there was perhaps something more surprising still in this sympathy born here in a single evening, like a flower that had budded and opened in a few minutes in the warmth of this little room. I could not help asking Robert when he spoke to me about Balbec whether it were really settled that he was to marry Mlle. d'Ambresac. He assured me that not only was it not settled, but there had never been any thought of such a match, he had never seen her, he did not know who she was. If at that moment I had happened to see any of the social gossipers who had told me of this coming event, they would promptly have announced the betrothal of Mlle. d'Ambresac to some one who was not Saint-Loup and that of Saint-Loup to some one who was not Mlle. d'Ambresac. I should have surprised them greatly had I reminded them of their incompatible and still so recent predictions. In order that this little game may continue, and multiply false reports by attaching the greatest possible number to every name in turn, nature has furnished those who play it with a memory as short as their credulity is long.

Saint-Loup had spoken to me of another of his friends who was present also, one with whom he was on particularly good terms just then, since they were the only two advocates in their mess of the retrial of Dreyfus.

Just as a brother of this friend of Saint-Loup, who had

been trained at the Schola Cantorum, thought about every
new musical work not at all what his father, his mother,
his cousins, his club friends thought, but exactly what the
other students thought at the Schola, so this non-commissioned nobleman (of whom Bloch formed an extraordinary opinion when I told him about him, because,
touched to hear that he belonged to the same party as
himself, he nevertheless imagined him on account of his
aristocratic birth and religious and military upbringing
to be as different as possible, endowed with the same
romantic attraction as a native of a distant country) had
a "mentality", as people were now beginning to say,
analogous to that of the whole body of Dreyfusards in
general and of Bloch in particular, on which the traditions
of his family and the interests of his career could retain
no hold whatever. Similarly one of Saint-Loup's cousins
had married a young Eastern princess who was said to
write poetry quite as fine as Victor Hugo's or Alfred de
Vigny's, and in spite of this was supposed to have a
different type of mind from what one would naturally
expect, the mind of an Eastern princess immured in an
Arabian Nights palace. For the writers who had the
privilege of meeting her was reserved the disappointment
or rather the joy of listening to conversation which gave
the impression not of Scheherazade but of a person of
genius of the type of Alfred de Vigny or Victor Hugo.

"That fellow? Oh, he's not like Saint-Loup, he's a
regular devil," my new friend informed me; "he's not
even straight about it. At first, he used to say: 'Just wait
a little, there's a man I know well, a clever, kind-hearted
fellow, General de Boisdeffre; you need have no hesitation in accepting his decision.' But as soon as he heard

that Boisdeffre had pronounced Dreyfus guilty, Boisdeffre ceased to count: clericalism, staff prejudices prevented his forming a candid opinion, although there is no one in the world (or was, rather, before this Dreyfus business) half so clerical as our friend. Next he told us that now we were sure to get the truth, the case had been put in the hands of Saussier, and he, a soldier of the Republic (our friend coming of an ultra-monarchist family, if you please), was a man of bronze, a stern unyielding conscience. But when Saussier pronounced Esterhazy innocent, he found fresh reasons to account for the decision, reasons damaging not to Dreyfus but to General Saussier. It was the militarist spirit that blinded Saussier (and I must explain to you that our friend is just as much militarist as clerical, or at least he was; I don't know what to think of him now). His family are all broken-hearted at seeing him possessed by such ideas."

"Don't you think," I suggested, turning half towards Saint-Loup so as not to appear to be cutting myself off from him, as well as towards his friend, and so that we might all three join in the conversation, "that the influence we ascribe to environment is particularly true of intellectual environment. One is the man of one's idea. There are far fewer ideas than men, therefore all men with similar ideas are alike. As there is nothing material in an idea, so the people who are only materially neighbours of the man with an idea can do nothing to alter it."

At this point I was interrupted by Saint-Loup, because another of the young men had leaned across to him with a smile and, pointing to me, exclaimed: "Duroc! Duroc all over!" I had no idea what this might mean, but I felt the expression on the shy young face to be more than friendly. While I was speaking, the approbation of the party seemed to Saint-Loup superfluous; he insisted on silence. And just as a conductor stops his orchestra with a rap from his baton because some one in the audience has made a noise, so he rebuked the author of this disturbance: "Gibergue, you must keep your mouth shut when people are speaking. You can tell us about it afterwards." And to me: "Please go on."

I gave a sigh of relief, for I had been afraid that he was going to make me begin all over again.

"And as an idea," I went on, "is a thing that cannot participate in human interests and would be incapable of deriving any benefit from them, the men who are governed by an idea are not influenced by material considerations."

When I had finished, "That's one in the eye for you, my boys," exclaimed Saint-Loup, who had been following me with his gaze with the same anxious solicitude as if I had been walking upon a tight-rope. "What were you going to say, Gibergue?"

"I was just saying that your friend reminded me of Major Duroc. I seemed to hear him speaking."

"Why, I've often thought so myself," replied Saint-Loup; "they have several points in common, but you'll find there are a thousand things in this fellow that Duroc hasn't got."

Saint-Loup was not satisfied with this comparison. In an ecstasy of joy, into which there no doubt entered the joy that he felt in making me shine before his friends, with extreme volubility, stroking me as though he were rubbing down a horse that had just come first past the post, he reiterated: "You're the cleverest man I know, do you hear?" He corrected himself, and added: "You and Elstir.—You don't mind my bracketing him with you, I hope. You understand—punctiliousness. It's like this: I say it to you as one might have said to Balzac: 'You are the greatest novelist of the century—you and Stendhal.' Excessive punctiliousness, don't you know, and at heart an immense admiration. No? You don't admit Stendhal?" he went on, with an ingenuous confidence in my judgment which found expression in a charming, smiling, almost childish glance of interrogation from his green eyes. "Oh, good! I see you're on my side; Bloch can't stand Stendhal. I think it's idiotic of him. The *Chartreuse* is after all an immense work, don't you think? I am so glad you agree with me. What is it you like best in the *Chartreuse,* answer me?" he appealed to me with a boyish impetuosity. And the menace of his physical strength made the question almost terrifying. "Mosca? Fabrice?" I answered timidly that Mosca reminded me a little of M. de Norpois. Whereupon peals of laughter from the young Siegfried Saint-Loup. And while I was going on to explain: "But Mosca is far more intelligent, not so pedantic," I heard Robert cry: "Bravo!" actually clapping his hands, and, helpless with laughter, gasp: "Oh, perfect! Admirable! You really are astounding."

I took a particular pleasure in talking to this young man, as for that matter to all Robert's friends and to Robert himself, about their barracks, the officers of the garrison, and the army in general. Thanks to the immensely enlarged scale on which we see the things, however petty they may be, in the midst of which we eat, and talk, and lead our real life; thanks to that formidable enlargement which they undergo, and the effect of which is that the rest of the world, not being present, cannot compete with them, and assumes in comparison the un-substantiality of a dream, I had begun to take an interest in the various personalities of the barracks, in the officers whom I saw in the square when I went to visit Saint-Loup, or, if I was awake then, when the regiment passed beneath my windows. I should have liked to know more about the major whom Saint-Loup so greatly admired, and about the course of military history which would have appealed to me "even from an aesthetic point of view". I knew that with Robert the spoken word was, only too often, a trifle hollow, but at other times implied the assimilation of valuable ideas which he was fully capable of grasping. Unfortunately, from the military point of view Robert was exclusively preoccupied at this time with the case of Dreyfus. He spoke little about it, since he alone of the party at table was a Dreyfusard; the others were violently opposed to the idea of a fresh trial, except my other neighbour, my new friend, and his opinions appeared to be somewhat vague. A firm admirer of the colonel, who was regarded as an exceptionally competent officer and had denounced the current agitation against the Army in several of his regimental orders, which won him the reputation of being an anti-Dreyfusard, my neighbour had heard that his commanding officer had let fall certain remarks which had led to the supposition that he had his doubts as to the guilt of Dreyfus and retained his admiration for Picquart. In the latter respect, at any rate, the rumour of Dreyfusism as applied to the colonel was as ill-founded as are all the rumours, springing from none knows where, which float around any great scandal. For, shortly afterwards, this colonel having been detailed to interrogate the former Chief of the Intelligence Branch, had treated him with a brutality and contempt the like of which had never been known before. However this might be (and naturally he had not taken the liberty of going direct to the colonel for his information), my neighbour had paid Saint-Loup the compliment of telling him—in the tone in which a Catholic lady might tell a Jewish lady that her parish priest denounced the po-groms in Russia and might openly admire the generosity of certain Israelites—that their colonel was not, with regard to Dreyfusism—to a certain kind of Dreyfusism, at least—the fanatical, narrow opponent that he had been made out to be.

"I am not surprised," was Saint-Loup's comment; "for he's a sensible man. But in spite of that he is blinded by the prejudices of his caste, and above all by his clericalism. Now," he turned to me, "Major Duroc, the lecturer on military history I was telling you about; there's a man who is whole-heartedly in support of our views, or so I'm told. And I should have been surprised to hear that he wasn't, for he's not only a brilliantly clever man, but a Radical-Socialist and a freemason."

Partly out of courtesy to his friends, whom these ex-pressions of Saint-Loup's faith in Dreyfus made uncom-fortable, and also because the subject was of more interest to myself, I asked my neighbour if it were true that this major gave a demonstration of military history which had a genuine aesthetic beauty. "It is absolutely true."

"But what do you mean by that?"

"Well, all that you read, let us say, in the narrative of a military historian, the smallest facts, the most trivial happenings, are only the outward signs of an idea which has to be analysed, and which often brings to light other ideas, like a palimpsest. So that you have a field for study as intellectual as any science you care to name, or any art, and one that is satisfying to the mind."

"Give me an example or two, if you don't mind."

"It is not very easy to explain," Saint-Loup broke in. "You read, let us say, that this or that Corps has tried . . . but before we go any farther, the serial number of the Corps, its order of battle are not without their significance. If it is not the first time that the operation has been attempted, and if for the same operation we find a different Corps being brought up, it is perhaps a sign that the previous Corps have been wiped out or have suffered heavy casualties in the said operation; that they are no longer in a fit state to carry it through successfully. Next, we must ask ourselves what was this Corps which is now out of action; if it was composed of shock troops, held in reserve for big attacks, a fresh Corps of inferior quality will have little chance of succeeding where the first has failed. Furthermore, if we are not at the start of a campaign, this fresh Corps may itself be a composite formation of odds and ends withdrawn from other Corps, which throws a light on the strength of the forces the belligerent still has at his disposal and the proximity of the moment when his forces shall be definitely inferior to the enemy's, which gives to the operation on which this Corps is about to engage a different meaning, because, if it is no longer in a condition to make good its losses, its successes even will only help mathematically to bring it nearer to its ultimate destruction. And then, the serial number of the Corps that it has facing it is of no less significance. If, for instance, it is a much weaker unit, which has already accounted for

several important units of the attacking force, the whole
nature of the operation is changed, since, even if it should
end in the loss of the position which the defending force
has been holding, simply to have held it for any length of
time may be a great success if a very small defending
force has been sufficient to disable highly important forces
on the other side. You can understand that if, in the
analysis of the Corps engaged on both sides, there are
all these points of importance, the study of the position
itself, of the roads, of the railways which it commands,
of the lines of communication which it protects, is of the
very highest. One must study what I may call the whole
geographical context," he added with a laugh. And indeed he was so delighted with this expression that, every
time he employed it, even months afterwards, it was
always accompanied by the same laugh. "While the
operation is being prepared by one of the belligerents, if
you read that one of his patrols has been wiped out in
the neighbourhood of the position by the other belligerent,
one of the conclusions which you are entitled to draw is
that one side was attempting to reconnoitre the defensive
works with which the other intended to resist his attack.
An exceptional burst of activity at a given point may
indicate the desire to capture that point, but equally well
the desire to hold the enemy in check there, not to retaliate at the point at which he has attacked you; or it
may indeed be only a feint, intended to cover by an increased activity the relief of troops in that sector. (Which
was a classic feint in Napoleon's wars.) On the other
hand, to appreciate the significance of any movement, its
probable object, and, as a corollary, the other movements
by which it will be accompanied or followed, it is not

immaterial to consult, not so much the announcements
issued by the Higher Command, which may be intended
to deceive the enemy, to mask a possible check, as the
manual of field operations in use in the country in question. We are always entitled to assume that the manoeuvre
which an army has attempted to carry out is that prescribed by the rules that are applicable to the circumstances. If, for instance, the rule lays down that a frontal
attack should be accompanied by a flank attack; if, after
the flank attack has failed, the Higher Command makes
out that it had no connexion with the main attack and
was merely a diversion, there is a strong likelihood that the
truth will be found by consulting the rules and not the
reports issued from Headquarters. And there are not only
the regulations governing each army to be considered,
but their traditions, their habits, their doctrines; the study
of diplomatic activities, with their perpetual action or
reaction upon military activities, must not be neglected
either. Incidents apparently insignificant, which at the
time are not understood, will explain to you how the
enemy, counting upon a support which these incidents
shew to have been withheld, was able to carry out only
a part of his strategic plan. So that, if you can read
between the lines of military history, what is a confused
jumble for the ordinary reader becomes a chain of reasoning as straightforward as a picture is for the picture-
lover who can see what the person portrayed is wearing
and has in his hands, while the visitor hurrying through
the gallery is bewildered by a blur of colour which gives
him a headache. But just as with certain pictures, in
which it is not enough to observe that the figure is holding
a chalice, but one must know why the painter chose to

place a chalice in his hands, what it is intended to symbolise, so these military operations, apart from their immediate object, are quite regularly traced, in the mind of the general responsible for the campaign, from the plans of earlier battles, which we may call the past experience, the literature, the learning, the etymology, the aristocracy (whichever you like) of the battles of to-day. Observe that I am not speaking for the moment of the local, the (what shall I call it?) spatial identity of battles. That exists also. A battle-field has never been, and never will be throughout the centuries, simply the ground upon which a particular battle has been fought. If it has been a battle-field, that was because it combined certain conditions of geographical position, of geological formation, drawbacks even, of a kind that would obstruct the enemy (a river, for instance, cutting his force in two), which made it a good field of battle. And so what it has been it will continue to be. A painter doesn't make a studio out of any old room; so you don't make a battle-field out of any old piece of ground. There are places set apart for the purpose. But, once again, this is not what I was telling you about; it was the type of battle which one follows, in a sort of strategic tracing, a tactical imitation, if you like. Battles like Ulm, Lodi, Leipzig, Cannae. I can't say whether there is ever going to be another war, or what nations are going to fight in it, but, if a war does come, you may be sure that it will include (and deliberately, on the commander's part) a Cannae, an Austerlitz, a Rosbach, a Waterloo. Some of our people say quite openly that Marshal von Schieffer and General Falkenhausen have prepared a Battle of Cannae against France, in the Hannibal style, pinning their enemy down along his whole front, and advancing on both flanks, especially through Belgium, while Bernhardi prefers the oblique order of Frederick the Great, Lenthen rather than Cannae. Others expound their views less crudely, but I can tell you one thing, my boy, that Beauconseil, the squadron commander I introduced you to the other day, who is an officer with a very great future before him, has swotted up a little Pratzen attack of his own; he knows it inside out, he is keeping it up his sleeve, and if he ever has an opportunity to put it into practice he will make a clean job of it and let us have it on a big scale. The break through in the centre at Rivoli, too; that's a thing that will crop up if there's ever another war. It's no more obsolete than the *Iliad*. I must add that we are practically condemned to make frontal attacks, because we can't afford to repeat the mistake we made in Seventy; we must assume the offensive, and nothing else. The only thing that troubles me is that if I see only the slower, more antiquated minds among us opposing this splendid doctrine, still, one of the youngest of my masters, who is a genius, I mean Mangin, would like us to leave room, provisionally of course, for the defensive. It is not very easy to answer him when he cites the example of Austerlitz, where the defence was merely a prelude to attack and victory."

The enunciation of these theories by Saint-Loup made me happy. They gave me to hope that perhaps I was not being led astray, in my life at Doncières, with regard to these officers whom I used to hear being discussed while I sat sipping a sauterne which bathed them in its charming golden glint, by the same magnifying power which had swollen to such enormous proportions in my eyes while I was at Balbec the King and Queen of the South Sea Island, the little group of the four epicures, the young gambler, Legrandin's brother-in-law, now shrunken so in my view as to appear non-existent. What gave me pleasure to-day would not, perhaps, leave me indifferent to-morrow, as had always happened hitherto; the creature that I still was at this moment was not, perhaps, doomed to immediate destruction, since to the ardent and fugitive passion which I had felt on these few evenings for everything connected with military life, Saint-Loup, by what he had just been saying to me, touching the art of war, added an intellectual foundation, of a permanent character, capable of attaching me to itself so strongly that I might, without any attempt to deceive myself, feel assured that after I had left Doncières I should continue to take an interest in the work of my friends there, and should not be long in coming to pay them another visit. At the same time, so as to make quite sure that this art of war was indeed an art in the true sense of the word:

"You interest me—I beg your pardon, *tu* interest me enormously," I said to Saint-Loup, "but tell me, there is one point that puzzles me. I feel that I could be keenly thrilled by the art of strategy, but if so I must first be sure that it is not so very different from the other arts, that knowing the rules is not everything. You tell me that plans of battles are copied. I do find something aesthetic, just as you said, in seeing beneath a modern battle the plan of an older one, I can't tell you how attractive it sounds. But then, does the genius of the commander count for nothing? Does he really do no more than apply the rules? Or, in point of science, are there great generals as there are great surgeons, who, when the symptoms exhibited by two states of ill-health are identical to the outward eye, nevertheless feel, for some infinitesimal reason, founded perhaps on their experience, but interpreted afresh, that in one case they ought to do one thing, in another case another; that in one case it is better to operate, in another to wait?"

"I should just say so! You will find Napoleon not attacking when all the rules ordered him to attack, but some obscure divination warned him not to. For instance, look at Austerlitz, or in 1806 take his instructions to Lannes. But you will find certain generals slavishly imitating one of Napoleon's movements and arriving at a diametrically opposite result. There are a dozen examples of that in 1870. But even for the interpretation of what the enemy *may* do, what he actually does is only a symptom which may mean any number of different things. Each of them has an equal chance of being the right thing, if one looks only to reasoning and science, just as in certain difficult cases all the medical science in the world will be powerless to decide whether the invisible tumour is malignant or not, whether or not the operation ought to be performed. It is his instinct, his divination— like Mme. de Thèbes (you follow me?)—which decides, in the great general as in the great doctor. Thus I've been telling you, to take one instance, what might be meant by a reconnaissance on the eve of a battle. But it may mean a dozen other things also, such as to make the enemy think you are going to attack him at one point whereas you intend to attack him at another, to put out a screen which will prevent him from seeing the preparations for your real operation, to force him to bring up

fresh troops, to hold them, to immobilise them in a different place from where they are needed, to form an
estimate of the forces at his disposal, to feel him, to force
him to shew his hand. Sometimes, indeed, the fact that
you employ an immense number of troops in an operation is by no means a proof that that is your true objective; for you may be justified in carrying it out, even if
it is only a feint, so that your feint may have a better
chance of deceiving the enemy. If I had time now to go
through the Napoleonic wars from this point of view, I
assure you that these simple classic movements which
we study here, and which you will come and see us
practising in the field, just for the pleasure of a walk,
you young rascal—no, I know you're not well, I apologise!
—well, in a war, when you feel behind you the vigilance,
the judgment, the profound study of the Higher Command, you are as much moved by them as by the simple
lamps of a lighthouse, only a material combustion, but an
emanation of the spirit, sweeping through space to warn
ships of danger. I may have been wrong, perhaps, in
speaking to you only of the literature of war. In reality,
as the formation of the soil, the direction of wind and
light tell us which way a tree will grow, so the conditions
in which a campaign is fought, the features of the country
through which you march, prescribe, to a certain extent,
and limit the number of the plans among which the
general has to choose. Which means that along a mountain range, through a system of valleys, over certain
plains, it is almost with the inevitability and the tremendous beauty of an avalanche that you can forecast the
line of an army on the march."

" Now you deny me that freedom of choice in the commander, that power of divination in the enemy who is trying to discover his plan, which you allowed me a moment ago."

"Not at all. You remember that book of philosophy we read together at Balbec, the richness of the world of possibilities compared with the real world. Very well. It is the same again with the art of strategy. In a given situation there will be four plans that offer themselves, one of which the general has to choose, as a disease may pass through various phases for which the doctor has to watch. And here again the weakness and greatness of the human elements are fresh causes of uncertainty. For of these four plans let us assume that contingent reasons (such as the attainment of minor objects, or time, which may be pressing, or the smallness of his effective strength and shortage of rations) lead the general to prefer the first, which is less perfect, but less costly also to carry out, is more rapid, and has for its terrain a richer country for feeding his troops. He may, after having begun with this plan, which the enemy, uncertain at first, will soon detect, find that success lies beyond his grasp, the difficulties being too great (that is what I call the element of human weakness), abandon it and try the second or third or fourth. But it may equally be that he has tried the first plan (and this is what I call human greatness) merely as a feint to pin down the enemy, so as to surprise him later at a point where he has not been expecting an attack. Thus at Ulm, Mack, who expected the enemy to advance from the west, was surrounded from the north where he thought he was perfectly safe. My example is not a very good one, as a matter of fact. And Ulm is a better type of enveloping battle, which the future will see reproduced, because it is not only a classic example from which generals will seek inspiration, but a form that is to some extent necessary (one of several necessities, which leaves room for choice, for variety) like a type of crystallisation. But it doesn't much matter, really, because these conditions are after all artificial. To go back to our philosophy book; it is like the rules of logic or scientific laws, reality does conform to it more or less, but bear in mind that the great mathematician Poincaré is by no means certain that mathematics are strictly accurate. As to the rules themselves, which I mentioned to you, they are of secondary importance really, and besides they are altered from time to time. We cavalrymen, for instance, have to go by the *Field Service* of 1895, which, you may say, is out of date since it is based on the old and obsolete doctrine which maintains that cavalry warfare has little more than a moral effect, in the panic that the charge creates in the enemy. Whereas the more intelligent of our teachers, all the best brains in the cavalry, and particularly the major I was telling you about, anticipate on the contrary that the decisive victory will be obtained by a real hand to hand encounter in which our weapons will be sabre and lance and the side that can hold out longer will win, not simply morally and by creating panic, but materially."

"Saint-Loup is quite right, and it is probable that the next *Field Service* will shew signs of this evolution," put in my other neighbour.

"I am not ungrateful for your support, for your opinions seem to make more impression upon my friend than mine," said Saint-Loup with a smile, whether because the growing attraction between his comrade and myself annoyed him slightly or because he thought it graceful to solemnise it with this official confirmation. " Perhaps I may have underestimated the importance of the rules; I don't know. They do change, that must be admitted. But in the mean time they control the military situation, the plans of campaign and concentration. If they reflect a false conception of strategy they may be the principal cause of defeat. All this is a little too technical for you," he remarked to me. " After all, you may say that what does most to accelerate the evolution of the art of war is wars themselves. In the course of a campaign, if it is at all long, you will see one belligerent profiting by the lessons furnished him by the successes and mistakes, perfecting the methods of the other, who will improve on him in turn. But all that is a thing of the past. With the terrible advance of artillery, the wars of the future, if there are to be any more wars, will be so short that, before we have had time to think of putting our lessons into practice, peace will have been signed."

" Don't be so touchy," I told Saint-Loup, reverting to the first words of this speech. " I was listening to you quite eagerly."

" If you will kindly not fly into a passion, and will allow me to speak," his friend went on, " I shall add to what you have just been saying that if battles copy and coincide with one another it is not merely due to the mind of the commander. It may happen that a mistake on his part (for instance, his failure to appreciate the strength of the enemy) will lead him to call upon his men for extravagant sacrifices, sacrifices which certain units will make with an abnegation so sublime that their part in the battle will be analogous to that played by some other unit in some other battle, and these will be quoted in history as interchangeable examples: to stick to 1870, we have the Prussian Guard at Saint-Privat, and the Turcos at Frœschviller and Wissembourg."

"Ah! Interchangeable; very neat! Excellent! The lad has brains," was Saint-Loup's comment.

I was not unmoved by these last examples, as always when, beneath the particular instance, I was afforded a glimpse of the general law. Still, the genius of the commander, that was what interested me, I was anxious to discover in what it consisted, what steps, in given circumstances, when the commander who lacked genius could not withstand the enemy, the inspired leader would take to re-establish his jeopardised position, which, according to Saint-Loup, was quite possible and had been done by Napoleon more than once. And to understand what military worth meant I asked for comparisons between the various generals whom I knew by name, which of them had most markedly the character of a leader, the gifts of a tactician; at the risk of boring my new friends, who however shewed no signs of boredom, but continued to answer me with an inexhaustible good-nature.

I felt myself isolated, not only from the great, freezing night which extended far around us and in which we heard from time to time the whistle of a train which only rendered more keen the pleasure of being where we were, or the chime of an hour which, happily, was still a long way short of that at which these young men would have to buckle on their sabres and go, but also from all my external obsessions, almost from the memory of Mme. de Guermantes, by the hospitality of Saint-Loup, to which that of his friends, reinforcing it, gave, so to speak, a greater solidity; by the warmth also of this little dining-room, by the savour of the well-chosen dishes that were set before us. They gave as much pleasure to my imagination as to my appetite; sometimes the little piece of still life from which they had been taken, the rugged holy water stoup of the oyster in which lingered a few drops of brackish water, or the knotted stem, the yellow leaves of a bunch of grapes still enveloped them, inedible, poetic and remote as a landscape, and producing, at different points in the course of the meal, the impressions of rest in the shade of a vine and of an excursion out to sea; on other evenings it was the cook alone who threw into relief these original properties of our food, which he presented in its natural setting, like a work of art; and a fish cooked in wine was brought in on a long earthen-ware dish, on which, as it stood out in relief on a bed of bluish herbs, unbreakable now but still contorted from having been dropped alive into boiling water, surrounded by a circle of satellite creatures in their shells, crabs, shrimps and mussels, it had the appearance of being part of a ceramic design by Bernard Palissy.

" I am jealous, furious," Saint-Loup attacked me, half smiling, half in earnest, alluding to the interminable conversations aside which I had been having with his friend. " Is it because you find him more intelligent than me; do you like him better than me? Well, I suppose he's everything now, and no one else is to have a look in!" Men who are enormously in love with a woman, who live in the society of woman-lovers, allow themselves pleasantries on which others, who would see less innocence in them, would never venture.

When the conversation became general, they avoided any reference to Dreyfus for fear of offending Saint-Loup. The following week, however, two of his friends were remarking what a curious thing it was that, living in so military an atmosphere, he was so keen a Dreyfusard, almost an anti-militarist: "The reason is," I suggested, not wishing to enter into details, "that the influence of environment is not so important as people think . . ." I intended of course to stop at this point, and not to reiterate the observations which I had made to Saint-Loup a few days earlier. Since, however, I had repeated these words almost textually, I proceeded to excuse myself by adding: "As, in fact, I was saying the other day . . ." But I had reckoned without the reverse side of Robert's polite admiration of myself and certain other persons. That admiration reached its fulfilment in so entire an assimilation of their ideas that, in the course of a day or two, he would have completely forgotten that those ideas were not his own. And so, in the matter of my modest theory, Saint-Loup, for all the world as though it had always dwelt in his own brain, and as though I were merely poaching on his preserves, felt it incumbent upon him to greet my discovery with warm approval.

"Why, yes; environment is of no importance."

And with as much vehemence as if he were afraid of my interrupting, or failing to understand him:

"The real influence is that of one's intellectual environment! One is the man of one's idea!"

He stopped for a moment, with the satisfied smile of one who has digested his dinner, dropped his eyeglass and, fixing me with a gimlet-like stare:

"All men with similar ideas are alike," he informed me, with a challenging air. Probably he had completely forgotten that I myself had said to him, only a few days earlier, what on the other hand he remembered so well.

I did not arrive at Saint-Loup's restaurant every evening in the same state of mind. If a memory, a sorrow that weigh on us are able to leave us so effectively that we are no longer aware of them, they can also return and sometimes remain with us for a long time. There were evenings when, as I passed through the town on my way to the restaurant, I felt so keen a longing for Mme. de Guermantes that I could scarcely breathe; you might have said that part of my breast had been cut open by a skilled anatomist, taken out, and replaced by an equal part of immaterial suffering, by an equivalent load of longing and love. And however neatly the wound may have been stitched together, there is not much comfort in life when regret for the loss of another person is substituted for one's entrails, it seems to be occupying more room than they, one feels it perpetually, and besides, what a contradiction in terms to be obliged to *think* a part of one's body. Only it seems that we are worth more, somehow. At the whisper of a breeze we sigh, from oppression, but from weariness also. I would look up at the sky. If it were clear, I would say to myself: "Perhaps she is in the country; she is looking at the same stars; and, for all I know, when I arrive at the restaurant Robert may say to me: 'Good news! I have just heard from my aunt; she wants to meet you; she is coming down here.'" It was not in the firmament alone that I enshrined the thought of Mme. de Guermantes. A passing breath of air, more fragrant than the rest, seemed to bring me a message from her, as, long ago, from Gilberte in the cornfields of Méséglise. We do not change; we introduce into the feeling with which we regard a person many slumbering elements which that feeling revives but which are foreign to it. Besides, with these feelings for particular people, there is always something in us that is trying to bring them nearer to the truth, that is to say, to absorb them in a more general feeling, common to the whole of humanity, with which people and the suffering that they cause us are merely a means to enable us to communicate. What brought a certain pleasure into my grief was that I knew it to be a tiny fragment of the universal love. Simply because I thought that I recognised sorrows which I had felt on Gilberte's account, or else when in the evenings at Combray Mamma would not stay in any room, and also the memory of certain pages of Bergotte, in the agony I now felt, to which Mme. de Guermantes, her coldness, her absence, were not clearly linked, as cause is to effect in the mind of a philosopher, I did not conclude that Mme. de Guermantes was not the cause of that agony. Is there not such a thing as a diffused bodily pain, extending, radiating out into other parts, which, however, it leaves, to vanish altogether, if the practitioner lays his finger on the precise spot from which it springs? And yet, until that moment, its extension gave it for us so vague, so fatal a semblance that, powerless to explain or even to locate it, we imagined that there was no possibility of its being healed. As I made my way to the restaurant I said to myself: "A fortnight already since I last saw Mme. de Guermantes." A fortnight which did not appear so enormous an interval save to me, who, when Mme. de Guermantes was concerned, reckoned time by minutes. For me it was no longer the stars and the breeze merely, but the arithmetical divisions of time that assumed a dolorous and poetic aspect. Each day now was like the loose crest of a crumbling mountain, down one side of which I felt that I could descend into oblivion, but down the other was borne by the necessity of seeing the Duchess again. And I was continually inclining one way or the other, having no stable equilibrium. One day I said to myself: "Perhaps there will be a letter to-night;" and on entering the dining-room I found courage to ask Saint-Loup:

"You don't happen to have had any news from Paris?"

"Yes," he replied gloomily; "bad news."

I breathed a sigh of relief when I realised that it was only he who was unhappy, and that the news came from his mistress. But I soon saw that one of its consequences would be to prevent Robert, for ever so long, from taking me to see his aunt.

I learned that a quarrel had broken out between him and his mistress, through the post presumably, unless she had come down to pay him a flying visit between trains. And the quarrels, even when relatively slight, which they had previously had, had always seemed as though they must prove insoluble. For she was a girl of violent temper, who would stamp her foot and burst into tears for reasons as incomprehensible as those that make children shut themselves into dark cupboards, not come out for dinner, refuse to give any explanation, and only redouble their sobs when, our patience exhausted, we visit them with a whipping. To say that Saint-Loup suffered terribly from this estrangement would be an understatement of the truth, which would give the reader a false impression of his grief. When he found himself alone, the only picture in his mind being that of his mistress parting from him with the respect which she had felt for him at the sight of his energy, the anxieties which he had had at first gave way before the irreparable, and the cessation of an anxiety is so pleasant a thing that the rupture, once it was certain, assumed for him something of the same kind of charm as a reconciliation. What he began to suffer from, a little later, was a secondary and accidental grief, the tide of which flowed incessantly from his own heart, at the idea that perhaps she would be glad to make it up, that it was not inconceivable that she was waiting for a word from him, that in the mean time, to be avenged on him, she would perhaps on a certain evening, in a certain place, do a certain thing, and that he had only to telegraph to her that he was coming for it not to happen, that others perhaps were taking advantage of the time which he was letting slip, and that in a few days it would be too late to recapture her, for she would be already bespoke. Among all these possibilities he was certain of nothing; his mistress preserved a silence which wrought him up to such a frenzy of grief that he began to ask himself whether she might not be in hiding at Doncières, or have sailed for the Indies.

It has been said that silence is a force; in another and widely different sense it is a tremendous force in the hands of those who are loved. It increases the anxiety of the lover who has to wait. Nothing so tempts us to approach another person as what is keeping us apart; and what barrier is there so insurmountable as silence? It has been said also that silence is a torture, capable of goading to madness him who is condemned to it in a prison cell. But what a torture—keener than that of having to keep silence—to have to endure the silence of the person one loves! Robert asked himself: "What can she be doing, never to send me a single word, like this? She hates me, perhaps, and will always go on hating me." And he reproached himself. Thus her silence did indeed drive him mad with jealousy and remorse. Besides, more cruel than the silence of prisons, that kind of silence is in itself a prison. An immaterial enclosure, I admit, but impenetrable, this interposed slice of empty atmosphere through which, despite its emptiness, the visual rays of the abandoned lover cannot pass. Is there a more terrible illumination than that of silence which shews us not one absent love but a thousand, and shews us each of them in the act of indulging in some fresh betrayal? Sometimes, in an abrupt relaxation of his strain, Robert would imagine that this period of silence was just coming to an end, that the long expected letter was on its way. He saw it, it arrived, he started at every sound, his thirst was already quenched, he murmured: "The letter! The letter!" After this glimpse of a phantom oasis of affection, he found himself once more toiling across the real desert of a silence without end.

He suffered in anticipation, without a single omission, all the griefs and pains of a rupture which at other moments he fancied he might somehow contrive to avoid, like people who put all their affairs in order with a view to a migration abroad which they never make, whose minds, no longer certain where they will find themselves living next day, flutter helplessly for the time being, detached from them, like a heart that is taken out of a

dying man and continues to beat, though disjoined from
the rest of his body. Anyhow, this hope that his mistress
would return gave him courage to persevere in the rupture,
as the belief that one will return alive from the battle
helps one to face death. And inasmuch as habit is, of
all the plants of human growth, the one that has least
need of nutritious soil in order to live, and is the first
to appear upon what is apparently the most barren rock,
perhaps had he begun by effecting their rupture as a
feint he would in the end have grown genuinely accustomed to it. But his uncertainty kept him in a state of
emotion which, linked with the memory of the woman
herself, was akin to love. He forced himself, nevertheless,
not to write to her, thinking perhaps that it was a less
cruel torment to live without his mistress than with her
in certain conditions, or else that, after the way in which
they had parted, it was necessary to wait for excuses
from her, if she was to keep what he believed her to
feel for him in the way, if not of love, at any rate of
esteem and regard. He contented himself with going to
the telephone, which had recently been installed at Doncières, and asking for news from, or giving instructions
to a lady's maid whom he had procured and placed with
his friend. These communications were, as it turned out,
complicated and took up much of his time, since, influenced by what her literary friends preached to her
about the ugliness of the capital, but principally for the
sake of her animals, her dogs, her monkey, her canaries
and her parrokeet, whose incessant din her Paris landlord had declined to tolerate for another moment, Robert's mistress had now taken a little house in the neighbourhood of Versailles. Meanwhile he, down at Don-

cières, no longer slept a wink all night. Once, in my room, overcome by exhaustion, he dozed off for a little. But suddenly he began to talk, tried to get up and run, to stop something from happening, said: " I hear her; you shan't . . . you shan't. . . ." He awoke. He had been dreaming, he explained to me, that he was in the country with the serjeant-major. His host had tried to keep him away from a certain part of the house. Saint-Loup had discovered that the serjeant-major had staying with him a subaltern, extremely rich and extremely vicious, whom he knew to have a violent passion for his mistress. And suddenly in his dream he had distinctly heard the spasmodic, regular cries which his mistress was in the habit of uttering at the moment of gratification. He had tried to force the serjeant-major to take him to the room in which she was. And the other had held him back, to keep him from going there, with an air of annoyance at such a want of discretion in a guest which, Robert said, he would never be able to forget.

" It was an idiotic dream," he concluded, still quite breathless.

All the same I could see that, during the hour that followed, he was more than once on the point of telephoning to his mistress to beg for a reconciliation. My father had now had the telephone for some time at home, but I doubt whether that would have been of much use to Saint-Loup. Besides, it hardly seemed to me quite proper to make my parents, or even a mechanical instrument installed in their house, play pander between Saint-Loup and his mistress, ladylike and high-minded as the latter might be. His bad dream began to fade from his memory.

With a fixed and absent stare, he came to see me on each of those cruel days which traced in my mind as they followed one after the other the splendid sweep of a staircase forged in hard metal on which Robert stood asking himself what decision his friend was going to take.

At length she wrote to ask whether he would consent to forgive her. As soon as he realised that a definite rupture had been avoided he saw all the disadvantages of a reconciliation. Besides, he had already begun to suffer less acutely, and had almost accepted a grief the sharp tooth of which he would have, in a few months perhaps, to feel again if their intimacy were to be resumed. He did not hesitate for long. And perhaps he hesitated only because he was now certain of being able to recapture his mistress, of being able to do it and therefore of doing it. Only she asked him, so that she might have time to recover her equanimity, not to come to Paris at the New Year. Now he had not the heart to go to Paris without seeing her. On the other hand, she had declared her willingness to go abroad with him, but for that he would need to make a formal application for leave, which Captain de Borodino was unwilling to grant.

"I'm sorry about it, because of your meeting with my aunt, which will have to be put off. I dare say I shall be in Paris at Easter."

"We shan't be able to call on Mme. de Guermantes then, because I shall have gone to Balbec. But, really, it doesn't matter in the least, I assure you."

"To Balbec? But you didn't go there till August."

"I know; but next year they're making me go there earlier, for my health."

All that he feared was that I might form a bad impression of his mistress, after what he had told me. "She is violent simply because she is too frank, too thorough in her feelings. But she is a sublime creature. You can't imagine what exquisite poetry there is in her. She goes every year to spend All Souls' Day at Bruges. 'Nice' of her, don't you think? If you ever do meet her you'll see what I mean; she has a greatness. . . ." And, as he was infected with certain of the mannerisms used in the literary circles in which the lady moved: "There is something sidereal about her, in fact something bardic; you know what I mean, the poet merging into the priest."

I was searching all through dinner for a pretext which would enable Saint-Loup to ask his aunt to see me without my having to wait until he came to Paris. Now such a pretext was furnished by the desire that I had to see some more pictures by Elstir, the famous painter whom Saint-Loup and I had met at Balbec. A pretext behind which there was, moreover, an element of truth, for if, on my visits to Elstir, what I had asked of his painting had been that it should lead me to the comprehension and love of things better than itself, a real thaw, an authentic square in a country town, live women on a beach (all the more would I have commissioned from it the portraits of the realities which I had not been able to fathom, such as a lane of hawthorn-blossoms, not so much that it might perpetuate their beauty for me as that it might reveal that beauty to me), now, on the other hand, it was the originality, the seductive attraction of those paintings that aroused my desire, and what I wanted above anything else was to look at other pictures by Elstir.

It seemed to me, also, that the least of his pictures were

something quite different from the masterpieces even of greater painters than himself. His work was like a realm apart, whose frontiers were not to be passed, matchless in substance. Eagerly collecting the infrequent periodicals in which articles on him and his work had appeared, I had learned that it was only recently that he had begun to paint landscapes and still life, and that he had started with mythological subjects (I had seen photographs of two of these in his studio), and had then been for long under the influence of Japanese art.

Several of the works most characteristic of his various manners were scattered about the provinces. A certain house at Les Andelys, in which there was one of his finest landscapes, seemed to me as precious, gave me as keen a desire to go there and see it as did a village in the Chartres district, among whose millstone walls was enshrined a glorious painted window; and towards the possessor of this treasure, towards the man who, inside his ugly house, on the main street, closeted like an astrologer, sat questioning one of those mirrors of the world which Elstir's pictures were, and who had perhaps bought it for many thousands of francs, I felt myself borne by that instinctive sympathy which joins the very hearts, the inmost natures of those who think alike upon a vital subject. Now three important works by my favourite painter were described in one of these articles as belonging to Mme. de Guermantes. So that it was, after all, quite sincerely that, on the evening on which Saint-Loup told me of his lady's projected visit to Bruges, I was able, during dinner, in front of his friends, to let fall, as though on the spur of the moment:

"Listen, if you don't mind. Just one last word on the

subject of the lady we were speaking about. You remember Elstir, the painter I met at Balbec?"

"Why, of course I do."

"You remember how much I admired his work?"

"I do, quite well; and the letter we sent him."

"Very well, one of the reasons—not one of the chief reasons, a subordinate reason—why I should like to meet the said lady—you do know who' I mean, don't you?"

"Of course I do. How involved you're getting."

"Is that she has in her house one very fine picture, at least, by Elstir."

"I say, I never knew that."

"Elstir will probably be at Balbec at Easter; you know he stays down there now all the year round, practically. I should very much like to have seen this picture before I leave Paris. I don't know whether you're on sufficiently intimate terms with your aunt: but couldn't you manage, somehow, to give her so good an impression of me that she won't refuse, and then ask her if she'll let me come and see the picture without you, since you won't be there?"

"That's all right. I'll answer for her; I'll make a special point of it."

"Oh, Robert, you are an angel; I do love you."

"It's very nice of you to love me, but it would be equally nice if you were to call me *tu*, as you promised, and as you began to do."

"I hope it's not your departure that you two are plotting together," one of Robert's friends said to me. "You know, if Saint-Loup does go on leave, it needn't make any difference, we shall still be here. It will be less amusing for you, perhaps, but we'll do all we can to make you forget his absence." As a matter of fact, just as we had decided that Robert's mistress would have to go to Bruges by herself, the news came that Captain de Borodino, obdurate hitherto in his refusal, had given authority for Serjeant Saint-Loup to proceed on long leave to Bruges. What had happened was this. The Prince, extremely proud of his luxuriant head of hair, was an assiduous customer of the principal hairdresser in the town, who had started life as a boy under Napoleon III's barber. Captain de Borodino was on the best of terms with the hairdresser, being, in spite of his air of majesty, quite simple in his dealings with his inferiors. But the hairdresser, through whose books the Prince's account had been running without payment for at least five years, swollen no less by bottles of Portugal and Eau des Souverains, irons, razors, and strops, than by the ordinary charges for shampooing, haircutting and the like, had a greater respect for Saint-Loup, who always paid on the nail and kept several carriages and saddle-horses. Having learned of Saint-Loup's vexation at not being able to go with his mistress, he had spoken strongly about it to the Prince at a moment when he was trussed up in a white surplice with his head held firmly over the back of the chair and his throat menaced by a razor. This narrative of a young man's gallant adventures won from the princely captain a smile of Bonapartish indulgence. It is hardly probable that he thought of his unpaid bill, but the barber's recommendation tended to put him in as good a humour as one from a duke would have put him in a bad. While his chin was still smothered in soap, the leave was promised, and the warrant was signed that evening. As for the hairdresser, who was in the habit of boasting all day long of his own exploits, and in order to do so claimed for himself, shewing an astonishing faculty for lying, distinctions that were pure fabrications, having for once rendered this signal service to Saint-Loup, not only did he refrain from publishing it broadcast, but, as if vanity were obliged to lie, and when there was no scope for lying gave place to modesty, he never mentioned the matter to Robert again.

All his friends assured me that, as long as I stayed at Doncières, or if I should come there again at any time, even although Robert were away, their horses, their quarters, their time would be at my disposal, and I felt that it was with the greatest cordiality that these young men put their comfort and youth and strength at the service of my weakness.

"Why on earth," they went on, after insisting that I should stay, "don't you come down here every year; you see how our quiet life appeals to you! Besides you're so keen about everything that goes on in the Regiment; quite the old soldier."

For I continued my eager demands that they would classify the different officers whose names I knew according to the degree of admiration which they seemed to deserve, just as, in my schooldays, I used to make the other boys classify the actors of the Théâtre-Français. If, in the place of one of the generals whom I had always heard mentioned at the head of the list, such as Galliffet or Négrier, one of Saint-Loup's friends, with a contemptuous: "But Négrier is one of the feeblest of our general officers," put the new, intact, appetising name of Pau or Geslin de Bourgogne, I felt the same joyful surprise as long ago when the outworn name of Thiron or Febvre was sent flying by the sudden explosion of the unfamiliar name of Amaury. " Better even than Négrier? But in what respect; give me an example? " I should have liked there to exist profound differences even among the junior officers of the regiment, and I hoped in the reason for these differences to seize the essential quality of what constituted military superiority. The one whom I should have been most interested to hear discussed, because he was the one whom I had most often seen, was the Prince de Borodino. But neither Saint-Loup nor his friends, if they did justice to the fine officer who kept his squadron up to the supreme pitch of efficiency, liked the man. Without speaking of him, naturally, in the same tone as of certain other officers, rankers and freemasons, who did not associate much with the rest and had, in comparison, an uncouth, barrack-room manner, they seemed not to include M. de Borodino among the officers of noble birth, from whom, it must be admitted, he differed considerably in his attitude even towards Saint-Loup. The others, taking advantage of the fact that Robert was only an N.C.O., and that therefore his influential relatives might be grateful were he invited to the houses of superior officers on whom ordinarily they would have looked down, lost no opportunity of having him to dine when any bigwig was expected who might be of use to a young cavalry serjeant. Captain de Borodino alone confined himself to his official relations (which, for that matter, were always excellent) with Robert. The fact was that the Prince, whose grandfather had been made a Marshal and a Prince-Duke by the Emperor, with whose family he had subsequently allied himself by marriage, while his father had married a cousin of Napoleon

III and had twice been a Minister after the Coup d'Etat, felt that in spite of all this he did not count for much with Saint-Loup and the Guermantes connexion, who in turn, since he did not look at things from the same point of view as they, counted for very little with him. He suspected that, for Saint-Loup, he himself was—he, a kinsman of the Hohenzollern—not a true noble but the grandson of a farmer, but at the same time he regarded Saint-Loup as the son of a man whose Countship had been confirmed by the Emperor—one of what were known in the Faubourg Saint-Germain as " touched-up " Counts —and who had besought him first for a Prefecture, then for some other post a long way down the list of subordinates to His Highness the Prince de Borodino, Minister of State, who was styled on his letters " Monseigneur " and was a nephew of the Sovereign.

Something more than a nephew, possibly. The first Princesse de Borodino was reputed to have bestowed her favours on Napoleon I, whom she followed to the Isle of Elba, and the second hers on Napoleon III. And if, in the Captain's placid countenance, one caught a trace of Napoleon I—if not in his natural features, at least in the studied majesty of the mask—the officer had, particularly in his melancholy and kindly gaze, in his drooping moustache, something that reminded one also of Napoleon III; and this in so striking a fashion that, having asked leave, after Sedan, to join the Emperor in captivity, and having been sent away by Bismarck, before whom he had been brought, the latter, happening to look up at the young man who was preparing to leave the room, was at once impressed by the likeness and, reconsidering his decision, recalled him and gave him the authorisation which he, in common with every one else, had just been refused.

If the Prince de Borodino was not prepared to make overtures to Saint-Loup nor to the other representatives of Faubourg Saint-Germain society that there were in the regiment (while he frequently invited two subalterns of plebeian origin who were pleasant companions) it was because, looking down upon them all from the height of his Imperial grandeur, he drew between these two classes of inferiors the distinction that one set consisted of inferiors who knew themselves to be such and with whom he was delighted to spend his time, being beneath his outward majesty of a simple, jovial humour, and the other of inferiors who thought themselves his superiors, a claim which he could not allow. And so, while all the other officers of the regiment made much of Saint-Loup, the Prince de Borodino, to whose care the young man had been recommended by Marshal X———, confined himself to being obliging with regard to the military duties which Saint-Loup always performed in the most exemplary fashion, but never had him to his house except on one special occasion when he found himself practically compelled to invite him, and when, as this occurred during my stay at Doncières, he asked him to bring me to dinner also. I had no difficulty that evening, as I watched Saint-Loup sitting at his Captain's table, in distinguishing, in their respective manners and refinements, the difference that existed between the two aristocracies: the old nobility and that of the Empire. The offspring of a caste the faults of which, even if he repudiated them with all the force of his intellect, had been absorbed into his blood, a caste which, having ceased to exert any real authority

for at least a century, saw nothing more now in the
protective affability which formed part of its regular
course of education, than an exercise, like horsemanship
or fencing, cultivated without any serious purpose, as a
sport; on meeting representatives of that middle class
on which the old nobility so far looked down as to believe
that they were flattered by its intimacy and would be
honoured by the informality of its tone, Saint-Loup would
take the hand of no matter who might be introduced
to him, though he had failed perhaps to catch the
stranger's name, in a friendly grip, and as he talked to
him (crossing and uncrossing his legs all the time, fling-
ing himself back in his chair in an attitude of absolute
unconstraint, one foot in the palm of his hand) call him
"my dear fellow." Belonging on the other hand to a
nobility whose titles still preserved their original meaning, provided that their holders still possessed the splendid
emoluments given in reward for glorious services and
bringing to mind the record of high offices in which one
is in command of numberless men and must know how
to deal with men, the Prince de Borodino—not perhaps
very distinctly or with any clear personal sense of superiority, but at any rate in his body, which revealed it by
its attitudes and behaviour generally—regarded his own
rank as a prerogative that was still effective; those same
commoners whom Saint-Loup would have slapped on the
shoulder and taken by the arm he addressed with a
majestic affability, in which a reserve instinct with grandeur tempered the smiling good-fellowship that came
naturally to him, in a tone marked at once by a genuine
kindliness and a stiffness deliberately assumed. This was
due, no doubt, to his being not so far removed from the

great Embassies, and the Court itself, at which his father had held the highest posts, whereas the manners of Saint-Loup, the elbow on the table, the foot in the hand, would not have been well received there; but principally it was due to the fact that he looked down less upon the middle classes because they were the inexhaustible source from which the first Emperor had chosen his Marshals and his nobles and in which the second had found a Rouher and a Fould.

Son, doubtless, or grandson of an Emperor, who had nothing more important to do than to command a squadron, the preoccupations of his putative father and grandfather could not, for want of an object on which to fasten themselves, survive in any real sense in the mind of M. de Borodino. But as the spirit of an artist continues to model, for many years after he is dead, the statue which he carved, so they had taken shape in him, were materialised, incarnate in him, it was they that his face reflected. It was with, in his voice, the vivacity of the first Emperor that he worded a reprimand to a corporal, with the dreamy melancholy of the second that he puffed out the smoke of a cigarette. When he passed in plain clothes through the streets of Doncières, a certain sparkle in his eyes escaping from under the brim of the bowler hat sent radiating round this captain of cavalry a regal incognito; people trembled when he strode into the serjeant-major's office, followed by the adjutant and the quartermaster, as though by Berthier and Masséna. When he chose the cloth for his squadron's breeches, he fastened on the master-tailor a gaze capable of baffling Talleyrand and deceiving Alexander; and at times, in the middle of an inspection, he would stop, let his handsome blue eyes cloud with dreams, twist his moustache, with the air of one building up a new Prussia and a new Italy. But a moment later, reverting from Napoleon III to Napoleon I, he would point out that the equipment was not properly polished, and would insist on tasting the men's rations. And at home, in his private life, it was for the wives of middle class officers (provided that their husbands were not freemasons) that he would bring out not only a dinner service of royal blue Sèvres, fit for an Ambassador (which had been given to his father by Napoleon, and appeared even more priceless in the commonplace house on a provincial street in which he was living, like those rare porcelains which tourists admire with a special delight in the rustic china-cupboard of some old manor that has been converted into a comfortable and prosperous farm house), but other gifts of the Emperor also: those noble and charming manners, which too would have won admiration in some diplomatic post abroad, if, for some men, it did not mean a lifelong condemnation to the most unjust form of ostracism, merely to be well born; his easy gestures, his kindness, his grace, and, embedding beneath an enamel that was of royal blue also glorious images, the mysterious, illuminated, living reliquary of his gaze. And, in treating of the social relations with the middle classes which the Prince had at Doncières, it may be as well to add these few words. The lieutenant-colonel played the piano beautifully; the senior medical officer's wife sang like a Conservatoire medallist. This latter couple, as well as the lieutenant-colonel and his wife, used to dine every week with M. de Borodino. They were flattered, unquestionably, knowing that when the Prince went to Paris on leave he dined with Mme. de Pourtalès, and the Murats, and people like that. "But," they said to themselves, "he's just a captain, after all; he's only too glad to get us to come. Still, he's a real friend, you know." But when M. de Borodino, who had long been pulling every possible wire to secure an appointment for himself nearer Paris, was posted to Beauvais, he packed up and went, and forgot as completely the two musical couples as he forgot the Doncières theatre and the little restaurant to which he used often to send out for his luncheon, and, to their great indignation, neither the lieutenant-colonel nor the senior medical officer, who had so often sat at his table, ever had so much as a single word from him for the rest of their lives.

One morning, Saint-Loup confessed to me that he had written to my grandmother to give her news of me, with the suggestion that, since there was telephonic connexion between Paris and Doncières, she might make use of it to speak to me. In short, that very day she was to give me a call, and he advised me to be at the post office at about a quarter to four. The telephone was not yet at that date as commonly in use as it is to-day. And yet habit requires so short a time to divest of their mystery the sacred forces with which we are in contact, that, not having had my call at once, the only thought in my mind was that it was very slow, and badly managed, and I almost decided to lodge a complaint. Like all of us nowadays I found not rapid enough for my liking in its abrupt changes the admirable sorcery for which a few moments are enough to bring before us, invisible but present, the person to whom we have been wishing to speak, and who, while still sitting at his table, in the town in which he lives (in my grandmother's case, Paris), under another sky than ours, in weather that is not necessarily the same, in the midst of circumstances and worries of which we know nothing, but of which he is going to inform us, finds himself suddenly transported hundreds of miles (he and all the surroundings in which he remains immured) within reach of our ear, at the precise moment which our fancy has ordained. And we are like the person in the fairy-tale to whom a sorceress, on his uttering the wish, makes appear with supernatural clearness his grandmother or his betrothed in the act of turning over a book, of shedding tears, of gathering flowers, quite close to the spectator and yet ever so remote, in the place in which she actually is at the moment. We need only, so that the miracle may be accomplished, apply our lips to the magic orifice and invoke—occasionally for rather longer than seems to us necessary, I admit—the Vigilant Virgins to whose voices we listen every day without ever coming to know their faces, and who are our Guardian Angels in the dizzy realm of darkness whose portals they so jealously keep; the All Powerful by whose intervention the absent rise up at our side, without our being permitted to set eyes on them; the Danaids of the Unseen who without ceasing empty, fill, transmit the urns of sound; the ironic Furies who, just as we were murmuring a confidence to a friend, in the hope that no one was listening, cry brutally: "I hear you!"; the ever infuriated servants of the Mystery, the umbrageous priestesses of the Invisible, the Young Ladies of the Telephone.

And, the moment our call has sounded, in the night filled with phantoms to which our ears alone are unsealed, a tiny sound, an abstract sound—the sound of distance overcome—and the voice of the dear one speaks to us.

It is she, it is her voice that is speaking, that is there. But how remote it is! How often have I been unable to listen without anguish, as though, confronted by the impossibility of seeing, except after long hours of journeying, her whose voice has been so close to my ear, I felt more clearly the sham and illusion of meetings apparently most pleasant, and at what a distance we may be from the people we love at the moment when it seems that we have only to stretch out our hand to seize and hold them. A real presence indeed that voice so near—in actual separation. But a premonition also of an eternal separation! Over and again, as I listened in this way, without seeing her who spoke to me from so far away, it has seemed to me that the voice was crying to me from depths out of which one does not rise again, and I have known the anxiety that was one day to wring my heart when a voice should thus return (alone, and attached no longer to a body which I was never more to see), to murmur, in my ear, words I would fain have kissed as they issued from lips for ever turned to dust.

This afternoon, alas, at Doncières, the miracle did not occur. When I reached the post office, my grandmother's call had already been received; I stepped into the box; the line was engaged; some one was talking who probably did not realise that there was nobody to answer him, for when I raised the receiver to my ear, the lifeless block began squeaking like Punchinello; I silenced it, as one silences a puppet, by putting it back on its hook, but, like Punchinello, as soon as I took it again in my hand, it resumed its gabbling. At length, giving it up as hopeless, by hanging up the receiver once and for all, I stifled the

convulsions of this vociferous stump which kept up its
chatter until the last moment, and went in search of the
operator, who told me to wait a little; then I spoke, and,
after a few seconds of silence, suddenly I heard that voice
which I supposed myself, mistakenly, to know so well;
for always until then, every time that my grandmother
had talked to me, I had been accustomed to follow what
she was saying on the open score of her face, in which the
eyes figured so largely; but her voice itself I was hearing
this afternoon for the first time. And because that voice
appeared to me to have altered in its proportions from
the moment that it was a whole, and reached me in this
way alone and without the accompaniment of her face
and features, I discovered for the first time how sweet
that voice was; perhaps, too, it had never been so sweet,
for my grandmother, knowing me to be alone and unhappy, felt that she might let herself go in the outpouring
of an affection which, on her principle of education, she
usually restrained and kept hidden. It was sweet, but
also how sad it was, first of all on account of its very
sweetness, a sweetness drained almost—more than any
but a few human voices can ever have been—of every
element of resistance to others, of all selfishness; fragile
by reason of its delicacy, it seemed at every moment ready
to break, to expire in a pure flow of tears; then, too, having it alone beside me, seen, without the mask of her
face, I noticed for the first time the sorrows that had
scarred it in the course of a lifetime.

Was it, however, solely the voice that, because it was
alone, gave me this new impression which tore my heart?
Not at all; it was rather that this isolation of the voice
was like a symbol, a presentation, a direct consequence

of another isolation, that of my grandmother, separated, for the first time in my life, from myself. The orders or prohibitions which she addressed to me at every moment in the ordinary course of my life, the tedium of obedience or the fire of rebellion which neutralised the affection that I felt for her were at this moment eliminated, and indeed might be eliminated for ever (since my grandmother no longer insisted on having me with her under her control, was in the act of expressing her hope that I would stay at Doncières altogether, or would at any rate extend my visit for as long as possible, seeing that both my health and my work seemed likely to benefit by the change); also, what I held compressed in this little bell that was ringing in my ear was, freed from the conflicting pressures which had, every day hitherto, given it a counterpoise, and from this moment irresistible, carrying me altogether away, our mutual affection. My grandmother, by telling me to stay, filled me with an anxious, an insensate longing to return. This freedom of action which for the future she allowed me and to which I had never dreamed that she would consent, appeared to me suddenly as sad as might be my freedom of action after her death (when I should still love her and she would for ever have abandoned me). "Granny!" I cried to her, "Granny!" and would fain have kissed her, but I had beside me only that voice, a phantom, as impalpable as that which would come perhaps to revisit me when my grandmother was dead. "Speak to me!" but then it happened that, left more solitary still, I ceased to catch the sound of her voice. My grandmother could no longer hear me; she was no longer in communication with me; we had ceased to stand face to face, to be audible to one another; I con-

tinued to call her, sounding the empty night, in which I
felt that her appeals also must be straying. I was shaken
by the same anguish which, in the distant past, I had felt
once before, one day when, a little child, in a crowd, I had
lost her, an anguish due less to my not finding her than
to the thought that she must be searching for me, must
be saying to herself that I was searching for her; an
anguish comparable to that which I was to feel on the
day when we speak to those who can no longer reply and
whom we would so love to have hear all the things that
we have not told them, and our assurance that we are
not unhappy. It seemed as though it were already a beloved ghost that I had allowed to lose herself in the
ghostly world, and, standing alone before the instrument,
I went on vainly repeating: "Granny! Granny!" as
Orpheus, left alone, repeats the name of his dead wife. I
decided to leave the post office, to go and find Robert at his
restaurant, in order to tell him that, as I was half expecting a telegram which would oblige me to return to Paris,
I wished at all costs to find out at what times the trains
left. And yet, before reaching this decision, I felt I must
make one attempt more to invoke the Daughters of the
Night, the Messengers of the Word, the Deities without
form or feature; but the capricious Guardians had not
deigned once again to unclose the miraculous portals, or
more probably, had not been able; in vain might they
untiringly appeal, as was their custom, to the venerable
inventor of printing and the young prince, collector of
impressionist paintings and driver of motor-cars (who
was Captain de Borodino's nephew); Gutenberg and
Wagram left their supplications unanswered, and I came
away, feeling that the Invisible would continue to turn a

deaf ear.

When I came among Robert and his friends, I withheld the confession that my heart was no longer with them, that my departure was now irrevocably fixed. Saint-Loup appeared to believe me, but I learned afterwards that he had from the first moment realised that my uncertainty was feigned and that he would not see me again next day. And while, letting their plates grow cold, his friends joined him in searching through the time-table for a train which would take me to Paris, and while we heard in the cold, starry night the whistling of the engines on the line, I certainly felt no longer the same peace of mind which on all these last evenings I had derived from the friendship of the former and the latter's distant passage. And yet they did not fail me this evening, performing the same office in a different way. My departure overpowered me less when I was no longer obliged to think of it by myself, when I felt that there was concentrated on what was to be done the more normal, more wholesome activity of my strenuous friends, Robert's brothers in arms, and of those other strong creatures, the trains, whose going and coming, night and morning, between Doncières and Paris, broke up in retrospect what had been too compact and insupportable in my long isolation from my grandmother into daily possibilities of return.

" I don't doubt the truth of what you're saying, or that you aren't thinking of leaving us just yet," said Saint-Loup, smiling; " but pretend you are going, and come and say good-bye to me to-morrow morning; early, otherwise there's a risk of my not seeing you; I'm going out to luncheon, I've got leave from the Captain; I shall have to be back in barracks by two, as we are to be on the march all afternoon. I suppose the man to whose house I'm going, a couple of miles out, will manage to get me back in time."

Scarcely had he uttered these words when a messenger came for me from my hotel; the telephone operator had sent to find me. I ran to the post office, for it was nearly closing time. The word "trunks" recurred incessantly in the answers given me by the officials. I was in a fever of anxiety, for it was my grandmother who had asked for me. The office was closing for the night. Finally I got my connexion. "Is that you, Granny?" A woman's voice, with a strong English accent, answered: "Yes, but I don't know your voice." Neither did I recognise the voice that was speaking to me; besides, my grandmother called me *tu,* and not *vous.* And then all was explained. The young man for whom his grandmother had called on the telephone had a name almost identical with my own, and was staying in an annex of my hotel. This call coming on the very day on which I had been telephoning to my grandmother, I had never for a moment doubted that it was she who was asking for me. Whereas it was by pure coincidence that the post office and the hotel had combined to make a twofold error.

The following morning I rose late, and failed to catch Saint-Loup, who had already started for the country house where he was invited to luncheon. About half past one, I had decided to go in any case to the barracks, so as to be there before he arrived, when, as I was crossing one of the avenues on the way there, I noticed, coming behind me in the same direction as myself, a tilbury which, as it overtook me, obliged me to jump out of its way; an N.C.O. was driving it, wearing an eyeglass; it was

Saint-Loup. By his side was the friend whose guest he had been at luncheon, and whom I had met once before at the hotel where we dined. I did not dare shout to Robert since he was not alone, but, in the hope that he would stop and pick me up, I attracted his attention by a sweeping wave of my hat, which might be regarded as due to the presence of a stranger. I knew that Robert was short-sighted; still, I should have supposed that, provided he saw me at all, he could not fail to recognise me; he did indeed see my salute, and returned it, but without stopping; driving on at full speed, without a smile, without moving a muscle of his face, he confined himself to keeping his hand raised for a minute to the peak of his cap, as though he were acknowledging the salute of a trooper whom he did not know personally. I ran to the barracks, but it was a long way; when I arrived, the regiment was parading on the square, on which I was not allowed to stand, and I was heart-broken at not having been able to say good-bye to Saint-Loup; I went up to his room, but he had gone; I was reduced to questioning a group of sick details, recruits who had been excused route-marches, the young graduate, one of the " old soldiers ", who were watching the regiment parade.

" You haven't seen Serjeant Saint-Loup, have you, by any chance? " I asked.

" He's gone on parade, sir," said the old soldier.

" I never saw him," said the graduate.

" You never saw him," exclaimed the old soldier, losing all interest in me, " you never saw our famous Saint-Loup, the figure he's cutting with his new breeches! When the Capstan sees that, officer's cloth, my word! "

" Oh, you're a wonder, you are; officer's cloth," replied

the young graduate, who, reported " sick in quarters ",
was excused marching and tried, not without some misgivings, to be on easy terms with the veterans. " This
officer's cloth you speak of is cloth like that, is it? "

" Sir? " asked the old soldier angrily.

He was indignant that the young graduate should
throw doubt on the breeches' being made of officer's
cloth, but, being a Breton, coming from a village that
went by the name of Penguern-Stereden, having learned
French with as much difficulty as if it had been English
or German, whenever he felt himself overcome by emotion he would go on saying " Sir? " to give himself time
to find words, then, after this preparation, let loose his
eloquence, confining himself to the repetition of certain
words which he knew better than others, but without
haste, taking every precaution to glose over his unfa-
miliarity with the pronunciation.

" Ah! It is cloth like that," he broke out, with a fury
the intensity of which increased as the speed of his utterance diminished. " Ah! It is cloth like that; when I tell
you that it is officer's cloth, when-I-tell-you-a-thing, if-I
tell-you-a-thing, it's because I know, I should think."

" Very well, then; " replied the young graduate, overcome by the force of this argument. " Keep your hair on,
old boy."

" There, look, there's the Capstan coming along. No,
but just look at Saint-Loup; the way he throws his leg
out; and his head. Would you call that a non-com? And
his eyeglass; oh, he's hot stuff, he is."

I asked these troopers, who did not seem at all embarrassed by my presence, whether I too might look out
of the window. They neither objected to my doing so

nor moved to make room for me. I saw Captain de Borodino go majestically by, putting his horse into a trot, and
apparently under the illusion that he was taking part in
the Battle of Austerlitz. A few loiterers had stopped by
the gate to see the regiment file out. Erect on his charger,
his face inclined to plumpness, his cheeks of an Imperial
fulness, his eye lucid, the Prince must have been the
victim of some hallucination, as I was myself whenever,
after the tramway-car had passed, the silence that followed
its rumble seemed to me to throb and echo with a vaguely
musical palpitation. I was wretched at not having said
good-bye to Saint-Loup, but I went nevertheless, for my
one anxiety was to return to my grandmother; always
until then, in this little country town, when I thought of
what my grandmother must be doing by herself, I had
pictured her as she was when with me, suppressing my
own personality but without taking into account the effects
of such a suppression; now, I had to free myself, at the
first possible moment, in her arms, from the phantom,
hitherto unsuspected and suddenly called into being by
her voice, of a grandmother really separated from me,
resigned, having, what I had never yet thought of her as
having, a definite age, who had just received a letter from
me in an empty house, as I had once before imagined
Mamma in a house by herself, when I had left her to go
to Balbec.

Alas, this phantom was just what I did see when,
entering the drawing-room before my grandmother had
been told of my return, I found her there, reading. I was
in the room, or rather I was not yet in the room since
she was not aware of my presence, and, like a woman
whom one surprises at a piece of work which she will lay

aside if anyone comes in, she had abandoned herself to a
train of thoughts which she had never allowed to be visible
by me. Of myself—thanks to that privilege which does not
last but which one enjoys during the brief moment of
return, the faculty of being a spectator, so to speak, of
one's own absence,—there was present only the witness,
the observer, with a hat and travelling coat, the stranger
who does not belong to the house, the photographer who
has called to take a photograph of places which one will
never see again. The process that mechanically occurred
in my eyes when I caught sight of my grandmother was
indeed a photograph. We never see the people who are
dear to us save in the animated system, the perpetual motion of our incessant love for them, which before allowing
the images that their faces present to reach us catches
them in its vortex, flings them back upon the idea that
we have always had of them, makes them adhere to it,
coincide with it. How, since into the forehead, the cheeks
of my grandmother I had been accustomed to read all the
most delicate, the most permanent qualities of her mind;
how, since every casual glance is an act of necromancy,
each face that we love a mirror of the past, how could I
have failed to overlook what in her had become dulled and
changed, seeing that in the most trivial spectacles of our
daily life, our eye, charged with thought, neglects, as
would a classical tragedy, every image that does not
assist the action of the play and retains only those that
may help to make its purpose intelligible. But if, in place
of our eye, it should be a purely material object, a photo-
graphic plate, that has watched the action, then what we
shall see, in the courtyard of the Institute, for example,
will be, instead of the dignified emergence of an Academi-

cian who is going to hail a cab, his staggering gait, his precautions to avoid tumbling upon his back, the parabola of his fall, as though he were drunk, or the ground frozen over. So is it when some casual sport of chance prevents our intelligent and pious affection from coming forward in time to hide from our eyes what they ought never to behold, when it is forestalled by our eyes, and they, arising first in the field and having it to themselves, set to work mechanically, like films, and shew us, in place of the loved friend who has long ago ceased to exist but whose death our affection has always hitherto kept concealed from us, the new person whom a hundred times daily that affection has clothed with a dear and cheating likeness. And, as a sick man who for long has not looked at his own reflexion, and has kept his memory of the face that he never sees refreshed from the ideal image of himself that he carries in his mind, recoils on catching sight in the glass, in the midst of an arid waste of cheek, of the sloping red structure of a nose as huge as one of the pyramids of Egypt, I, for whom my grandmother was still myself, I who had never seen her save in my own soul, always at the same place in the past, through the transparent sheets of contiguous, overlapping memories, suddenly in our drawing-room which formed part of a new world, that of time, that in which dwell the strangers of whom we say " He's begun to age a good deal," for the first time and for a moment only, since she vanished at once, I saw, sitting on the sofa, beneath the lamp, red-faced, heavy and common, sick, lost in thought, following the lines of a book with eyes that seemed hardly sane, a dejected old woman whom I did not know.

My request to be allowed to inspect the Elstirs in Mme.

de Guermantes's collection had been met by Saint-Loup with: "I will answer for her." And indeed, as ill luck would have it, it was he and he alone who did answer. We answer readily enough for other people when, setting our mental stage with the little puppets that represent them, we manipulate these to suit our fancy. No doubt even then we take into account the difficulties due to another person's nature being different from our own, and we do not fail to have recourse to some plan of action likely to influence that nature, an appeal to his material interest, persuasion, the rousing of emotion, which will neutralise contrary tendencies on his part. But these differences from our own nature, it is still our own nature that is imagining them, these difficulties, it is we that are raising them; these compelling motives, it is we that are applying them. And so with the actions which before our mind's eye we have made the other person rehearse, and which make him act as we choose; when we wish to see him perform them in real life, the case is altered, we come up against unseen resistances which may prove insuperable. One of the strongest is doubtless that which may be developed in a woman who is not in love with him by the disgust inspired in her, a fetid, insurmountable loathing, by the man who is in love with her; during the long weeks in which Saint-Loup still did not come to Paris, his aunt, to whom I had no doubt of his having written begging her to do so, never once asked me to call at her house to see the Elstirs.

I perceived signs of coldness on the part of another occupant of the building. This was Jupien. Did he consider that I ought to have gone in and said how d'ye do to him, on my return from Doncières, before even going

189

upstairs to our own flat? My mother said no, that there was nothing unusual about it. Françoise had told her that he was like that, subject to sudden fits of ill humour, without any cause. These invariably passed off after a little time.

Meanwhile the winter was drawing to an end. One morning, after several weeks of showers and storms, I heard in my chimney—instead of the wind, formless, elastic, sombre, which convulsed me with a longing to go to the sea—the cooing of the pigeons that were nesting in the wall outside; shimmering, unexpected, like a first hyacinth, gently tearing open its fostering heart that there might shoot forth, purple and satin-soft, its flower of sound, letting in like an opened window into my bedroom still shuttered and dark the heat, the dazzling brightness, the fatigue of a first fine day. That morning, I was surprised to find myself humming a music-hall tune which had never entered my head since the year in which I had been going to Florence and Venice. So profoundly does the atmosphere, as good days and bad recur, act on our organism and draw from dim shelves, where we had forgotten them, the melodies written there which our memory could not decipher. Presently a more conscious dreamer accompanied this musician to whom I was listening inside myself, without having recognised at first what he was playing.

I quite realised that it was not for any reason peculiar to Balbec that on my arrival there I had failed to find in its church the charm which it had had for me before I knew it; that at Florence or Parma or Venice my imagination could no more take the place of my eyes when I looked at the sights there. I realised this. Similarly, one

New Year's afternoon, as night fell, standing before a column of playbills, I had discovered the illusion that lies in our thinking that certain solemn holidays differ essentially from the other days in the calendar. And yet I could not prevent my memory of the time during which I had looked forward to spending Easter in Florence from continuing to make that festival the atmosphere, so to speak, of the City of Flowers, to give at once to Easter Day something Florentine and to Florence something Paschal. Easter was still a long way off; but in the range of days that stretched out before me the days of Holy Week stood out more clearly at the end of those that merely came between. Touched by a far flung ray, like certain houses in a village which one sees from a distance when the rest are in shadow, they had caught and kept all the sun.

The weather had now become milder. And my parents themselves, by urging me to take more exercise, gave me an excuse for resuming my morning walks. I had meant to give them up, since they meant my meeting Mme. de Guermantes. But it was for this very reason that I kept thinking all the time of those walks, which led to my finding, every moment, a fresh reason for taking them, a reason that had no connexion with Mme. de Guermantes and no difficulty in convincing me that, had she never existed, I should still have taken a walk, without fail, at that hour every morning.

Alas, if to me meeting any person other than herself would not have mattered, I felt that to her meeting anyone in the world except myself would have been endurable. It happened that, in the course of her morning walks, she received the salutations of plenty of fools whom she regarded as such. But the appearance of these in her path seemed to her, if not to hold out any promise of pleasure, to be at any rate the result of mere accident. And she stopped them at times, for there are moments in which one wants to escape from oneself, to accept the hospitality offered by the soul of another person, provided always that the other, however modest and plain it may be, is a different soul, whereas in my heart she was exasperated to feel that what she would have found was herself. And so, even when I had, for taking the same way as she, another reason than my desire to see her, I trembled like a guilty man as she came past; and sometimes, so as to neutralise anything extravagant that there might seem to have been in my overtures, I would barely acknowledge her bow, or would fasten my eyes on her face without raising my hat, and succeed only in making her angrier than ever, and begin to regard me as insolent and ill-bred besides.

She was now wearing lighter, or at any rate brighter clothes, and would come strolling down the street in which already, as though it were spring, in front of the narrow shops that were squeezed in between the huge fronts of the old aristocratic mansions, over the booths of the butter-woman and the fruit-woman and the vegetable-woman, awnings were spread to protect them from the sun. I said to myself that the woman whom I could see far off, walking, opening her sunshade, crossing the street, was, in the opinion of those best qualified to judge, the greatest living exponent of the art of performing those movements and of making out of them something exquisitely lovely. Meanwhile she was advancing towards me, unconscious of this widespread reputation, her narrow, stubborn body, which had absorbed none of it, was bent stiffly forward under a scarf of violet silk; her clear, sullen eyes looked absently in front of her, and had perhaps caught sight of me; she was biting her lip; I saw her straighten her muff, give alms to a beggar, buy a bunch of violets from a flower-seller, with the same curiosity that I should have felt in watching the strokes of a great painter's brush. And when, as she reached me, she gave me a bow that was accompanied sometimes by a faint smile, it was as though she had sketched in colour for me, adding a personal inscription to myself, a drawing that was a masterpiece of art. Each of her gowns seemed to me her natural, necessary surroundings, like the projection around her of a particular aspect of her soul. On one of these Lenten mornings, when she was on her way out to luncheon, I met her wearing a gown of bright red velvet, cut slightly open at the throat. The face of Mme. de Guermantes appeared to be dreaming, beneath its pile of fair hair. I was less sad than usual because the melancholy of her expression, the sort of claustration which the startling hue of her gown set between her and the rest of the world, made her seem somehow lonely and unhappy, and this comforted me. The gown struck me as being the materialisation round about her of the scarlet rays of a heart which I did not recognise as hers and might have been able, perhaps, to console; sheltered in the mystical light of the garment with its gently flowing folds, she made me think of some Saint of the early ages of Christianity. After which I felt ashamed of afflicting with the sight of myself this holy martyr. " But, after all, the streets are public."

The streets are public, I reminded myself, giving a different meaning to the words, and marvelling that indeed in the crowded thoroughfare often soaked with rain, which made it beautiful and precious as a street sometimes is in the old towns of Italy, the Duchesse de Guermantes mingled with the public life of the world moments of her own secret life, shewing herself thus to all and sundry, jostled by every passer-by, with the splendid gratuitousness of the greatest works of art. As I had been out in the morning, after staying awake all night, in the afternoon my parents would tell me to lie down for a little and try to sleep. There is no need, when one is trying to find sleep, to give much thought to the quest, but habit is very useful, and even freedom from thought. But in these afternoon hours both were lacking. Before going to sleep, I devoted so much time to thinking that I should not be able to sleep, that even after I was asleep a little of my thought remained. It was no more than a glimmer in the almost total darkness, but it was bright enough to cast a reflexion in my sleep, first of the idea that I could not sleep, and then, a reflexion of this reflexion, that it was in my sleep that I had had the idea that I was not asleep, then, by a further refraction, my awakening . . . to a fresh doze in which I was trying to tell some friends who had come into my room that, a moment earlier, when I was asleep, I had imagined that I was not asleep. These shades were barely distinguishable; it would have required a keen—and quite useless—delicacy of perception to seize them all. Similarly, in later years, at Venice, long after the sun had set, when it seemed to be quite dark, I have seen, thanks to the echo, itself imperceptible, of a last note of light, held indefinitely on the surface of the canals, as though some optical pedal were being pressed, the reflexion of the palaces unfurled, as though for all time, in a darker velvet, on the crepuscular greyness of the water. One of my dreams was the synthesis of what my imagination had often sought to depict, in my waking hours, of a certain seagirt place and its mediaeval past. In my sleep I saw a gothic fortress rising from a sea whose waves were stilled as in a painted window. An arm of the sea cut the town in two; the green water stretched to my feet; it bathed on the opposite shore the foundations of an oriental church, and beyond it houses which existed already in the fourteenth century, so that to go across to them would have been to ascend the stream of time. This dream in which nature had learned from art, in which the sea had turned gothic, this dream in which I longed to attain, in which I believed that I was attaining to the impossible, it seemed to me that I had often dreamed it before. But as it is the property of what we imagine in our sleep to multiply itself in the past, and to appear, even when novel, familiar, I supposed that I was mistaken. I noticed, however, that I did frequently have this dream.

The limitations, too, that are common to all sleep were reflected in mine, but in a symbolical manner; I could not in the darkness make out the faces of the friends who were in the room, for we sleep with our eyes shut; I, who could carry on endless arguments with myself while I dreamed, as soon as I tried to speak to these friends felt the words stick in my throat, for we do not speak distinctly in our sleep; I wanted to go to them, and I could not move my limbs, for we do not walk when we are asleep either; and suddenly I was ashamed to be seen by them, for we sleep without our clothes. So, my eyes blinded, my lips sealed, my limbs fettered, my body naked, the figure of sleep which my sleep itself projected had the appearance of those great allegorical figures (in one of which Giotto has portrayed Envy with a serpent in her mouth) of which Swann had given me photographs.

Saint-Loup came to Paris for a few hours only. He came with assurances that he had had no opportunity of mentioning me to his cousin. "She's not being at all nice just now, Oriane isn't," he explained, with innocent self-betrayal. "She's not my old Oriane any longer, they've gone and changed her. I assure you, it's not worth while bothering your head about her. You pay her far too great a compliment. You wouldn't care to meet my cousin Poictiers?" he went on, without stopping to reflect that this could not possibly give me any pleasure. "Quite an intelligent young woman, she is; you'ld like her. She's married to my cousin, the Duc de Poictiers, who is a good fellow, but a bit slow for her. I've told her about you. She said I was to bring you to see her. She's much better looking than Oriane, and younger, too. Really a nice person, don't you know, really a good sort." These were ex- pressions recently—and all the more ardently—taken up by Robert, which meant that the person in question had a delicate nature. "I don't go so far as to say she's a Dreyfusard, you must remember the sort of people she lives among; still, she did say to me: 'If he is innocent, how ghastly for him to be shut up on the Devil's Isle.' You see what I mean, don't you? And then she's the sort of woman who does a tremendous lot for her old gov- ernesses; she's given orders that they're never to be sent in by the servants' stair, when they come to the house. She's a very good sort, I assure you. The real reason why Oriane doesn't like her is that she feels she's the cleverer of the two."

Although completely absorbed in the pity which she felt for one of the Guermantes footmen—who had no chance of going to see his girl, even when the Duchess was out, for it would immediately have been reported to her from the lodge,—Françoise was heartbroken at not having been in the house at the moment of Saint-Loup's visit, but this was because now she herself paid visits also. She never failed to go out on the days when I most wanted her. It was always to see her brother, her niece and, more particularly, her own daughter, who had recently come to live in Paris. The intimate nature of these visits itself increased the irritation that I felt at being deprived of her services, for I had a foreboding that she would speak of them as being among those duties from which there was no dispensation, according to the laws laid down at Saint-André-des-Champs. And so I never listened to her excuses without an ill humour which was highly unjust to her, and was brought to a climax by the way Françoise had of saying not: " I have been to see my brother," or " I have been to see my niece," but " I have been to see the brother," " I just looked in as I passed to bid good day to the niece " (or " to my niece the butcheress "). As for her daughter, Françoise would have been glad to see her return to Combray. But this recent Parisian, making use, like a woman of fashion, of abbreviations, though hers were of a vulgar kind, protested that the week she was going shortly to spend at Combray would seem quite long enough without so much as a sight of " the *Intran* ". She was still less willing to go to Françoise's sister, who lived in a mountainous country, for "mountains," said the daughter, giving to the adjective a new and terrible meaning, " aren't really interesting." She could not make up her mind to go back to Méséglise, where "the people are so stupid," where in the market the gossips at their stalls would call cousins with her, and say "Why, it's never poor Bazireau's daughter?" She would sooner die than go back and bury herself down there, now that she had "tasted the life of Paris," and Françoise, traditionalist as she was, smiled complacently nevertheless at the spirit of innovation that was incarnate in this new Parisian when she said: "Very well, mother, if you don't get your day out, you have only to send me a pneu."

The weather had turned chilly again. "Go out? What for? To catch your death?" said Françoise, who preferred to remain in the house during the week which her daughter and brother and the butcher-niece had gone to spend at Combray. Being, moreover, the last surviving adherent of the sect in whom persisted obscurely the doctrine of my aunt Léonie—a natural philosopher—Françoise would add, speaking of this unseasonable weather: "It is the remnant of the wrath of God!" But I responded to her complaints only in a languid smile; all the more indifferent to these predictions, in that whatever befell it would be fine for me; already I could see the morning sun shine on the slope of Fiesole, I warmed myself in its rays; their strength obliged me to half-open, half-shut my eyelids, smiling the while, and my eyelids, like alabaster lamps, were filled with a rosy glow. It was not only the bells that came from Italy, Italy had come with them. My faithful hands would not lack flowers to honour the anniversary of the pilgrimage which I ought to have made long ago, for since, here in Paris, the weather had turned cold again as in another year at the time of our preparations for departure at the end of Lent, in the liquid, freezing air which bathed the chestnuts and planes on the boulevards, the tree in the courtyard of our house, there were already opening their petals, as in a bowl of pure water, the narcissi, the jonquils, the anemones of the Ponte Vecchio.

My father had informed us that he now knew, from his friend A. J., where M. de Norpois was going when he met him about the place.

"It's to see Mme. de Villeparisis, they are great friends; I never knew anything about it. It seems she's a delightful person, a most superior woman. You ought to go and call on her," he told me. "Another thing that surprised me very much. He spoke to me of M. de Guermantes as quite a distinguished man; I had always taken him for a boor. It seems, he knows an enormous amount, and has perfect taste, only he's very proud of his name and his connexions. But for that matter, according to Norpois, he has a tremendous position, not only here but all over Europe. It appears, the Austrian Emperor and the Tsar treat him just like one of themselves. Old Norpois told me that Mme. de Villeparisis had taken quite a fancy to you, and that you would meet all sorts of interesting people in her house. He paid a great tribute to you; you will see him if you go there, and he may have some good advice for you even if you are going to be a writer. For you're not likely to do anything else; I can see that. It might turn out quite a good career; it's not what I should have chosen for you, myself; but you'll be a man in no time now, we shan't always be here to look after you, and we mustn't prevent you from following your vocation."

If only I had been able to start writing! But whatever the conditions in which I approached the task (as, too, alas, the undertakings not to touch alcohol, to go to bed early, to sleep, to keep fit), whether it were with enthusiasm, with method, with pleasure, in depriving myself of a walk, or postponing my walk and keeping it in reserve as a reward of industry, taking advantage of an hour of good health, utilising the inactivity forced on me by a day of illness, what always emerged in the end from all my effort was a virgin page, undefiled by any writing, ineluctable as that forced card which in certain tricks one invariably is made to draw, however carefully one may first have shuffled the pack. I was merely the instruments of habits of not working, of not going to bed, of not sleeping, which must find expression somehow, cost what it might; if I offered them no resistance, if I contented myself with the pretext they seized from the first opportunity that the day afforded them of acting as they chose, I escaped without serious injury, I slept for a few hours after all, towards morning, I read a little, I did not over-exert myself; but if I attempted to thwart them, if I pretended to go to bed early, to drink only water, to work, they grew restive, they adopted strong measures, they made me really ill, I was obliged to double my dose of alcohol, did not lie down in bed for two days and nights on end, could not even read, and I vowed that another time I would be more reasonable, that is to say less wise, like the victim of an assault who allows himself to be robbed for fear, should he offer resistance, of being murdered.

My father, in the mean time, had met M. de Guermantes once or twice, and, now that M. de Norpois had told him that the Duke was a remarkable man, had begun to pay more attention to what he said. As it happened, they met in the courtyard and discussed Mme. de Villeparisis. "He tells me, she's his aunt; 'Viparisi,' he pronounces it. He tells me, too, she's an extraordinarily able woman. In fact he said she kept a School of Wit," my father announced to us, impressed by the vagueness of this expression, which he had indeed come across now and then in volumes of memoirs, but without attaching to it any definite meaning. My mother, so great was her respect for him, when she saw that he did not dismiss as of no importance the fact that Mme. de Villeparisis kept a School of Wit, decided that this must be of some consequence. Albeit from my grandmother she had known all the time the exact amount of the Marquise's intellectual worth, it was immediately enhanced in her eyes. My grandmother, who was not very well just then, was not in favour at first of the suggested visit, and afterwards lost interest in the matter. Since we had moved into our new flat, Mme. de Villeparisis had several times asked my grandmother to call upon her. And invariably my grandmother had replied that she was not going out just at present, in one of those letters which, by a new habit of hers which we did not understand, she no longer sealed herself, but employed Françoise to lick the envelopes for her. As for myself, without any very clear picture in my mind of this School of Wit, I should not have been greatly surprised to find the old lady from Balbec installed behind a desk, as, for that matter, I eventually did.

My father would have been glad to know, into the bargain, whether the Ambassador's support would be worth many votes to him at the Institute, for which he had thoughts of standing as an independent candidate. To tell the truth, while he did not venture to doubt that he would have M. de Norpois's support, he was by no means certain of it. He had thought it merely malicious gossip when they assured him at the Ministry that M. de Norpois, wishing to be himself the only representative there of the Institute, would put every possible obstacle in the way of my father's candidature, which besides would be particularly awkward for him at that moment, since he was supporting another candidate already. And yet, when M. Leroy-Beaulieu had first advised him to stand, and had reckoned up his chances, my father had been struck by the fact that, among the colleagues upon whom he could count for support, the eminent economist had not mentioned M. de Norpois. He dared not ask the Ambassador point-blank, but hoped that I should return from my call on Mme. de Villeparisis with his election as good as secured. This call was now imminent. That M. de Norpois would carry on propaganda calculated to assure my father the votes of at least two thirds of the Academy seemed to him all the more probable since the Ambassador's willingness to oblige was proverbial, those who liked him least admitting that no one else took such pleasure in being of service. And besides, at the Ministry, his protective influence was extended over my father far more markedly than over any other official.

My father had also another encounter about this time, but one at which his extreme surprise ended in equal indignation. In the street one day he ran into Mme. Sazerat, whose life in Paris her comparative poverty restricted to occasional visits to a friend. There was no one who bored my father quite so intensely as did Mme. Sazerat, so much so that Mamma was obliged, once a year, to intercede with him in sweet and suppliant tones: " My dear, I really must invite Mme. Sazerat to the house, just once; she won't stay long; " and even: " Listen, dear, I am going to ask you to make a great sacrifice; do go and call upon Mme. Sazerat. You know I hate bothering you, but it would be so nice of you." He would laugh, raise various objections, and go to pay the call. And so, for all that Mme. Sazerat did not appeal to him, on catching sight of her in the street my father went towards her, hat in hand; but to his profound astonishment Mme. Sazerat confined her greeting to the frigid bow enforced by politeness towards a person who is guilty of some disgraceful action or has been condemned to live, for the future, in another hemisphere. My father had come home speechless with rage. Next day my mother met Mme. Sazerat in some one's house. She did not offer my mother her hand, but only smiled at her with a vague and melancholy air as one smiles at a person with whom one used to play as a child, but with whom one has since severed all one's relations because she has led an abandoned life, has married a convict or (what is worse still) a co-respondent. Now, from all time my parents had accorded to Mme. Sazerat, and inspired in her, the most profound respect. But (and of this my mother was ignorant) Mme. Sazerat, alone of her kind at Combray, was a Dreyfusard. My father, a friend of M. Méline, was convinced that Dreyfus was guilty. He had flatly refused to listen to some of his colleagues who had asked him to sign a petition demanding a fresh trial. He never spoke to me for a week, after learning that I had chosen to take a different line. His opinions were well known. He came near to being looked upon as a Nationalist. As for my grandmother, in whom alone of the family a generous doubt was likely to be kindled, whenever anyone spoke to her of the possible innocence of Dreyfus, she gave a shake of her head, the meaning of which we did not at the time understand, but which was like the gesture of a person who has been interrupted while thinking of more serious things. My mother, torn between her love for my father and her hope that I might turn out to have brains, preserved an impartiality which she expressed by silence. Finally my grandfather, who adored the Army (albeit his duties with the National Guard had been the bugbear of his riper years), could never, at Combray, see a regiment go by the garden railings without baring his head as the colonel and the colours passed. All this was quite enough to make Mme. Sazerat, who knew every incident of the disinterested and honourable careers of my father and grandfather, regard them as pillars of Injustice. We pardon the crimes of individuals, but not their participation in a collective crime. As soon as she knew my father to be an anti-Dreyfusard she set between him and herself continents and centuries. Which explains why, across such an interval of time and space, her bow had been imperceptible to my father, and why it had not occurred to her to hold out her hand, or to say a few words which would never have carried across the worlds that lay between.

Saint-Loup, who was coming anyhow to Paris, had promised to take me to Mme. de Villeparisis's, where I hoped, though I had not said so to him, that we might meet Mme. de Guermantes. He invited me to luncheon in a restaurant with his mistress, whom we were afterwards to accompany to a rehearsal. We were to go out in the morning and call for her at her home on the outskirts of Paris.

I had asked Saint-Loup that the restaurant to which we went for luncheon (in the lives of young noblemen with money to spend the restaurant plays as important a part as do bales of merchandise in Arabian stories), might, if possible, be that to which Aimé had told me that he would be going as head waiter until the Balbec season started. It was a great attraction to me who dreamed of so many expeditions and made so few to see again some one who formed part not merely of my memories of Balbec but of Balbec itself, who went there year after year, who when ill health or my studies compelled me to stay in Paris would be watching, just the same, through the long July afternoons while he waited for the guests to come in to dinner, the sun creep down the sky and set in the sea, through the glass panels of the great dining-room, behind which, at the hour when the light died, the motionless wings of vessels, smoky blue in the distance, looked like exotic and nocturnal moths in a show-case. Himself magnetised by his contact with the strong lodestone of Balbec, this head waiter became in turn a magnet attracting me. I hoped by talking to him to get at once into communication with Balbec, to have realised here in Paris something of the delights of travel.

I left the house early, with Françoise complaining bitterly because the footman who was engaged to be married had once again been prevented, the evening before, from going to see his girl. Françoise had found him in tears; he had been itching to go and strike the porter, but had restrained himself, for he valued his place.

Before reaching Saint-Loup's, where he was to be waiting for me at the door, I ran into Legrandin, of whom we had lost sight since our Combray days, and who, though now grown quite grey, had preserved his air of youthful candour. Seeing me, he stopped:

"Ah! So it's you," he exclaimed, "a man of fashion, and in a frock coat too! That is a livery in which my independent spirit would be ill at ease. It is true that you are a man of the world, I suppose, and go out paying calls! To go and dream, as I do, before some half ruined tomb, my flowing tie and jacket are not out of place. You know how I admire the charming quality of your soul; that is why I tell you how deeply I regret that you should go forth and deny it among the Gentiles. By being capable of remaining for a moment in the nauseating atmosphere—which I am unable to breathe—of a drawing-room, you pronounce on your own future the condemnation, the damnation of the Prophet. I can see it all, you frequent the 'light hearts', the houses of the great, that is the vice of our middle class to-day. Ah! Those aristocrats! The Terror was greatly to blame for not cutting the heads off every one of them. They are all sinister debauchees, when they are not simply dreary idiots. Still, my poor boy, if that sort of thing amuses you! While you are on your way to your tea-party your old friend will be more fortunate than you, for alone in an outlying suburb he will be watching the pink moon rise in a violet sky. The truth is that I scarcely belong to this Earth upon which I feel myself such an exile; it takes all the force of the law of gravity to hold me here, to keep me from escaping into another sphere. I belong to a different planet. Good-bye; do not take amiss the old-time frankness of the peasant of the Vivonne, who has also remained a peasant of the Danube. To prove to you that I am your sincere well-wisher, I am going to send you my last novel.

But you will not care for it; it is not deliquescent enough, not *fin de siècle* enough for you; it is too frank, too honest; what you want is Bergotte, you have confessed it, high game for the jaded palates of pleasure-seeking epicures. I suppose I am looked upon, in your set, as an old campaigner; I do wrong to put my heart into what I write, that is no longer done; besides, the life of the people is not distinguished enough to interest your little snobbicules. Go, get you gone, try to recall at times the words of Christ: ' Do this and ye shall live.' Farewell, Friend."

It was not with any particular resentment against Legrandin that I parted from him. Certain memories are like friends in common, they can bring about reconciliations; set down amid fields starred with buttercups, upon which were piled the ruins of feudal greatness, the little wooden bridge still joined us, Legrandin and me, as it joined the two banks of the Vivonne.

After coming out of a Paris in which, although spring had begun, the trees on the boulevards had hardly put on their first leaves, it was a marvel to Saint-Loup and myself, when the circle train had set us down at the suburban village in which his mistress was living, to see every cottage garden gay with huge festal altars of fruit trees in blossom. It was like one of those peculiar, poetical, ephemeral, local festivals which people travel long distances to attend on certain fixed occasions, only this one was held by Nature. The bloom of the cherry tree is stuck so close to its branches, like a white sheath, that from a distance, among the other trees that shewed as yet scarcely a flower or leaf, one might have taken it, on this day of sunshine that was still so cold, for snow, melted everywhere else, which still clung to the bushes.

But the tall pear trees enveloped each house, each modest courtyard in a whiteness more vast, more uniform, more dazzling, as if all the dwellings, all the enclosed spaces in the village were on their way to make, on one solemn date, their first communion.

It had been a country village, and had kept its old mayor's office sunburned and brown, in front of which, in the place of maypoles and streamers, three tall pear trees were, as though for some civic and local festival, gallantly beflagged with white satin. These villages in the environs of Paris still have at their gates parks of the seventeenth and eighteenth centuries which were the "follies" of the stewards and favourites of the great. A fruit-grower had utilised one of these which was sunk below the road for his trees, or had simply, perhaps, preserved the plan of an immense orchard of former days. Laid out in quincunxes, these pear trees, less crowded and not so far on as those that I had seen, formed great quadrilaterals—separated by low walls—of snowy blossom, on each side of which the light fell differently, so that all these airy roofless chambers seemed to belong to a Palace of the Sun, such as one might unearth in Crete or somewhere; and made one think also of the different ponds of a reservoir, or of those parts of the sea which man, for some fishery, or to plant oyster-beds has subdivided, when one saw, varying with the orientation of the boughs, the light fall and play upon their trained arms as upon water warm with spring, and coax into unfolding here and there, gleaming amid the open, azure-panelled trellis of the branches, the foaming whiteness of a creamy, sunlit flower.

Never had Robert spoken to me so tenderly of his friend

as he did during this walk. She alone had taken root in his heart; his future career in the Army, his position in society, his family, he was not, of course, indifferent altogether to these, but they were of no account compared with the veriest trifle that concerned his mistress. That alone had any importance in his eyes, infinitely more importance than the Guermantes and all the kings of the earth put together. I do not know whether he had formulated the doctrine that she was of a superior quality to anyone else, but I do know that he considered, took trouble only about what affected her. Through her and for her he was capable of suffering, of being happy, perhaps of doing murder. There was really nothing that interested, that could excite him except what his mistress wished, was going to do, what was going on, discernable at most in fleeting changes of expression, in the narrow expanse of her face and behind her privileged brow. So nice-minded in all else, he looked forward to the prospect of a brilliant marriage, solely in order to be able to continue to maintain her, to keep her always. If one had asked oneself what was the value that he set on her, I doubt whether one could ever have imagined a figure high enough. If he did not marry her, it was because a practical instinct warned him that as soon as she had nothing more to expect from him she would leave him, or would at least live as she chose, and that he must retain his hold on her by keeping her in suspense from day to day. For he admitted the possibility that she did not love him. No doubt the general affection called love must have forced him—as it forces all men—to believe at times that she did. But in his heart of hearts he felt that this love which she felt for him did not exhaust the possibility of her remaining with him only on account of his money, and that on the day when she had nothing more to expect from him she would make haste (the dupe of her friends and their literary theories, and loving him all the time, really—he thought) to leave him. " If she is nice to me to-day," he confided to me, " I am going to give her something that she'll like. It's a necklace she saw at Boucheron's. It's rather too much for me just at present—thirty thousand francs. But, poor puss, she gets so little pleasure out of life. She will be jolly pleased with it, I know. She mentioned it to me and told me she knew somebody who would perhaps give it to her. I don't believe that is true, really, but I wasn't taking any risks, so I've arranged with Boucheron, who is our family jeweller, to keep it for me. I am glad to think that you're going to meet her; she's nothing so very wonderful to look at, you know," (I could see that he thought just the opposite and had said this only so as to make me, when I did see her, admire her all the more) "what she has got is a marvellous judgment; she'll perhaps be afraid to talk much before you, but, by Jove! the things she'll say to me about you afterwards, you know she says things one can go on thinking about for hours; there's really something about her that's quite Pythian."

On our way to her house we passed by a row of little gardens, and I was obliged to stop, for they were all aflower with pear and cherry blossom; as empty, no doubt, and lifeless only yesterday as a house that no tenant has taken, they were suddenly peopled and adorned by these newcomers, arrived during the night, whose lovely white garments we could see through the railings along the garden paths.

" Listen; I can see you'ld rather stop and look at that

stuff, and grow poetical about it," said Robert, "so just
wait for me here, will you; my friend's house is quite close,
I will go and fetch her."

While I waited I strolled up and down the road, past
these modest gardens. If I raised my head I could see,
now and then, girls sitting in the windows, but outside, in
the open air, and at the height of a half-landing, here and
there, light and pliant, in their fresh pink gowns, hanging
among the leaves, young lilac-clusters were letting themselves be swung by the breeze without heeding the passer-
by who was turning his eyes towards their green mansions.
I recognised in them the platoons in violet uniform
posted at the entrance to M. Swann's park, past the little
white fence, in the warm afternoons of spring, like an
enchanting rustic tapestry. I took a path which led me
into a meadow. A cold wind blew keenly along it, as at
Combray, but from the midst of the rich, moist, country
soil, which might have been on the bank of the Vivonne,
there had nevertheless arisen, punctual at the trysting
place like all its band of brothers, a great white pear tree
which waved smilingly in the sun's face, like a curtain
of light materialised and made palpable, its flowers shaken
by the breeze but polished and frosted with silver by the
sun's rays.

Suddenly Saint-Loup appeared, accompanied by his
mistress, and then, in this woman who was for him all the
love, every possible delight in life, whose personality, mysteriously enshrined in a body as in a Tabernacle, was the
object that still occupied incessantly the toiling imagination of my friend, whom he felt that he would never really
know, as to whom he was perpetually asking himself what
could be her secret self, behind the veil of eyes and flesh,

in this woman I recognised at once " Rachel when from the
Lord ", her who, but a few years since—women change
their position so rapidly in that world, when they do
change—used to say to the procuress: " To-morrow evening, then, if you want me for anyone, you will send
round, won't you? "

And when they had " come round " for her, and she
found herself alone in the room with the " anyone ", she
had known so well what was required of her that after
locking the door, as a prudent woman's precaution or a
ritual gesture, she would begin to take off all her things,
as one does before the doctor who is going to sound one's
chest, never stopping in the process unless the " some one ",
not caring for nudity, told her that she might keep on her
shift, as specialists do sometimes who, having an extremely fine ear and being afraid of their patient's catching a chill, are satisfied with listening to his breathing and
the beating of his heart through his shirt. On this woman
whose whole life, all her thoughts, all her past, all the
men who at one time or another had had her were to me
so utterly unimportant that if she had begun to tell me
about them I should have listened to her only out of politeness, and should barely have heard what she said, I felt
that the anxiety, the torment, the love of Saint-Loup had
been concentrated in such a way as to make—out of what
was for me a mechanical toy, nothing more—the cause of
endless suffering, the very object and reward of existence.
Seeing these two elements separately (because I had known
" Rachel when from the Lord " in a house of ill fame),
I realised that many women for the sake of whom men
live, suffer, take their lives, may be in themselves or for
other people what Rachel was for me. The idea that any

one could be tormented by curiosity with regard to her life stupefied me. I could have told Robert of any number of her unchastities, which seemed to me the most uninteresting things in the world. And how they would have pained him! And what had he not given to learn them, without avail!

I realised also then all that the human imagination can put behind a little scrap of face, such as this girl's face was, if it is the imagination that was the first to know it; and conversely into what wretched elements, crudely material and utterly without value, might be decomposed what had been the inspiration of countless dreams if, on the contrary, it should be so to speak controverted by the slightest actual acquaintance. I saw that what had appeared to me to be not worth twenty francs when it had been offered to me for twenty francs in the house of ill fame, where it was then for me simply a woman desirous of earning twenty francs, might be worth more than a million, more than one's family, more than all the most coveted positions in life if one had begun by imagining her to embody a strange creature, interesting to know, difficult to seize and to hold. No doubt it was the same thin and narrow face that we saw, Robert and I. But we had arrived at it by two opposite ways, between which there was no communication, and we should never both see it from the same side. That face, with its stares, its smiles, the movements of its lips, I had known from outside as being simply that of a woman of the sort who for twenty francs would do anything that I asked. And so her stares, her smiles, the movements of her lips had seemed to me significant merely of the general actions of a class without any distinctive quality. And beneath them I should not have had the curiosity to look for a person. But what to me had in a sense been offered at the start, that consenting face, had been for Robert an ultimate goal towards which he had made his way through endless hopes and doubts, suspicions, dreams. He gave more than a million francs in order to have for himself, in order that there might not be offered to others what had been offered to me, as to all and sundry, for a score. That he too should not have enjoyed it at the lower price may have been due to the chance of a moment, the instant in which she who seemed ready to yield herself makes off, having perhaps an assignation elsewhere, some reason which makes her more difficult of access that day. Should the man be a sentimentalist, then, even if she has not observed it, but infinitely more if she has, the direst game begins. Unable to swallow his disappointment, to make himself forget about the woman, he starts afresh in pursuit, she flies him, until a mere smile for which he no longer ventured to hope is bought at a thousand times what should have been the price of the last, the most intimate favours. It happens even at times in such a case, when one has been led by a mixture of simplicity in one's judgment and cowardice in the face of suffering to commit the crowning folly of making an inaccessible idol of a girl, that these last favours, or even the first kiss one is fated never to obtain, one no longer even ventures to ask for them for fear of destroying one's chances of Platonic love. And it is then a bitter anguish to leave the world without having ever known what were the embraces of the woman one has most passionately loved. As for Rachel's favours, however, Saint-Loup had by mere accident succeeded in winning them all. Certainly if he had now learned that they had been offered to all the world for a louis, he would have suffered, of course, acutely, but would still have given a million francs for the right to keep them, for nothing that he might have learned could have made him emerge—since that is beyond human control and can be brought to pass only in spite of it by the action of some great natural law —from the path he was treading, from which that face could appear to him only through the web of the dreams that he had already spun. The immobility of that thin face, like that of a sheet of paper subjected to the colossal pressure of two atmospheres, seemed to me to be being maintained by two infinities which abutted on her without meeting, for she held them apart. And indeed, when Robert and I were both looking at her we did not both see her from the same side of the mystery.

It was not " Rachel when from the Lord "—who seemed to me a small matter—it was the power of the human imagination, the illusion on which were based the pains of love; these I felt to be vast. Robert noticed that I appeared moved. I turned my eyes to the pear and cherry trees of the garden opposite, so that he might think that it was their beauty that had touched me. And it did touch me in somewhat the same way; it also brought close to me things of the kind which we not only see with our eyes but feel also in our hearts. These trees that I had seen in the garden, likening them in my mind to strange deities, had not my mistake been like the Magdalene's when, in another garden, she saw a human form and " thought it was the gardener ". Treasurers of our memories of the age of gold, keepers of the promise that reality is not what we suppose, that the splendour of poetry, the wonderful radiance of innocence may shine in it and may be the recompense which we strive to earn, these great white creatures, bowed in a marvellous fashion above the shade propitious for rest, for angling or for reading, were they not rather angels? I exchanged a few words with Saint-Loup's mistress. We cut across the village. Its houses were sordid. But by each of the most wretched, of those that looked as though they had been scorched and branded by a rain of brimstone, a mysterious traveller, halting for a day in the accursed city, a resplendent angel stood erect, extending broadly over it the dazzling protection of the wings of flowering innocence: it was a pear tree. Saint-Loup drew me a little way in front to explain:

" I should have liked if you and I could have been alone together, in fact I would much rather have had luncheon just with you, and stayed with you until it was time to go to my aunt's. But this poor girl of mine here, it is such a pleasure to her, and she is so decent to me, don't you know, I hadn't the heart to refuse her. You'll like her, however, she's literary, you know, a most sensitive nature, and besides it's such a pleasure to be with her in a restaurant, she is so charming, so simple, always delighted with everything."

I fancy nevertheless that, on this same morning, and then probably for the first and last time, Robert did detach himself for a moment from the woman whom out of successive layers of affection he had gradually created, and beheld suddenly at some distance from himself another Rachel, outwardly the double of his but entirely different, who was nothing more or less than a little light of love. We had left the blossoming orchard and were making for the train which was to take us to Paris when, at the station, Rachel, who was walking by herself, was

recognised and accosted by a pair of common little
"tarts" like herself, who first of all, thinking that she
was alone, called out: "Hello, Rachel, you come with us;
Lucienne and Germaine are in the train, and there's room
for one more. Come on. We're all going to the rink,"
and were just going to introduce to her two counter-
jumpers, their lovers, who were escorting them, when,
noticing that she seemed a little uneasy, they looked up
and beyond her, caught sight of us, and with apologies bade her a good-bye to which she responded in
a somewhat embarrassed, but still friendly tone. They
were two poor little "tarts" with collars of sham otter
skin, looking more or less as Rachel must have looked
when Saint-Loup first met her. He did not know them, or
their names even, and seeing that they appeared to be
extremely intimate with his mistress he could not help
wondering whether she too might not once have had, had
not still perhaps her place in a life of which he had never
dreamed, utterly different from the life she led with him,
a life in which one had women for a louis apiece, whereas
he was giving more than a hundred thousand francs a
year to Rachel. He caught only a fleeting glimpse of that
life, but saw also in the thick of it a Rachel other than
her whom he knew, a Rachel like the two little "tarts"
in the train, a twenty-franc Rachel. In short, Rachel had
for the moment duplicated herself in his eyes, he had
seen, at some distance from his own Rachel, the little
"tart" Rachel, the real Rachel, assuming that Rachel
the "tart" was more real than the other. It may then
have occurred to Robert that from the hell in which he
was living, with the prospect of a rich marriage, of the sale
of his name, to enable him to go on giving Rachel a hun-

dred thousand francs every year, he might easily perhaps have escaped, and have enjoyed the favours of his mistress, as the two counter-jumpers enjoyed those of their girls, for next to nothing. But how was it to be done? She had done nothing to forfeit his regard. Less generously rewarded she would be less kind to him, would stop saying and writing the things that so deeply moved him, things which he would quote, with a touch of ostentation, to his friends, taking care to point out how nice it was of her to say them, but omitting to mention that he was maintaining her in the most lavish fashion, or even that he ever gave her anything at all, that these inscriptions on photographs, or greetings at the end of telegrams were but the conversion into the most exiguous, the most precious of currencies of a hundred thousand francs. If he took care not to admit that these rare kindnesses on Rachel's part were handsomely paid for by himself, it would be wrong to say—and yet, by a crude piece of reasoning, we do say it, absurdly, of every lover who pays in cash for his pleasure, and of a great many husbands—that this was from self-esteem or vanity. Saint-Loup had enough sense to perceive that all the pleasures which appeal to vanity he could have found easily and without cost to himself in society, on the strength of his historic name and handsome face, and that his connexion with Rachel had rather, if anything, tended to ostracise him, led to his being less sought after. No; this self-esteem which seeks to appear to be receiving gratuitously the outward signs of the affection of her whom one loves is simply a consequence of love, the need to figure in one's own eyes and in other people's as loved in return by the person whom one loves so well. Rachel rejoined us, leaving the two " tarts " to

get into their compartment; but, no less than their sham
otter skins and the self-conscious appearance of their
young men, the names Lucienne and Germaine kept the
new Rachel alive for a moment longer. For a moment
Robert imagined a Place Pigalle existence with unknown
associates, sordid love affairs, afternoons spent in simple
amusements, excursions or pleasure-parties, in that Paris
in which the sunny brightness of the streets from the
Boulevard de Clichy onwards did not seem the same as
the solar radiance in which he himself strolled with his
mistress, but must be something different, for love, and
suffering which is one with love have, like intoxication, the
power to alter for us inanimate things. It was almost an
unknown Paris in the heart of Paris itself that he suspected, his connexion appeared to him like the explora-
tion of a strange form of life, for if when with him Rachel
was somewhat similar to himself, it was nevertheless a
part of her real life that she lived with him, indeed the
most precious part, in view of his reckless expenditure on
her, the part that made her so greatly envied by her friends
and would enable her one day to retire to the country or
to establish herself in the leading theatres, when she had
made her pile. Robert longed to ask her who Lucienne
and Germaine were, what they would have said to her if
she had joined them in their compartment, how they would
all have spent a day which would have perhaps ended, as a
supreme diversion, after the pleasures of the rink, at the
Olympia Tavern, if Robert and I had not been there. For
a moment the purlieus of the Olympia, which until then
had seemed to him merely deadly dull, aroused curiosity in
him and pain, and the sunshine of this spring day beating
upon the Rue Caumartin where, possibly, if she had not

known Robert, Rachel might have gone in the course of the evening and have earned a louis, filled him with a vague longing. But what use was it to ply Rachel with questions when he already knew that her answer would be merely silence, or a lie, or something extremely painful for him to hear, which would yet explain nothing. The porters were shutting the doors; we jumped into a first-class carriage; Rachel's magnificent pearls reminded Robert that she was a woman of great price, he caressed her, restored her to her place in his heart where he could contemplate her, internalised, as he had always done hitherto—save during this brief instant in which he had seen her in the Place Pigalle of an impressionist painter—and the train began to move.

It was, by the way, quite true that she was " literary ". She never stopped talking to me about books, new art and Tolstoyism except to rebuke Saint-Loup for drinking so much wine:

" Ah! If you could live with me for a year, we'd see a fine change. I should keep you on water and you'ld be ever so much better."

" Right you are. Let's begin now."

" But you know quite well I have to work all day! " For she took her art very seriously. " Besides, what would your people say? "

And she began to abuse his family to me in terms which for that matter seemed to me highly reasonable, and with which Saint-Loup, while disobeying her orders in the matter of champagne, entirely concurred. I, who was so much afraid of the effect of wine on him, and felt the good influence of his mistress, was quite prepared to advise him to let his family go hang. Tears sprang to the young

ROBERT DE SAINT-LOUP AND RACHEL

woman's eyes; I had been rash enough to refer to
Dreyfus.

"The poor martyr!" she almost sobbed; "it will be
the death of him in that dreadful place."

"Don't upset yourself, Zézette, he will come back, he
will be acquitted all right, they will admit they've made a
mistake."

"But long before then he'll be dead! Oh, well at any
rate his children will bear a stainless name. But just think
of the agony he must be going through; that's what makes
my heart bleed. And would you believe that Robert's
mother, a pious woman, says that he ought to be left on
the Devil's Isle, even if he is innocent; isn't it appalling?"

"Yes, it's absolutely true, she does say that," Robert
assured me. "She's my mother, I've no fault to find with
her, but it's quite clear she hasn't got a sensitive nature,
like Zézette."

As a matter of fact these luncheons which were said
to be "such a pleasure" always ended in trouble. For as
soon as Saint-Loup found himself in a public place with
his mistress, he would imagine that she was looking at
every other man in the room, and his brow would darken;
she would remark his ill-humour, which she may have
thought it amusing to encourage, or, as was more probable,
by a foolish piece of conceit preferred, feeling wounded by
his tone, not to appear to be seeking to disarm; and would
make a show of being unable to take her eyes off some
man or other, not that this was always a mere pretence.
In fact, the gentleman who, in theatre or café, happened
to sit next to them, or, to go no farther, the driver of the
cab they had engaged need only have something attractive
about him, no matter what, and Robert, his perception

quickened by jealousy, would have noticed it before his mistress; he would see in him immediately one of those foul creatures whom he had denounced to me at Balbec, who corrupted and dishonoured women for their own amusement, would beg his mistress to take her eyes off the man, thereby drawing her attention to him. And sometimes she found that Robert had shewn such good judgment in his suspicion that after a little she even left off teasing him in order that he might calm down and consent to go off by himself on some errand which would give her time to begin conversation with the stranger, often to make an assignation, sometimes even to bring matters quickly to a head. I could see as soon as we entered the restaurant that Robert was looking troubled. The fact of the matter was that he had at once remarked, what had escaped our notice at Balbec, namely that, standing among his coarser colleagues, Aimé, with a modest brilliance, emitted, quite unconsciously of course, that air of romance which emanates until a certain period in life from fine hair and a grecian nose, features thanks to which he was distinguishable among the crowd of waiters. The others, almost all of them well on in years, presented a series of types, extraordinarily ugly and criminal, of hypocritical priests, sanctimonious confessors, more numerously of comic actors of the old school, whose sugar-loaf foreheads are scarcely to be seen nowadays outside the collections of portraits that hang in the humbly historic green-rooms of little, out of date theatres, where they are represented in the parts of servants or high priests, though this restaurant seemed, thanks to a selective method of recruiting and perhaps to some system of hereditary nomination, to have preserved their solemn type in a sort of College of Augurs. As ill luck would have it, Aimé having recognised us, it was he who came to take our order, while the procession of operatic high priests swept past us to other tables. Aimé inquired after my grandmother's health; I asked for news of his wife and children. He gave it with emotion, being a family man. He had an intelligent, vigorous, but respectful air. Robert's mistress began to gaze at him with a strange attentiveness. But Aimé's sunken eyes, in which a slight short-sightedness gave one the impression of veiled depths, shewed no sign of consciousness in his still face. In the provincial hotel in which he had served for many years before coming to Balbec, the charming sketch, now a trifle discoloured and faded, which was his face, and which, for all those years, like some engraved portrait of Prince Eugène, had been visible always at the same place, at the far end of a dining-room that was almost always empty, could not have attracted any very curious gaze. He had thus for long remained, doubtless for want of sympathetic admirers, in ignorance of the artistic value of his face, and but little inclined for that matter to draw attention to it, for he was temperamentally cold. At the most, some passing Parisian, stopping for some reason in the town, had raised her eyes to his, had asked him perhaps to bring something to her in her room before she left for the station, and in the pellucid, monotonous, deep void of this existence of a faithful husband and servant in a country town had hidden the secret of a caprice without sequel which no one would ever bring to light. And yet Aimé must have been conscious of the insistent emphasis with which the eyes of the young actress were fastened upon him now. Anyhow, it did not escape Robert,

beneath whose skin I saw gathering a flush, not vivid like
that which burned his cheeks when he felt any sudden
emotion, but faint, diffused.

" Anything specially interesting about that waiter,
Zézette? " he inquired, after sharply dismissing Aimé.
" One would think you were studying the part."

"There you are, beginning again; I knew it was
coming."

" Beginning what again, my dear girl? I may have been
mistaken; I haven't said anything, I'm sure. But I have
at least the right to warn you against the fellow, seeing
that I knew him at Balbec (otherwise I shouldn't give a
damn), and a bigger scoundrel doesn't walk the face of
the earth."

She seemed anxious to pacify Robert and began to
engage me in a literary conversation in which he joined. I
found that it did not bore me to talk to her, for she had
a thorough knowledge of the books that I most admired,
and her opinion of them agreed more or less with my own;
but as I had heard Mme. de Villeparisis declare that she
had no talent, I attached but little importance to this evidence of culture. She discoursed wittily on all manner of
topics, and would have been genuinely entertaining had
she not affected to an irritating extent the jargon of the
sets and studios. She applied this, moreover, to everything
under the sun; for instance, having acquired the habit of
saying of a picture, if it were impressionist, or an opera,
if Wagnerian, "Ah! That is *good!*" one day when a
young man had kissed her on the ear, and, touched by her
pretence of being thrilled, had affected modesty, she said:
" Yes, as a sensation I call it distinctly *good*." But what
most surprised me was that the expressions peculiar to

224

Robert (which, moreover, had come to him, perhaps, from literary men whom she knew) were used by her to him and by him to her as though they had been a necessary form of speech, and without any conception of the point-lessness of an originality that is universal.

In eating, she managed her hands so clumsily that one assumed that she must appear extremely awkward upon the stage. She recovered her dexterity only when making love, with that touching prescience latent in women who love the male body so intensely that they immediately guess what will give most pleasure to that body, which is yet so different from their own.

I ceased to take part in the conversation when it turned upon the theatre, for on that topic Rachel was too ma-licious for my liking. She did, it was true, take up in a tone of commiseration—against Saint-Loup, which proved that he was accustomed to hearing Rachel attack her—the defence of Berma, saying: "Oh, no, she's a wonderful person, really. Of course, the things she does no longer appeal to us, they don't correspond quite to what we are looking for, but one must think of her at the period to which she belongs; we owe her a great deal. She has done good work, you know. And besides she's such a fine woman, she has such a good heart; naturally she doesn't care about the things that interest us, but she has had in her time, with a rather impressive face, a charming quality of mind." (Our fingers, by the way, do not play the same accompaniment to all our aesthetic judgments. If it is a picture that is under discussion, to shew that it is a fine work with plenty of paint, it is enough to stick out one's thumb. But the "charming quality of mind" is more exacting. It requires two fingers, or rather two finger-

nails, as though one were trying to flick off a particle of
dust.) But, with this single exception, Saint-Loup's mistress referred to the best-known actresses in a tone of
ironical superiority which annoyed me because I believed
—quite mistakenly, as it happened—that it was she who
was inferior to them. She was clearly aware that I must
regard her as an indifferent actress, and on the other hand
have a great regard for those she despised. But she
shewed no resentment, because there is in all great talent
while it is still, as hers was then, unrecognised, however
sure it may be of itself, a vein of humility, and because we
make the consideration that we expect from others pro-
portionate not to our latent powers but to the position to
which we have attained. (I was, an hour or so later, at
the theatre, to see Saint-Loup's mistress shew great deference towards those very artists against whom she was
now bringing so harsh a judgment to bear.) And so, in
however little doubt my silence may have left her, she
insisted nevertheless on our dining together that evening,
assuring me that never had anyone's conversation delighted her so much as mine. If we were not yet in the
theatre, to which we were to go after luncheon, we had the
sense of being in a green-room hung with portraits of old
members of the company, so markedly were the waiters'
faces those which, one thought, had perished with a whole
generation of obscure actors of the Palais-Royal; they
had a look, also, of Academicians; stopping before a side
table one of them was examining a dish of pears with
the expression of detached curiosity that M. de Jussieu
might have worn. Others, on either side of him, were
casting about the room that gaze instinct with curiosity
and coldness which Members of the Institute, who have

arrived early, throw at the public, while they exchange a
few murmured words which one fails to catch. They were
faces well known to all the regular guests. One of them,
however, was being pointed out, a newcomer with distended nostrils and a smug upper lip, who looked like a
cleric; he was entering upon his duties there for the
first time, and everyone gazed with interest at this newly
elected candidate. But presently, perhaps to drive Robert
away so that she might be alone with Aimé, Rachel began
to make eyes at a young student, who was feeding with
another man at a neighbouring table.

"Zézette, let me beg you not to look at that young man
like that," said Saint-Loup, on whose face the hesitating
flush of a moment ago had been gathered now into a
scarlet tide which dilated and darkened his swollen features, "if you must make a scene here, I shall simply finish
eating by myself and join you at the theatre afterwards."

At this point a messenger came up to tell Aimé that
he was wanted to speak to a gentleman in a carriage
outside. Saint-Loup, ever uneasy, and afraid now that it
might be some message of an amorous nature that was to
be conveyed to his mistress, looked out of the window
and saw there, sitting up in his brougham, his hands
tightly buttoned in white gloves with black seams, a
flower in his buttonhole, M. de Charlus.

"There; you see!" he said to me in a low voice, "my
family hunt me down even here. Will you, please—I can't
very well do it myself, but you can, as you know the
head waiter so well and he's certain to give us away—
ask him not to go to the carriage. He can always send
some other waiter who doesn't know me. I know my
uncle; if they tell him that I'm not known here, he'll

never come inside to look for me, he loathes this sort of place. Really, it's pretty disgusting that an old petticoat-chaser like him, who is still at it, too, should be perpetually lecturing me and coming to spy on me!"

Aimé on receiving my instructions sent one of his underlings to explain that he was busy and could not come out at the moment, and (should the gentleman ask for the Marquis de Saint-Loup) that they did not know any such person. But Saint-Loup's mistress, who had failed to catch our whispered conversation and thought that it was still about the young man at whom Robert had been finding fault with her for making eyes, broke out in a torrent of rage.

"Oh, indeed! So it's the young man over there, now, is it? Thank you for telling me; it's a real pleasure to have this sort of thing with one's meals! Don't listen to him, please; he's rather cross to-day, and, you know," she went on, turning to me, "he just says it because he thinks it smart, that it's the gentlemanly thing to appear jealous always."

And she began with feet and fingers to shew signs of nervous irritation.

"But, Zézette, it is I who find it unpleasant. You are making us all ridiculous before that gentleman, who will begin to imagine you're making overtures to him, and an impossible bounder he looks, too."

"Oh, no, I think he's charming; for one thing, he's got the most adorable eyes, and a way of looking at women—you can feel he must love them."

"You can at least keep quiet until I've left the room, if you have lost your senses," cried Robert. "Waiter, my things."

I did not know whether I was expected to follow him. "No, I want to be alone," he told me in the same tone in which he had just been addressing his mistress, and as if he were quite furious with me. His anger was like a single musical phrase to which in an opera several lines are sung which are entirely different from one another, if one studies the words, in meaning and character, but which the music assimilates by a common sentiment. When Robert had gone, his mistress called Aimé and asked him various questions. She then wanted to know what I thought of him.

"An amusing expression, hasn't he? Do you know what I should like; it would be to know what he really thinks about things, to have him wait on me often, to take him travelling. But that would be all. If we were expected to love all the people who attract us, life would be pretty ghastly, wouldn't it? It's silly of Robert to get ideas like that. All that sort of thing, it's only just what comes into my head, that's all; Robert has nothing to worry about." She was still gazing at Aimé. "Do look, what dark eyes he has. I should love to know what there is behind them."

Presently came a message that Robert was waiting for her in a private room, to which he had gone to finish his luncheon, by another door, without having to pass through the restaurant again. I thus found myself alone, until I too was summoned by Robert. I found his mistress stretched out on a sofa laughing under the kisses and caresses that he was showering on her. They were drinking champagne. "Hallo, you!" she cried to him, having recently picked up this formula which seemed to her the last word in playfulness and wit. I had fed badly,

I was extremely uncomfortable, and albeit Legrandin's words had had no effect on me I was sorry to think that I was beginning in a back room of a restaurant and should be finishing in the wings of a theatre this first afternoon of spring. Looking first at the time to see that she was not making herself late, she offered me a glass of champagne, handed me one of her Turkish cigarettes and unpinned a rose for me from her bodice. Whereupon I said to myself: "I have nothing much to regret, after all; these hours spent in this young woman's company are not wasted, since I have had from her, charming gifts which could not be bought too dear, a rose, a scented cigarette and a glass of champagne." I told myself this because I felt that it endowed with an aesthetic character and thereby justified, saved these hours of boredom. I ought perhaps to have reflected that the very need which I felt of a reason that would console me for my boredom was sufficient to prove that I was experiencing no aesthetic sensation. As for Robert and his mistress, they appeared to have no recollection of the quarrel which had been raging between them a few minutes earlier, or of my having been a witness of it. They made no allusion to it, sought no excuse for it any more than for the contrast with it which their present conduct formed. By dint of drinking champagne with them, I began to feel a little of the intoxication that used to come over me at Rive-belle, though probably not quite the same. Not only every kind of intoxication, from that which the sun or travelling gives us to that which we get from exhaustion or wine, but every degree of intoxication—and each must have a different figure, like the numbers of fathoms on a chart—lays bare in us exactly at the depth to which it reaches a different kind of man. The room which Saint-Loup had taken was small, but the mirror which was its sole ornament was of such a kind that it seemed to reflect thirty others in an endless vista; and the electric bulb placed at the top of the frame must at night, when the light was on, followed by the procession of thirty flashes similar to its own, give to the drinker, even when alone, the idea that the surrounding space was multiplying itself simultaneously with his sensations heightened by intoxication, and that, shut up by himself in this little cell, he was reigning nevertheless over something far more extensive in its indefinite luminous curve than a passage in the Jardin de Paris. Being then myself at this moment the said drinker, suddenly, looking for him in the glass, I caught sight of him, hideous, a stranger, who was staring at me. The joy of intoxication was stronger than my disgust; from gaiety or bravado I smiled at him, and simultaneously he smiled back at me. And I felt myself so much under the ephemeral and potent sway of the minute in which our sensations are so strong, that I am not sure whether my sole regret was not at the thought that this hideous self of whom I had just caught sight in the glass was perhaps there for the last time on earth, and that I should never meet the stranger again in the whole course of my life.

Robert was annoyed only because I was not being more brilliant before his mistress.

"What about that fellow you met this morning, who combines snobbery with astronomy; tell her about him, I've forgotten the story," and he watched her furtively.

"But, my dear boy, there's nothing more than what you've just said."

"What a bore you are. Then tell her about Françoise in the Champs-Elysées. She'll enjoy that."

"Oh, do! Bobby is always talking about Françoise." And taking Saint-Loup by the chin, she repeated, for want of anything more original, drawing the said chin nearer to the light: "Hallo, you!"

Since actors had ceased to be for me exclusively the depositaries, in their diction and playing, of an artistic truth, they had begun to interest me in themselves; I amused myself, pretending that what I saw before me were the characters in some old humorous novel, by watching, struck by the fresh face of the young man who had just come into the stalls, the heroine listen distractedly to the declaration of love which the juvenile lead in the piece was addressing to her, while he, through the fiery torrent of his impassioned speech, still kept a burning gaze fixed on an old lady seated in a stage box, whose magnificent pearls had caught his eye; and thus, thanks especially to the information that Saint-Loup gave me as to the private lives of the players, I saw another drama, mute but expressive, enacted beneath the words of the spoken drama which in itself, although of no merit, interested me also; for I could feel in it that there were budding and opening for an hour in the glare of the footlights, created out of the agglutination on the face of an actor of another face of grease paint and pasteboard, on his own human soul the words of a part.

These ephemeral vivid personalities which the characters are in a play that is entertaining also, whom one loves, admires, pities, whom one would like to see again after one has left the theatre, but who by that time are already disintegrated into a comedian who is no longer

in the position which he occupied in the play, a text
which no longer shews one the comedian's face, a coloured
powder which a handkerchief wipes off, who have returned in short to elements that contain nothing of them,
since their dissolution, effected so soon after the end of
the show, make us—like the dissolution of a dear friend—
begin to doubt the reality of our ego and meditate on
the mystery of death.

One number in the programme I found extremely trying. A young woman whom Rachel and some of her
friends disliked was, with a set of old songs, to make
a first appearance on which she had based all her hopes
for the future of herself and her family. This young
woman was blessed with unduly, almost grotesquely prominent hips and a pretty but too slight voice, weakened
still farther by her excitement and in marked contrast
to her muscular development. Rachel had posted among
the audience a certain number of friends, male and female,
whose business it was by their sarcastic comments to put
the novice, who was known to be timid, out of countenance, to make her lose her head so that her turn should
prove a complete failure, after which the manager would
refuse to give her a contract. At the first notes uttered
by the wretched woman, several of the male audience,
recruited for that purpose, began pointing to her backward
profile with jocular comments, several of the women,
also in the plot, laughed out loud, each flute-like note
from the stage increased the deliberate hilarity, which
grew to a public scandal. The unhappy woman, sweat-
ing with anguish through her grease-paint, tried for a
little longer to hold out, then stopped and looked round
the audience with an appealing gaze of misery and anger

which succeeded only in increasing the uproar. The instinct to imitate others, the desire to shew their own wit and daring added to the party several pretty actresses who had not been forewarned but now threw at the others glances charged with malicious connivance, and sat convulsed with laughter which rang out in such violent peals that at the end of the second song, although there were still five more on the programme, the stage manager rang down the curtain. I tried to make myself pay no more heed to the incident than I had paid to my grandmother's sufferings when my great-aunt, to tease her, used to give my grandfather brandy, the idea of deliberate wickedness being too painful for me to bear. And yet, just as our pity for misfortune is perhaps not very exact since in our imagination we recreate a whole world of grief by which the unfortunate who has to struggle against it has no time to think of being moved to self-pity, so wickedness has probably not in the mind of the wicked man that pure and voluptuous cruelty which it so pains us to imagine. Hatred inspires him, anger gives him an ardour, an activity in which there is no great joy; he must be a sadist to extract any pleasure from it; ordinarily, the wicked man supposes himself to be punishing the wickedness of his victim; Rachel imagined certainly that the actress whom she was making suffer was far from being of interest to any one, and that anyhow, in having her hissed off the stage, she was herself avenging an outrage on good taste and teaching an unworthy comrade a lesson. Nevertheless, I preferred not to speak of this incident since I had had neither the courage nor the power to prevent it, and it would have been too painful for me, by saying any good of their victim, to approximate to a gratification of the lust for cruelty the sentiments which animated the tormentors who had strangled this career in its infancy.

But the opening scene of this afternoon's performance interested me in quite another way. It made me realise in part the nature of the illusion of which Saint-Loup was a victim with regard to Rachel, and which had set a gulf between the images that he and I respectively had in mind of his mistress, when we beheld her that morning among the blossoming pear trees. Rachel was playing a part which involved barely more than her walking on in the little play. But seen thus, she was another woman. She had one of those faces to which distance—and not necessarily that between stalls and stage, the world being in this respect only a larger theatre—gives form and outline and which, seen close at hand, dissolve back into dust. Standing beside her one saw only a nebula, a milky way of freckles, of tiny spots, nothing more. At a proper distance, all this ceased to be visible and, from cheeks that withdrew, were reabsorbed into her face, rose like a crescent moon a nose so fine, so pure that one would have liked to be the object of Rachel's attention, to see her again as often as one chose, to keep her close to one, provided that one had not already seen her differently and at close range. This was not my case but it had been Saint-Loup's when he first saw her on the stage. Then he had asked himself how he might approach her, how come to know her, there had opened in him a whole fairy realm—that in which she lived—from which emanated an exquisite radiance but into which he might not penetrate. He had left the theatre telling himself that it would be madness to write to her, that she would not answer his letter, quite prepared to give his fortune and his name for the creature who was living in him in a world so vastly superior to those too familiar realities, a world made beautiful by desire and dreams of happiness, when at the back of the theatre, a little old building which had itself the air of being a piece of scenery, from the stage door he saw debouch the gay and daintily hatted band of actresses who had just been playing. Young men who knew them were waiting for them outside. The number of pawns on the human chessboard being less than the number of combinations that they are capable of forming, in a theatre from which are absent all the people we know and might have expected to find, there turns up one whom we never imagined that we should see again and who appears so opportunely that the coincidence seems to us providential, although no doubt some other coincidence would have occurred in its stead had we been not in that place but in some other, where other desires would have been aroused and we should have met some other old acquaintance to help us to satisfy them. The golden portals of the world of dreams had closed again upon Rachel before Saint-Loup saw her emerge from the theatre, so that the freckles and spots were of little importance. They vexed him nevertheless, especially as, being no longer alone, he had not now the same opportunity to dream as in the theatre. But she, for all that he could no longer see her, continued to dictate his actions, like those stars which govern us by their attraction even during the hours in which they are not visible to our eyes. And so his desire for the actress with the fine features which had no place now even in Robert's memory had the result that, dashing towards the old friend whom chance had brought to the spot, he insisted upon an introduction to the person with no features and with freckles, since she was the same person, telling himself that later on he would take care to find out which of the two this same person really was. She was in a hurry, she did not on this occasion say a single word to Saint-Loup, and it was only some days later that he finally contrived, by inducing her to leave her companions, to escort her home. He loved her already. The need for dreams, the desire to be made happy by her of whom one has dreamed, bring it about that not much time is required before one entrusts all one's chances of happiness to her who a few days since was but a fortuitous apparition, unknown, unmeaning, upon the boards of the theatre.

When, the curtain having fallen, we moved on to the stage, alarmed at finding myself there for the first time, I felt the need to begin a spirited conversation with Saint-Loup. In this way my attitude, as I did not know what one ought to adopt in a setting that was strange to me, would be entirely dominated by our talk, and people would think that I was so absorbed in it, so un-observant of my surroundings, that it was quite natural that I should not shew the facial expressions proper to a place in which, to judge by what I appeared to be saying, I was barely conscious of standing; and seizing, to make a beginning, upon the first topic that came to my mind:

"You know," I said, "I did come to say good-bye to you the day I left Doncières; I've not had an opportunity to mention it. I waved to you in the street."

"Don't speak about it," he replied, "I was so sorry. I passed you just outside the barracks, but I couldn't stop because I was late already. I assure you, I felt quite wretched about it."

So he had recognised me! I saw again in my mind the wholly impersonal salute which he had given me, raising his hand to his cap, without a glance to indicate that he knew me, without a gesture to shew that he was sorry he could not stop. Evidently this fiction, which he had adopted at that moment, of not knowing me must have simplified matters for him greatly. But I was amazed to find that he had been able to compose himself to it so swiftly and without any instinctive movement to betray his original impression. I had already observed at Balbec that, side by side with that childlike sincerity of his face, the skin of which by its transparence rendered visible the sudden tide of certain emotions, his body had been admirably trained to perform a certain number of well-bred dissimulations, and that, like a consummate actor, he could, in his regimental and in his social life, play alternately quite different parts. In one of his parts he loved me tenderly, he acted towards me almost as if he had been my brother; my brother he had been, he was now again, but for a moment that day he had been another person who did not know me and who, holding the reins, his glass screwed to his eye, without a look or a smile had lifted his disengaged hand to the peak of his cap to give me correctly the military salute.

The stage scenery, still in its place, among which I was passing, seen thus at close range and without the advantage of any of those effects of lighting and distance on which the eminent artist whose brush had painted it had calculated, was a depressing sight, and Rachel, when I came near her, was subjected to a no less destructive force. The curves of her charming nose had stood out in perspective, between stalls and stage, like the relief of the scenery. It was no longer herself, I recognised her only thanks to her eyes, in which her identity had taken refuge. The form, the radiance of this young star, so brilliant a moment ago, had vanished. On the other hand—as though we came close to the moon and it ceased to present the appearance of a disk of rosy gold— on this face, so smooth a surface until now, I could distinguish only protuberances, discolourations, cavities. Despite the incoherence into which were resolved at close range not only the feminine features but the painted canvas, I was glad to be there to wander among the scenery, all that setting which at one time my love of nature had prompted me to dismiss as tedious and artificial until the description of it by Goethe in *Wilhelm Meister* had given it a sort of beauty in my eyes; and I had already observed with delight, in the thick of a crowd of journalists or men of fashion, friends of the actresses, who were greeting one another, talking, smoking, as though in a public thoroughfare, a young man in a black velvet cap and hortensia coloured skirt, his cheeks chalked in red like a page from a Watteau album, who with his smiling lips, his eyes raised to the ceiling, as he sprang lightly into the air, seemed so entirely of another species than the rational folk in every day clothes, in the midst of whom he was pursuing like a madman the course of his ecstatic dream, so alien to the preoccupations of their life, so anterior to the habits of their civilisation, so enfranchised from all the laws of nature, that it was as restful and as fresh a spectacle as watching a butterfly straying along a crowded street to follow with one's eyes, between the strips of canvas, the natural arabesques traced by his winged capricious painted oscillations. But at that moment Saint-Loup conceived the idea that his mistress was paying undue attention to this dancer, who was engaged now in practising for the last time the figure of fun with which he was going to take the stage, and his face darkened.

"You might look the other way," he warned her gloomily. "You know that none of those dancer-fellows is worth the rope they can at least fall off and break their necks, and they're the sort of people who go about afterwards boasting that you've taken notice of them. Besides, you know very well you've been told to go to your dressing-room and change. You'll be missing your call again."

A group of men—journalists—noticing the look of fury on Saint-Loup's face, came nearer, amused, to listen to what we were saying. And as the stage-hands had just set up some scenery on our other side we were forced into close contact with them.

"Oh, but I know him; he's a friend of mine," cried Saint-Loup's mistress, her eyes still fixed on the dancer. "Look how well made he is, do watch those little hands of his dancing away by themselves like his whole body!"

The dancer turned his head towards her, and his human person appeared beneath the sylph that he was endeavouring to be, the clear grey jelly of his eyes trembled and sparkled between eyelids stiff with paint, and a smile extended the corners of his mouth into cheeks plastered with rouge; then, to amuse the girl, like a singer who hums to oblige us the air of the song in which we have told her that we admired her singing, he began to repeat the movement of his hands, counterfeiting himself with the fineness of a parodist and the good humour of a child.

"Oh, that's too lovely, the way he copies himself," she cried, clapping her hands.

"I implore you, my dearest girl," Saint-Loup broke in, in a tone of utter misery, "do not make a scene here, I can't stand it; I swear, if you say another word I won't go with you to your room, I shall walk straight out; come, don't be so naughty. . . . You oughtn't to stand about in the cigar smoke like that, it'll make you ill," he went on, to me, with the solicitude he had shewn for me in our Balbec days.

"Oh! What a good thing it would be if you did go."

"I warn you, if I do I shan't come back."

"That's more than I should venture to hope."

"Listen; you know, I promised you the necklace if you behaved nicely to me, but the moment you treat me like this. . . ."

"Ah! Well, that doesn't surprise me in the least. You gave me your promise; I ought to have known you'ld never keep it. You want the whole world to know you're made of money, but I'm not a money-grubber like you. You can keep your blasted necklace; I know some one else who'll give it to me."

"No one else can possibly give it to you; I've told Boucheron he's to keep it for me, and I have his promise not to let anyone else have it."

"There you are, trying to blackmail me, you've arranged everything I see. That's what they mean by Marsantes, *Mater Semita*, it smells of the race," retorted Rachel, quoting an etymology which was founded on a wild misinterpretation, for *Semita* means "path" and not " Semite ", but one which the Nationalists applied to Saint-Loup on account of the Dreyfusard views for which, so far as that went, he was indebted to the actress. She was less entitled than anyone to apply the word " Jew " to Mme. de Marsantes, in whom the ethnologists of society could succeed in finding no trace of Judaism apart from her connexion with the Lévy-Mirepoix family. " But this isn't the last of it, I can tell you. An agreement like that isn't binding. You have acted treacherously towards me. Boucheron shall be told of it and he'll be paid twice as much for his necklace. You'll hear from me before long; don't you worry."

Robert was in the right a hundred times over. But circumstances are always so entangled that the man who is in the right a hundred times may have been once in the wrong. And I could not help recalling that unpleasant and yet quite innocent expression which he had used at Balbec: " In that way I keep a hold over her."

" You don't understand what I mean about the necklace. I made no formal promise: once you start doing everything you possibly can to make me leave you, it's only natural, surely, that I shouldn't give it to you; I fail to understand what treachery you can see in that, or what my ulterior motive is supposed to be. You can't seriously maintain that I brag about my money, I'm always telling you that I'm only a poor devil without a cent to my name. It's foolish of you to take it in that way, my dear. What possible interest can I have in hurting you? You know very well that my one interest in life is yourself."

" Oh, yes, yes, please go on," she retorted ironically, with the sweeping gesture of a barber wielding his razor. And turning to watch the dancer:

"Isn't he too wonderful with his hands. A woman like me couldn't do the things he's doing now." She went closer to him and, pointing to Robert's furious face: "Look, he's hurt," she murmured, in the momentary elation of a sadic impulse to cruelty totally out of keeping with her genuine feelings of affection for Saint-Loup.

"Listen; for the last time, I swear to you it doesn't matter what you do—in a week you'll be giving anything to get me back—I shan't come; it's a clean cut, do you hear, it's irrevocable; you will be sorry one day, when it's too late."

Perhaps he was sincere in saying this, and the torture of leaving his mistress may have seemed to him less cruel than that of remaining with her in certain circumstances.

"But, my dear boy," he went on, to me, "you oughtn't to stand about here, I tell you, it will make you cough."

I pointed to the scenery which barred my way. He touched his hat and said to one of the journalists:

"Would you mind, sir, throwing away your cigar; the smoke is bad for my friend."

His mistress had not waited for him to accompany her; on her way to her dressing-room she turned round and:

"Do they do those tricks with women too, those nice little hands?" she flung to the dancer from the back of the stage, in an artificially melodious tone of girlish innocence. "You look just like one yourself, I'm sure I could have a wonderful time with you and a girl I know."

"There's no rule against smoking that I know of; if people aren't well, they have only to stay at home," said the journalist.

The dancer smiled mysteriously back at the actress.

" Oh! Do stop! You'll make me quite mad," she cried
to him. " Then there will be trouble."

" In any case, sir, you are not very civil," observed
Saint-Loup to the journalist, still with a courteous suavity,
in the deliberate manner of a man judging retrospectively
the rights and wrongs of an incident that is already closed.

At that moment I saw Saint-Loup raise his arm vertically above his head as if he had been making a signal
to some one whom I could not see, or like the conductor
of an orchestra, and indeed—without any greater transition than when, at a simple wave of the baton, in a sym-
phony or a ballet, violent rhythms succeed a graceful
andante—after the courteous words that he had just
uttered he brought down his hand with a resounding
smack upon the journalist's cheek.

Now that to the measured conversations of the diplomats, to the smiling arts of peace had succeeded the
furious onthrust of war, since blows lead to blows, I
should not have been surprised to see the combatants
swimming in one another's blood. But what I could not
understand (like people who feel that it is not according
to the rules when a war breaks out between two countries
after some question merely of the rectification of a
frontier, or when a sick man dies after nothing more
serious than a swelling of the liver) was how Saint-Loup
had contrived to follow up those words, which implied a
distinct shade of friendliness, with an action which in no
way arose out of them, which they had not, so to speak,
announced, that action of an arm raised in defiance not
only of the rights of man but of the law of cause and
effect, that action created *ex nihilo*. Fortunately the journalist who, staggering back from the violence of the blow,

had turned pale and hesitated for a moment, did not retaliate. As for his friends, one of them had promptly turned away his head and was looking fixedly into the wings for some one who evidently was not there; the second pretended that a speck of dust had got into his eye, and began rubbing and squeezing his eyelid with every sign of being in pain; while the third had rushed off, exclaiming: "Good heavens, I believe the curtain's going up; we shan't get into our seats."

I wanted to speak to Saint-Loup, but he was so full of his indignation with the dancer that it adhered exactly to the surface of his eyeballs; like a subcutaneous structure it distended his cheeks with the result that, his internal agitation expressing itself externally in an entire immobility, he had not even the power of relaxation, the "play" necessary to take in a word from me and to answer it. The journalist's friends, seeing that the incident was at an end, gathered round him again, still trembling. But, ashamed of having deserted him, they were absolutely determined that he should be made to suppose that they had noticed nothing. And so they dilated, one upon the speck of dust in his eye, one upon his false alarm when he had thought that the curtain was going up, the third upon the astonishing resemblance between a man who had just gone by and the speaker's brother. Indeed they seemed quite to resent their friend's not having shared their several emotions.

"What, didn't it strike you? You must be going blind."

"What I say is that you're a pack of curs," growled the journalist whom Saint-Loup had punished.

Forgetting the poses they had adopted, to be consistent with which they ought—but they did not think of it—to have pretended not to understand what he meant, they fell back on certain expressions traditional in the circumstances: "What's all the excitement? Keep your hair on, old chap. Don't take the bit in your teeth."

I had realised that morning beneath the pear blossom how illusory were the grounds upon which Robert's love for "Rachel when from the Lord" was based; I was bound now to admit how very real were the sufferings to which that love gave rise. Gradually the feeling that had obsessed him for the last hour, without a break, began to diminish, receded into him, an unoccupied pliable zone appeared in his eyes. I had stopped for a moment at a corner of the Avenue Gabriel from which I had often in the past seen Gilberte appear. I tried for a few seconds to recall those distant impressions, and was hurrying at a "gymnastic" pace to overtake Saint-Loup when I saw that a gentleman, somewhat shabbily attired, appeared to be talking to him confidentially. I concluded that this was a personal friend of Robert; at the same time they seemed to be drawing even closer to one another; suddenly, as a meteor flashes through the sky, I saw a number of ovoid bodies assume with a giddy swiftness all the positions necessary for them to form, before Saint-Loup's face and body, a flickering constellation. Flung out like stones from a catapult, they seemed to me to be at the very least seven in number. They were merely, however, Saint-Loup's pair of fists, multiplied by the speed with which they were changing their places in this—to all appearance ideal and decorative—arrangement. But this elaborate display was nothing more than a pummelling which Saint-Loup was administering, the true character of which, aggressive rather than aesthetic, was first revealed

to me by the aspect of the shabbily dressed gentleman who
appeared to be losing at once his self-possession, his lower
jaw and a quantity of blood. He gave fictitious explanations to the people who came up to question him, turned
his head and, seeing that Saint-Loup had made off and
was hastening to rejoin me, stood gazing after him with
an offended, crushed, but by no means furious expression
on his face. Saint-Loup, on the other hand, was furious,
although he himself had received no blow, and his eyes
were still blazing with anger when he reached me. The
incident was in no way connected (as I had supposed)
with the assault in the theatre. It was an impassioned
loiterer who, seeing the fine looking young soldier that
Saint-Loup was, had made overtures to him. My friend
could not get over the audacity of this "clique" who
no longer even waited for the shades of night to cover
their operations, and spoke of the suggestion that had
been made to him with the same indignation as the
newspapers use in reporting an armed assault and rob-
bery, in broad daylight, in the centre of Paris. And yet
the recipient of his blow was excusable in one respect,
for the trend of the downward slope brings desire so
rapidly to the point of enjoyment that beauty by itself
appears to imply consent. Now, that Saint-Loup was
beautiful was beyond dispute. Castigation such as he had
just administered has this value, for men of the type that
had accosted him, that it makes them think seriously of
their conduct, though never for long enough to enable
them to amend their ways and thus escape correction at
the hands of the law. And so, although Saint-Loup's arm
had shot out instinctively, without any preliminary
thought, all such punishments, even when they reinforce

the law, are powerless to bring about any uniformity in morals.

These incidents, particularly the one that was weighing most on his mind, seemed to have prompted in Robert a desire to be left alone for a while. After a moment's silence he asked me to leave him, and to go by myself to call on Mme. de Villeparisis. He would join me there, but preferred that we should not enter the room together, so that he might appear to have only just arrived in Paris, instead of having spent half the day already with me.

As I had supposed before making the acquaintance of Mme. de Villeparisis at Balbec, there was a vast difference between the world in which she lived and that of Mme. de Guermantes. Mme. de Villeparisis was one of those women who, born of a famous house, entering by marriage into another no less famous, do not for all that enjoy any great position in the social world, and, apart from a few duchesses who are their nieces or sisters-in-law, perhaps even a crowned head or two, old family friends, see their drawing-rooms filled only by third rate people, drawn from the middle classes or from a nobility either provincial or tainted in some way, whose presence there has long since driven away all such smart and snobbish folk as are not obliged to come to the house by ties of blood or the claims of a friendship too old to be ignored. Certainly I had no difficulty after the first few minutes in understanding how Mme. de Villeparisis, at Balbec, had come to be so well informed, better than ourselves even, as to the smallest details of the tour through Spain which my father was then making with M. de Norpois. Even this, however, did not make it possible to rest content with the theory that the intimacy

—of more than twenty years' standing—between Mme. de Villeparisis and the Ambassador could have been responsible for the lady's loss of caste in a world where the smartest women boasted the attachment of lovers far less respectable than him, not to mention that it was probably years since he had been anything more to the Marquise than just an old friend. Had Mme. de Villeparisis then had other adventures in days gone by? Being then of a more passionate temperament than now, in a calm and religious old age which nevertheless owed some of its mellow colouring to those ardent, vanished years, had she somehow failed, in the country neighbourhood where she had lived for so long, to avoid certain scandals unknown to the younger generation who simply took note of their effect in the unequal and defective composition of a visiting list bound, otherwise, to have been among the purest of any taint of mediocrity? That " sharp tongue " which her nephew ascribed to her, had it in those far-off days made her enemies? Had it driven her into taking advantage of certain successes with men so as to avenge herself upon women? All this was possible; nor could the exquisitely sensitive way in which— giving so delicate a shade not merely to her words but to her intonation—Mme. de Villeparisis spoke of modesty or generosity be held to invalidate this supposition; for the people who not only speak with approval of certain virtues but actually feel their charm and shew a marvellous comprehension of them (people in fact who will, when they come to write their memoirs, present a worthy picture of those virtues) are often sprung from but not actually part of the silent, simple, artless generation which practised them. That generation is reflected in them but is not continued. Instead of the character which it possessed we find a sensibility, an intelligence which are not conducive to action. And whether or not there had been in the life of Mme. de Villeparisis any of those scandals, which (if there had) the lustre of her name would have blotted out, it was this intellect, resembling rather that of a writer of the second order than that of a woman of position, that was undoubtedly the cause of her social degradation.

It is true that they were not specially elevating, the qualities, such as balance and restraint, which Mme. de Villeparisis chiefly extolled; but to speak of restraint in a manner that shall be entirely adequate, the word " restraint " is not enough, we require some of the qualities of authorship which presuppose a quite unrestrained exaltation; I had remarked at Balbec that the genius of certain great artists was completely unintelligible to Mme. de Villeparisis; and that all she could do was to make delicate fun of them and to express her incomprehension in a graceful and witty form. But this wit and grace, at the point to which she carried them, became themselves—on another plane, and even although they were employed to belittle the noblest masterpieces—true artistic qualities. Now the effect of such qualities on any social position is a morbid activity of the kind which doctors call elective, and so disintegrating that the most firmly established pillars of society are hard put to it to hold out for any length of time. What artists call intellect seems pure presumption to the fashionable world which, unable to place itself at the sole point of view from which they, the artists, look at and judge things, incapable of understanding the particular attraction to which they yield when they choose an expression or start a friendship, feel in their company an exhaustion, an irritation, from which antipathy very shortly springs. And yet in her conversation, and the same may be said of the *Memoirs* which she afterwards published, Mme. de Villeparisis shewed nothing but a sort of grace that was eminently social. Having passed by great works without mastering, sometimes without even noticing them, she had preserved from the period in which she had lived and which, more-over, she described with great aptness and charm, little more than the most frivolous of the gifts that they had had to offer her. But a narrative of this sort, even when it treats exclusively of subjects that are not intellectual, is still a work of the intellect, and to give in a book or in conversation, which is almost the same thing, a deliberate impression of frivolity, a serious touch is required which a purely frivolous person would be incapable of supplying. In a certain book of reminiscences written by a woman and regarded as a masterpiece, the phrase that people quote as a model of airy grace has always made me suspect that, in order to arrive at such a pitch of light-ness, the author must originally have had a rather stodgy education, a boring culture, and that as a girl she probably appeared to her friends an insufferable prig. And between certain literary qualities and social failure the connexion is so inevitable that when we open Mme. de Villeparisis's *Memoirs* to-day, on any page a fitting epithet, a sequence of metaphors will suffice to enable the reader to reconstruct the deep but icy bow which must have been bestowed on the old Marquise on the staircases of the Embassies by a snob like Mme. Leroi, who perhaps may have left a card on her when she went to call on the Guermantes, but never set foot in her house for fear of losing caste among all the doctors' or solicitors' wives whom she would find there. A bluestocking Mme. de Villeparisis had perhaps been in her earliest youth, and, intoxicated with the ferment of her own knowledge, had perhaps failed to realise the importance of not applying to people in society, less intelligent and less educated than herself, those cutting strokes which the injured party never forgets.

Moreover, talent is not a separate appendage which one artificially attaches to those qualities which make for social success, in order to create from the whole what people in society call a "complete woman". It is the living product of a certain moral complexion, from which as a rule many moral qualities are lacking and in which there predominates a sensibility of which other manifestations such as we do not notice in a book may make themselves quite distinctly felt in the course of a life, certain curiosities for instance, certain whims, the desire to go to this place or that for one's own amusement and not with a view to the extension, the maintenance or even the mere exercise of one's social relations. I had seen at Balbec Mme. de Villeparisis hemmed in by a bodyguard of her own servants without even a glance, as she passed, at the people sitting in the hall of the hotel. But I had had a presentiment that this abstention was due not to indifference, and it seemed that she had not always confined herself to it. She would get a sudden craze to know some one or other because she had seen him and thought him good-looking, or merely because she had been told that he was amusing, or because he had struck her as different from the people she knew, who at this period, when she had not yet begun to appreciate them because she imagined that they would never fail her, belonged, all of them, to the purest cream of the Faubourg Saint-Germain. To the bohemian, the humble middle-class gentleman whom she had marked out with her favour she was obliged to address invitations the importance of which he was unable to appreciate, with an insistence which began gradually to depreciate her in the eyes of the snobs who were in the habit of estimating the smartness of a house by the people whom its mistress excluded rather than by those whom she entertained. Certainly, if at a given moment in her youth Mme. de Villeparisis, surfeited with the satisfaction of belonging to the fine flower of the aristocracy, had found a sort of amusement in scandalising the people among whom she lived, and in deliberately impairing her own position in society, she had begun to attach its full importance to that position once it was definitely lost. She had wished to shew the Duchesses that she was better than they, by saying and doing all the things that they dared not say or do. But now that they all, save such as were closely related to her, had ceased to call, she felt herself diminished, and sought once more to reign, but with another sceptre than that of wit. She would have liked to attract to her house all those women whom she had taken such pains to drive away. How many women's lives, lives of which little enough is known (for we all live in different worlds according to our ages, and the discretion of their elders prevents the young from forming any clear idea of the past and so completing the cycle), have been divided in this way into contrasted periods, the last being entirely devoted to the reconquest of what in the second has been so light-heartedly flung on the wind. Flung on the wind in what way? The young people are all the less capable of imagining it, since they see before them an elderly and respectable Marquise de Villeparisis and have no idea that the grave diarist of the present day, so dignified beneath her pile of snowy hair, can ever have been a gay midnight-reveller who was perhaps the delight in those days, devoured the fortunes perhaps of men now sleeping in their graves; that she should also have set to work, with a persevering and natural industry, to destroy the position which she owed to her high birth does not in the least imply that even at that remote period Mme. de Villeparisis did not attach great importance to her position. In the same way the web of isolation, of inactivity in which a neurasthenic lives may be woven by him from morning to night without therefore seeming endurable, and while he is hastening to add another mesh to the net which holds him captive, it is possible that he is dreaming only of dancing, sport and travel. We are at work every moment upon giving its form to our life, but we do so by copying unintentionally, like the example in a book, the features of the person that we are and not of him who we should like to be. The disdainful bow of Mme. Leroi might to some extent be expressive of the true nature of Mme. de Villeparisis; it in no way corresponded to her ambition.

No doubt at the same moment at which Mme. Leroi was—to use an expression beloved of Mme. Swann—" cutting " the Marquise, the latter could seek consolation in remembering how Queen Marie-Amélie had once said to her: " You are just like a daughter to me." But such marks of royal friendship, secret and unknown to the

world, existed for the Marquise alone, dusty as the diploma
of an old Conservatoire medallist. The only true social
advantages are those that create life, that can disappear
without the person who has benefited by them needing
to try to keep them or to make them public, because on
the same day a hundred others will take their place.
And for all that she could remember the Queen's using
those words to her, she would nevertheless have bartered
them gladly for the permanent faculty of being asked
everywhere which Mme. Leroi possessed, as in a restaurant a great but unknown artist whose genius is written
neither in the lines of his bashful face nor in the antiquated cut of his threadbare coat, would willingly be
even the young stock-jobber, of the lowest grade of society,
who is sitting with a couple of actresses at a neighbouring
table to which in an obsequious and incessant chain come
hurrying manager, head waiter, pages and even the scul-
lions who file out of the kitchen to salute him, as in the
fairy-tales, while the wine waiter advances, dust-covered
like his bottles, limping and dazed, as if on his way up
from the cellar he had twisted his foot before emerging
into the light of day.

It must be remarked, however, that in Mme. de Villeparisis's drawing-room the absence of Mme. Leroi, if it
distressed the lady of the house, passed unperceived by
the majority of her guests. They were entirely ignorant
of the peculiar position which Mme. Leroi occupied, a
position known only to the fashionable world, and never
doubted that Mme. de Villeparisis's receptions were, as
the readers of her *Memoirs* to-day are convinced that they
must have been, the most brilliant in Paris.

On the occasion of this first call which, after leaving

Saint-Loup, I went to pay on Mme. de Villeparisis, following the advice given by M. de Norpois to my father, I found her in her drawing-room hung with yellow silk, against which the sofas and the admirable armchairs upholstered in Beauvais tapestry stood out with the almost purple redness of ripe raspberries. Side by side with the Guermantes and Villeparisis portraits one saw those—gifts from the sitters themselves—of Queen Marie-Amélie, the Queen of the Belgians, the Prince de Joinville and the Empress of Austria. Mme. de Villeparisis herself, capped with an old-fashioned bonnet of black lace (which she preserved with the same instinctive sense of local or historical colour as a Breton innkeeper who, however Parisian his customers may have become, feels it more in keeping to make his maids dress in coifs and wide sleeves), was seated at a little desk on which in front of her, as well as her brushes, her palette and an unfinished flower-piece in water-colours, were arranged in glasses, in saucers, in cups, moss-roses, zinnias, maidenhair ferns, which on account of the sudden influx of callers she had just left off painting, and which had the effect of being piled on a florist's counter in some eighteenth-century mezzotint. In this drawing-room, which had been slightly heated on purpose because the Marquise had caught cold on the journey from her house in the country, there were already when I arrived a librarian with whom Mme. de Villeparisis had spent the morning in selecting the autograph letters to herself from various historical personages which were to figure in facsimile as documentary evidence in the *Memoirs* which she was preparing for the press, and a historian, solemn and tongue-tied, who hearing that she had inherited and still possessed a portrait of the Duchesse de Montmorency, had come to ask her permission to reproduce it as a plate in his work on the Fronde; a party strengthened presently by the addition of my old friend Bloch, now a rising dramatist, upon whom she counted to secure the gratuitous services of actors and actresses at her next series of afternoon parties. It was true that the social kaleidoscope was in the act of turning and that the Dreyfus case was shortly to hurl the Jews down to the lowest rung of the social ladder. But, for one thing, the anti-Dreyfus cyclone might rage as it would, it is not in the first hour of a storm that the waves are highest. In the second place, Mme. de Villeparisis, leaving a whole section of her family to fulminate against the Jews, had hitherto kept herself entirely aloof from the Case and never gave it a thought. Lastly, a young man like Bloch, whom no one knew, might pass unperceived, whereas leading Jews, representatives of their party, were already threatened. He had his chin pointed now by a goat-beard, wore double glasses and a long frock coat, and carried a glove like a roll of papyrus in his hand. The Rumanians, the Egyptians, the Turks may hate the Jews. But in a French drawing-room the differences between those peoples are not so apparent, and an Israelite making his entry as though he were emerging from the heart of the desert, his body crouching like a hyaena's, his neck thrust obliquely forward, spreading himself in profound " salaams ", completely satisfies a certain taste for the oriental. Only it is essential that the Jew should not be actually " in " society, otherwise he will readily assume the aspect of a lord and his manners become so Gallicised that on his face a rebellious nose, growing like a nasturtium in any but the right direction, will make one think rather of Mascarille's nose than of Solomon's. But Bloch, not having been rendered supple by the gymnastics of the Faubourg, nor ennobled by a crossing with England or Spain, remained for a lover of the exotic as strange and savoury a spectacle, in spite of his European costume, as one of Decamps's Jews. Marvellous racial power which from the dawn of time thrusts to the surface, even in modern Paris, on the stage of our theatres, behind the pigeonholes of our public offices, at a funeral, in the street, a solid phalanx, setting their mark upon our modern ways of hairdressing, absorbing, making us forget, disciplining the frock coat which on them remains not at all unlike the garment in which Assyrian scribes are depicted in ceremonial attire on the frieze of a monument at Susa before the gates of the Palace of Darius. (Later in the afternoon Bloch might have imagined that it was out of anti-semitic malice that M. de Charlus inquired whether his first name was Jewish, whereas it was simply from aesthetic interest and love of local colour.) But, to revert for a moment, when we speak of racial persistence we do not accurately convey the impression we receive from Jews, Greeks, Persians, all those peoples whom it is better to leave with their differences. We know from classical paintings the faces of the ancient Greeks, we have seen Assyrians on the walls of a palace at Susa. And so we feel, on encountering in a Paris drawing-room Orientals belonging to one or other group, that we are in the presence of creatures whom the forces of necromancy must have called to life. We knew hitherto only a superficial image; behold it has gained depth, it extends into three dimensions, it moves. The young Greek lady, daughter of a rich banker and the latest favourite of society, looks exactly like one of those dancers who in the chorus of a ballet at once historical and aesthetic symbolise in flesh and blood the art of Hellas; and yet in the theatre the setting makes these images somehow trite; the spectacle, on the other hand, to which the entry into a drawing-room of a Turkish lady or a Jewish gentleman admits us, by animating their features makes them appear stranger still, as if they really were creatures evoked by the effort of a medium. It is the soul (or rather the pigmy thing to which—up to the present, at any rate—the soul is reduced in this sort of materialisation), it is the soul of which we have caught glimpses hitherto in museums alone, the soul of the ancient Greeks, of the ancient Hebrews, torn from a life at once insignificant and transcendental, which seems to be enacting before our eyes this disconcerting pantomime. In the young Greek lady who is leaving the room what we seek in vain to embrace is the figure admired long ago on the side of a vase. I felt that if I had in the light of Mme. de Villeparisis's drawing-room taken photographs of Bloch, they would have furnished of Israel the same image—so disturbing because it does not appear to emanate from humanity, so deceiving because all the same it is so strangely like humanity—which we find in spirit photographs. There is nothing, to speak more generally, not even the insignificance of the remarks made by the people among whom we spend our lives, that does not give us a sense of the supernatural, in our every-day world where even a man of genius from whom we expect, gathered as though around a turning table, to learn the secret of the Infinite utters only these words—the same that had just issued from the lips of Bloch: "Take care of my top hat."

"Oh, Ministers, my dear sir," Mme. de Villeparisis was saying, addressing herself specially to my friend, and picking up the thread of a conversation which had been broken by my arrival: "nobody ever wanted to see them. I was only a child at the time, but I can remember so well the King begging my grandfather to invite M. Decazes to a rout at which my father was to dance with the Duchesse de Berry. 'It will give me pleasure, Florimond,' said the King. My grandfather, who was a little deaf, thought he had said M. de Castries, which seemed a perfectly natural thing to ask. When he understood that it was M. Decazes, he was furious at first, but he gave in, and wrote a note the same evening to M. Decazes, begging him to pay my grandfather the compliment and give him the honour of his presence at the ball which he was giving the following week. For we were polite, sir, in those days, and no hostess would have dreamed of simply sending her card and writing on it 'Tea' or 'Dancing' or 'Music'. But if we understood politeness we were not incapable of impertinence either. M. Decazes accepted, but the day before the ball it was given out that my grandfather felt indisposed and had cancelled his invitations. He had obeyed the King, but he had not had M. Decazes at his ball. . . . Yes, sir, I remember M. Molé very well, he was a clever man— he shewed that in his reception of M. de Vigny at the Academy—but he was very pompous, and I can see him now coming downstairs to dinner in his own house with his tall hat in his hand."

"Ah! that is typically suggestive of what must have

been a pretty perniciously philistine epoch, for it was no doubt a universal habit to carry one's hat in one's hand in one's own house," observed Bloch, anxious to make the most of so rare an opportunity of learning from an eyewitness details of the aristocratic life of another day, while the librarian, who was a sort of intermittent secretary to the Marquise, gazed at her tenderly as though he were saying to the rest of us: " There, you see what she's like, she knows everything, she has met everybody, you can ask her anything you like, she's quite amazing."

"Oh, dear, no," replied Mme. de Villeparisis, drawing nearer to her as she spoke the glass containing the maidenhair which presently she would begin again to paint, " it was a habit M. Molé had; that was all. I never saw my father carry his hat in the house, except of course when the King came, because the King being at home wherever he is the master of the house is only a visitor then in his own drawing-room."

" Aristotle tells us in the second chapter of . . ." ventured M. Pierre, the historian of the Fronde, but so timidly that no one paid any attention. Having been suffering for some weeks from a nervous insomnia which resisted every attempt at treatment, he had given up going to bed, and, half-dead with exhaustion, went out only whenever his work made it imperative. Incapable of repeating at all often these expeditions which, simple enough for other people, cost him as much effort as if, to make them, he was obliged to come down from the moon, he was surprised to be brought up so frequently against the fact that other people's lives were not organised on a constant and permanent basis so as to furnish the maximum utility to the sudden outbursts of his own. He sometimes found the doors shut of a library which he had reached only after setting himself artificially on his feet and in a frock coat like some automaton in a story by Mr. Wells. Fortunately he had found Mme. de Villeparisis at home and was going to be shewn the portrait.

Meanwhile he was cut short by Bloch. "Indeed," the latter remarked, referring to what Mme. de Villeparisis had said as to the etiquette for royal visits. "Do you know, I never knew that," as though it were strange that he should not have known it always.

"Talking of that sort of visit, you heard the stupid joke my nephew Basin played on me yesterday morning?" Mme. de Villeparisis asked the librarian. "He told my people, instead of announcing him, to say that it was the Queen of Sweden who had called to see me."

"What! He made them tell you just like that! I say, he must have a nerve," exclaimed Bloch with a shout of laughter, while the historian smiled with a stately timidity.

"I was quite surprised, because I had only been back from the country a few days; I had specially arranged, just to be left in peace for a little, that no one was to be told that I was in Paris, and I asked myself how the Queen of Sweden could have heard so soon," went on Mme. de Villeparisis, leaving her guests amazed to find that a visit from the Queen of Sweden was in itself nothing out of the common to their hostess.

Earlier in the day Mme. de Villeparisis might have been collaborating with the librarian in arranging the illustrations to her *Memoirs*; now she was, quite unconsciously, trying their effect on an average public typical of that from which she would eventually have to enlist

her readers. Hers might be different in many ways from
a really fashionable drawing-room in which you would
have been struck by the absence of a number of middle
class ladies to whom Mme. de Villeparisis was "at
home", and would have noticed instead such brilliant
leaders of fashion as Mme. Leroi had in course of time
managed to secure, but this distinction is not perceptible in
her *Memoirs*, from which certain unimportant friendships
of the author have disappeared because there is never any
occasion to refer to them; while the absence of those who
did not come to see her leaves no gap because, in the
necessarily restricted space at the author's disposal, only
a few persons can appear, and if these persons are royal
personages, historic personalities, then the utmost impression of distinction which any volume of memoirs can
convey to the public is achieved. In the opinion of Mme.
Leroi, Mme. de Villeparisis's parties were third-rate; and
Mme. de Villeparisis felt the sting of Mme. Leroi's opinion.
But hardly anyone to-day remembers who Mme. Leroi
was, her opinions have vanished into thin air, and it is
the drawing-room of Mme. de Villeparisis, frequented as
it was by the Queen of Sweden, and as it had been by
the Duc d'Aumale, the Duc de Broglie, Thiers, Mon-
talembert, Mgr. Dupanloup, which will be looked upon
as one of the most brilliant of the nineteenth century by
that posterity which has not changed since the days of
Homer and Pindar, and for which the enviable things
are exalted birth, royal or quasi-royal, and the friendship
of kings, the leaders of the people and other eminent men.
   Now of all this Mme. de Villeparisis had her share in
the people who still came to her house and in the memories—sometimes slightly "touched up"—by means of

which she extended her social activity into the past. And then there was M. de Norpois who, while unable to restore his friend to any substantial position in society, did indeed bring to her house such foreign or French statesmen as might have need of his services and knew that the only effective method of securing them was to pay court to Mme. de Villeparisis. Possibly Mme. Leroi also knew these European celebrities. But, as a well-mannered woman who avoids anything that suggests the bluestocking, she would as little have thought of mentioning the Eastern question to her Prime Ministers as of discussing the nature of love with her novelists and philosophers. " Love? " she had once replied to a pushing lady who had asked her: " What are your views on love? " —" Love? I make it, constantly, but I never talk about it." When she had any of these literary or political lions in her house she contented herself, as did the Duchesse de Guermantes, with setting them down to play poker. They often preferred this to the serious conversations on general ideas in which Mme. de Villeparisis forced them to engage. But these conversations, ridiculous as in the social sense they may have been, have furnished the *Memoirs* of Mme. de Villeparisis with those admirable passages, those dissertations on politics which read so well in volumes of autobiography, as they do in Corneille's tragedies. Furthermore, the parties of the Villeparisis of this world are alone destined to be handed down to posterity, because the Lerois of this world cannot write, and, if they could, would not have the time. And if the literary bent of the Villeparisis is the cause of the Lerois' disdain, the disdain of the Lerois does, in its turn, a singular service to the literary bent of the Villeparisis by affording the bluestockings that leisure which the career of letters requires. God, Whose Will it is that there should be a few books in the world well written, breathes with that purpose such disdain into the hearts of the Lerois, for He knows that if these should invite the Villeparisis to dinner the latter would at once rise from their writing tables and order their carriages to be round at eight.

Presently there came into the room, with slow and solemn step, an old lady of tall stature who, beneath the raised brim of her straw hat, revealed a monumental pile of snowy hair in the style of Marie-Antoinette. I did not then know that she was one of three women who were still to be seen in Parisian society and who, like Mme. de Villeparisis, while all of the noblest birth, had been reduced, for reasons which were now lost in the night of time and could have been told us only by some old gallant of their period, to entertaining only certain of the dregs of society who were not sought after elsewhere. Each of these ladies had her own " Duchesse de Guermantes ", the brilliant niece who came regularly to pay her respects, but none of them could have succeeded in attracting to her house the " Duchesse de Guermantes " of either of the others. Mme. de Villeparisis was on the best of terms with these three ladies, but she did not like them. Perhaps the similarity between their social position and her own gave her an impression of them which was not pleasing. Besides, soured bluestockings as they were, seeking by the number and frequency of the drawing-room comedies which they arranged in their houses to give themselves the illusion of a regular salon, there had grown up among them a rivalry which the decay of her fortune in the course of a somewhat tempestuous existence reduced for each of them, when it was a question of securing the kind assistance of a professional actor or actress, into a sort of struggle for life. Furthermore, the lady with the Marie-Antoinette hair, whenever she set eyes on Mme. de Villeparisis, could not help being reminded of the fact that the Duchesse de Guermantes did not come to her Fridays. Her consolation was that at these same Fridays she could always count on having, blood being thicker than water, the Princesse de Poix, who was her own personal Guermantes, and who never went near Mme. de Villeparisis, albeit Mme. de Poix was an intimate friend of the Duchess.

Nevertheless from the mansion on the Quai Malaquais to the drawing-rooms of the Rue de Tournon, the Rue de la Chaise and the Faubourg Saint-Honoré, a bond as compelling as it was hateful united the three fallen goddesses, as to whom I would fain have learned by searching in some dictionary of social mythology through what gallant adventure, what sacrilegious presumption, they had incurred their punishment. Their common brilliance of origin, the common decay of their present state entered largely, no doubt, into the necessity which compelled them, while hating one another, to frequent one another's society. Besides, each of them found in the others a convenient way of being polite to her own guests. How should these fail to suppose that they had scaled the most inaccessible peak of the Faubourg when they were introduced to a lady with a string of titles whose sister was married to a Duc de Sagan or a Prince de Ligne? Especially as there was infinitely more in the newspapers about these sham salons than about the genuine ones. Indeed these old ladies' " men about town "

nephews—and Saint-Loup the foremost of them—when
asked by a friend to introduce him to people, would
answer at once " I will take you to see my aunt Villeparisis," (or whichever it was) " you meet interesting
people there." They knew very well that this would
mean less trouble for themselves than trying to get the
said friends invited by the smart nieces or sisters-in-law
of these ladies. Certain very old men, and young women
who had heard it from those men, told me that if these
ladies were no longer received in society it was because
of the extraordinary irregularity of their conduct, which,
when I objected that irregular conduct was not necessarily a barrier to social success, was represented to me
as having gone far beyond anything that we know to-day.
The misconduct of these solemn dames who held themselves so erect assumed on the lips of those who hinted
at it something that I was incapable of imagining, pro-
portionate to the magnitude of prehistoric days, to the
age of the mammoth. In a word, these three Parcae with
their white or blue or red locks had spun the fatal threads
of an incalculable number of gentlemen. I felt that the
people of to-day exaggerated the vices of those fabulous
times, like the Greeks who created Icarus, Theseus,
Heracles out of men who had been but little different
from those who long afterwards deified them. But one
does not tabulate the sum of a person's vices until he has
almost ceased to be in a fit state to practise them, when
from the magnitude of his social punishment, which is
then nearing the completion of its term and which alone
one can estimate, one measures, one imagines, one exag-
gerates that of the crime that has been committed. In
that gallery of symbolical figures which is " society ", the

really light women, the true Messalinas, invariably present
the solemn aspect of a lady of at least seventy, with an
air of lofty distinction, who entertains everyone she can
but not everyone she would like to have, to whose house
women will never consent to go whose own conduct falls
in any way short of perfection, to whom the Pope regularly sends his Golden Rose, and who as often as not
has written—on the early days of Lamartine—an essay
that has been crowned by the French Academy. " How
d'ye do, Alix? " Mme. de Villeparisis greeted the Marie-
Antoinette lady, which lady cast a searching glance round
the assembly to see whether there was not in this drawing-
room any item that might be a valuable addition to her
own, in which case she would have to discover it for herself, for Mme. de Villeparisis, she was sure, would be
spiteful enough to try to keep it from her. Thus Mme. de
Villeparisis took good care not to introduce Bloch to the
old lady for fear of his being asked to produce the same
play that he was arranging for her in the drawing-room
of the Quai Malaquais. Besides it was only tit for tat.
For, the evening before, the old lady had had Mme.
Ristori, who had recited, and had taken care that Mme.
de Villeparisis, from whom she had filched the Italian
artist, should not hear of this function until it was over.
So that she should not read it first in the newspapers and
feel annoyed, the old lady had come in person to tell
her about it, shewing no sense of guilt. Mme. de Villeparisis, considering that an introduction of myself was not
likely to have the same awkward results as that of Bloch,
made me known to the Marie-Antoinette of the Quai
Malaquais. The latter, who sought, by making the fewest
possible movements, to preserve in her old age those

lines, as of a Coysevox goddess, which had years ago charmed the young men of fashion and which spurious poets still celebrated in rhymed charades—and had acquired the habit of a lofty and compensating stiffness common to all those whom a personal degradation obliges to be continually making advances—just perceptibly lowered her head with a frigid majesty, and, turning the other way, took no more notice of me than if I had not existed. By this crafty attitude she seemed to be assuring Mme. de Villeparisis: "You see, I'm nowhere near him; please understand that I'm not interested—in any sense of the word, you old cat—in little boys." But when, twenty minutes later, she left the room, taking advantage of the general conversation, she slipped into my ear an invitation to come to her box the following Friday with another of the three, whose high-sounding name—she had been born a Choiseul, moreover—had a prodigious effect on me.

"I understand, sir, that you are thinkin' of writin' somethin' about Mme. la Duchesse de Montmorency," said Mme. de Villeparisis to the historian of the Fronde in that grudging tone which she allowed, quite unconsciously, to spoil the effect of her great and genuine kindness, a tone due to the shrivelling crossness, the sense of grievance that is a physiological accompaniment of age, as well as to the affectation of imitating the almost rustic speech of the old nobility: "I'm goin' to let you see her portrait, the original of the copy they have in the Louvre."

She rose, laying down her brushes beside the flowers, and the little apron which then came into sight at her waist, and which she wore so as not to stain her dress with

269

paints, added still further to the impression of an old
peasant given by her bonnet and her big spectacles, and
offered a sharp contrast to the luxury of her appointments,
the butler who had brought in the tea and cakes, the
liveried footman for whom she now rang to light up the
portrait of the Duchesse de Montmorency, Abbess of one
of the most famous Chapters in the East of France.
Everyone had risen. "What is rather amusin'," said our
hostess, "is that in these Chapters where our great-aunts
were so often made Abbesses, the daughters of the King
of France would not have been admitted. They were very
close corporations." "Not admit the King's daughters,"
cried Bloch in amazement, "why ever not?" "Why, because the House of France had not enough quarterin's
after that low marriage." Bloch's bewilderment increased.
"A low marriage? The House of France? When was
that?" "Why, when they married into the Medicis,"
replied Mme. de Villeparisis in the most natural manner.
"It's a fine picture, ain't it, and in a perfect state of
preservation," she added.

"My dear," put in the Marie-Antoinette lady, "surely
you remember that when I brought Liszt to see you he
said that it was this one that was the copy."

"I should bow to any opinion of Liszt on music, but
not on painting. Besides, he was quite off his head then,
and I don't remember his ever saying anything of the
sort. But it wasn't you that brought him here. I had
met him any number of times at dinner at Princess Sayn-
Wittgenstein's."

Alix's shot had missed fire; she stood silent, erect and
motionless. Plastered with layers of powder, her face had
the appearance of a face of stone. And, as the profile

was noble, she seemed, on a triangular and moss-grown pedestal hidden by her cape, the time-worn stucco goddess of a park.

"Ah, I see another fine portrait," began the historian. The door opened and the Duchesse de Guermantes entered the room.

"Well, how are you?" Mme. de Villeparisis greeted her without moving her head, taking from her apron-pocket a hand which she held out to the newcomer; and then ceasing at once to take any notice of her niece, in order to return to the historian: "That is the portrait of the Duchesse de La Rochefoucauld. . . . "

A young servant with a bold manner and a charming face (but so finely chiselled, to ensure its perfection, that the nose was a little red and the rest of the skin slightly flushed as though they were still smarting from the recent and sculptural incision) came in bearing a card on a salver.

"It is that gentleman who has been several times to see Mme. la Marquise."

"Did you tell him I was at home?"

"He heard the voices."

"Oh, very well then, shew him in. It's a man who was introduced to me," she explained. "He told me he was very anxious to come to the house. I certainly never said he might. But here he's taken the trouble to call five times now; it doesn't do to hurt people's feelings. Sir," she went on to me, "and you, Sir," to the historian of the Fronde, "let me introduce my niece, the Duchesse de Guermantes."

The historian made a low bow, as I did also, and since he seemed to suppose that some friendly remark ought to follow this salute, his eyes brightened and he was preparing to open his mouth when he was once more frozen by the sight of Mme. de Guermantes who had taken advantage of the independence of her torso to throw it forward with an exaggerated politeness and bring it neatly back to a position of rest without letting face or eyes appear to have noticed that anyone was standing before them; after breathing a gentle sigh she contented herself with manifesting the nullity of the impression that had been made on her by the sight of the historian and myself by performing certain movements of her nostrils with a precision that testified to the absolute inertia of her unoccupied attention.

The importunate visitor entered the room, making straight for Mme de Villeparisis with an ingenuous, fervent air: it was Legrandin.

"Thank you so very much for letting me come and see you," he began, laying stress on the word "very". "It is a pleasure of a quality altogether rare and subtle that you confer on an old solitary; I assure you that its repercussion . . ." He stopped short on catching sight of me.

"I was just shewing this gentleman a fine portrait of the Duchesse de La Rochefoucauld, the wife of the author of the *Maxims*; it's a family picture."

Mme. de Guermantes meanwhile had greeted Alix, with apologies for not having been able, that year as in every previous year, to go and see her. "I hear all about you from Madeleine," she added.

"She was at luncheon with me to-day," said the Marquise of the Quai Malaquais, with the satisfying reflexion that Mme. de Villeparisis could never say that.

Meanwhile I had been talking to Bloch, and fearing,

from what I had been told of his father's change of
attitude towards him, that he might be envying my life,
I said to him that his must be the happier of the two.
My remark was prompted solely by my desire to be
friendly. But such friendliness readily convinces those
who cherish a high opinion of themselves of their own
good fortune, or gives them a desire to convince other
people. " Yes, I do lead a delightful existence," Bloch
assured me with a beatified smile. " I have three great
friends; I do not wish for one more; an adorable mistress;
I am infinitely happy. Rare is the mortal to whom Father
Zeus accords so much felicity." I fancy that he was anxious principally to extol himself and to make me envious.
Perhaps too there was some desire to shew originality
in his optimism. It was evident that he did not wish
to reply in the commonplace phraseology that everybody
uses: " Oh, it was nothing, really," and so forth, when,
to my question: " Was it a good show? " put with regard
to an afternoon dance at his house to which I had been
prevented from going, he replied in a level, careless tone,
as if the dance had been given by some one else: " Why,
yes, it was quite a good show, couldn't have been better.
It was really charming!"

" What you have just told us interests me enormously,"
said Legrandin to Mme. de Villeparisis, " for I was saying
to myself only the other day that you shewed a marked
likeness to him in the clear-cut turn of your speech, in
a quality which I will venture to describe by two contradictory terms, monumental rapidity and immortal in-
stantaneousness. I should have liked this afternoon to
take down all the things you say; but I shall remember
them. They are, in a phrase which comes, I think, from

Joubert, friends of the memory. You have never read Joubert? Oh! he would have admired you so! I will take the liberty this evening of sending you a set of him, it is a privilege to make you a present of his mind. He had not your strength. But he had a great deal of charm all the same."

I would have gone up to Legrandin at once and spoken to him, but he kept as far away from me as he could, no doubt in the hope that I might not overhear the stream of flattery which, with a remarkable felicity of expression, he kept pouring out, whatever the topic, to Mme. de Villeparisis.

She shrugged her shoulders, smiling, as though he had been trying to make fun of her, and turned to the historian.

"And this is the famous Marie de Rohan, Duchesse de Chevreuse, who was married first of all to M. de Luynes."

"My dear, speaking of Mme. de Luynes reminds me of Yolande; she came to me yesterday evening, and if I had known that you weren't engaged I'ld have sent round to ask you to come. Mme. Ristori turned up quite by chance, and recited some poems by Queen Carmen Sylva in the author's presence. It was too beautiful!"

"What treachery!" thought Mme. de Villeparisis. "Of course that was what she was whispering about the other day to Mme. de Beaulaincourt and Mme. de Chaponay. I had no engagement," she replied, "but I should not have come. I heard Ristori in her great days, she's a mere wreck now. Besides I detest Carmen Sylva's poetry. Ristori came here once, the Duchess of Aosta brought her, to recite a canto of the *Inferno,* by Dante. In that sort of thing she's incomparable."

Alix bore the blow without flinching. She remained marble. Her gaze was piercing and blank, her nose proudly arched. But the surface of one cheek was scaling. A faint, strange vegetation, green and pink, was invading her chin. Perhaps another winter would level her with the dust.

"Now, sir, if you are fond of painting, look at the portrait of Mme. de Montmorency," Mme. de Villeparisis said to Legrandin, to stop the flow of compliments which was beginning again.

Seizing her opportunity, while his back was turned, Mme. de Guermantes pointed to him, with an ironical, questioning look at her aunt.

"It's M. Legrandin," murmured Mme. de Villeparisis, "he has a sister called Mme. de Cambremer, not that that conveys any more to you than it does to me."

"What! Oh, but I know her quite well!" exclaimed Mme. de Guermantes, and put her hand over her lips. "That is to say, I don't know her, but for some reason or other Basin, who meets the husband heaven knows where, took it into his head to tell the wretched woman she might call on me. And she did. I can't tell you what it was like. She informed me that she had been to London, and gave me a complete catalogue of all the things in the British Museum. And this very day, the moment I leave your house, I'm going, just as you see me now, to drop a card on the monster. And don't for a moment suppose that it's an easy thing to do. On the pretence that she's dying of some disease she's always at home, it doesn't matter whether you arrive at seven at night or nine in the morning, she's ready for you with a dish of strawberry tarts.

" No, but seriously, you know, she is a monstrosity,"
Mme. de Guermantes replied to a questioning glance from
her aunt. " She's an impossible person, she talks about
' plumitives ' and things like that." " What does ' plumitive' mean?" asked Mme. de Villeparisis. " I haven't
the slightest idea!" cried the Duchess in mock indignation.
" I don't want to know. I don't speak that sort of language." And seeing that her aunt really did not know
what a plumitive was, to give herself the satisfaction of
shewing that she was a scholar as well as a purist, and
to make fun of her aunt, now, after making fun of Mme.
de Cambremer: " Why, of course," she said, with a half-
laugh which the last traces of her pretended ill humour
kept in check, " everybody knows what it means; a
plumitive is a writer, a person who holds a pen. But it's a
dreadful word. It's enough to make your wisdom teeth
drop out. Nothing will ever make me use words like that.

" And so that's the brother, is it? I hadn't realized that
yet. But after all it's not inconceivable. She has the same
doormat docility and the same mass of information
like a circulating library. She's just as much of a flatterer
as he is, and just as boring. Yes, I'm beginning to see the
family likeness now quite plainly."

" Sit down, we're just going to take a dish of tea," said
Mme. de Villeparisis to her niece. " Help yourself; you
don't want to look at the pictures of your great-grand-
mothers, you know them as well as I do."

Presently Mme. de Villeparisis sat down again at her
desk and went on with her painting. The rest of the party
gathered round her, and I took the opportunity to go up
to Legrandin and, seeing no harm myself in his presence
in Mme. de Villeparisis's drawing-room and never dream-

ing how much my words would at once hurt him and make him believe that I had deliberately intended to hurt him, say: " Well, sir, I am almost excused for coming to a tea-party when I find you here too." M. Legrandin concluded from this speech (at least this was the opinion which he expressed of me a few days later) that I was a thoroughly spiteful little wretch who delighted only in doing mischief.

" You might at least have the civility to begin by saying how d'ye do to me," he replied, without offering me his hand and in a coarse and angry voice which I had never suspected him of possessing, a voice which bearing no traceable relation to what he ordinarily said did bear another more immediate and striking relation to something that he was feeling at the moment. What happens is that since we are determined always to keep our feelings to ourselves, we have never given any thought to the manner in which we should express them. And suddenly there is within us a strange and obscene animal making its voice heard, the tones of which may inspire as much terror in the listener who receives the involuntary elliptical irresistible communication of our defect or vice as would the sudden avowal indirectly and uncouthly proffered by a criminal who can no longer refrain from confessing a murder of which one had never imagined him to be guilty. I knew, of course, that idealism, even subjective idealism did not prevent great philosophers from still having hearty appetites or from presenting themselves with untiring perseverance for election to the Academy. But really Legrandin had no occasion to remind people so often that he belonged to another planet when all his convulsive movements of anger or affability were governed by the desire to occupy a good position on this.

" Naturally, when people pester me twenty times on end to go anywhere," he went on in lower tones, " although I am perfectly free to do what I choose, still I can't behave like an absolute boor."

Mme. de Guermantes had sat down. Her name, accompanied as it was by her title, added to her corporeal dimensions the duchy which projected itself rŏund about her and brought the shadowy, sun-splashed coolness of the woods of Guermantes into this drawing-room, to surround the tuffet on which she was sitting. I felt surprised only that the likeness of those woods was not more discernible on the face of the Duchess, about which there was nothing suggestive of vegetation, and at the most the ruddy discolouration of her cheeks—which ought rather, surely, to have been emblazoned with the name Guermantes—was the effect, but did not furnish a picture of long gallops in the open air. Later on, when she had ceased to interest me, I came to know many of the Duchess's peculiarities, notably (to speak for the moment only of that one of which I already at this time felt the charm though without yet being able to discover what it was) her eyes, in which was held captive as in a picture the blue sky of an afternoon in France, broadly expansive, bathed in light even when no sun shone; and a voice which one would have thought, from its first hoarse sounds, to be almost plebeian, through which there trailed, as over the steps of the church at Combray or the pastry-cook's in the square, the rich and lazy gold of a country sun. But on this first day I discerned nothing, the warmth of my attention volatilised at once the little that I might otherwise have been able to extract from her, in which I should have found some indication of the name Guermantes. In any case, I told myself that it was indeed she who was designated for all the world by the title Duchesse de Guermantes: the inconceivable life which that name signified, this body did indeed contain; it had just introduced that life into a crowd of different creatures, in this room which enclosed it on every side and on which it produced so violent a reaction that I thought I could see, where the extent of that mysterious life ceased, a fringe of effervescence outline its frontiers: round the circumference of the circle traced on the carpet by the balloon of her blue peking skirt, and in the bright eyes of the Duchess at the point of intersection of the preoccupations, the memories, the incomprehensible, scornful, amused and curious thoughts which filled them from within and the outside images that were reflected on their surface. Perhaps I should have been not quite so deeply stirred had I met her at Mme. de Villeparisis's at an evening party, instead of seeing her thus on one of the Marquise's " days ", at one of those tea-parties which are for women no more than a brief halt in the course of their afternoon's outing, when, keeping on the hats in which they have been driving through the streets, they waft into the close atmosphere of a drawing-room the quality of the fresh air outside, and give one a better view of Paris in the late afternoon than do the tall, open windows through which one can hear the bowling wheels of their victorias: Mme. de Guermantes wore a boating-hat trimmed with cornflowers, and what they recalled to me was not, among the tilled fields round Combray where I had so often gathered those flowers, on the slope adjoining the Tansonville hedge, the suns of bygone years, it was the scent and dust of twilight as they had been an hour ago, when Mme. de Guermantes drove through them, in the Rue de la Paix. With a smiling, disdainful, vague air, and a grimace on her pursed lips, with the point of her sunshade, as with the extreme tip of an antenna of her mysterious life, she was tracing circles on the carpet; then, with that indifferent attention which begins by eliminating every point of contact with what one is actually studying, her gaze fastened upon each of us in turn; then inspected the sofas and armchairs, but softened this time by that human sympathy which is aroused by the presence, however insignificant, of a thing one knows, a thing that is almost a person; these pieces of furniture were not like us, they belonged vaguely to her world, they were bound up with the life of her aunt; then from the Beauvais furniture her gaze was carried back to the person sitting on it, and resumed then the same air of perspicacity and that same disapproval which the respect that Mme. de Guermantes felt for her aunt would have prevented her from expressing in words, but which she would obviously have felt had she discovered on the chairs, instead of our presence, that of a spot of grease or a layer of dust.

That admirable writer G—— entered the room; he had come to pay a call on Mme. de Villeparisis which he regarded as a tiresome duty. The Duchess, although delighted to see him again, gave him no sign of welcome, but instinctively he made straight for her, the charm that she possessed, her tact, her simplicity making him look upon her as a woman of exceptional intelligence. He was bound, moreover, in common politeness to go and talk to her, for, since he was a pleasant and a distinguished man, Mme. de Guermantes frequently invited him to luncheon even when there were only her husband and herself besides, or in

the autumn to Guermantes, making use of this intimacy
to have him to dinner occasionally with Royalties who
were curious to meet him. For the Duchess liked to entertain certain eminent men, on condition always that they
were bachelors, a condition which, even when married,
they invariably fulfilled for her, for, as their wives, who
were bound to be more or less common, would have been
a blot on a drawing-room in which there were never any
but the most fashionable beauties in Paris, it was always
without them that their husbands were invited; and the
Duke, to avoid hurting any possible susceptibility, used
to explain to these involuntary widowers that the Duchess
never had women in the house, could not endure feminine
society, almost as though this had been under doctor's
orders, and as he might have said that she could not stay
in a room in which there were smells, or eat salt food, or
travel with her back to the engine, or wear stays. It was
true that these eminent men used to see at the Guermantes' the Princesse de Parme, the Princesse de Sagan
(whom Françoise, hearing her constantly mentioned, had
taken to calling, in the belief that this feminine ending
was required by the laws of accidence, " the Sagante "),
and plenty more, but their presence was accounted for
by the explanation that they were relatives, or such very
old friends that it was impossible to exclude them. Whether
or not they were convinced by the explanations which the
Duc de Guermantes had given of the singular malady
that made it impossible for the Duchess to associate with
other women, the great men duly transmitted them to
their wives. Some of these thought that this malady was
only an excuse to cloak her jealousy, because the Duchess
wished to reign alone over a court of worshippers. Others

more simple still thought that perhaps the Duchess had some peculiar habit, a scandalous past it might be, that women did not care to go to her house and that she gave the name of a whim to what was stern necessity. The better among them, hearing their husbands expatiate on the Duchess's marvellous brain, assumed that she must be so far superior to the rest of womankind that she found their society boring since they could not talk intelligently about anything. And it was true that the Duchess was bored by other women, if their princely rank did not render them specially interesting. But the excluded wives were mistaken when they imagined that she chose to entertain men alone in order to be free to discuss with them literature, science and philosophy. For she never referred to these, at least with the great intellectuals. If, by virtue of a family tradition such as makes the daughters of great soldiers preserve, in the midst of their most frivolous distractions, a respect for military matters, she, the granddaughter of women who had been on terms of friendship with Thiers, Mérimée and Augier, felt that a place must always be kept in her drawing-room for men of intellect, she had on the other hand derived from the manner, at once condescending and intimate, in which those famous men had been received at Guermantes the foible of looking on men of talent as family friends whose talent does not dazzle one, to whom one does not speak of their work, and who would not be at all interested if one did. Moreover the type of mind illustrated by Mérimée and Meilhac and Halévy, which was hers also, led her by reaction from the verbal sentimentality of an earlier generation to a style in conversation that rejects everything to do with fine language and the expression of lofty thoughts, so that she made it a sort of element of good breeding when she was with a poet or a musician to talk only of the food that they were eating or the game of cards to which they would afterwards sit down. This abstention had, on a third person not conversant with her ways, a disturbing effect which amounted to mystification. Mme. de Guermantes, having asked him whether it would amuse him to come to luncheon to meet this or that famous poet, devoured by curiosity he would arrive at the appointed hour. The Duchess was talking to the poet about the weather. They sat down to luncheon. " Do you like this way of doing eggs? " she asked the poet. On hearing his approval, which she shared, for everything in her own house appeared to her exquisite, including a horrible cider which she imported from Guermantes: " Give Monsieur some more eggs," she would tell the butler, while the anxious fellow-guest sat waiting for what must surely have been the object of the party, since they had arranged to meet, in spite of every sort of difficulty, before the Duchess, the poet and he himself left Paris. But the meal went on, one after another the courses were cleared away, not without having first provided Mme. de Guermantes with opportunities for clever witticisms or apt stories. Meanwhile the poet went on eating, and neither Duke nor Duchess shewed any sign of remembering that he was a poet. And presently the luncheon came to an end and the party broke up, without a word having been said about the poetry which, for all that, everyone admired but to which, by a reserve analogous to that of which Swann had given me a foretaste, no one might refer. This reserve was simply a matter of good form. But for the fellow-guest, if he thought at all about the matter, there was something strangely melancholy about it all, and these meals in the Guermantes household made him think of the hours which timid lovers often spend together in talking trivialities until it is time to part, without—whether from shyness, from audacity or from awkwardness—the great secret which they would have been happier had they confessed ever succeeding in passing from their hearts to their lips. It must, however, be added that this silence with regard to the serious matters which one was always waiting in vain to see approached, if it might pass as characteristic of the Duchess, was by no means constant with her. Mme. de Guermantes had spent her girlhood in a society somewhat different, equally aristocratic but less brilliant and above all less futile than that in which she now lived, and one of wide culture. It had left beneath her present frivolity a sort of bed-rock of greater solidity, invisibly nutritious, to which indeed the Duchess would repair in search (very rarely, though, for she detested pedantry) of some quotation from Victor Hugo or Lamartine which, extremely appropriate, uttered with a look of true feeling from her fine eyes, never failed to surprise and charm her audience. Sometimes, even, without any pretence of authority, pertinently and quite simply, she would give some dramatist and Academician a piece of sage advice, would make him modify a situation or alter an ending.

If, in the drawing room of Mme. de Villeparisis, just as in the church at Combray, on the day of Mlle. Percepied's wedding, I had difficulty in discovering, in the handsome, too human face of Mme. de Guermantes the unknown element of her name, I at least thought that, when she spoke, her conversation, profound, mysterious, would have a strangeness as of a mediaeval tapestry or a gothic window. But in order that I should not be disappointed by the words which I should hear uttered by a person who called herself Mme. de Guermantes, even if I had not been in love with her, it would not have sufficed that those words were fine, beautiful and profound, they would have had to reflect that amaranthine colour of the closing syllable of her name, that colour which I had on my first sight of her been disappointed not to find in her person and had driven to take refuge in her mind. Of course I had already heard Mme. de Villeparisis, Saint-Loup, people whose intelligence was in no way extraordinary, pronounce without any precaution this name Guermantes, simply as that of a person who was coming to see them or with whom they had promised to dine, without seeming to feel that there were latent in her name the glow of yellowing woods in autumn and a whole mysterious tract of country. But this must have been an affectation on their part, as when the classic poets give us no warning of the profound purpose which they had, all the same, in writing, an affectation which I myself also strove to imitate, saying in the most natural tone: " The Duchesse de Guermantes," as though it were a name that was just like other names. And then everybody assured me that she was a highly intelligent woman, a clever talker, that she was one of a little group of most interesting people: words which became accomplices of my dream. For when they spoke of an intelligent group, of clever talk, it was not at all the sort of intelligence that I knew that I imagined, not even that of the greatest minds, it was not at all with men like Bergotte that I peopled this group. No, by intelligence I understood an ineffable faculty gilded by the sun, impregnated with a sylvan coolness. Indeed, had she made the most intelligent remarks (in the sense in which I understood the word when it was used of a philosopher or critic), Mme. de Guermantes would perhaps have disappointed even more keenly my expectation of so special a faculty than if, in the course of a trivial conversation, she had confined herself to discussing kitchen recipes or the furnishing of a country house, to mentioning the names of neighbours and relatives of her own, which would have given me a picture of her life.

"I thought I should find Basin here, he was meaning to come and see you to-day," said Mme. de Guermantes to her aunt.

"I haven't set eyes on your husband for some days," replied Mme. de Villeparisis in a somewhat nettled tone. "In fact, I haven't seen him—well, I have seen him once, perhaps—since that charming joke he played on me of making my servants announce him as the Queen of Sweden."

Mme. de Guermantes formed a smile by contracting the corners of her mouth as though she were biting her veil.

"We met her at dinner last night at Blanche Leroi's. You wouldn't know her now, she's positively enormous; I'm sure she must have something the matter with her."

"I was just telling these gentlemen that you said she looked like a frog."

Mme. de Guermantes uttered a sort of raucous sound intended to signify that she acknowledged the compliment.

"I don't remember making such a charming comparison, but if she was one before, now she's the frog that has succeeded in swelling to the size of the ox. Or rather, it isn't quite that, because all her swelling is concentrated in front of her waist, she's more like a frog in an interesting condition."

"Ah, that is quite clever," said Mme. de Villeparisis, secretly proud that her guests should be witnessing this display of her niece's wit.

"It is purely *arbitrary*, though," answered Mme. de Guermantes, ironically detaching this selected epithet, as Swann would have done, "for I must admit I never saw a frog in the family way. Anyhow, the frog in question, who, by the way, is not asking for a king, for I never saw her so skittish as she's been since her husband died, is coming to dine with us one day next week. I promised I'ld let you know in good time."

Mme. de Villeparisis gave vent to a confused growl, from which emerged: "I know she was dining with the Mecklenburgs the night before last. Hannibal de Bréauté was there. He came and told me about it, and was quite amusing, I must say."

"There was a man there who's a great deal wittier than Babal," said Mme. de Guermantes who, in view of her close friendship with M. de Bréauté-Consalvi, felt that she must advertise their intimacy by the use of this abbreviation. "I mean M. Bergotte."

I had never imagined that Bergotte could be regarded as witty; in fact, I thought of him always as mingling with the intellectual section of humanity, that is to say infinitely remote from that mysterious realm of which I had caught a glimpse through the purple hangings of a theatre box, behind which, making the Duchess smile, M. de Bréauté was holding with her, in the language of the gods, that unimaginable thing, a conversation between people of the Faubourg Saint-Germain. I was stupefied to see the balance upset, and Bergotte rise above M. de Bréauté. But above all I was dismayed to think that I had avoided Bergotte on the evening of *Phèdre*, that I had not gone up and spoken to him, when I heard Mme. de Guermantes say to Mme. de Villeparisis:

" He is the only person I have any wish to know," went on the Duchess, in whom one could always, as at the turn of a mental tide, see the flow of curiosity with regard to well-known intellectuals sweep over the ebb of her aristocratic snobbishness. " It would be such a pleasure."

The presence of Bergotte by my side, which it would have been so easy for me to secure but which I had thought liable to give Mme. de Guermantes a bad impression of myself, would no doubt, on the contrary, have had the result that she would have signalled to me to join her in her box, and would have invited me to bring the eminent writer, one day, to luncheon.

" I gather that he didn't behave very well, he was presented to M. de Cobourg, and never uttered a word to him," said Mme. de Guermantes, dwelling on this odd characteristic as she might have recounted that a Chinaman had blown his nose on a sheet of paper. " He never once said ' Monseigneur ' to him," she added, with an air of amusement at this detail, as important to her mind as the refusal of a Protestant, during an audience with the Pope, to go on his knees before his Holiness.

Interested by these idiosyncrasies of Bergotte, she did not, however, appear to consider them reprehensible, and seemed rather to find a certain merit in them, though she would have been put to it to say of what sort. Despite this unusual mode of appreciating Bergotte's originality, it was a fact which I was later on not to regard as wholly negligible that Mme. de Guermantes, greatly to the surprise of many of her friends, did consider Bergotte more witty than M. de Bréauté. Thus it is that such judgments, subversive, isolated, and yet after all just, are delivered in the world of fashion by those rare minds that are superior to the rest. And they sketch then the first rough outlines of the hierarchy of values as the next generation will establish it, instead of abiding eternally by the old standards.

The Comte d'Argencourt, Chargé d'Affaires at the Belgian Legation and a remote connexion of Mme. de Villeparisis, came limping in, followed presently by two young men, the Baron de Guermantes and H. H. the Duc de Châtellerault, whom Mme. de Guermantes greeted with: "How d'ye do, young Châtellerault," in a careless tone and without moving from her tuffet, for she was a great friend of the young Duke's mother, which had given him a deep and lifelong respect for her. Tall, slender, with golden hair and sunny complexions, thoroughly of the Guermantes type, these two young men looked like a condensation of the light of the spring evening which was flooding the spacious room. Following a custom which was the fashion at that time they laid their silk hats on the floor, by their feet. The historian of the Fronde thought that they were embarrassed, like a peasant coming into the mayor's office and not knowing what to do with his hat. Feeling that he ought in charity to come to the rescue of the awkwardness and timidity which he ascribed to them:

"No, no," he said, "don't leave them on the floor, they'll be trodden on."

A glance from the Baron de Guermantes, tilting the plane of his pupils, shot suddenly from them a wave of pure and piercing azure which froze the well-meaning historian.

"What is that person's name?" I was asked by the Baron, who had just been introduced to me by Mme. de Villeparisis.

"M. Pierre," I whispered.

"Pierre what?"

"Pierre: it's his name, he's a historian, a most distinguished man."

"Really? You don't say so."

"No, it's a new fashion with these young men to put their hats on the floor," Mme. de Villeparisis explained. "I'm like you, I can never get used to it. Still, it's better than my nephew Robert, who always leaves his in the hall. I tell him when I see him come in that he looks just like a clockmaker, and I ask him if he's come to wind the clocks."

"You were speaking just now, Madame la Marquise, of M. Molé's hat; we shall soon be able, like Aristotle, to compile a chapter on hats," said the historian of the Fronde, somewhat reassured by Mme. de Villeparisis's intervention, but in so faint a voice that no one but myself overheard him.

"She really is astonishing, the little Duchess," said M. d'Argencourt, pointing to Mme. de Guermantes who was talking to G——. Whenever there's a famous man in the room you're sure to find him sitting with her. Evidently that must be the lion of the party over there. It can't always be M. de Borelli, of course, or M. Schlumberger or M. d'Avenel. But then it's bound to be M.

Pierre Loti or M. Edmond Rostand. Yesterday evening at the Doudeauvilles', where by the way she was looking splendid in her emerald tiara and a pink dress with a long train, she had M. Deschanel on one side and the German Ambassador on the other: she was holding forth to them about China; the general public, at a respectful distance where they couldn't hear what was being said, were wondering whether there wasn't going to be war. Really, you'd have said she was a Queen, holding her circle."

Everyone had gathered round Mme. de Villeparisis to watch her painting.

"Those flowers are a truly celestial pink," said Legrandin, "I should say sky-pink. For there is such a thing as sky-pink just as there is sky-blue. But," he lowered his voice in the hope that he would not be heard by anyone but the Marquise, "I think I shall still give my vote to the silky, living flesh tint of your rendering of them. You leave Pisanello and Van Huysun a long way behind, with their laborious, dead herbals."

An artist, however modest, is always willing to hear himself preferred to his rivals, and tries only to see that justice is done them.

"What makes you think that is that they painted the flowers of their period, which we don't have now, but they did it with great skill."

"Ah! The flowers of their period! That is a most ingenious theory," exclaimed Legrandin.

"I see you're painting some fine chetry blossoms—or are they mayflowers?" began the historian of the Fronde, not without hesitation as to the flower, but with a note of confidence in his voice, for he was beginning to forget the incident of the hats.

"No; they're apple blossom," said the Duchesse de Guermantes, addressing her aunt.

"Ah! I see you're a good countrywoman like me; you can tell one flower from another."

"Why yes, so they are! But I thought the season for apple blossom was over now," said the historian, seeking wildly to cover his mistake.

"Oh dear, no; far from it, it's not out yet; the trees won't be in blossom for another fortnight, not for three weeks perhaps," said the librarian who, since he helped with the management of Mme. de Villeparisis's estates, was better informed upon country matters.

"At least three weeks," put in the Duchess; "even round Paris, where they're very far forward. Down in Normandy, don't you know, at his father's place," she went on, pointing to the young Duc de Châtellerault, "where they have some splendid apple trees close to the seashore, like a Japanese screen, they're never really pink until after the twentieth of May."

"I never see them," said the young Duke, "because they give me hay fever. Such a bore."

"Hay fever? I never heard of that before," said the historian.

"It's the fashionable complaint just now," the librarian informed him.

"That all depends, you won't get it at all, probably, if it's a good year for apples. You know Le Normand's saying: 'When it's a good year for apples . . . ,'" put in M. d'Argencourt who, not being really French, was always trying to give himself a Parisian air.

"You're quite right," Mme. de Villeparisis told her

THE MARQUISE DE VILLEPARISIS

niece, "these are from the South. It was a florist who sent them round and asked me to accept them as a present. You're surprised, I dare say, Monsieur Valmère," she turned to the librarian, "that a florist should make me a present of apple blossom. Well, I may be an old woman, but I'm not quite on the shelf yet, I have still a few friends," she went on with a smile that might have been taken as a sign of her simple nature but meant rather, I could not help feeling, that she thought it effective to pride herself on the friendship of a mere florist when she moved in such distinguished circles.

Bloch rose and went over to look at the flowers which Mme. de Villeparisis was painting.

"Never mind, Marquise," said the historian, sitting down again, "even though we should have another of those Revolutions which have stained so many pages of our history with blood—and, upon my soul, in these days one can never tell," he added, with a circular and circumspect glance, as though to make sure that there was no "disaffected" person in the room, though he had not the least suspicion that there actually was, "with a talent like yours and your five languages you would be certain to get on all right." The historian of the Fronde was feeling quite refreshed, for he had forgotten his insomnia. But he suddenly remembered that he had not slept for the last six nights, whereupon a crushing weariness, born of his mind, paralysed his limbs, made him bow his shoulders, and his melancholy face began to droop like an old man's.

Bloch tried to express his admiration in an appropriate gesture, but only succeeded in knocking over with his elbow the glass containing the spray of apple blossom, and all the water was spilled on the carpet.

"Really, you have the fingers of a fairy," went on (to the Marquise) the historian who, having his back turned to me at that moment, had not noticed Bloch's clumsiness.

But Bloch took this for a sneer at himself, and to cover his shame in insolence retorted: "It's not of the slightest importance; I'm not wet."

Mme. de Villeparisis rang the bell and a footman came to wipe the carpet and pick up the fragments of glass. She invited the two young men to her theatricals, and also Mme. de Guermantes, with the injunction:

"Remember to tell Gisèle and Berthe" (the Duchesses d'Auberjon and de Portefin) "to be here a little before two to help me," as she might have told the hired waiters to come early to arrange the tables.

She treated her princely relatives, as she treated M. de Norpois, without any of the little courtesies which she shewed to the historian, Cottard, Bloch and myself, and they seemed to have no interest for her beyond the possibility of serving them up as food for our social curiosity. This was because she knew that she need not put herself out to entertain people for whom she was not a more or less brilliant woman but the touchy old sister—who needed and received tactful handling—of their father or uncle. There would have been no object in her trying to shine before them, she could never have deceived them as to the strength and weakness of her position, for they knew (none so well) her whole history and respected the illustrious race from which she sprang. But, above all, they had ceased to be anything more for her than a dead stock which would not bear fruit again, they would not let her know their new friends, or share their pleasures. She could obtain from them only their occasional presence, or the possibility of speaking of them, at her five o'clock tea-parties as, later on, in her *Memoirs,* of which these parties were only a sort of rehearsal, a preliminary reading aloud of the manuscript before a selected audience. And the society which all these noble kinsmen and kinswomen served to interest, to dazzle, to enthral, the society of the Cottards, of the Blochs, of the dramatists who were in the public eye at the moment, of the historians of the Fronde and such matters; it was in this society that there existed for Mme. de Villeparisis—failing that section of the fashionable world which did not call upon her—the movement, the novelty, all the entertainment of life, it was from people like these that she was able to derive social benefits (which made it well worth her while to let them meet, now and then, though without ever coming to know her, the Duchesse de Guermantes), dinners with remarkable men whose work had interested her, a light opera or a pantomime staged complete by its author in her drawing-room, boxes for interesting shows. Bloch got up to go. He had said aloud that the incident of the broken flower-glass was of no importance, but what he said to himself was different, more different still what he thought: " If people can't train their servants to put flowers where they won't be knocked over and wet their guests and probably cut their hands, it's much better not to go in for such luxuries," he muttered angrily. He was one of those susceptible, highly strung persons who cannot bear to think of themselves as having made a blunder which, though they do not admit even to themselves that they have made it, is enough to spoil their whole day. In a black rage, he was just making up his mind never to go into society again. He had reached the point at which some distraction was imperative. Fortunately in another minute Mme. de Villeparisis was to press him to stay. Either because she was aware of the general feeling among her friends, and had noticed the tide of anti-semitism that was beginning to rise, or simply from carelessness, she had not introduced him to any of the people in the room. He, however, being little used to society, felt bound before leaving the room to take leave of them all, to shew his manners, but without any friendliness; he lowered his head several times, buried his bearded chin in his collar, scrutinised each of the party in turn through his glasses with a cold, dissatisfied glare. But Mme. de Villeparisis stopped him; she had still to discuss with him the little play which was to be performed in her house, and also she did not wish him to leave before he had had the pleasure of meeting M. de Norpois (whose failure to appear puzzled her), although as an inducement to Bloch this introduction was quite superfluous, he having already decided to persuade the two actresses whose names he had mentioned to her to come and sing for nothing in the Marquise's drawing-room, to enhance their own reputations, at one of those parties to which all that was best and noblest in Europe thronged. He had even offered her, in addition, a tragic actress "with pure eyes, fair as Hera," who would recite lyrical prose with a sense of plastic beauty. But on hearing this lady's name Mme. de Villeparisis had declined, for it was that of Saint-Loup's mistress.

"I have better news," she murmured in my ear, "I really believe he's quite cooled off now, and that before very long they'll be parted—in spite of an officer who has played an abominable part in the whole business," she added. For Robert's family were beginning to look with a deadly hatred on M. de Borodino, who had given him leave, at the hairdresser's instance, to go to Bruges, and accused him of giving countenance to an infamous intrigue. "It's really too bad of him," said Mme. de Villeparisis with that virtuous accent common to all the Guermantes, even the most depraved. "Too, too bad," she repeated, giving the word a trio of 't's. One felt that she had no doubt of the Prince's being present at all their orgies. But, as kindness of heart was the old lady's dominant quality, her expression of frowning severity towards the horrible captain, whose name she articulated with an ironical emphasis: "The Prince de Borodino!"—speaking as a woman for whom the Empire simply did not count, melted into a gentle smile at myself with a mechanical twitch of the eyelid indicating a vague understanding between us.

"I have a great admiration for de Saint-Loup-en-Bray," said Bloch, "dirty dog as he is, because he's so extremely well-bred. I have a great admiration, not for him but for well-bred people, they're so rare," he went on, without thinking, since he was himself so extremely ill-bred, what offence his words were giving. "I will give you an example which I consider most striking of his perfect breeding. I met him once with a young gentleman just as he was about to spring into his wheelèd chariot, after he himself had buckled their splendid harness on a pair of steeds, whose mangers were heaped with oats and barley, who had no need of the flashing whip to urge them on. He introduced us, but I did not catch the gentleman's name; one never does catch people's names when one's introduced to them," he explained with a laugh, this being one of his father's witticisms. "De Saint-Loup-en-Bray was perfectly calm, made no fuss about the young gentleman, seemed absolutely at his ease. Well, I found out, by pure chance, a day or two later, that the young gentleman was the son of Sir Rufus Israels!"

The end of this story sounded less shocking than its preface, for it remained quite incomprehensible to everyone in the room. The fact was that Sir Rufus Israels, who seemed to Bloch and his father an almost royal personage before whom Saint-Loup ought to tremble, was in the eyes of the Guermantes world a foreign upstart, tolerated in society, on whose friendship nobody would ever have dreamed of priding himself, far from it.

"I learned this," Bloch informed us, "from the person who holds Sir Rufus's power of attorney; he is a friend of my father, and quite an extraordinary man. Oh, an absolutely wonderful individual," he assured us with that affirmative energy, that note of enthusiasm which one puts only into those convictions that did not originate with oneself.

"Tell me," Bloch went on, lowering his voice, to myself, "how much do you suppose Saint-Loup has? Not that it matters to me in the least, you quite understand, don't you. I'm interested from the Balzacian point of view. You don't happen to know what it's in, French stocks, foreign stocks, or land or what?"

I could give him no information whatsoever. Suddenly raising his voice, Bloch asked if he might open the windows, and without waiting for an answer, went across the room to do so. Mme. de Villeparisis protested that he must not, that she had a cold. "Of course, if it's bad for you!" Bloch was downcast. "But you can't say it's not hot in here." And breaking into a laugh he put into the gaze with which he swept the room an appeal for support against Mme. de Villeparisis. He received none, from these well-bred people. His blazing eyes, having failed to seduce any of the guests from their allegiance, faded with resignation to their normal gravity of expression; he acknowledged his defeat with: "What's the temperature? Seventy-two, at least, I should say. I'm not surprised. I'm simply dripping. And I have not, like the sage Antenor, son of the river Alpheus, the power to plunge myself in the paternal wave to stanch my sweat before laying my body in a bath of polished marble and anointing my limbs with fragrant oils." And with that need which people feel to outline for the use of others medical theories the application of which would be beneficial to their own health: "Well, if you believe it's good for you! I must say, I think you're quite wrong. It's exactly what gives you your cold."

Bloch was overjoyed at the idea of meeting M. de Norpois. He would like, he told us, to get him to talk about the Dreyfus case. "There's a mentality at work there which I don't altogether understand, and it would be quite sensational to get an interview out of this eminent diplomat," he said in a tone of sarcasm, so as not to appear to be rating himself below the Ambassador.

Mme. de Villeparisis was sorry that he had said this so loud, but minded less when she saw that the librarian, whose strong Nationalist views kept her, so to speak, on leash, was too far off to have overheard. She was more shocked to hear Bloch, led on by that demon of ill-breed-

ing which made him permanently blind to the consequences of what he said, inquiring, with a laugh at the
paternal pleasantry: "Haven't I read a learned treatise
by him in which he sets forth a string of irrefutable
arguments to prove that the Japanese war was bound to
end in a Russian victory and a Japanese defeat? He's
fairly paralytic now, isn't he? I'm sure he's the old boy
I've seen taking aim at his chair before sliding across
the room to it, as if he was on wheels."

"Oh, dear, no! Not in the least like that! Just wait a
minute," the Marquise went on, "I don't know what he
can be doing."

She rang the bell and, when the servant had appeared,
as she made no secret, and indeed liked to advertise the
fact that her old friend spent the greater part of his time
in her house: "Go and tell M. de Norpois to come in,"
she ordered him, "he is sorting some papers in my
library; he said he would be twenty minutes, and I've
been waiting now for an hour and three-quarters. He will
tell you about the Dreyfus case, anything you want to
know," she said gruffly to Bloch. "He doesn't approve
much of the way things are going."

For M. de Norpois was not on good terms with the
Government of the day, and Mme. de Villeparisis, although he had never taken the liberty of bringing any
actual Ministers to her house (she still preserved all the
unapproachable dignity of a great lady, and remained outside and above the political relations which he was obliged
to cultivate), was kept well informed by him of everything that went on. Then, too, the politicians of the day
would never have dared to ask M. de Norpois to introduce them to Mme. de Villeparisis. But several of them

had gone down to see him at her house in the country when they needed his advice or help at critical conjunctures. One knew the address. One went to the house. One did not see its mistress. But at dinner that evening she would say:

" I hear they've been down here bothering you. I trust things are going better."

" You are not in a hurry? " she now asked Bloch.

" No, not at all. I wanted to go because I am not very well; in fact there is some talk of my taking a cure at Vichy for my biliary ducts," he explained, articulating the last words with a fiendish irony.

" Why, that's where my nephew Châtellerault's got to go, you must fix it up together. Is he still in the room? He's a nice boy, you know," said Mme. de Villeparisis, and may quite well have meant what she said, feeling that two people whom she knew had no reason not to be friends with each other.

" Oh, I dare say he wouldn't care about that—I don't really know him—at least I barely know him. He is sitting over there," stammered Bloch in an ecstasy of confusion.

The butler could not have delivered his mistress's message properly, for M. de Norpois, to make believe that he had just come in from the street, and had not yet seen his hostess, had picked up the first hat that he had found in the hall, and came forward to kiss Mme. de Villeparisis's hand with great ceremony, asking after her health with all the interest that people shew after a long separation. He was not aware that the Marquise had already destroyed any semblance of reality in this charade, which she cut short by taking M. de Norpois and Bloch into an adjoining room. Bloch, who had observed all the courtesy that was being shewn to a person whom he had not yet discovered to be M. de Norpois, had said to me, trying to seem at his ease: "Who is that old idiot?" Perhaps, too, all this bowing and scraping by M. de Norpois had really shocked the better element in Bloch's nature, the freer and more straightforward manners of a younger generation, and he was partly sincere in condemning it as absurd. However that might be, it ceased to appear absurd, and indeed delighted him the moment it was himself, Bloch, to whom the salutations were addressed.

"Monsieur l'Ambassadeur," said Mme. de Villeparisis, "I should like you to know this gentleman. Monsieur Bloch, Monsieur le Marquis de Norpois." She made a point, despite her casual usage of M. de Norpois, of addressing him always as "Monsieur l'Ambassadeur," as a social convention as well as from an exaggerated respect for his Ambassadorial rank, a respect which the Marquis had inculcated in her, and also with an instinctive application to him of the special manner, less familiar and more ceremonious, in relation to one particular man which, in the house of a distinguished woman, in contrast to the liberties that she takes with her other guests, marks that man out instantly as her lover.

M. de Norpois drowned his azure gaze in his white beard, bent his tall body deep down as though he were bowing before all the famous and (to him) imposing connotations of the name Bloch, and murmured: "I am delighted . . ." whereat his young listener, moved, but feeling that the illustrious diplomat was going too far, hastened to correct him, saying: "Not at all! On the contrary, it is I who am delighted." But this ceremony, which

M. de Norpois, in his friendship for Mme. de Villeparisis, repeated for the benefit of every fresh person that his old friend introduced to him, did not seem to her adequate to the deserts of Bloch, to whom she said:

"Just ask him anything you want to know; take him into the other room if it's more convenient; he will be delighted to talk to you. I think you wished to speak to him about the Dreyfus case," she went on, no more considering whether this would suit M. de Norpois than she would have thought of asking leave of the Duchesse de Montmorency's portrait before having it lighted up for the historian, or of the tea before pouring it into a cup.

"You must speak loud," she warned Bloch, "he's a little deaf, but he will tell you anything you want to know; he knew Bismarck very well, and Cavour. That is so, isn't it;" she raised her voice, "you knew Bismarck well?"

"Have you got anything on the stocks?" M. de Norpois asked me with a knowing air as he shook my hand warmly. I took the opportunity to relieve him politely of the hat which he had felt obliged to bring ceremonially into the room, for I saw that it was my own which he had inadvertently taken. "You shewed me a somewhat laboured little thing in which you went in for a good deal of hairsplitting. I gave you my opinion quite frankly; what you had written was literally not worth the trouble of putting it on paper. Are you thinking of letting us have anything else? You were greatly smitten with Bergotte, if I remember rightly." "You're not to say anything against Bergotte," put in the Duchess. "I don't dispute his talent as a painter; no one would, Duchess. He understands all about etching, if not brush-work on a large scale like

M. Cherbuliez. But it seems to me that in these days we have a tendency to confuse the arts, and forget that the novelist's business is rather to weave a plot and edify his readers than to fiddle away at producing a frontispiece or tailpiece in drypoint. I shall be seeing your father on Sunday at our good friend A. J.'s," he went on, turning again to myself.

I had hoped for a moment, when I saw him talking to Mme. de Guermantes, that he would perhaps afford me, for getting myself asked to her house, the help he had refused me for getting to Mme. Swann's. "Another of my great favourites," I told him, " is Elstir. It seems the Duchesse de Guermantes has some wonderful examples of his work, particularly that admirable *Bunch of Radishes* which I remember at the Exhibition and should so much like to see again; what a masterpiece that is!" And indeed, if I had been a prominent person and had been asked to state what picture I liked best, I should have named this *Bunch of Radishes*. "A masterpiece?" cried M. de Norpois with a surprised and reproachful air. "It makes no pretence of being even a picture, it is merely a sketch." (He was right.) "If you label a clever little thing of that sort 'masterpiece', what have you got to say about Hébert's *Virgin* or Dagnan-Bouveret?"

"I heard you refusing to let him bring Robert's woman," said Mme. de Guermantes to her aunt, after Bloch had taken the Ambassador aside. "I don't think you'll miss much, she's a perfect horror, as you know, without a vestige of talent, and besides she's grotesquely ugly."

"Do you mean to say, you know her, Duchess?" asked M. d'Argencourt.

"Yes, didn't you know that she performed in my house before the whole of Paris, not that that's anything for me to be proud of," explained Mme. de Guermantes with a laugh, glad nevertheless, since the actress was under discussion, to let it be known that she herself had had the first fruits of her foolishness. "Hallo, I suppose I ought to be going now," she added, without moving.

She had just seen her husband enter the room, and these words were an allusion to the absurdity of their appearing to be paying a call together, like a newly married couple, rather than to the often strained relations that existed between her and the enormous fellow she had married, who, despite his increasing years, still led the life of a gay bachelor. Ranging over the considerable party that was gathered round the tea-table the genial, cynical gaze—dazzled a little by the brightness of the setting sun—of the little round pupils lodged in the exact centre of his eyes, like the " bulls " which the excellent marksman that he was could always hit with such perfect aim and precision, the Duke came forward with a bewildered cautious slowness as though, alarmed by so brilliant a gathering, he was afraid of treading on ladies' skirts and interrupting conversations. A permanent smile —suggesting a " Good King of Yvetot "—slightly pompous, a half-open hand floating like a shark's fin by his side, which he allowed to be vaguely clasped by his old friends and by the strangers who were introduced to him, enabled him, without his having to make a single movement, or to interrupt his genial, lazy, royal progress, to reward the assiduity of them all by simply murmuring: " How do, my boy; how do, my dear friend; charmed, Monsieur Bloch; how do, Argencourt; " and, on coming to myself, who was the most highly favoured, when he had been told my name: "How do, my young neighbour, how's your father? What a splendid fellow he is!" He made no great demonstration except to Mme. de Villeparisis, who gave him good-day with a nod of her head, drawing one hand from a pocket of her little apron.

Being formidably rich in a world where everyone was steadily growing poorer, and having secured the permanent attachment to his person of the idea of this enormous fortune, he displayed all the vanity of the great nobleman reinforced by that of the man of means, the refinement and breeding of the former just managing to control the latter's self-sufficiency. One could understand, moreover, that his success with women, which made his wife so unhappy, was not due merely to his name and fortune, for he was still extremely good looking, and his profile retained the purity, the firmness of outline of a Greek god's.

"Do you mean to tell me she performed in your house?" M. d'Argencourt asked the Duchess.

"Well, don't you see, she came to recite, with a bunch of lilies in her hand, and more lilies on her *dwess*." Mme. de Guermantes shared her aunt's affectation of pronouncing certain words in an exceedingly rustic fashion, but never rolled her 'r's like Mme. de Villeparisis.

Before M. de Norpois, under constraint from his hostess, had taken Bloch into the little recess where they could talk more freely, I went up to the old diplomat for a moment and put in a word about my father's Academic chair. He tried first of all to postpone the conversation to another day. I pointed out that I was going to Balbec. "What? Going again to Balbec? Why, you're a regular globe-trotter." He listened to what I had to say. At the name of Leroy-Beaulieu, he looked at me suspiciously. I conjectured that he had perhaps said something disparaging to M. Leroy-Beaulieu about my father and was afraid of the economist's having repeated it to him. All at once he seemed animated by a positive affection for my father. And after one of those opening hesitations out of which suddenly a word explodes as though in spite of the speaker, whose irresistible conviction prevails over his half-hearted efforts at silence: " No, no," he said to me with emotion, " your father *must not* stand. In his own interest he must not; it is not fair to himself; he owes a certain respect to his own really great merits, which would be compromised by such an adventure. He is too big a man for that. If he should be elected, he will have everything to lose and nothing to gain. He is not an orator, thank heaven. And that is the one thing that counts with my dear colleagues, even if you only talk platitudes. Your father has an important goal in life; he should march straight ahead towards it, and not allow himself to turn aside to beat bushes, even the bushes (more thorny for that matter than flowery) of the grove of Academe. Besides, he would not get many votes. The Academy likes to keep a postulant waiting for some time before taking him to its bosom. For the present, there is nothing to be done. Later on, I don't say. But he must wait until the Society itself comes in quest of him. It makes a practice, not a very fortunate practice, a fetish rather, of the *farà da sè of* our friends across the Alps. Leroy-Beaulieu spoke to me about all this in a way I did not at all like. I pointed out to him, a little sharply perhaps, that a man accustomed as he is to dealing with colonial imports and metals could not be expected to understand the part played by the imponderables, as Bismarck used to say. But, whatever happens, your father must on no account put himself forward as a candidate. *Principis obsta.* His friends would find themselves placed in a delicate position if he suddenly called upon them for their votes. Indeed," he broke forth, with an air of candour, fixing his blue eyes on my face, " I am going to say a thing that you will be surprised to hear coming from me, who am so fond of your father. Well, simply because I am fond of him (we are known as the inseparables—*Arcades ambo*), simply because I know the immense service that he can still render to his country, the reefs from which he can steer her if he remains at the helm; out of affection, out of high regard for him, out of patriotism, I should not vote for him. I fancy, moreover, that I have given him to understand that I should not." (I seemed to discern in his eyes the stern Assyrian profile of Leroy-Beaulieu.) " So that to give him my vote now would be a sort of recantation on my part." M. de Norpois repeatedly dismissed his brother Academicians as old fossils. Other reasons apart, every member of a club or academy likes to ascribe to his fellow members the type of character that is the direct converse of his own, less for the advantage of being able to say: "Ah! If it only rested with me!" than for the satisfaction of making the election which he himself has managed to secure seem more difficult, a greater distinction. " I may tell you," he concluded, " that in the best interests of you all, I should prefer to see your father triumphantly elected in ten or fifteen years' time." Words which I assumed to have been dictated if not by jealousy, at any rate by an utter lack of any willingness to oblige, and which later on I was to recall when the course of events had given them a different meaning.

" You haven't thought of giving the Institute an address on the price of bread during the Fronde, I suppose," the historian of 'that movement timidly inquired of M. de Norpois. "You could make a considerable success of a subject like that," (which was to say, " you would give me a colossal advertisement,") he added, smiling at the Ambassador pusillanimously, but with a warmth of feeling which made him raise his eyelids and expose a double horizon of eye. I seemed to have seen this look before, and yet I had met the historian for the first time this afternoon. Suddenly I remembered having seen the same expression in the eyes of a Brazilian doctor who claimed to be able to cure choking fits of the kind from which I suffered by some absurd inhalation of the essential oils of plants. When, in the hope that he would pay more attention to my case, I had told him that I knew Professor Cottard, he had replied, as though speaking in Cottard's interest: " Now this treatment of mine, if you were to tell him about it, would give him the material for a most sensational paper for the Academy of Medicine! " He had not ventured to press the matter but had stood gazing at me with the same air of interrogation, timid, anxious, appealing, which it had just puzzled me to see on the face of the historian of the Fronde. Obviously the two men were not acquainted and had little or nothing in common, but psychological like physical laws have a more or less general application. And the requisite conditions are the same; an identical expression lights the eyes of different human animals, as a single sunrise lights different places, a long way apart, which have no connexion with one another. I did not hear the Ambassador's reply, for the whole party, with a good deal of noise, had again gathered round Mme. de Villeparisis to watch her at work.

"You know who' we're talking about, Basin?" the Duchess asked her husband.

"I can make a pretty good guess," said the Duke.

"Ah! As an actress she's not, I'm afraid, in what one would call the great tradition."

"You can't imagine," went on Mme. de Guermantes to M. d'Argencourt, "anything more ridiculous."

"In fact, it was drolatic," put in M. de Guermantes, whose odd vocabulary enabled people in society to declare that he was no fool and literary people, at the same time, to regard him as a complete imbecile.

"What I fail to understand," resumed the Duchess, "is how in the world Robert ever came to fall in love with her. Oh, of course I know one mustn't discuss that sort of thing," she added, with the charming pout of a philosopher and sentimentalist whose last illusion had long been shattered. "I know that anybody may fall in love with anybody else. And," she went on, for, though she might still laugh at modern literature, it, either by its dissemination through the popular press or else in the course of conversation, had begun to percolate into her mind, "that is the really nice thing about love, because it's what makes it so 'mysterious'."

"Mysterious! Oh, I must confess, cousin, that's a bit beyond me," said the Comte d'Argencourt.

"Oh dear, yes, it's a very mysterious thing, love," declared the Duchess, with the sweet smile of a good-natured woman of the world, but also with the rooted

conviction with which a Wagnerian assures a bored gentleman from the Club that there is something more than just
noise in the *Walküre*. "After all, one never does know
what makes one person fall in love with another; it may
not be at all what we think," she added with a smile, re-
pudiating at once by this interpretation the idea she had
just suggested. "After all, one never knows anything, does
one?" she concluded with an air of weary scepticism.
"Besides, one understands, doesn't one; one simply can't
explain other people's choices in love."

But having laid down this principle she proceeded at
once to abandon it and to criticise Saint-Loup's choice.

"All the same, don't you know, it is amazing to me that
a man can find any attraction in a person who's simply
silly."

Bloch, hearing Saint-Loup's name mentioned and gathering that he was in Paris, promptly made a remark about
him so outrageous that everybody was shocked. He was
beginning to nourish hatreds, and one felt that he would
stop at nothing to gratify them. Once he had established
the principle that he himself was of great moral worth
and that the sort of people who frequented La Boulie (an
athletic club which he supposed to be highly fashionable)
deserved penal servitude, every blow he could get in
against them seemed to him praiseworthy. He went so
far once as to speak of a lawsuit which he was anxious
to bring against one of his La Boulie friends. In the
course of the trial he proposed to give certain evidence
which would be entirely untrue, though the defendant
would be unable to impugn his veracity. In this way
Bloch (who, incidentally, never put his plan into action)
counted on baffling and infuriating his antagonist. What

harm could there be in that, since he whom he sought to injure was a man who thought only of doing the "right thing", a La Boulie man, and against people like that any weapon was justified, especially in the hands of a Saint, such as Bloch himself.

"I say, though, what about Swann?" objected M. d'Argencourt, who having at last succeeded 'in understanding the point of his cousin's speech, was impressed by her accuracy of observation, and was racking his brains for instances of men who had fallen in love with women in whom he himself had seen no attraction.

"Oh, but Swann's case was quite different," the Duchess protested. "It was a great surprise, I admit, because she's just a well-meaning idiot, but she was never silly, and she was at one time good looking."

"Oh, oh!" muttered Mme. de Villeparisis.

"You never thought so? Surely, she had some charming points, very fine eyes, good hair, she used to dress, and does still dress wonderfully. Nowadays, I quite agree, she's horrible, but she has been a lovely woman in her time. Not that that made me any less sorry when Charles married her, because it was so unnecessary." The Duchess had not intended to say anything out of the common, but as M. d'Argencourt began to laugh she repeated these last words—either because she thought them amusing or because she thought it nice of him to laugh—and looked up at him with a coaxing smile, to add the enchantment of her femininity to that of her wit. She went on: "Yes, really, it wasn't worth the trouble, was it; still, after all, she did have some charm and I can quite understand anybody's falling in love with her, but if you saw Robert's girl, I assure you, you'ld simply die of laughter. Oh, I know somebody's going to quote Augier at me: 'What matters the bottle so long as one gets drunk?' Well, Robert may have got drunk, all right, but he certainly hasn't shewn much taste in his choice of a bottle! First of all, would you believe that she actually expected me to fit up a staircase right in the middle of my drawing-room. Oh, a mere nothing—what?—and she announced that she was going to lie flat on her stomach on the steps. And then, if you'd heard the things she recited, I only remember one scene, but I'm sure nobody could imagine anything like it: it was called the *Seven Princesses*."

"*Seven Princesses*! Dear, dear, what a snob she must be!" cried M. d'Argencourt. "But, wait a minute, why, I know the whole play. The author sent a copy to the King, who couldn't understand a word of it and called on me to explain it to him.

"It isn't, by any chance, by Sar Peladan?" asked the historian of the Fronde, meaning to make a subtle and topical allusion, but in so low a tone that his question passed unnoticed.

"So you know the *Seven Princesses*, do you?" replied the Duchess. "I congratulate you! I only know one, but she's quite enough; I have no wish to make the acquaintance of the other six. If they are all like the one I've seen!"

"What a goose!" I thought to myself. Irritated by the coldness of her greeting, I found a sort of bitter satisfaction in this proof of her complete inability to understand Maeterlinck. "To think that's the woman I walk miles every morning to see. Really, I'm too kind. Well, it's my turn now not to want to see her." Thus I reasoned with myself; but my words ran counter to my thoughts; they were purely conversational words such as we say to ourselves at those moments when, too much excited to remain quietly alone, we feel the need, for want of another listener, to talk to ourselves, without meaning what we say, as we talk to a stranger.

"I can't tell you what it was like," the Duchess went on; "you simply couldn't help laughing. Not that anyone tried; rather the other way, I'm sorry to say, for the young person was not at all pleased and Robert has never really forgiven me. Though I can't say I'm sorry, actually, because if it had been a success the lady would perhaps have come again, and I don't quite see Marie-Aynard approving of that."

This was the name given in the family to Robert's mother, Mme. de Marsantes, the widow of Aynard de Saint-Loup, to distinguish her from her cousin, the Princesse de Guermantes-Bavière, also a Marie, to whose Christian name her nephews and cousins and brothers-in-law added, to avoid confusion, either that of her husband or another of her own, making her Marie-Gilbert or Marie-Hedwige.

"To begin with, there was a sort of rehearsal the night before, which was a wonderful affair!" went on Mme. de Guermantes in ironical pursuit of her theme. "Just imagine, she uttered a sentence, no, not so much, not a quarter of a sentence, and then she stopped; she didn't open her mouth—I'm not exaggerating—for a good five minutes."

"Oh, I say," cried M. d'Argencourt.

"With the utmost politeness I took the liberty of hinting to her that this might seem a little unusual. And she said—I give you her actual words—'One ought always to repeat a thing as though one were just composing it oneself.' When you think of it, that really is monumental."

"But I understood she wasn't at all bad at reciting poetry," said one of the two young men.

"She hasn't the ghost of a notion what poetry is," replied Mme. de Guermantes. "However, I didn't need to listen to her to tell that. It was quite enough to see her come in with her lilies. I knew at once that she couldn't have any talent when I saw those lilies!"

Everybody laughed.

"I hope, my dear aunt, you aren't angry with me, over my little joke the other day about the Queen of Sweden. I've come to ask your forgiveness."

"Oh, no, I'm not at all angry, I even give you leave to eat at my table, if you're hungry.—Come along, M. Valmère, you're the daughter of the house," Mme. de Villeparisis went on to the librarian, repeating a time-honoured pleasantry.

M. de Guermantes sat upright in the armchair in which he had come to anchor, his hat on the carpet by his side, and examined with a satisfied smile the plate of little cakes that was being held out to him.

"Why, certainly, now that I am beginning to feel at home in this distinguished company, I will take a sponge-cake; they look excellent."

"This gentleman makes you an admirable daughter," commented M. d'Argencourt, whom the spirit of imitation prompted to keep Mme. de Villeparisis's little joke in circulation.

The librarian handed the plate of cakes to the historian of the Fronde.

"You perform your functions admirably," said the latter, startled into speech, and hoping also to win the sympathy of the crowd. At the same time he cast a covert glance of connivance at those who had anticipated him.

"Tell me, my dear aunt," M. de Guermantes inquired of Mme. de Villeparisis, "who was that rather good-looking man who was going out just now as I came in? I must know him, because he gave me a sweeping bow, but I couldn't place him at all; you know I never can remember names, it's such a nuisance," he added, in a tone of satisfaction.

"M. Legrandin."

"Oh, but Oriane has a cousin whose mother, if I'm not mistaken, was a Grandin. Yes, I remember quite well, she was a Grandin de l'Eprevier."

"No," replied Mme. de Villeparisis, "no relation at all. These are plain Grandins. Grandins of nothing at all. But they'ld be only too glad to be Grandins of anything you chose to name. This one has a sister called Mme. de Cambremer."

"Why, Basin, you know quite well who' my aunt means," cried the Duchess indignantly. "He's the brother of that great graminivorous creature you had the weird idea of sending to call on me the other day. She stayed a solid hour; I thought I should go mad. But I began by thinking it was she who was mad when I saw a person I didn't know come browsing into the room looking exactly like a cow."

"Listen, Oriane; she asked me what afternoon you were at home; I couldn't very well be rude to her; and besides, you do exaggerate so, she's not in the least like a cow," he added in a plaintive tone, though not without a quick smiling glance at the audience.

He knew that his wife's lively wit needed the stimulus of contradiction, the contradiction of common sense which protests that one cannot (for instance) mistake a woman seriously for a cow; by this process Mme. de Guermantes, enlarging upon her original idea, had been inspired to produce many of her most brilliant sayings. And the Duke in his innocent fashion helped her, without seeming to do so, to bring off her effects like, in a railway carriage, the unacknowledged partner of the three-card player.

"I admit she doesn't look like *a* cow, she looks like a dozen," exclaimed Mme. de Guermantes. "I assure you, I didn't know what to do when I saw a herd of cattle come marching into my drawing-room in a hat and heard them ask me how I was. I had half a mind to say: 'Please, herd of cattle, you must be making a mistake, you can't possibly know me, because you're a herd of cattle,' but after racking my brains over her I came to the conclusion that your Cambremer woman must be the Infanta Dorothea, who had said she was coming to see me one day, and is rather bovine also, so that I was just on the point of saying: 'Your Royal Highness' and using the third person to a herd of cattle. The cut of her dewlap reminded me rather, too, of the Queen of Sweden. But this massed attack had been prepared for by long range artillery fire, according to all the rules of war. For I don't know how long before, I was bombarded with her cards; I used to find them lying about all over the house, on all the tables and chairs, like prospectuses. I couldn't think what they were supposed to be advertising. You saw nothing in the house but 'Marquis et Marquise de Cambremer' with some address or other which I've forgotten; you may be quite sure nothing will ever take me there."

" But it's a great distinction to look like a Queen," said the historian of the Fronde.

"Gad, sir, Kings and Queens, in these days, don't amount to much," said M. de Guermantes, partly because he liked to be thought broad-minded and modern, and also so as to not to seem to attach any importance to his own royal friendships, which he valued highly.

Bloch and M. de Norpois had returned from the other room and came towards us.

"Well, sir," asked Mme. de Villeparisis, "have you been talking to him about the Dreyfus case?"

M. de Norpois raised his eyes to the ceiling, but with a smile, as though calling on heaven to witness the monstrosity of the caprices to which his Dulcinea compelled him to submit. Nevertheless he spoke to Bloch with great affability of the terrible, perhaps fatal period through which France was passing. As this presumably meant that M. de Norpois (to whom Bloch had confessed his belief in the innocence of Dreyfus) was an ardent anti-Dreyfusard, the Ambassador's geniality, his air of tacit admission that his listener was in the right, of never doubting that they were both of the same opinion, of being prepared to join forces with him to overthrow the Government, flattered Bloch's vanity and aroused his curiosity. What were the important points which M. de Norpois never specified but on which he seemed implicitly to affirm that he was in agreement with Bloch; what opinion, then, did he hold of the case, that could bring them together? Bloch was all the more astonished at the mysterious unanimity which seemed to exist between him and M. de Norpois, in that it was not confined to politics, Mme. de Villeparisis having spoken at some length to M. de Norpois of Bloch's literary work.

"You are not of your age," the former Ambassador told him, "and I congratulate you upon that. You are not of this age in which disinterested work no longer exists, in which writers offer the public nothing but obscenities or ineptitudes. Efforts such as yours ought to be encouraged, and would be, if we had a Government."

Bloch was flattered by this picture of himself swimming alone amid a universal shipwreck. But here again he would have been glad of details, would have liked to know what were the ineptitudes to which M. de Norpois referred. Bloch had the feeling that he was working along the same lines as plenty of others; he had never supposed himself to be so exceptional. He returned to the Dreyfus case, but did not succeed in elucidating M. de Norpois's own views. He tried to induce him to speak of the officers whose names were appearing constantly in the newspapers at that time; they aroused more curiosity than the politicians who were involved also, because they were not, like the politicians, well known already, but, wearing a special garb, emerging from the obscurity of a different kind of life and a religiously guarded silence, simply stood up and spoke and disappeared again, like Lohengrin landing from a skiff drawn by a swan. Bloch had been able, thanks to a Nationalist lawyer of his acquaintance, to secure admission to several hearings of the Zola trial. He would arrive there in the morning and stay until the court rose, with a packet of sandwiches and a flask of coffee, as though for the final examination for a degree, and this change of routine stimulating a nervous excitement which the coffee and the emotional interest of the trial worked up to a climax, he would come out so enamoured of everything that had happened in court that, in the evening, as

he sat at home, he would long to immerse himself again
in that beautiful dream and would hurry out, to a restaurant frequented by both parties, in search of friends with
whom he would go over interminably the whole of the
day's proceedings, and make up, by a supper ordered in
an imperious tone which gave him the illusion of power,
for the hunger and exhaustion of a day begun so early
and unbroken by any interval for luncheon. The human
mind, hovering perpetually between the two planes of
experience and imagination, seeks to fathom the ideal life
of the people it knows and to know the people whose life
it has had to imagine. To Bloch's questions M. de Norpois replied:

" There are two officers involved in the case now being
tried of whom I remember hearing some time ago from a
man in whose judgment I felt great confidence, and who
praised them both highly—I mean M. de Miribel. They
are Lieutenant-Colonel Henry and Lieutenant-Colonel
Picquart."

" But," exclaimed Bloch, " the divine Athena, daughter
of Zeus, has put in the mind of one the opposite of what
is in the mind of the other. And they are fighting against
one another like two lions. Colonel Picquart had a splendid position in the Army, but his Moira has led him to the
side that was not rightly his. The sword of the Nationalists
will carve his tender flesh, and he will be cast out as food
for the beasts of prey and the birds that wax fat upon
the bodies of men."

M. de Norpois made no reply.

" What are those two palavering about over there? "
M. de Guermantes asked Mme. de Villeparisis, indicating
M. de Norpois and Bloch.

" The Dreyfus case."

" The devil they are. By the way, do you know who is a red-hot supporter of Dreyfus? I give you a thousand guesses. My nephew Robert! I can tell you that, at the Jockey, when they heard of his goings on, there was a fine gathering of the clans, a regular hue and cry. And as he's coming up for election next week . . ."

" Of course," broke in the Duchess, if they're all like Gilbert, who keeps on saying that all the Jews ought to be sent back to Jerusalem."

" Indeed; then the Prince de Guermantes is quite of my way of thinking," put in M. d'Argencourt.

The Duke made a show of his wife, but did not love her. Extremely self-centred, he hated to be interrupted, besides he was in the habit, at home, of treating her brutally. Convulsed with the twofold rage of a bad husband when his wife speaks to him, and a good talker when he is not listened to, he stopped short and transfixed the Duchess with a glare which made everyone feel uncomfortable.

" What makes you think we want to hear about Gilbert and Jerusalem? It's nothing to do with that. But," he went on in a gentler tone, " you will agree that if one of our family were to be pilled at the Jockey, especially Robert, whose father was chairman for ten years, it would be a pretty serious matter. What can you expect, my dear, it's got 'em on the raw, those fellows; they're all over it. I don't blame them, either; personally, you know that I have no racial prejudice, all that sort of thing seems to me out of date, and I do claim to move with the times; but damn it all, when one goes by the name of ' Marquis de Saint-Loup ' one isn't a Dreyfusard; what more can

I say?"

M. de Guermantes uttered the words: "When one goes by the name of Marquis de Saint-Loup," with some emphasis. He knew very well that it was a far greater thing to go by that of Duc de Guermantes. But if his self-esteem had a tendency to exaggerate if anything the superiority of the title Duc de Guermantes over all others, it was perhaps not so much the rules of good taste as the laws of imagination that urged him thus to attenuate it. Each of us sees in the brightest colours what he sees at a distance, what he sees in other people. For the general laws which govern perspective in imagination apply just as much to dukes as to ordinary mortals. And not only the laws of imagination, but those of speech. Now, either of two laws of speech may apply here, one being that which makes us express ourselves like others of our mental category and not of our caste. Under this law M. de Guermantes might be, in his choice of expressions, even when he wished to talk about the nobility, indebted to the humblest little tradesman, who would have said: "When one goes by the name of Duc de Guermantes," whereas an educated man, a Swann, a Legrandin would not have said it. A duke may write novels worthy of a grocer, even about life in high society, titles and pedigrees being of no help to him there, and the epithet "aristocratic" be earned by the writings of a plebeian. Who had been, in this instance, the inferior from whom M. de Guermantes had picked up "when one goes by the name", he had probably not the least idea. But another law of speech is that, from time to time, as there appear and then vanish diseases of which nothing more is ever heard, there come into being, no one knows how, spontaneously perhaps or

by an accident like that which introduced into France a
certain weed from America, the seeds of which, caught
in the wool of a travelling rug, fell on a railway embank-
ment, forms of speech which one hears in the same decade
on the lips of people who have not in any way combined
together to use them. So, just as in a certain year I heard
Bloch say, referring to himself, that "the most charming
people, the most brilliant, the best known, the most exclusive had discovered that there was only one man in
Paris whom they felt to be intelligent, pleasant, whom
they could not do without—namely Bloch," and heard
the same phrase used by countless other young men who
did not know him and varied it only by substituting their
own names for his, so I was often to hear this "when
one goes by the name".

"What can one expect," the Duke went on, "with the
influence he's come under; it's easy to understand."

"Still it is rather comic," suggested the Duchess, "when
you think of his mother's attitude, how she bores us to
tears with her Patrie Française, morning, noon and night."

"Yes, but there's not only his mother to be thought of,
you can't humbug us like that. There's a damsel, too, a
fly-by-night of the worst type; she has far more influence
over him than his mother, and she happens to be a compatriot of Master Dreyfus. She has passed on her state of
mind to Robert."

"You may not have heard, Duke, that there is a new
word to describe that sort of mind," said the librarian,
who was Secretary to the Antirevisionist Committee.
"They say 'mentality'. It means exactly the same thing,
but it has this advantage that nobody knows what
you're talking about. It is the very latest expression

just now, the 'last word' as people say." Meanwhile, having heard Bloch's name, he was watching him question M. de Norpois with misgivings which aroused others as strong though of a different order in the Marquise. Trembling before the librarian, and always acting the anti-Dreyfusard in his presence, she dreaded what he would say were he to find out that she had asked to her house a Jew more or less affiliated to the "Syndicate".

"Indeed," said the Duke, "'mentality', you say; I must make a note of that; I shall use it some day." This was no figure of speech, the Duke having a little pocket-book filled with such "references" which he used to consult before dinner-parties. "I like 'mentality'. There are a lot of new words like that which people suddenly start using, but they never last. I read somewhere the other day that some writer was 'talentuous'. You may perhaps know what it means; I don't. And since then I've never come across the word again."

"But 'mentality' is more widely used than 'talentuous'," the historian of the Fronde made his way into the conversation. "I am on a Committee at the Ministry of Education at which I have heard it used several times, as well as at my Club, the Volney, and indeed at dinner at M. Emile Ollivier's."

"I, who have not the honour to belong to the Ministry of Education," replied the Duke with a feigned humility but with a vanity so intense that his lips could not refrain from curving in a smile, nor his eyes from casting round his audience a glance sparkling with joy, the ironical scorn in which made the poor historian blush, "I who have not the honour to belong to the Ministry of Education," he repeated, relishing the sound of his words, " nor to the

Volney Club (my only clubs are the Union and the Jockey
—you aren't in the Jockey, I think, sir?" he asked the
historian, who, blushing a still deeper red, scenting an
insult and failing to understand it, began to tremble in
every limb.) " I, who am not even invited to dine with
M. Emile Ollivier, I must confess that I had never heard
' mentality '. I'm sure you're in the same boat, Argencourt.

" You know," he went on, " why they can't produce the
proofs of Dreyfus's guilt. Apparently it's because the War
Minister's wife was his mistress, that's what people are
saying."

" Ah! I thought it was the Prime Minister's wife," said
M. d'Argencourt.

" I think you're all equally tiresome about this wretched
case," said the Duchesse de Guermantes, who, in the social
sphere, was always anxious to shew that she did not allow
herself to be led by anyone. " It can't make any difference
to me, so far as the Jews are concerned, for the simple
reason that I don't know any of them, and I intend to
remain in that state of blissful ignorance. But on the other
hand I do think it perfectly intolerable that just because
they're supposed to hold ' sound ' views and don't deal
with Jewish tradesmen, or have ' Down with the Jews '
printed on their sunshades, we should have a swarm of
Durands and Dubois and so forth, women we should
never have known but for this business, forced down our
throats by Marie-Aynard or Victurnienne. I went to see
Marie-Aynard a couple of days ago. It used to be so nice
there. Nowadays one finds all the people one has spent
one's life trying to avoid, on the pretext that they're
against Dreyfus, and others of whom you have no idea

who they can be."

"No; it was the War Minister's wife; at least, that's the bedside rumour," went on the Duke, who liked to flavour his conversation with certain expressions which he imagined to be of the old school. "Personally, of course, as everyone knows, I take just the opposite view to my cousin Gilbert. I am not feudal like him, I would go about with a negro if he was a friend of mine, and I shouldn't care two straws what anybody thought; still after all you will agree with me that when one goes by the name of Saint-Loup one doesn't amuse oneself by running clean against the rails of public opinion, which has more sense than Voltaire or even my nephew. Nor does one go in for what I may be allowed to call these acrobatics of conscience a week before one comes up for a club. It is a bit stiff, really! No, it is probably that little wench of his that has put him on his high horse. I expect she told him that he would be classed among the 'intellectuals'. The intellectuals, they're the very cream of those gentry. It's given rise, by the way, to a rather amusing pun, though a very naughty one."

And the Duke murmured, lowering his voice, for his wife's and M. d'Argencourt's benefit, "Mater Semita," which had already made its way into the Jockey Club, for, of all the flying seeds in the world, that to which are attached the most solid wings, enabling it to be disseminated at the greatest distance from its parent branch, is still a joke.

"We might ask this gentleman, who has a *nerudite* air, to explain it to us," he went on, indicating the historian. "But it is better not to repeat it, especially as there's not a vestige of truth in the suggestion. I am not so ambitious as my cousin Mirepoix, who claims that she can trace the descent of her family before Christ to the Tribe of Levi, and I will undertake to prove that there has never been a drop of Jewish blood in our family. Still there is no good in our shutting our eyes to the fact, you may be sure that my dear nephew's highly original views are liable to make a considerable stir at Landerneau. Especially as Fezensac is ill just now, and Duras will be running the election; you know how he likes to make nuisances," concluded the Duke, who had never succeeded in learning the exact meaning of certain phrases, and supposed "making nuisances" to mean "making difficulties".

Bloch tried to pin M. de Norpois down on Colonel Picquart.

"There can be no two opinions;" replied M. de Norpois, "his evidence had to be taken. I am well aware that, by maintaining this attitude, I have drawn screams of protest from more than one of my colleagues, but to my mind the Government were bound to let the Colonel speak. One can't dance lightly out of a blind alley like that, or if one does there's always the risk of falling into a ditch. As for the officer himself, his statement gave one, at the first hearing, a most excellent impression. When one saw him, looking so well in that smart Chasseur uniform, come into court and relate in a perfectly simple and frank tone what he had seen and what he had deduced, and say: 'On my honour as a soldier'" (here M. de Norpois's voice shook with a faint patriotic throb) "'such is my conviction,' it is impossible to deny that the impression he made was profound."

"There; he is a Dreyfusard, there's not the least doubt of it," thought Bloch.

"But where he entirely forfeited all the sympathy that he had managed to attract was when he was confronted with the registrar, Gribelin. When one heard that old public servant, a man who had only one answer to make," (here M. de Norpois began to accentuate his words with the energy of his sincere convictions) "when one listened to him, when one saw him look his superior officer in the face, not afraid to hold his head up to him, and say to him in a tone that admitted of no response: 'Colonel, sir, you know very well that I have never told a lie, you know that at this moment, as always, I am speaking the truth,' the wind changed; M. Picquart might move heaven and earth at the subsequent hearings; he made a complete fiasco."

"No; evidently he's an anti-Dreyfusard; it's quite obvious," said Bloch to himself. "But if he considers Picquart a traitor and a liar, how can he take his revelations seriously, and quote them as if he found them charming and believed them to be sincere. And if, on the other hand, he sees in him an honest man easing his conscience, how can he suppose him to have been lying when he was confronted with Gribelin?"

"In any case, if this man Dreyfus is innocent," the Duchess broke in, "he hasn't done much to prove it. What idiotic, raving letters he writes from that island. I don't know whether M. Esterhazy is any better, but he does shew some skill in his choice of words, a different tone altogether. That can't be very pleasant for the supporters of M. Dreyfus. What a pity for them there's no way of exchanging innocents." Everybody laughed. "You heard what Oriane said?" the Duc de Guermantes inquired eagerly of Mme. de Villeparisis. "Yes; I think it most amusing." This was not enough for the Duke. "Well, I don't know, I can't say that I thought it amusing; or rather it doesn't make the slightest difference to me whether a thing is amusing or not. I don't care about wit." M. d'Argencourt protested. "It is probably because I've been a Member of Parliament, where I have listened to brilliant speeches that meant absolutely nothing. I learned there to value, more than anything, logic. That's probably why they didn't elect me again. Amusing things leave me cold." "Basin, don't play the heavy father like that, my child, you know quite well that no one admires wit more than you do." "Please let me finish. It is just because I am unmoved by a certain type of humour, that I am often struck by my wife's wit. For you will find it based, as a rule, upon sound observation. She reasons like a man; she states her case like a writer."

Possibly the explanation of M. de Norpois's speaking in this way to Bloch, as though they had been in agreement, may have lain in the fact that he himself was so keen an anti-Dreyfusard that, finding the Government not anti-Dreyfusard enough, he was its enemy just as much as the Dreyfusards. Perhaps because the object to which he devoted himself in politics was something more profound, situated on another plane, from which Dreyfusism appeared as an unimportant modality which did not deserve the attention of a patriot interested in large questions of foreign policy. Perhaps, rather, because the maxims of his political wisdom being applicable only to questions of form, of procedure, of expediency, they were as powerless to solve questions of fact as in philosophy pure logic is powerless to tackle the problems of existence; or else because that very wisdom made him see danger in handling such subjects and so, in his caution, he preferred to speak only of minor incidents. But where Bloch made a mistake was in thinking that M. de Norpois, even had he been less cautious by nature and of a less exclusively formal cast of mind, could (supposing he would) have told him the truth as to the part played by Henry, Picquart or du Paty de Clam, or as to any of the different aspects of the case. The truth, indeed, as to all these matters Bloch could not doubt that M. de Norpois knew. How could he fail to know it seeing that he was a friend of all the Ministers? Naturally, Bloch thought that the truth in politics could be approximately reconstructed by the most luminous minds, but he imagined, like the man in the street, that it resided permanently, beyond the reach of argument and in a material form, in the secret files of the President of the Republic and the Prime Minister, who imparted it to their Cabinet. Now, even when a political truth does take the form of written documents, it is seldom that these have any more value than a radiographic plate on which the layman imagines that the patient's disease is inscribed in so many words, when, as a matter of fact, the plate furnishes simply one piece of material for study, to be combined with a number of others, which the doctor's reasoning powers will take into consideration as a whole and upon them found his diagnosis. So, too, the truth in politics, when one goes to well-informed men and imagines that one is about to grasp it, eludes one. Indeed, later on (to confine ourselves to the Dreyfus case), when so startling an event occurred as Henry's confession, followed by his suicide, this fact was at once interpreted in opposite ways by the Dreyfusard Ministers, and by Cavaignac and Cuignet who had

themselves made the discovery of the forgery and conducted the examination; still more so among the Dreyfusard Ministers themselves, men of the same shade of
Dreyfusism, judging not only from the same documents
but in the same spirit, the part played by Henry was explained in two entirely different ways, one set seeing in
him an accomplice of Esterhazy, the others assigning that
part to du Paty de Clam, thus rallying in support of a
theory of their opponent Cuignet and in complete opposition to their supporter Reinach. All that Bloch could
elicit from M. de Norpois was that if it were true that the
Chief of Staff, M. de Boisdeffre, had had a secret communication sent to M. Rochefort, it was evident that a
singularly regrettable irregularity had occurred.

" You may be quite sure that the War Minister must
(*in petto* at any rate) be consigning his Chief of Staff
to the infernal powers. An official disclaimer would not
have been (to my mind) a work of supererogation. But
the War Minister expresses himself very bluntly on the
matter *inter pocula*. There are certain subjects, moreover, about which it is highly imprudent to create an
agitation over which one cannot retain control afterwards."

" But those documents are obviously forged," put in
Bloch.

M. de Norpois made no reply to this, but announced
that he did not approve of the manifestations that were
being made by Prince Henri d'Orléans:

" Besides, they can only ruffle the calm of the pre-
torium, and encourage agitations which, looked at from
either point of view, would be deplorable. Certainly we
must put a stop to the anti-militarist conspiracy, but we
cannot possibly tolerate, either, a brawl encouraged by

those elements on the Right who instead of serving the patriotic ideal themselves are hoping to make it serve them. Heaven be praised, France is not a South American Republic, and the need has not yet been felt here for a military pronunciamento."

Bloch could not get him to speak on the question of Dreyfus's guilt, nor would he utter any forecast as to the judgment in the civil trial then proceeding. On the other hand, M. de Norpois seemed only too ready to indicate the consequences of this judgment.

"If it is a conviction," he said, "it will probably be quashed, for it is seldom that, in a case where there has been such a number of witnesses, there is not some flaw in the procedure which counsel can raise on appeal. To return to Prince Henri's outburst, I greatly doubt whether it has met with his father's approval."

"You think Chartres is for Dreyfus?" asked the Duchess with a smile, her eyes rounded, her cheeks bright, her nose buried in her plate, her whole manner deliciously scandalised.

"Not at all; I meant only that there runs through the whole family, on that side, a political sense which we have seen, in the admirable Princesse Clémentine, carried to its highest power, and which her son, Prince Ferdinand, has kept as a priceless inheritance. You would never have found the Prince of Bulgaria clasping Major Esterhazy to his bosom."

"He would have preferred a private soldier," murmured Mme. de Guermantes, who often met the Bulgarian monarch at dinner at the Prince de Joinville's, and had said to him once, when he asked if she was not envious: "Yes, Sir, of your bracelets."

" You aren't going to Mme. de Sagan's ball this evening? " M. de Norpois asked Mme. de Villeparisis, to cut
short his conversation with Bloch. My friend had not
failed to interest the Ambassador, who told us afterwards,
not without a quaint simplicity, thinking no doubt of the
traces that survived in Bloch's speech of the neo-Homeric
manner which he had on the whole outgrown: " He is
rather amusing, with that way of speaking, a trifle old
fashioned, a trifle solemn. You expect him to come out
with ' The Learned Sisters ', like Lamartine or Jean-
Baptiste Rousseau. It has become quite uncommon in
the youth of the present day, as it was indeed in the
generation before them. We ourselves were inclined to be
romantic." But however exceptional his companion may
have seemed to him, M. de Norpois decided that the conversation had lasted long enough.

" No, sir, I don't go to balls any more," she replied
with a charming grandmotherly smile. " You're going, all
of you, I suppose? You're the right age for that sort of
thing," she added, embracing in a comprehensive glance
M. de Châtellerault, his friend and Bloch. " Still, I was
asked," she went on, pretending, just for fun, to be flattered by the distinction. " In fact, they came specially
to ask me." (" They " being the Princesse de Sagan.)

" I haven't had a card," said Bloch, thinking that Mme.
de Villeparisis would at once offer to procure him one, and
that Mme. de Sagan would be glad to see at her ball the
friend of a woman whom she had called in person to
invite.

The Marquise made no reply, and Bloch did not press
the point, for he had another, more serious matter to
discuss with her, and, with that in view, had already asked

her whether he might call again in a couple of days. Having heard the two young men say that they had both just resigned from the Rue Royale Club, which was letting in every Tom, Dick and Harry, he wished to ask Mme. de Villeparisis to arrange for his election there.

" Aren't they rather bad form, rather stuck-up snobs, these Sagans? " he inquired in a tone of sarcasm.

" Not at all, they're the best we can do for you in that line," M. d'Argencourt, who adopted all the catch-words of Parisian society, assured him.

" Then," said Bloch, still half in irony, " I suppose it's one of the solemnities, the great social fixtures of the season."

Mme. de Villeparisis turned merrily to Mme. de Guermantes.

" Tell us, is it a great social solemnity, Mme. de Sagan's ball? "

" It's no good asking me," answered the Duchess, " I have never yet succeeded in finding out what a social solemnity is. Besides, society isn't my strong point."

" Indeed; I thought it was just the other way," said Bloch, who supposed Mme. de Guermantes to be speaking seriously.

He continued, to the desperation of M. de Norpois, to ply him with questions about the Dreyfus case. The Ambassador declared that, looking at it from outside, he got the impression from du Paty de Clam of a somewhat cloudy brain, which had perhaps not been very happily chosen to conduct that delicate operation, which required so much coolness and discernment, a judicial inquiry.

" I know that the Socialist Party are crying aloud for his head on a charger, as well as for the immediate release of the prisoner from the Devil's Isle. But I think that we are not yet reduced to the necessity of passing the Caudine Forks of MM. Gérault-Richard and Company. So far, the whole case has been an utter mystery, I don't say that on one side just as much as on the other there has not been some pretty dirty work to be hushed up. That certain of your client's more or less disinterested protectors may have the best intentions I will not attempt to deny, but you know that hell is paved with such things," he added, with a look of great subtlety. "It is essential that the Government should give the impression that they are not in the hands of the factions of the Left, and that they are not going to surrender themselves, bound hand and foot, at the demand of some pretorian guard or other, which, believe me, is not the same thing as the Army. It stands to reason that, should any fresh evidence come to light, a new trial would be ordered. And what follows from that? Obviously, that to demand a new trial is to force an open door. When the day comes, the Government will speak with no uncertain voice or will let fall into abeyance what is their essential prerogative. Cock and bull stories will no longer be enough. We must appoint judges to try Dreyfus. And that will be an easy matter because, although we have acquired the habit, in our sweet France, where we love to belittle ourselves, of thinking or letting it be thought that, in order to hear the words Truth and Justice, it is necessary to cross the Channel, which is very often only a roundabout way of reaching the Spree, there are judges to be found outside Berlin. But once the machinery of Government has been set in motion, will you have ears for the voice of authority? When it bids you perform your duty as a citizen will you have ears for its voice, will you take your stand in the ranks of law and order? When its patriotic appeal sounds, will you have the wisdom not to turn a deaf ear but to answer: 'Present!'?"

M. de Norpois put these questions to Bloch with a vehemence which, while it alarmed my friend, flattered him also; for the Ambassador spoke to him with the air of one addressing a whole party, questioned him as though he had been in the confidence of that party and might be held responsible for the decisions which it would adopt. "Should you fail to disarm," M. de Norpois went on, without waiting for Bloch's collective answer, "should you, before even the ink had dried on the decree ordering the fresh trial of the case, obeying it matters not what insidious word of command, fail, I say, to disarm, and band yourselves, rather, in a sterile opposition which seems to some minds the *ultima ratio* of policy, should you retire to your tents and burn your boats, you would be doing so to your own damnation. Are you the prisoners of those who foment disorder? Have you given them pledges?" Bloch was in doubt how to answer. M. de Norpois gave him no time. "If the negative be true, as I should like to think, and if you have a little of what seems to me to be lamentably lacking in certain of your leaders and your friends, namely political sense, then, on the day when the Criminal Court assembles, if you do not allow yourselves to be dragooned by the fishers in troubled waters, you will have won your battle. I do not guarantee that the whole of the General Staff is going to get away unscathed, but it will be so much to the good if some of them at least can save their faces without setting the heather on fire.

"It stands to reason, moreover, that it is with the Government that it rests to pronounce judgment, and to close the list—already too long—of unpunished crimes, not certainly at the bidding of Socialist agitators, nor yet of any obscure military mouthpiece," he added, looking Bloch boldly in the face, perhaps with the instinct that leads all Conservatives to establish support for themselves in the enemy's camp. "Government action is not to be dictated by the highest bidder, from wherever the bid may come. The Government are not, thank heaven, under the orders of Colonel Driant, nor, at the other end of the scale, under M. Clemenceau's. We must curb the professional agitators and prevent them from raising their heads again. France, the vast majority here in France, desires only to be allowed to work in orderly conditions. As to that, there can be no question whatever. But we must not be afraid to enlighten public opinion; and if a few sheep, of the kind our friend Rabelais knew so well, should dash headlong into the water, it would be as well to point out to them that the water in question was troubled, that it had been troubled deliberately by an agency not within our borders, in order to conceal the dangers lurking in its depths. And the Government ought not to give the impression that they are emerging from their passivity in self-defence when they exercise the right which is essentially their own, I mean that of setting the wheels of justice in motion. The Government will accept all your suggestions. If it is proved that there has been a judicial error, they can be sure of an overwhelming majority which would give them room to act with freedom."

"You, sir," said Bloch, turning to M. d'Argencourt, to

whom he had been made known, with the rest of the party, on that gentleman's arrival, "you are a Dreyfusard, of course; they all are, abroad."

"It is a question that concerns only the French themselves, don't you think?" replied M. d'Argencourt with that peculiar form of insolence which consists in ascribing to the other person an opinion which one must, obviously, know that he does not hold since he has just expressed one directly its opposite.

Bloch coloured; M. d'Argencourt smiled, looking round the room, and if this smile, so long as it was directed at the rest of the company, was charged with malice at Bloch's expense, it became tempered with cordiality when finally it came to rest on the face of my friend, so as to deprive him of any excuse for annoyance at the words which he had heard uttered, though those words remained just as cruel. Mme. de Guermantes murmured something to M. d'Argencourt which I could not hear, but which must have referred to Bloch's religion, for there flitted at that moment over the face of the Duchess that expression to which one's fear of being noticed by the person of whom one is speaking gives a certain hesitancy and unreality, while there is blended with it the inquisitive, malicious amusement inspired in one by a group of human beings to which one feels oneself to be fundamentally alien. To retrieve himself, Bloch turned to the Duc de Châtellerault. "You, sir, as a Frenchman, you must be aware that people abroad are all Dreyfusards, although everyone pretends that in France we never know what is going on abroad. Anyhow, I know I can talk freely to you; Saint-Loup told me so." But the young Duke, who felt that every one was turning against Bloch, and was a

coward as people often are in society, employing a mor-
dant and precious form of wit which he seemed, by a
sort of collateral atavism, to have inherited from M. de
Charlus, replied: "You must not ask me, sir, to discuss the
Dreyfus case with you; it is a subject which, on principle,
I never mention except to Japhetics." Everyone smiled,
except Bloch, not that he was not himself in the habit of
making scathing references to his Jewish origin, to that
side of his ancestry which came from somewhere near
Sinai. But instead of one of these epigrams (doubtless
because he had not one ready) the operation of the internal machine brought to Bloch's lips something quite
different. And we caught only: "But how on earth did
you know? Who told you?" as though he had been the
son of a convict. Whereas, given his name, which had not
exactly a Christian sound, and his face, his surprise argued
a certain simplicity of mind.

What M. de Norpois had said not having completely
satisfied him, he went up to the librarian and asked him
whether Mme. de Villeparisis did not sometimes have in her
house M. du Paty de Clam or M. Joseph Reinach. The
librarian made no reply; he was a Nationalist, and never
ceased preaching to the Marquise that the social revolu-
tion might break out at any moment, and that she ought
to shew more caution in the choice of her friends. He
asked himself whether Bloch might not be a secret emis-
sary of the Syndicate, come to collect information, and
went off at once to repeat to Mme. de Villeparisis the
questions that Bloch had put to him. She decided that,
at the best, he was ill-bred and might be in a position to
compromise M. de Norpois. Also, she wished to give
satisfaction to the librarian, the only person of whom she

went in fear, by whom she was being indoctrinated, though without any marked success (every morning he read her M. Judet's article in the *Petit Journal*). She decided, therefore, to make it plain to Bloch that he need not come to the house again, and had no difficulty in finding, among her social repertory, the scene by which a great lady shews anyone her door, a scene which does not in any way involve the raised finger and blazing eyes that people imagine. As Bloch came up to her to say good-bye, buried in her deep armchair, she seemed only half-awakened from a vague somnolence. Her sunken eyes gleamed with only the feeble though charming light of a pair of pearls. Bloch's farewell, barely pencilling on the Marquise's face a languid smile, drew from her not a word, nor did she offer him her hand. This scene left Bloch in utter bewilderment, but as he was surrounded by a circle of spectators he felt that it could not be prolonged without disadvantage to himself, and, to force the Marquise, the hand which she had made no effort to take he himself thrust out at her. Mme. de Villeparisis was startled. But doubtless, while still bent upon giving an immediate satisfaction to the librarian and the anti-Dreyfusard clan, she wished at the same time to provide for the future, and so contented herself with letting her eyelids droop over her closing eyes.

" I believe she's asleep," said Bloch to the librarian who, feeling that he had the support of the Marquise, assumed an indignant air. " Good-bye, madame," shouted Bloch.

The old lady made the slight movement with her lips of a dying woman who wants to open her mouth but whose eye can no longer recognise people. Then she turned, overflowing with a restored vitality, to M. d'Argencourt, while Bloch left the room, convinced that she must be "soft" in the head. Full of curiosity and anxious to have more light thrown upon so strange an incident, he came to see her again a few days later. She received him in the most friendly fashion, because she was a goodnatured woman, because the librarian was not there, because she had in mind the little play which Bloch was going to produce for her, and finally because she had acted once and for all the little scene of the indignant lady that she had wished to act, a scene that had been universally admired and discussed the same evening in various drawing-rooms, but in a version which had already ceased to bear any resemblance to the truth.

"You were speaking just now of the *Seven Princesses*, Duchess; you know (not that it's anything to be proud of) that the author of that—what shall I call it?—that production is a compatriot of mine," said M. d'Argencourt with a fine scorn blended with satisfaction at knowing more than anyone else in the room about the author of a work which had been under discussion. "Yes, he's a Belgian, by nationality," he went on.

"Indeed! No, we don't accuse you of any responsibility for the *Seven Princesses*. Fortunately for yourself and your compatriots you are not like the author of that absurdity. I know several charming Belgians, yourself, your King, who is inclined to be shy, but full of wit, my Ligne cousins, and heaps of others, but you, I am thankful to say, do not speak the same language as the author of the *Seven Princesses*. Besides, if you want to know, it's not worth talking about, because really there is absolutely nothing in it. You know the sort of people who are always trying to seem obscure, and even plan to make themselves ridiculous to conceal the fact that they have not an idea in their heads. If there was anything behind it all, I may tell you that I'm not in the least afraid of a little daring," she added in a serious tone, " provided that there is some idea in it. I don't know if you've seen Borelli's piece. Some people seem to have been shocked by it, but I must say, even if they stone me through the streets for saying it," she went on, without stopping to think that she ran no very great risk of such a punishment, " I found it immensely interesting. But the *Seven Princesses*! It's all very well, one of them having a fondness for my nephew, I cannot carry family feeling quite . . ."

The Duchess broke off abruptly, for a lady came in who was the Comtesse de Marsantes, Robert's mother. Mme. de Marsantes was regarded in the Faubourg Saint-Germain as a superior being, of a goodness, a resignation that were positively angelic. So I had been told, and had had no particular reason to feel surprised, not knowing at the same time that she was the sister of the Duc de Guermantes. Later, I have always been taken aback, whenever I have learned that such women, melancholy, pure, victimised, venerated like the ideal forms of saints in church windows, had flowered from the same genealogical stem as brothers brutal debauched and vile. Brothers and sisters, when they are closely alike in features as were the Duc de Guermantes and Mme. de Marsantes, ought (I felt) to have a single intellect in common, the same heart, as a person would have who might vary between good and evil moods but in whom one could not, for all that, expect to find a vast breadth of outlook if he had a narrow mind, or a sublime abnegation if his heart was hard.

Mme. de Marsantes attended Brunetière's lectures. She fascinated the Faubourg Saint-Germain and, by her saintly life, edified it as well. But the morphological link of handsome nose and piercing gaze led one, nevertheless, to classify Mme. de Marsantes in the same intellectual and moral family as her brother the Duke. I could not believe that the mere fact of her being a woman, and perhaps those of her having had an unhappy life and won everyone's sympathy could make a person be so different from the rest of her family, as in the old romances, where all the virtues and graces are combined in the sister of wild and lawless brothers. It seemed to me that nature, less unconventional than the old poets, must make use almost exclusively of the elements common to the family, and I was unable to credit her with enough power of invention to construct, out of materials analogous to those that composed a fool and clod, a lofty mind without the least strain of clownishness, a saint unsoiled by any brutality. Mme. de Marsantes was wearing a gown of white surah embroidered with large palms, on which stood out flowers of a different material, these being black. This was because, three weeks earlier, she had lost her cousin, M. de Montmorency, a bereavement which did not prevent her from paying calls or even from going to small dinners, but always in mourning. She was a great lady. Atavism had filled her with the frivolity of generations of life at court, with all the superficial, rigorous duties that that implies. Mme. de Marsantes had not had the strength of character to regret for any length of time the death of her father and mother, but she would not for anything in the world have appeared in colours in the month following that of a cousin. She was more than pleasant to me, both because I was Robert's friend and because I did not move in the same world as he. This pleasantness was accompanied by a pretence of shyness, by that sort of intermittent withdrawal of the voice, the eyes, the mind which a woman draws back to her like a skirt that has indiscreetly spread, so as not to take up too much room, to remain stiff and erect even in her suppleness, as a good upbringing teaches. A good upbringing which must not, however, be taken too literally, many of these ladies passing very swiftly into a complete dissolution of morals without ever losing the almost childlike correctness of their manners. Mme. de Marsantes was a trifle irritating in conversation since, whenever she had occasion to speak of a plebeian, as for instance Bergotte or Elstir, she would say, isolating the word, giving it its full value, intoning it on two different notes with a modulation peculiar to the Guermantes: " I have had the *honour*, the great *hon*-our of meeting Monsieur Bergotte," or " of making the acquaintance of Monsieur Elstir," whether that her hearers might marvel at her humility or from the same tendency that Mme. de Guermantes shewed to revert to the use of obsolete forms, as a protest against the slovenly usages of the present day, in which people never professed themselves sufficiently "honoured". Whichever of these was the true reason, one felt that when Mme. de Marsantes said: " I have had the *honour*, the great *hon*-our," she felt she was playing an important part and shewing that she could take in the names of distinguished men as she would have welcomed the men themselves at her home in the country, had they happened to be in the neighbourhood. On the other hand, as her family connexion was numerous, as she was devoted to all her relatives, as, slow in speech and fond of explaining things at length, she was always trying to make clear the exact degree of kinship, she found herself (without any desire to create an effect and without really caring to talk about anyone except touching peasants and sublime gamekeepers) referring incessantly to all the mediatised houses in Europe, a failing which people less brilliantly connected than herself could not forgive, and, if they were at all intellectual, derided as a sign of stupidity.

In the country, Mme. de Marsantes was adored for the good that she did, but principally because the purity of a strain of blood into which for many generations there had flowed only what was greatest in the history of France had taken from her manner everything that the lower orders call " manners ", and had given her a perfect simplicity. She never shrank from kissing a poor woman who was in trouble, and would tell her to come up to the castle for a cartload of wood. She was, people said, the perfect Christian. She was determined to find an immensely rich wife for Robert. Being a great lady means playing the great lady, that is to say, to a certain extent, playing at simplicity. It is a pastime which costs an extremely high price, all the more because simplicity charms people only on condition that they know that you are not bound to live simply, that is to say that you are very rich. Some one said to me afterwards, when I had told him of my meeting her: " You saw of course that she must have been lovely as a young woman." But true beauty is so individual, so novel always, that one does not recognize it as beauty. I said to myself this afternoon only that she had a tiny nose, very blue eyes, a long neck and a sad expression.

"Listen," said Mme. de Villeparisis to the Duchesse de Guermantes, "I'm expecting a woman at any moment whom you don't wish to know. I thought I'ld better warn you, to avoid any unpleasantness. But you needn't be afraid, I shall never have her here again, only I was obliged to let her come to-day. It's Swann's wife."

Mme. Swann, seeing the dimensions that the Dreyfus case had begun to assume, and fearing that her husband's racial origin might be used against herself, had besought him never again to allude to the prisoner's innocence. When he was not present she went farther and used to profess the most ardent Nationalism; in doing which she was only following the example of Mme. Verdurin, in whom a middle-class anti-semitism, latent hitherto, had awakened and grown to a positive fury. Mme. Swann had won by this attitude the privilege of membership in several of the women's leagues that were beginning to be formed in anti-semitic society, and had succeeded in making friends with various members of the aristocracy. It may seem strange that, so far from following their example, the Duchesse de Guermantes, so close a friend of Swann, had on the contrary always resisted his desire, which he had not concealed from her, to introduce to her his wife. But we shall see in due course that this arose from the peculiar nature of the Duchess, who held that she was not "bound to" do things, and laid down with despotic force what had been decided by her social "free will", which was extremely arbitrary.

"Thank you for telling me," said the Duchess. "It would indeed be most unpleasant. But as I know her by sight I shall be able to get away in time."

"I assure you, Oriane, she is really quite nice; an

excellent woman," said Mme. de Marsantes.

"I have no doubt she is, but I feel no need to assure myself of it."

"Have you been invited to Lady Israels's?" Mme de Villeparisis asked the Duchess, to change the conversation.

"Why, thank heaven, I don't know the woman," replied Mme. de Guermantes. "You must ask Marie-Aynard. She knows her. I never could make out why."

"I did indeed know her at one time," said Mme. de Marsantes. "I confess my faults. But I have decided not to know her any more. It seems she's one of the very worst of them, and makes no attempt to conceal it. Besides, we have all been too trusting, too hospitable. I shall never go near anyone of that race again. While we had old friends, country cousins, people of our own flesh and blood on whom we shut our doors, we threw them open to Jews. And now we see what thanks we get from them. But I've no right to speak; I have an adorable son, and, like a young fool, he says and does all the maddest things you can imagine," she went on, having caught some allusion by M. d'Argencourt to Robert. "But, talking of Robert, haven't you seen him?" she asked Mme. de Villeparisis; "being Saturday, I thought he'ld be coming to Paris on leave, and in that case he would be sure to pay you a visit."

As a matter of fact Mme. de Marsantes thought that her son would not obtain leave that week; but knowing that, even if he did, he would never dream of coming to see Mme. de Villeparisis, she hoped, by making herself appear to have expected to find him in the room, to procure his forgiveness from her susceptible aunt for all the visits that he had failed to pay her.

"Robert here! But I have never had a single word from him; I don't think I've seen him since Balbec."

"He is so busy; he has so much to do," pleaded Mme. de Marsantes.

A faint smile made Mme. de Guermantes's eyelashes quiver as she studied the circle which, with the point of her sunshade, she was tracing on the carpet. Whenever the Duke had been too openly unfaithful to his wife, Mme. de Marsantes had always taken up the cudgels against her own brother on her sister-in-law's behalf. The latter had a grateful and bitter memory of this protection, and was not herself seriously shocked by Robert's pranks. At this point the door opened again and Robert himself entered the room.

"Well, talk of the Saint!" said Mme. de Guermantes.

Mme. de Marsantes, who had her back to the door, had not seen her son come in. When she did catch sight of him, her motherly bosom was convulsed with joy, as by the beating of a wing, her body half rose from her seat, her face quivered and she fastened on Robert eyes big with astonishment:

"What! You've come! How delightful! What a surprise!"

"Ah! *Talk of the Saint!*—I see," cried the Belgian diplomat, with a shout of laughter.

"Delicious, ain't it?" came tartly from the Duchess, who hated puns, and had ventured on this one only with a pretence of making fun of herself.

"Good afternoon, Robert," she said, "I believe he's forgotten his aunt."

They talked for a moment, probably about myself, for as Saint-Loup was leaving her to join his mother

Mme. de Guermantes turned to me:

"Good afternoon; how are you?" was her greeting.

She allowed to rain on me the light of her azure gaze, hesitated for a moment, unfolded and stretched towards me the stem of her arm, leaned forward her body which sprang rapidly backwards like a bush that has been pulled down to the ground and, on being released, returns to its natural position. Thus she acted under the fire of Saint-Loup's eyes, which kept her under observation and were making frantic efforts to obtain some further concession still from his aunt. Fearing that our conversation might fail altogether, he joined in, to stimulate it, and answered for me:

"He's not very well just now, he gets rather tired; I think he would be a great deal better, by the way, if he saw you more often, for I can't help telling you that he admires you immensely."

"Oh, but that's very nice of him," said Mme. de Guermantes in a deliberately casual tone, as if I had brought her her cloak. "I am most flattered."

"Look, I must go and talk to my mother for a minute; take my chair," said Saint-Loup, thus forcing me to sit down next to his aunt.

We are both silent.

"I see you sometimes in the morning," she said, as though she were telling me something that I did not know, and I for my part had never seen her. "It's so good for one, a walk."

"Oriane," began Mme. de Marsantes in a low tone, "you said you were going on to Mme. de Saint-Ferréol's; would you be so very kind as to tell her not to expect me to dinner, I shall stay at home now that I've got

349

Robert. And one other thing, but I hardly like to ask you, if you would leave word as you pass to tell them to send out at once for a box of the cigars Robert likes. 'Corona', they're called. I've none in the house."

Robert came up to us; he had caught only the name of Mme. de Saint-Ferréol.

"Who in the world is Mme. de Saint-Ferréol?" he inquired, in a surprised but decisive tone, for he affected a studied ignorance of everything to do with society.

"But, my dear boy, you know quite well," said his mother, "She's Vermandois's sister. It was she gave you that nice billiard table you liked so much."

"What, she's Vermandois's sister, I had no idea of that. Really, my family are amazing," he went on, turning so as to include me in the conversation and adopting unconsciously Bloch's intonation just as he borrowed his ideas, "they know the most unheard-of people, people called Saint-Ferréol" (emphasising the final consonant of each word) "and names like that; they go to balls, they drive in victorias, they lead a fabulous existence. It's prodigious."

Mme. de Guermantes made in her throat a slight, short, sharp sound, as of an involuntary laugh which one chokes back, meaning thereby to shew that she paid just as much tribute as the laws of kinship imposed on her to her nephew's wit. A servant came in to say that the Prince von Faffenheim-Munsterburg-Weinigen had sent word to M. de Norpois that he was waiting.

"Bring him in, sir," said Mme. de Villeparisis to the old Ambassador, who started in quest of the German Minister.

"Stop, sir; do you think I ought to shew him the

miniature of the Empress Charlotte?"

"Why, I'm sure he'll be delighted," said the Ambassador in a tone of conviction, and as though he were envying the fortunate Minister the favour that was in store for him.

"Oh, I know he's very *sound*," said Mme. de Marsantes, "and that is so rare among foreigners. "But I've found out all about him. He is anti-semitism personified."

The Prince's name preserved in the boldness with which its opening syllables were—to borrow an expression from music—attacked, and in the stammering repetition that scanned them, the impulse, the mannered simplicity, the heavy delicacies of the Teutonic race, projected like green boughs over the "heim" of dark blue enamel which glowed with the mystic light of a Rhenish window behind the pale and finely wrought gildings of the German eighteenth century. This name included, among the several names of which it was composed, that of a little German watering-place to which as a child I had gone with my grandmother, at the foot of a mountain honoured by the feet of Goethe, from the vineyards of which we used to drink, at the Kurhof, their illustrious vintages with elaborate and sonorous names, like the epithets which Homer applies to his heroes. And so, scarcely had I heard the Prince's name spoken than, before I had recalled the watering-place, the name itself seemed to shrink, to grow rich with humanity, to find large enough a little place in my memory to which it clung, familiar, earth to earth, picturesque, savoury, light, with something about it, too, that was authorised, prescribed. And then, M. de

Guermantes, in explaining who the Prince was, quoted a number of his titles, and I recognised the name of a village threaded by the river on which, every evening, my cure finished for the day, I used to go in a boat amid the mosquitoes, and that of a forest so far away that the doctor would not allow me to make the excursion to it. And indeed it was comprehensible that the suzerainty of the lord extended to the surrounding places and associated afresh in the enumeration of his titles the names which one could read, close together, upon a map. Thus beneath the visor of the Prince of the Holy Roman Empire and Knight of Franconia it was the face of a dear and smiling land, on which had often lingered for me the light of the six-o'clock sun, that I saw, at any rate before the Prince, Rheingraf and Elector Palatine, had entered the room. For I speedily learned that the revenues which he drew from the forest and river, peopled with gnomes and undines, and from the enchanted mountain on which rose the ancient Burg that cherished memories of Luther and Lewis the Germanic, he employed in keeping five Charron motor-cars, a house in Paris and one in London, a box on Mondays at the Opera and another for the " Tuesdays " at the " Français ". He did not seem to me, nor did he seem to regard himself as different from other men of similar fortune and age who had a less poetic origin. He had their culture, their ideals, he was proud of his rank, but purely on account of the advantages it conferred on him, and had now only one ambition in life, to be elected a Corresponding Member of the Academy of Moral and Political Sciences, which was the reason of his coming to see Mme. de Villeparisis. If he, whose wife was a

leader of the most exclusive set in Berlin, had begged
to be introduced to the Marquise, it was not the result
of any desire on his part for her acquaintance. Devoured
for years past by this ambition to be elected to the
Institute, he had unfortunately never been in a position
to reckon above five the number of Academicians who
seemed prepared to vote for him. He knew that M. de
Norpois could by himself dispose of at least ten others,
a number which he was capable, by skillful negotiations,
of increasing still further. And so the Prince, who had
known him in Russia when they were both there as
Ambassadors, had gone to see him and had done everything in his power to win him over. But in vain might
he multiply his friendly overtures, procure for the Marquis Russian decorations, quote him in articles on foreign
politics; he had had before him an ingrate, a man in
whose eyes all these attentions appeared to count as
nothing, who had not advanced the prospects of his
candidature one inch, had not even promised him his
own vote. No doubt M. de Norpois received him with
extreme politeness, indeed begged that he would not put
himself out and "take the trouble to come so far out
of his way," went himself to the Prince's residence, and
when the Teutonic Knight had launched his: "I should
like immensely to be your colleague," replied in a tone
of deep emotion: "Ah! I should be most happy!" And
no doubt a simpleton, a Dr. Cottard would have said
to himself: "Well, here he is in my house; it was he
who insisted on coming, because he regards me as a
more important person than himself; he tells me that
he would be happy to see me in the Academy; words
do have some meaning after all, damn it, probably if

he doesn't offer to vote for me it is because it hasn't occurred to him. He lays so much stress on my great influence; presumably he imagines that larks drop into my mouth ready roasted, that I have all the support I want, and that is why he doesn't offer me his; but I have only got to get him with his back to the wall, and just say to him quietly: 'Very well, vote for me, will you?' and he will be obliged to do it."

But Prince von Faffenheim was no simpleton. He was what Dr. Cottard would have called "a fine diplomat" and he knew that M. de Norpois was no less fine a one than himself, nor a man who would have failed to realise without needing to be told that he could confer a favour on a candidate by voting for him. The Prince, in his Embassies and as Foreign Minister, had conducted, on his country's behalf instead of, as in the present instance, his own, many of those conversations in which one knows beforehand just how far one is prepared to go and at what point one will decline to commit oneself. He was not unaware that, in this diplomatic language, to talk meant to offer. And it was for this reason that he had arranged for M. de Norpois to receive the Cordon of Saint Andrew. But if he had had to report to his Government the conversation which he had subsequently had with M. de Norpois, he would have stated in his dispatch: "I realised that I had gone the wrong way to work." For as soon as he had returned to the subject of the Institute, M. de Norpois had repeated:

"I should like nothing better; nothing could be better, for my colleagues. They ought, I consider, to feel genuinely honoured that you should have thought of them. It is a really interesting candidature, a little outside our

ordinary course. As you know, the Academy is very
conventional, it takes fright at everything which has
at all a novel sound. Personally, I deplore this. How
often have I had occasion to say as much to my colleagues! I cannot be sure, God forgive me, that I did not
even once let the word 'hide-bound' escape me," he
added, in an undertone, with a scandalised smile, almost
aside, as in a scene on the stage, casting at the Prince
a rapid, sidelong glance from his blue eyes, like a veteran
actor studying the effect on his audience. "You understand, Prince, that I should not care to allow a personality so eminent as yourself to embark on a venture
which was hopeless from the start. So long as my colleagues' ideas linger so far behind the times, I consider
that the wiser course will be to abstain. But you may
rest assured that if I were ever to discern a mind that
was a little more modern, a little more alive, shewing
itself in that college, which is tending to become a mau-
soleum, if I could reckon upon any possible chance of
your success, I should be the first to inform you of it."

"The Cordon was a mistake," thought the Prince;
"the negotiations have not advanced in the least; that
is not what he wanted. I have not yet laid my hand on
the right key."

This was a kind of reasoning of which M. de Norpois,
formed in the same school as the Prince, would also
have been capable. One may mock at the pedantic silli-
ness with which diplomats of the Norpois type go into
ecstasies over some piece of official wording which is,
for all practical purposes, meaningless. But their chil-
dishness has this compensation; diplomats know that, in
the loaded scales which assure that European or other

equilibrium which we call peace, good feeling, sounding speeches, earnest entreaties weigh very little; and that the heavy weight, the true determinant consists in something else, in the possibility which the adversary does (if he is strong enough) or does not enjoy of satisfying, in exchange for what one oneself wants, a desire. With this order of truths, which an entirely disinterested person, such as my grandmother for instance, would not have understood, M. de Norpois and Prince von Faffenheim had frequently had to deal. Chargé d'Affaires in countries with which we had been within an ace of going to war, M. de Norpois, in his anxiety as to the turn which events were about to take, knew very well that it was not by the word "Peace", nor by the word "War" that it would be revealed to him, but by some other, apparently commonplace word, a word of terror or blessing, which the diplomat, by the aid of his cipher, would immediately read and to which, to safeguard the honour of France, he would respond in another word, quite as commonplace, but one beneath which the Minister of the enemy nation would at once see written: "War." Moreover, in accordance with a time-honoured custom, analogous to that which gave to the first meeting between two young people promised to one another in marriage the form of a chance encounter at a performance in the Théâtre du Gymnase, the dialogue in the course of which destiny was to dictate the word "War" or the word "Peace" was held, as a rule, not in the ministerial sanctum but on a bench in a Kurgarten where the Minister and M. de Norpois went independently to a thermal spring to drink at its source their little tumblers of some curative water. By a sort of tacit convention they met at the hour appointed for their cure, began by taking together a short stroll which, beneath its innocent appearance, each of the speakers knew to be as tragic as an order for mobilisation. And so, in a private matter like this nomination for election to the Institute, the Prince had employed the same system of induction which had served him in his public career, the same method of reading beneath superimposed symbols.

And certainly it would be wrong to pretend that my grandmother and the few who resembled her would have been alone in their failure to understand this kind of calculation. For one thing, the average human being, practising a profession the lines of which have been laid down for him from the start, comes near, by his want of intuition, to the ignorance which my grandmother owed to her lofty disinterestedness. Often one has to come down to "kept" persons, male or female, before one finds the hidden spring of actions or words apparently of the most innocent nature in self-interest, in the bare necessity to keep alive. What man does not know that when a woman whom he is going to pay says to him: "Don't let's talk about money," the speech must be regarded as what is called in music "a silent beat" and that if, later on, she declares: "You are far too much trouble; you are always keeping things from me; I've done with you," he must interpret this as: "Some one else has been offering her more." And yet this is only the language of a lady of easy virtue, not so far removed from the ladies in society. The *apache* furnishes more striking examples. But M. de Norpois and the German Prince, if *apaches* and their ways were unknown to them, had been accustomed to living on the same plane as nations, which are also, despite their greatness, creatures of selfishness and cunning, kept in order only by force, by consideration of their material interests which may drive them to murder, a murder that is often symbolic also, since its mere hesitation or refusal to fight may spell for a nation the word " Perish ". But inasmuch as all this is not set forth in Yellow and otherwise coloured Books, the people as a whole are naturally pacific; should they be warlike, it is instinctively, from hatred, from a sense of injury, not for the reasons which have made up the mind of their ruler, on the advice of his Norpois.

The following winter the Prince was seriously ill; he recovered, but his heart was permanently affected.

" The devil! " he said to himself, " I can't afford to lose any time over the Institute. If I wait too long, I may be dead before they elect me. That really would be unpleasant."

He composed, on the foreign politics of the last twenty years, an essay for the *Revue des Deux Mondes,* in which he referred more than once, and in the most flattering terms, to M. de Norpois. The French diplomat called upon him to thank him. He added that he did not know how to express his gratitude. The Prince said to himself, like a man who has been trying to fit various keys into a stubborn lock: " Still not the right one! " and, feeling somewhat out of breath as he shewed M. de Norpois to the door, thought: 'Damn it, these fellows will see me in my grave before letting me in. We must hurry up."

That evening, he met M. de Norpois again at the Opera.

" My dear Ambassador," he began to him, " you told me to-day that you did not know what you could do to prove your gratitude; it was a great exaggeration, for you owe me none, but I am going to be so indelicate as to take you at your word."

M. de Norpois had no less high an esteem for the Prince's tact than the Prince had for his. He understood at once that it was not a request that Prince von Faffenheim was about to present to him, but an offer, and with a radiant affability made ready to hear it.

"Well now, you will think me highly indiscreet. There are two people to whom I am greatly attached—in quite different ways, as you will understand in a moment—two people both of whom have recently settled in Paris, where they intend to remain for the future: my wife, and the Grand Duchess John. They are thinking of giving a few dinners, chiefly in honour of the King and Queen of England, and what they would have liked more than anything in the world would have been to be able to offer their guests the company of a person for whom, without knowing her, they both of them feel a great admiration. I confess that I did not know how I was going to gratify their wish when I learned just now, by the most extraordinary accident, that you were a friend of this person. I know that she lives a most retired life, and sees only a very few people—'happy few,' as Stendhal would say—but if you were to give me your backing, with the generosity that you have always shewn me, I am sure that she would allow you to present me to her and to convey to her the wishes of both the Grand Duchess and the Princess. Perhaps she would consent to dine with us, when the Queen of England comes, and then (one never knows) if we don't bore her too much, to spend the Easter holidays with us at Beaulieu, at the Grand Duchess John's. The person I allude to is called the Marquise de Villeparisis. I confess that the hope of becoming one of the frequenters of such a school of wit would console me, would make me contemplate without regret the abandoning of my attempt at the Institute. For in her house, too, I understand, there is a regular flow of intellect and brilliant talk."

With an inexpressible sense of pleasure the Prince felt that the lock no longer resisted, and that at last the key was turning.

"Such an alternative is wholly unnecessary, my dear Prince," replied M. de Norpois; "nothing is more in harmony with the Institute than the house you speak of, which is a regular hotbed of Academicians. I shall convey your request to Mme. la Marquise de Villeparisis: she will undoubtedly be flattered. As for her dining with you, she goes out very little, and that will perhaps be more difficult to arrange. But I shall present you to her and you can plead your cause in person. You must on no account give up the Academy; to-morrow fortnight, as it happens, I shall be having luncheon, before going on with him to an important meeting, at Leroy-Beaulieu's, without whom nobody can be elected; I had already allowed myself in conversation with him to let fall your name, with which, naturally, he was perfectly familiar. He raised certain objections. But it so happens that he requires the support of my group at the next election, and I fully intend to return to the charge; I shall tell him quite openly of the wholly cordial ties that unite us, I shall not conceal from him that, if you were to stand, I should ask all my friends to vote for you," (here the Prince breathed a deep sigh of relief) "and he knows that I have friends. I consider that if I were to succeed in obtaining his assistance your chances would become very strong. Come that evening, at six, to Mme. de Ville-parisis's; I will introduce you to her and I can give you an account then of my conversation with him."

Thus it was that Prince von Faffenheim had been led to call upon Mme. de Villeparisis. My profound disillusionment occurred when he spoke. It had never struck me that, if an epoch in history has features both particular and general which are stronger than those of a nationality, so that in a biographical dictionary with illustrations, which go so far as to include an authentic portrait of Minerva, Leibniz with his wig and ruff differs little from Marivaux or Samuel Bernard, a nationality has particular features stronger than those of a caste. In the present instance these were rendered before me not by a discourse in which I had expected, before I saw him, to hear the rustling of the elves and the dance of the kobolds, but by a transposition which certified no less plainly that poetic origin: the fact that, as he bowed, short, red, corpulent, over the hand of Mme. de Villeparisis, the Rheingraf said to her: "Aow to you too, Matame la Marquise," in the accent of an Alsatian porter.

"Won't you let me give you a cup of tea or a little of this cake; it is so good?" Mme. de Guermantes asked me, anxious to have shewn herself as friendly as possible. "I do the honours in this house just as if it was mine," she explained in an ironical tone which gave a slightly guttural sound to her voice, as though she were trying to stifle a hoarse laugh.

"Sir," said Mme. de Villeparisis to M. de Norpois, "you won't forget that you have something to say to the Prince about the Academy?"

Mme. de Guermantes lowered her eyes and gave a semicircular turn to her wrist to look at the time.

"Gracious! I must fly at once if I'm to get to Mme. de Saint-Ferréol's, and I'm dining with Mme. Leroi."

And she rose without bidding me good-bye. She had just caught sight of Mme. Swann, who appeared considerably embarrassed at finding me in the room. She remembered, doubtless, that she had been the first to assure me that she was convinced of Dreyfus's innocence.

"I don't want my mother to introduce me to Mme. Swann," Saint-Loup said to me. "She's an ex-whore. Her husband's a Jew, and she comes here to pose as a Nationalist. Hallo, here's uncle Palamède."

The arrival of Mme. Swann had a special interest for me, due to an incident which had occurred a few days earlier and which I am obliged to record on account of the consequences which it was to have at a much later date, as the reader will learn in due course. Well, a few days before this visit to Mme. de Villeparisis, I had myself received a visitor whom I little expected, namely Charles Morel, the son (though I had never heard of his existence) of my great-uncle's old servant. This great-uncle (he in whose house I had met the lady in pink) had died the year before. His servant had more than once expressed his intention of coming to see me; I had no idea of the object of his visit, but should have been glad to see him for I had learned from Françoise that he had a genuine veneration for my uncle's memory and made a pilgrimage regularly to the cemetery in which he was buried. But, being obliged, for reasons of health, to retire to his home in the country, where he expected to remain for some time, he delegated the duty to his son. I was surprised to see come into my room a handsome young fellow of eighteen, dressed with expensive rather than good taste, but looking, all the same, like anything in the world except the son of a gentleman's servant. He made a point, moreover, at the start of our conversation, of severing all connexion with the domestic class from which he sprang, by informing me, with a smile of satisfaction, that he had won the first prize at the Conservatoire. The object of his visit to me was as follows: his father, when going through the effects of my uncle Adolphe, had set aside some which, he felt, could not very well be sent to my parents but were at the same time of a nature likely to interest a young man of my age. These were the photographs of the famous actresses, the notorious courtesans whom my uncle had known, the last fading pictures of that gay life of a man about town which he divided by a watertight compartment from his family life. While young Morel was shewing them to me, I noticed that he addressed me as though he were speaking to an equal. He derived from saying " you " to me as often, and " sir " as seldom as possible the pleasure natural in one whose father had never ventured, when addressing my parents, upon anything but the third person. Almost all these photographs bore an inscription such as: " To my best friend." One actress, less grateful and more circumspect than the rest, had written: " To the best of friends," which enabled her (so I was assured) to say afterwards that my uncle was in no sense and had never been her best friend but was merely the friend who had done the most little services for her, the friend she made use of, a good, kind man, in other words an old fool. In vain might young Morel seek to divest himself of his lowly origin, one felt that the shade of my uncle Adolphe, venerable and gigantic in the eyes of the old servant, had never ceased to hover, almost a holy vision, over the childhood and boyhood of the son. While I was turning over the photographs Charles Morel examined my room. And as I was looking for some place in which I might keep them, "How is it," he asked me (in a tone in which the reproach had no need to find expression, so implicit was it in the words themselves), "that I don't see a single photograph of your uncle in your room?" I felt the blood rise to my cheeks and stammered: "Why, I don't believe I have such a thing." "What, you haven't one photograph of your uncle Adolphe, who was so devoted to you! I will send you one of my governor's—he has quantities of them— and I hope you will set it up in the place of honour above that chest of drawers, which came to you from your uncle." It is true that, as I had not even a photograph of my father or mother in my room, there was nothing so very shocking in there not being one of my uncle Adolphe. But it was easy enough to see that for old Morel, who had trained his son in the same way of thinking, my uncle was the important person in the family, my parents only reflecting a diminished light from his. I was in higher favour, because my uncle used constantly to say that I was going to turn out a sort of Racine, or Vaulabelle, and Morel regarded me almost as an adopted son, as a child by election of my uncle. I soon discovered that this young man was extremely "pushing". Thus at this first meeting he asked me, being something of a composer as well and capable of setting short poems to music, whether I knew any poet who had a good position in society. I mentioned one. He did not know the work of this poet and had never heard his name, of which he made a note. Well, I found out that shortly afterwards he wrote to the poet telling him that, a fanatical admirer of his work, he, Morel, had composed a musical setting for one of his sonnets and would be grateful if the author would arrange for its performance at the Comtesse so-and-so's. This was going a little too fast, and exposing his hand. The poet, taking offence, made no reply.

For the rest, Charles Morel seemed to have, besides his ambition, a strong leaning towards more concrete realities. He had noticed, as he came through the court-yard, Jupien's niece at work upon a waistcoat, and al-though he explained to me only that he happened to want a fancy waistcoat at that very moment, I felt that the girl had made a vivid impression on him. He had no hesitation about asking me to come downstairs and in-troduce him to her, "but not as a connexion of your family, you follow me, I rely on your discretion not to drag in my father, say just a distinguished artist of your acquaintance, you know how important it is to make a good impression on tradespeople." Albeit he had sug-gested to me that, not knowing him well enough to call him, he quite realised, "dear friend," I might address him, before the girl, in some such terms as "not dear master, of course, . . . although . . . well, if you like, dear distinguished artist," once in the shop, I avoided "qualify-ing" him, as Saint-Simon would have expressed it, and contented myself with reiterating his "you". He picked out from several patterns of velvet one of the brightest red imaginable and so loud that, for all his bad taste, he was never able to wear the waistcoat when it was made. The girl settled down to work again with her two

prentices ", but it struck me that the impression had
n mutual, and that Charles Morel, whom she regarded
of her own " station " (only smarter and richer), had
oved singularly attractive to her. As I had been greatly
rprised to find among the photographs which his father
d sent me one of the portrait of Miss Sacripant (other-
ise Odette) by Elstir, I said to Charles Morel as I went
with him to the outer gate: " I don't suppose you can
tell me, but did my uncle know this lady well? I don't
see at what stage in his life I can fit her in exactly; and
it interests me, because of M. Swann . . ." " Why, if I
wasn't forgetting to tell you that my father asked me
specially to draw your attention to that lady's picture.
As a matter of fact, she was ' lunching ' with your uncle
the last time you ever saw him. My father was in two
minds whether to let you in. It seems you made a great
impression on the wench, and she hoped to see more of
you. But just at that time there was some trouble in the
family, by what my father tells me, and you never set
eyes on your uncle again." He broke off with a smile of
farewell, across the courtyard, at Jupien's niece. She was
watching him and admiring, no doubt, his thin face and
regular features, his fair hair and sparkling eyes. I, as
I gave him my hand, was thinking of Mme. Swann and
saying to myself with amazement, so far apart, so different were they in my memory, that I should have
henceforth to identify her with the " Lady in pink."

M. de Charlus was not long in taking his place by the
side of Mme. Swann. At every social gathering at which
he appeared and, contemptuous towards the men, courted
by the women, promptly attached himself to the smartest
of the latter, whose garments he seemed almost to put

on as an ornament to his own, the Baron's frock coat
or swallowtails made one think of a portrait by some
great painter of a man dressed in black but having by
his side, thrown over a chair, the brilliantly coloured cloak
which he is about to wear at some costume ball. This
partnership, generally with some royal lady, secured for
M. de Charlus various privileges which he liked to enjoy.
For instance, one result of it was that his hostesses, at
theatricals or concerts, allowed the Baron alone to have
a front seat, in a row of ladies, while the rest of the men
were crowded together at the back of the room. And then
besides, completely absorbed, it seemed, in repeating, at
the top of his voice, amusing stories to the enraptured
lady, M. de Charlus was dispensed from the necessity of
going to shake hands with any of the others, was set free,
in other words, from all social duties. Behind the scented
barrier in which the beauty of his choice enclosed him,
he was isolated amid a crowded drawing-room, as, in a
crowded theatre or concert-hall, behind the rampart of
a box; and when anyone came up to greet him, through,
so to speak, the beauty of his companion, it was permis-
sible for him to reply quite curtly and without interrupting his business of conversation with a lady. Certainly
Mme. Swann was scarcely of the rank of the people with
whom he liked thus to flaunt himself. But he professed
admiration for her, friendship for Swann, he knew that
she would be flattered by his attentions and was himself
flattered at being compromised by the prettiest woman
in the room.

Mme. de Villeparisis meanwhile was not too well pleased
to receive a visit from M. de Charlus. He, while admitting
serious defects in his aunt's character, was genuinely fond

ɔf her. But every now and then, carried away by anger, by an imaginary grievance, he would sit down and write to her, without making any attempt to resist his impulse, letters full of the most violent abuse, in which he made the most of trifling incidents which until then he seemed never even to have noticed. Among other examples I may instance the following, which my stay at Balbec brought tɔ my knowledge: Mme. de Villeparisis, fearing that she had not brought enough money with her to Balbec to enable her to prolong her holiday there, and not caring, since she was of a thrifty disposition and shrank from unnecessary expenditure, to have money sent to her from Paris, had borrowed three thousand francs from M. de Charlus. A month later, annoyed, for some trivial reason, with his aunt, he asked her to repay him this sum by telegraph. He received two thousand nine hundred and ninety-odd francs. Meeting his aunt a few days later in Paris, in the course of a friendly conversation, he drew her attention, with the utmost politeness, to the mistake that her banker had made when sending the money. " But there was no mistake," replied Mme. de Villeparisis, " the money order cost six francs seventy-five." " Oh, of course, if it was intentional, it is all right," said M. de Charlus, " I mentioned it only in case you didn't know, because in that case, if the bank had done the same thing with anyone who didn't know you as well as I do, it might have led to unpleasantness." " No, no, there was no mistake." " After all, you were quite right," M. de Charlus concluded easily, stooping to kiss his aunt's hand. And in fact he bore no resentment and was only amused at this little instance of her thrift. But some time afterwards, imagining that, in a family matter, his aunt had been trying to get the better of him and had "worked up a regular conspiracy" against him, as she took shelter, foolishly enough, behind the lawyers with whom he suspected her of having plotted to undo him, he had written her a letter boiling over with insolence and rage. "I shall not be satisfied with having my revenge," he added as a postscript; "I shall take care to make you a laughing-stock. To-morrow I shall tell everyone the story of the money order and the six francs seventy-five you kept back from me out of the three thousand I lent you; I shall disgrace you publicly." Instead of so doing, he had gone to his aunt the next day to beg her pardon, having already regretted a letter in which he had used some really terrible language. But apart from this, to whom could he have told the story of the money order? Seeking no longer vengeance but a sincere reconciliation, now was the time for him to keep silence. But already he had repeated the story everywhere, while still on the best of terms with his aunt; he had told it without any malice, as a joke, and because he was the soul of indiscretion. He had repeated the story, but without Mme. de Villeparisis's knowledge. With the result that, having learned from his letter that he intended to disgrace her by making public a transaction in which he had told her with his own lips that she had acted rightly, she concluded that he had been deceiving her from the first, and had lied when he pretended to be fond of her. This storm had now died down, but neither of them knew what opinion exactly the other had of her or him. This sort of intermittent quarrel is of course somewhat exceptional. Of a different order were the quarrels of Bloch and his friends. Of a different order again were those of M. de Charlus, as we shall presently see, with people wholly unlike Mme. de Villeparisis. In spite of which we must bear in mind that the opinions which we hold of one another, our relations with friends and kinsfolk are in no sense permanent, save in appearance, but are as eternally fluid as the sea itself. Whence all the rumours of divorce between couples who have always seemed so perfectly united and will soon afterwards speak of one another with affection, hence all the terrible things said by one friend of another from whom we supposed him to be inseparable and with whom we shall find him once more reconciled before we have had time to recover from our surprise; all the ruptures of alliances, after so short a time, between nations.

" I say, my uncle and Mme. Swann are getting warm over there!" remarked Saint-Loup. " And look at Mamma in the innocence of her heart going across to disturb them. To the pure all things are pure, I suppose!"

I studied M. de Charlus. The tuft of his grey hair, his eye, the brow of which was raised by his monocle to emit a smile, the red flowers in his buttonhole formed, so to speak, the three mobile apices of a convulsive and striking triangle. I had not ventured to bow to him, for he had given me no sign of recognition. And yet, albeit he had not turned his head in my direction, I was convinced that he had seen me; while he repeated some story to Mme. Swann, whose sumptuous, pansy-coloured cloak floated actually over the Baron's knee, his roving eye, like that of a street hawker who is watching all the time for the " tecs " to appear, had certainly explored every corner of the room and taken note of all the people who were in it. M. de Châtellerault came up to bid him good day without any indication on M. de Charlus's face that he had seen the young Duke until he was actually standing in front of him. In this way, in fairly numerous gatherings such as this, M. de Charlus kept almost continuously on show a smile without any definite direction or particular object, which, pre-existing before the greetings of new arrivals, found itself, when these entered its zone, devoid of any indication of friendliness towards them. Nevertheless, it was obviously my duty to go across and speak to Mme. Swann. But as she was not certain whether I already knew Mme. de Marsantes and M. de Charlus, she was distinctly cold, fearing no doubt that I might ask her to introduce me to them. I then made my way to M. de Charlus, and at once regretted it, for though he could not have helped seeing me he shewed no sign whatsoever. As I stood before him and bowed I found standing out from his body, which it prevented me from approaching by the full length of his outstretched arm, a finger widowed, one would have said, of an episcopal ring, of which he appeared to be offering, for the kiss of the faithful, the consecrated site, and I was made to appear to have penetrated, without leave from the Baron and by an act of trespass for which he would hold me permanently responsible, the anonymous and vacant dispersion of his smile. This coldness was hardly of a kind to encourage Mme. Swann to melt from hers.

" How tired and worried you look," said Mme. de Marsantes to her son who had come up to greet M. de Charlus.

And indeed the expression in Robert's eyes seemed every minute to reach a depth from which it rose at once like a diver who has touched bottom. This bottom which hurt Robert so when he touched it that he left it at once, to return to it a moment later, was the thought that he had quarrelled with his mistress.

"Never mind," his mother went on, stroking his cheek, "never mind; it's good to see my little boy again."

But this show of affection seeming to irritate Robert, Mme. de Marsantes led her son away to the other end of the room where in an alcove hung with yellow silk a group of Beauvais armchairs massed their violet-hued tapestries like purple irises in a field of buttercups. Mme. Swann, finding herself alone and having realised that I was a friend of Saint-Loup, beckoned to me to come and sit beside her. Not having seen her for so long I did not know what to talk to her about. I was keeping an eye on my hat, among the crowd of hats that littered the carpet, and I asked myself with a vague curiosity to whom one of them could belong which was not that of the Duc de Guermantes and yet in the lining of which a capital 'G' was surmounted by a ducal coronet. I knew who everyone in the room was, and could not think of anyone whose hat this could possibly be.

"What a pleasant man M. de Norpois is," I said to Mme. Swann, looking at the Ambassador. "It is true, Robert de Saint-Loup says he's a pest, but . . ."

"He is quite right," she replied.

Seeing from her face that she was thinking of something which she was keeping from me, I plied her with questions. For the satisfaction of appearing to be greatly taken up by some one in this room where she knew hardly anyone, she took me into a corner.

"I am sure this is what M. de Saint-Loup meant," she began, "but you must never tell him I said so, for he would think me indiscreet, and I value his esteem

very highly; I am an 'honest Injun,' don't you know.
The other day, Charlus was dining at the Princesse de
Guermantes's; I don't know how it was, but your name
was mentioned. M. de Norpois seems to have told them—
it's all too silly for words, don't go and worry yourself to
death over it, nobody paid any attention, they all knew
only too well the mischievous tongue that said it—that
you were a hypocritical little flatterer."

I have recorded a long way back my stupefaction at
the discovery that a friend of my father, such as M. de
Norpois was, could have expressed himself thus in speaking of me. I was even more astonished to learn that my
emotion on that evening long ago when I had asked him
about Mme. Swann and Gilberte was known to the Princesse de Guermantes, whom I imagined never to have
heard of my existence. Each of our actions, our words,
our attitudes is cut off from the " world ", from the people
who have not directly perceived it, by a medium the per-
meability of which is of infinite variation and remains
unknown to ourself; having learned by experience that
some important utterance which we eagerly hoped would
be disseminated (such as those so enthusiastic speeches
which I used at one time to make to all comers and on
every occasion on the subject of Mme. Swann) has found
itself, often simply on account of our anxiety, immediately hidden under a bushel, how immeasurably less do
we suppose that some tiny word, which we ourself have
forgotten, or else a word never uttered by us but formed
on its course by the imperfect refraction of a different
word, can be transported without ever halting for any
obstacle to infinite distances—in the present instance to
the Princesse de Guermantes—and succeed in diverting

at our expense the banquet of the gods. What we actually recall of our conduct remains unknown to our nearest neighbour; what we have forgotten that we ever said, or indeed what we never did say flies to provoke hilarity even in another planet, and the image that other people form of our actions and behaviour is no more like that which we form of them ourself, than is like an original drawing a spoiled copy in which, at one point, for a black line, we find an empty gap, and for a blank space an unaccountable contour. It may be, all the same, that what has not been transcribed is some non-existent feature which we behold merely in our purblind self-esteem, and that what seems to us added is indeed a part of ourself, but so essential a part as to have escaped our notice. So that this strange print which seems to us to have so little resemblance to ourself bears sometimes the same stamp of truth, scarcely flattering, indeed, but profound and useful, as a photograph taken by X-rays. Not that that is any reason why we should recognise ourself in it. A man who is in the habit of smiling in the glass at his handsome face and stalwart figure, if you shew him their radiograph, will have, face to face with that rosary of bones, labelled as being the image of himself, the same suspicion of error as the visitor to an art gallery who, on coming to the portrait of a girl, reads in his catalogue: "Dromedary resting." Later on, this discrepancy between our portraits, according as it was our own hand that drew them or another, I was to register in the case of others than myself, living placidly in the midst of a collection of photographs which they themselves had taken while round about them grinned frightful faces, invisible to them as a rule, but plunging them in stupor

if an accident were to reveal them with the warning:
" This is you."

A few years earlier I should have been only too glad
to tell Mme. Swann in what connexion I had fawned
upon M. de Norpois, since the connexion had been my
desire to know her. But I no longer felt this desire, I
was no longer in love with Gilberte. On the other hand
I had not succeeded in identifying Mme. Swann with the
lady in pink of my childhood. Accordingly I spoke of the
woman who was on my mind at the moment.

" Did you see the Duchesse de Guermantes just now? "
I asked Mme. Swann.

But since the Duchess did not bow to Mme. Swann
when they met, the latter chose to appear to regard
her as a person of no importance, whose presence in a
room one did not even remark.

" I don't know; I didn't *realise* her," she replied sourly,
using an expression borrowed from England.

I was anxious nevertheless for information with regard
not only to Mme. de Guermantes but to all the people
who came in contact with her, and (for all the world like
Bloch), with the tactlessness of people who seek in their
conversation not to give pleasure to others but to elucidate,
from sheer egoism, facts that are interesting to themselves,
in my effort to form an exact idea of the life of Mme. de
Guermantes I questioned Mme. de Villeparisis about
Mme. Leroi.

" Oh, yes, I know who' you mean," she replied with an
affectation of contempt, " the daughter of those rich tim-
ber people. I've heard that she's begun to go about quite
a lot lately, but I must explain to you that I am rather
old now to make new acquaintances. I have known such

interesting, such delightful people in my time that really
I do not believe Mme. Leroi would be any addition to
what I already have." Mme. de Marsantes, who was playing lady in waiting to the Marquise, presented me to
the Prince, and, while she was still doing so, M. de Norpois also presented me in the most glowing terms. Perhaps
he found it convenient to do me a courtesy which could
in no way damage his credit since I had just been presented, perhaps it was because he thought that a foreigner,
even so distinguished a foreigner, was unfamiliar with
French society and might think that he was having introduced to him a young man of fashion, perhaps to
exercise one of his prerogatives, that of adding the weight
of his personal recommendation as an Ambassador, or
in his taste for the archaic to revive in the Prince's honour
the old custom, flattering to his rank, that two sponsors
were necessary if one wished to be presented.

Mme. de Villeparisis appealed to M. de Norpois, feeling it imperative that I should have his assurance that
she had nothing to regret in not knowing Mme. Leroi.

"Am I not right, M. l'Ambassadeur, Mme. Leroi is
quite uninteresting, isn't she, quite out of keeping with
the people who come here; I was quite right not to make
friends with her, wasn't I?"

Whether from independence or because he was tired,
M. de Norpois replied merely in a bow full of respect
but devoid of meaning.

"Sir," went on Mme. de Villeparisis with a laugh,
"there are some absurd people in the world. Would you
believe that I had a visit this afternoon from a gentleman
who tried to persuade me that he found more pleasure in
kissing my hand than a young woman's?"

I guessed at once that this was Legrandin. M. de Norpois smiled with a slight quiver of the eyelid, as though such a remark had been prompted by a concupiscence so natural that one could not find fault with the person who had uttered it, almost as though it were the beginning of a romance which he was prepared to forgive, if not to encourage, with the perverse indulgence of a Voisenon or the younger Crébillon.

"Many young women's hands would be incapable of doing what I see there," said the Prince, pointing to Mme. de Villeparisis's unfinished water-colours. And he asked her whether she had seen the flower paintings by Fantin-Latour which had recently been exhibited.

"They are of the first order, and indicate, as people say nowadays, a fine painter, one of the masters of the palette," declared M. de Norpois; "I consider, all the same, that they stand no comparison with these, in which I find it easier to recognise the colouring of the flower."

Even supposing that the partiality of an old lover, the habit of flattering people, the critical standard admissible in a small circle had dictated this speech to the ex-Ambassador, it proved upon what an absolute vacuum of true taste the judgment of people in society is based, so arbitrary that the smallest trifle can make it rush to the wildest absurdities, on the way to which it is stopped, held up by no genuinely felt impression.

"I claim no credit for knowing about flowers, I've lived all my life among the fields," replied Mme. de Villeparisis modestly. "But," she added graciously, turning to the Prince, "If I did, when I was quite a girl, form a rather more serious idea of them than children generally do in the country, I owe that to a distinguished fellow-country-man of yours, Herr von Schlegel. I met him at Broglie, when I was staying there once with my aunt Cordelia (Marshal de Castellane's wife, don't you know?). I remember so well M. Lebrun, M. de Salvandy, M. Doudan, getting him to talk about flowers. I was only a little girl, I wasn't able to follow all he said. But he liked playing with me, and when he went back to your country he sent me a beautiful botany book to remind me of a drive we took together in a phaeton to the Val Richer, when I fell asleep on his knee. I have got the book still, and it taught me to observe many things about flowers which I should not have noticed otherwise. When Mme. de Barante published some of Mme. de Broglie's letters, charming and affected like herself, I hoped to find among them some record of those conversations with Herr von Schlegel. But she was a woman who looked for nothing from nature but arguments in support of religion."

Robert called me away to the far end of the room where he and his mother were.

"You have been good to me," I said, "how can I thank you? Can we dine together to-morrow?"

"To-morrow? Yes, if you like, but it will have to be with Bloch. I met him just now on the doorstep; he was rather stiff with me at first because I had quite forgotten to answer his last two letters. (At least, he didn't tell me that that was what had annoyed him, but I guessed it.) But after that he was so friendly to me that I simply can't disappoint him. Between ourselves, on his side at least, I can feel it's a life and death friendship." Nor do I consider that Robert was altogether mistaken. Furious detraction was often, with Bloch, the effect of a keen affection which he had supposed to be unreturned. And

as he had little power of imagining the lives of other
people, and never dreamed that one might have been ill,
or away from home, or otherwise occupied, a week's
silence was at once interpreted by him as meaning a
deliberate coldness. And so I have never believed that
his most violent outbursts as a friend, or in later years
as a writer, went very deep. They rose to a paroxysm if
one replied to them with an icy dignity, or by a platitude
which encouraged him to redouble his onslaught, but
yielded often to a warmly sympathetic attitude. "As for
being good," went on Saint-Loup, "you say I have been
to you, but I haven't been good at all, my aunt tells me
that it's you who avoid her, that you never utter a word
to her. She wonders whether you have anything against
her."

Fortunately for myself, if I had been taken in by this
speech, our departure, which I believed to be imminent,
for Balbec would have prevented my making any attempt
to see Mme. de Guermantes again, to assure her that I had
nothing against her, and so to put her under the necessity
of proving that it was she who had something against me.
But I had only to remind myself that she had not even
offered to let me see her Elstirs. Besides, this was not
a disappointment; I had never expected her to begin
talking to me about them; I knew that I did not appeal
to her, that I need have no hope of ever making her
like me; the most that I had been able to look forward
to was that, thanks to her kindness, I might there and
then receive, since I should not be seeing her again before
I left Paris, an entirely pleasing impression, which I could
take with me to Balbec indefinitely prolonged, intact,
instead of a memory broken by anxiety and sorrow.

Mme. de Marsantes kept on interrupting her conversation with Robert to tell me how often he had spoken to her about me, how fond he was of me; she treated me with a deference which almost hurt me because I felt it to be prompted by her fear of being embroiled, on my account, with this son whom she had not seen all day, with whom she was eager to be alone, and over whom she must accordingly have supposed that the influence which she wielded was not equal to and must conciliate mine. Having heard me, earlier in the afternoon, make some reference to Bloch's uncle, M. Nissim Bernard, Mme. de Marsantes inquired whether it was he who had at one time lived at Nice.

"In that case, he knew M. de Marsantes there before our marriage," she told me. "My husband used often to speak of him as an excellent man, with such a delicate, generous nature."

"To think that for once in his life he wasn't lying! It's incredible," would have been Bloch's comment.

All this time I should have liked to explain to Mme. de Marsantes that Robert felt infinitely more affection for her than for myself, and that had she shewn any hostility towards me it was not in my nature to attempt to set him against her, to detach him from her. But now that Mme. de Guermantes had left the room, I had more leisure to observe Robert, and I noticed then for the first time that, once again, a sort of flood of anger seemed to be coursing through him, rising to the surface of his stern and sombre features. I was afraid lest, remembering the scene in the theatre that afternoon, he might be feeling humiliated in my presence at having allowed himself to be treated so harshly by his mistress without making any rejoinder.

Suddenly he broke away from his mother, who had put her arm round his neck, and, coming towards me, led me behind the little flower-strewn counter at which Mme. de Villeparisis had resumed her seat, making a sign to me to follow him into the smaller room. I was hurrying after him when M. de Charlus, who must have supposed that I was leaving the house, turned abruptly from Prince von Faffenheim, to whom he had been talking, and made a rapid circuit which brought him face to face with me. I saw with alarm that he had taken the hat in the lining of which were a capital 'G' and a ducal coronet. In the doorway into the little room he said, without looking at me:

"As I see that you have taken to going into society, you must do me the pleasure of coming to see me. But it's a little complicated," he went on with a distracted, calculating air, as if the pleasure had been one that he was afraid of not securing again once he had let slip the opportunity of arranging with me the means by which it might be realised. "I am very seldom at home; you will have to write to me. But I should prefer to explain things to you more quietly. I am just going. Will you walk a short way with me? I shall only keep you a moment."

"You'ld better take care, sir," I warned him; "you have picked up the wrong hat by mistake."

"Do you want to stop me taking my own hat?" I assumed, a similar mishap having recently occurred to myself, that someone else having taken his hat he had seized upon one at random, so as not to go home bare-headed, and that I had placed him in a difficulty by exposing his strategem. I told him that I must say a few words to

Saint-Loup. "He is still talking to that idiot the Duc de Guermantes," I added. "That really is charming; I shall tell my brother." "Oh! you think that would interest M. de Charlus?" (I imagined that, if he had a brother, that brother must be called Charlus also. Saint-Loup had indeed explained his family tree to me at Balbec, but I had forgotten the details.) "Who has been talking to you about M. de Charlus?" replied the Baron in an arrogant tone. "Go to Robert.

"I hear," he went on, "that you took part this morning in one of those orgies that he has with a woman who is disgracing him. You would do well to use your influence with him to make him realise the pain he is causing his poor mother, and all of us, by dragging our name in the dirt."

I should have liked to reply that at this degrading luncheon the conversation had been entirely about Emerson, Ibsen and Tolstoy, and that the young woman had lectured Robert to make him drink nothing but water. In the hope of bringing some balm to Robert, whose pride had, I felt, been wounded, I sought to find an excuse for his mistress. I did not know that at that moment, in spite of his anger with her, it was on himself that he was heaping reproaches. But it always happens, even in quarrels between a good man and a worthless woman, and when the right is all on one side, that some trifle crops up which enables the woman to appear not to have been in the wrong on one point. And as she ignores all the other points, the moment the man begins to feel the need of her company, or is demoralised by separation from her, his weakness will make his conscience more exacting, he will remember the absurd reproaches that have been flung at him and will ask himself whether they have not some foundation in fact.

"I've come to the conclusion I was wrong about that matter of the necklace," Robert said to me. "Of course, I never meant for a moment to do anything wrong, but, I know very well, other people don't look at things in the same way as oneself. She had a very hard time when she was young. In her eyes, I was bound to appear just the rich man who thinks he can get anything he wants with his money, and with whom a poor person cannot compete, whether in trying to influence Boucheron or in a lawsuit. Of course she has been horribly cruel to me, when I have never thought of anything but her good. But I do see clearly, she believes that I wanted to make her feel that one could keep a hold on her with money, and that's not true. And she's so fond of me; what must she be thinking of me? Poor darling, if you only knew, she has such charming ways, I simply can't tell you, she has often done the most adorable things for me. How wretched she must be feeling now! In any case, whatever happens in the long run, I don't want to let her think me a cad; I shall dash off to Boucheron's and get the necklace. You never know; very likely when she sees me with it, she will admit that she's been in the wrong. Don't you see, it's the idea that she is suffering at this moment that I can't bear. What one suffers oneself one knows; that's nothing. But with her—to say to oneself that she's suffering and not to be able to form any idea of what she feels—I think I shall go mad in a minute—I'ld much rather never see her again than let her suffer. She can be happy without me, if she must; that's all I ask. Listen; you know, to me everything that concerns her is enormously important, it becomes something cosmic; I shall run to the jeweller's and then go and ask her to forgive me. But until I get down there what will she be thinking of me? If she could only know that I was on my way! What about your going down there and telling her? For all we know, that might settle the whole business. Perhaps," he went on with a smile, as though he hardly ventured to believe in so idyllic a possibility, "we can all three dine together in the country. But we can't tell yet. I never know how to handle her. Poor child, I shall perhaps only hurt her more than ever. Besides, her decision may be irrevocable."

Robert swept me back to his mother.

"Good-bye," he said to her. "I've got to go now. I don't know when I shall get leave again. Probably not for a month. I shall write as soon as I know myself."

Certainly Robert was not in the least of the type of son who, when he goes out with his mother, feels that an attitude of exasperation towards her ought to balance the smiles and bows which he bestows on strangers. Nothing is more common than this odious form of vengeance on the part of those who appear to believe that rudeness to one's own family is the natural complement to one's ceremonial behaviour. Whatever the wretched mother may say, her son, as though he had been taken to the house against his will and wished to make her pay dearly for his presence, refutes immediately, with an ironical, precise, cruel contradiction, the timidly ventured assertion; the mother at once conforms, though without thereby disarming him, to the opinion of this superior being of whom she will continue to boast to everyone, when he is not present, as having a charming nature, and who all the same spares her none of his keenest thrusts. Saint-Loup was not at all like this; but the anguish which Rachel's absence provoked in him brought it about that, for different reasons, he was no less harsh with his mother than the sons I have been describing are with theirs. And as she listened to him I saw the same throb, like that of a mighty wing, which Mme. de Marsantes had been unable to repress when her son first entered the room, convulse her whole body once again; but this time it was an anxious face, eyes wide with grief that she fastened on him.

"What, Robert, you're going away? Seriously? My little son! The one day I've seen anything of you!"

And then quite softly, in the most natural tone, in a voice from which she strove to banish all sadness so as not to inspire her son with a pity which would perhaps have been painful to him, or else useless and might serve only to irritate him, like an argument prompted by plain common sense she added:

"You know, it's not at all nice of you."

But to this simplicity she added so much timidity, to shew him that she was not trespassing on his freedom, so much affection, so that he should not reproach her with spoiling his pleasures, that Saint-Loup could not fail to observe in himself as it were the possibility of a similar wave of affection, that was to say an obstacle to his spending the evening with his lady. And so he grew angry:

"It's unfortunate, but, nice or not, that's how it is."

And he heaped on his mother the reproaches which no doubt he felt that he himself perhaps deserved; thus it is that egoists have always the last word; having laid down at the start that their determination is unshakeable, the more the sentiment in them to which one appeals to make them abandon it is touched, the more fault they find, not with themselves who resist the appeal but with those persons who put them under the necessity of resisting it, with the result that their own firmness may be carried to the utmost degree of cruelty, which only aggravates all the more in their eyes the culpability of the person who is so indelicate as to be hurt, to be in the right, and to cause them thus treacherously the pain of acting against their natural instinct of pity. But of her own accord Mme. de Marsantes ceased to insist, for she felt that she would not be able to keep him.

" I shall leave you here," he said to me, " but you're not to keep him long, Mamma, because he's got to go somewhere else in a minute."

I was fully aware that my company could not afford any pleasure to Mme. de Marsantes, but I preferred, by not going with Robert, not to let her suppose that I was involved in these pleasures which deprived her of him. I should have liked to find some excuse for her son's conduct, less from affection for him than from pity for her. But it was she who spoke first:

" Poor boy," she began, " I am sure I must have hurt him dreadfully. You see, Sir, mothers are such selfish creatures, after all he hasn't many pleasures, he comes so little to Paris. Oh, dear, if he hadn't gone already I should have liked to stop him, not to keep him of course, but just to tell him that I'm not vexed with him, that I think he was quite right. Will you excuse me if I go and look over the staircase? "

I accompanied her there.

"Robert! Robert!" she called. "No; he's gone; we are too late."

At that moment I would as gladly have undertaken a mission to make Robert break with his mistress as, a few hours earlier, to make him go and live with her altogether. In one case Saint-Loup would have regarded me as a false friend, in the other his family would have called me his evil genius. Yet I was the same man, at an interval of a few hours.

We returned to the drawing-room. Seeing that Saint-Loup was not with us, Mme. de Villeparisis exchanged with M. de Norpois that dubious, derisive and not too pitying glance with which people point out to one another an over-jealous wife or an over-loving mother (spectacles which to outsiders are amusing), as much as to say: "There now, there's been trouble."

Robert went to his mistress, taking with him the splendid ornament which, after what had been said on both sides, he ought not to have given her. But it came to the same thing, for she would not look at it, and even after their reconciliation he could never persuade her to accept it. Certain of Robert's friends thought that these proofs of disinterestedness which she furnished were deliberately planned to draw him closer to her. And yet she was not greedy about money, except perhaps to be able to spend it without thought. I have seen her bestow recklessly on people whom she believed to be in need the most insensate charity. "At this moment," Robert's friends would say to him, seeking to balance by their malicious words a disinterested action on Rachel's part, "at this moment she will be in the promenade at the Folies-Bergères. She's an enigma, that girl is, a regular sphinx."

After all, how many women who are not disinterested, since they are kept by men, have we not seen, with a delicacy that flowers from their sordid existence, set with their own hands a thousand little limits to the generosity of their lovers?

Robert knew of scarcely any of the infidelities of his mistress, and tortured his mind over what were mere nothings compared with the real life of Rachel, a life which began every day only after he had left her. He knew of scarcely any of these infidelities. One could have told him of them without shaking his confidence in Rachel. For it is a charming law of nature which manifests itself in the heart of the most complex social organisms, that we live in perfect ignorance of those we love. On one side of the mirror the lover says to himself: "She is an angel, she will never yield herself to me, I may as well die—and yet she does care for me; she cares so much that perhaps—but no, it can never possibly happen." And in the exaltation of his desire, in the anguish of waiting, what jewels he flings at the feet of this woman, how he runs to borrow money to save her from inconvenience; meanwhile, on the other side of the screen, through which their conversation will no more carry than that which visitors exchange outside the glass wall of an aquarium, the public are saying: "You don't know her? I congratulate you, she has robbed, in fact ruined I don't know how many men. There isn't a worse girl in Paris. She's a common swindler. And cunning isn't the word!" And perhaps the public are not entirely wrong in their use of the last epithet, for indeed the sceptical man who is not really in love with the woman and whom she merely attracts says to his friends: "No, no, my dear fellow,

she is not in the least a prostitute ; I don't say she hasn'
had an adventure or two in her time, but she's not a
woman one pays, she'd be a damned sight too expensive
if she was. With her it's fifty thousand francs or nothing."
Well, he has spent fifty thousand francs on her, he has
had her once, but she (finding, moreover, a willing accomplice in the man himself) has managed to persuade
him that he is one of those who have had her for nothing.
Such is society, in which every one of us has two aspects,
in which the most obvious, the most notorious faults will
never be known by a certain other person save embedded
in, under the protection of a shell, a smooth cocoon, a delicious curiosity of nature. There were in Paris two thoroughly respectable men to whom Saint-Loup no longer
bowed, and could not refer without a tremor in his voice,
calling them exploiters of women: this was because they
had both been ruined by Rachel.

" I blame myself for one thing only," Mme. de Marsantes murmured in my ear, " and that was my telling him
that he wasn't nice to me. He, such an adorable, unique
son, there's no one else like him in the world, the only
time I see him, to have told him he wasn't nice to me, I
would far rather he'd beaten me, because I am sure that
whatever pleasure he may be having this evening, and
he hasn't many, will be spoiled for him by that unfair
word. But, Sir, I mustn't keep you, since you're in a
hurry."

Anxiously, Mme. de Marsantes bade me good-bye.
These sentiments bore upon Robert; she was sincere. But
she ceased to be, to become a great lady once more.

" I have been so *interested,* so *glad* to have this little
talk with you. Thank you! Thank you! "

And with a humble air she fastened on me a look of gratitude, of exhilaration, as though my conversation were one of the keenest pleasures that she had experienced in her life. These charming glances went very well with the black flowers on her white skirt; they were those of a great lady who knew her business.

"But I am in no hurry," I replied; "besides, I must wait for M. de Charlus; I am going with him."

Mme. de Villeparisis overheard these last words. They appeared to vex her. Had the matter in question not been one which could not possibly give rise to such a sentiment, it might have struck me that what seemed to be at that moment alarmed in Mme. de Villeparisis was her modesty. But this hypothesis never even entered my mind. I was delighted with Mme. de Guermantes, with Saint-Loup, with Mme. de Marsantes, with M. de Charlus, with Mme. de Villeparisis; I did not stop to reflect, and I spoke light-heartedly and at random.

"You're going from here with my nephew Palamède?" she asked me.

Thinking that it might produce a highly favourable impression on Mme. de Villeparisis if she learned that I was on intimate terms with a nephew whom she esteemed so greatly, "He has asked me to go home with him," I answered blithely. "I am so glad. Besides, we are greater friends than you think, and I've quite made up my mind that we're going to be better friends still."

From being vexed, Mme. de Villeparisis seemed to have grown anxious. "Don't wait for him," she said to me, with a preoccupied air. "He is talking to M. de Faffenheim. He's certain to have forgotten what he said to you. You'd much better go, now, quickly, while his back is turned."

The first emotion shewn by Mme. de Villeparisis w
have suggested, but for the circumstances, offended me
esty. Her insistence, her opposition might well, if one ha
studied her face alone, have appeared to be dictated by
virtue. I was not, myself, in any hurry to join Robert and
his mistress. But Mme. de Villeparisis seemed to make
such a point of my going that, thinking perhaps that she
had some important business to discuss with her nephew,
I bade her good-bye. Next to her M. de Guermantes,
superb and Olympian, was ponderously seated. One would
have said that the notion, omnipresent in all his members,
of his vast riches gave him a particular high density,
as though they had been melted in a crucible into a single
human ingot to form this man whose value was so
immense. At the moment of my saying good-bye to him
he rose politely from his seat, and I could feel the dead
weight of thirty millions which his old-fashioned French
breeding set in motion, raised, until it stood before me. I
seemed to be looking at that statue of Olympian Zeus
which Pheidias is said to have cast in solid gold. Such
was the power that good breeding had over M. de Guermantes, over the body of M. de Guermantes at least, for
it had not an equal mastery over the ducal mind. M. de
Guermantes laughed at his own jokes, but did not unbend
to other people's.

As I went downstairs I heard behind me a voice calling
out to me:

"So this is how you wait for me, is it?"

It was M. de Charlus.

"You don't mind if we go a little way on foot?" he
asked dryly, when we were in the courtyard. "We can
walk until I find a cab that suits me."

ou wished to speak to me about something, Sir?"

Oh yes, as a matter of fact there were some things I shed to say to you, but I am not so sure now whether I shall. As far as you are concerned, I am sure that they might be the starting-point which would lead you to inestimable benefits. But I can see also that they would bring into my existence, at an age when one begins to value tranquillity, a great loss of time, great inconvenience. I ask myself whether you are worth all the pains that I should have to take with you, and I have not the pleasure of knowing you well enough to be able to say. Perhaps also to you yourself what I could do for you does not appear sufficiently attractive for me to give myself so much trouble, for I repeat quite frankly that for me it can only be trouble."

I protested that, in that case, he must not dream of it. This summary end to the discussion did not seem to be to his liking.

"That sort of politeness means nothing," he rebuked me coldly. "There is nothing so pleasant as to give oneself trouble for a person who is worth one's while. For the best of us, the study of the arts, a taste for old things, collections, gardens are all mere ersatz, succedanea, alibis. In the heart of our tub, like Diogenes, we cry out for a man. We cultivate begonias, we trim yews, as a last resort, because yews and begonias submit to treatment. But we should like to give our time to a plant of human growth, if we were sure that he was worth the trouble. That is the whole question: you must know something about yourself. Are you worth my trouble or not?"

"I would not for anything in the world, Sir, be a cause of anxiety to you," I said to him, "but so far as I am con-

cerned you may be sure that everything which c[...]
me from you will be a very great pleasure to me. [...]
deeply touched that you should be so kind as to [...]
notice of me in this way and try to help me."

Greatly to my surprise, it was almost with effusion tha[...]
he thanked me for this speech, slipping his arm through
mine with that intermittent familiarity which had already
struck me at Balbec, and was in such contrast to the coldness of his tone.

"With the want of consideration common at your age,"
he told me, "you are liable to say things at times which
would open an unbridgeable gulf between us. What you
have said just now, on the other hand, is exactly the sort
of thing that touches me, and makes me want to do a
great deal for you."

As he walked arm in arm with me and uttered these
words, which, albeit tinged with contempt, were so affec-
tionate, M. de Charlus now fastened his gaze on me with
that intense fixity which had struck me the first morning,
when I saw him outside the casino at Balbec, and indeed
many years before that, through the pink hawthorns,
standing beside Mme. Swann, whom I supposed then to
be his mistress, in the park at Tansonville; now let it
stray around him and examine the cabs which at this time
of the day were passing in considerable numbers on the
way to their stables, looking so determinedly at them that
several stopped, the drivers supposing that he wished to
engage them. But M. de Charlus immediately dismissed
them.

"They're not what I want," he explained to me, "it's
all a question of the colour of their lamps, and the direction they're going in. I hope, Sir," he went on, "that you

in any way misinterpret the purely disinterested
.aritable nature of the proposal which I am going
.ake to you."

. was struck by the similarity of his diction to Swann's,
.oser now than at Balbec.

"You have enough intelligence, I suppose, not to
imagine that it is from want of society, from any fear of
solitude and boredom that I have recourse to you. I do
not, as a rule, care to talk about myself, but you may
possibly have heard—it was alluded to in a leading article
in *The Times,* which made a considerable impression—
that the Emperor of Austria, who has always honoured
me with his friendship, and is good enough to insist on
keeping up terms of cousinship with me, declared the other
day in an interview which was made public that if the
Comte de Chambord had had by his side a man as thoroughly conversant with the undercurrents of European
politics as myself he would be King of France to-day. I
have often thought, sir, that there was in me, thanks not
to my own humble talents but to circumstances which you
may one day have occasion to learn, a sort of secret record
of incalculable value, of which I have not felt myself at
liberty to make use, personally, but which would be a
priceless acquisition to a young man to whom I would
hand over in a few months what it has taken me more
than thirty years to collect, what I am perhaps alone in
possessing. I do not speak of the intellectual enjoyment
which you would find in learning certain secrets which a
Michelet of our day would give years of his life to know,
and in the light of which certain events would assume for
him an entirely different aspect. And I do not speak
only of events that have already occurred, but of the chain

of circumstances." (This was a favourite express[...]
M. de Charlus, and often, when he used it, he join[...]
hands as if in prayer, but with his fingers stiffene[...]
though to illustrate by their complexity the said circu[...]
stances, which he did not specify, and the chain tha[...]
linked them.) "I could give you an explanation that no
one has dreamed of, not only of the past but of the
future." M. de Charlus broke off to question me about
Bloch, whom he had heard discussed, though without appearing to be listening, in his aunt's drawing-room. And
with that ironical accent he so skilfully detached what he
was saying that he seemed to be thinking of something
else altogether, and to be speaking mechanically, simply
out of politeness. He asked if my friend was young, good
looking and so forth. Bloch, if he had heard him, would
have been more puzzled even than with M. de Norpois,
but for very different reasons, to know whether M. de
Charlus was for or against Dreyfus. " It is not a bad idea,
if you wish to learn about life," went on M. de Charlus
when he had finished questioning me, " to include among
your friends an occasional foreigner." I replied that Bloch
was French. " Indeed," said M. de Charlus, " I took him
to be a Jew." His assertion of this incompatibility made
me suppose that M. de Charlus was more anti-Dreyfusard
than anyone I had met. He protested, however, against
the charge of treason levelled against Dreyfus. But his
protest took this form: " I understand the newspapers to
say that Dreyfus has committed a crime against his country—so I understand, I pay no attention to the newspapers, I read them as I wash my hands, without finding
that it is worth my while to take any interest in what I
am doing. In any case, the crime is non-existent, your

compatriot would have committed a crime if he
rayed Judaea, but what has he to do with France?"
nted out that if there should be a war the Jews
ld be mobilised just as much as anyone else. "Per-
ps so, and I am not sure that it would not be an im-
prudence. If we bring over Senegalese and Malagasies, I
hardly suppose that their hearts will be in the task of
defending France, which is only natural. Your Dreyfus
might rather be convicted of a breach of the laws of hospitality. But we need not discuss that. Perhaps you could
ask your friend to allow me to be present at some great
festival in the Temple, at a circumcision, with Jewish
chants. He might perhaps take a hall, and give me some
biblical entertainment, as the young ladies of Saint-Cyr
performed scenes taken from the Psalms by Racine, to
amuse Louis XIV. You might even arrange parties to give
us a good laugh. For instance a battle between your friend
and his father, in which he would smite him as David
smote Goliath. That would make quite an amusing farce.
He might even, while he was about it, deal some stout
blows at his hag (or, as my old nurse would say, his
"haggart") of a mother. That would be an excellent
show, and would not be unpleasing to us, eh, my young
friend, since we like exotic spectacles, and to thrash that
non-European creature would be giving a well-earned
punishment to an old camel." As he poured out this terrible, almost insane language, M. de Charlus squeezed
my arm until it ached. I reminded myself of all that his
family had told me of his wonderful kindness to this old
nurse, whose Molieresque vocabulary he had just quoted,
and thought to myself that the connexions, hitherto, I
felt, little studied, between goodness and wickedness in the

same heart, various as they might be, would be an in
ing subject for research.

I warned him that, anyhow, Mme. Bloch no long
existed, while as for M. Bloch, I questioned to what exten
he would enjoy a sport which might easily result in his
being blinded. M. de Charlus seemed annoyed. " That,"
he said, " is a woman who made a great mistake in dying.
As for blinding him, surely the Synagogue is blind, it does
not perceive the truth of the Gospel. In any case, think,
at this moment, when all these unhappy Jews are trembling before the stupid fury of the Christians, what an
honour it would be for him to see a man like myself condescend to be amused by their sports." At this point I
caught sight of M. Bloch senior, who was coming towards
us, probably on his way to meet his son. He did not see
us, but I offered to introduce him to M. de Charlus. I
had no conception of the torrent of rage which my words
were to let loose. " Introduce him to me! But you must
have singularly little idea of social values! People do not
get to know me as easily as that. In the present instance,
the awkwardness would be twofold, on account of the
youth of the introducer and the unworthiness of the person introduced. At the most, if I am ever permitted to
enjoy the Asiatic spectacle which I suggested to you,
I might address to the horrible creature a few words
indicative of generous feeling. But on condition that he
allows himself to be thoroughly thrashed by his son. I
might go so far as to express my satisfaction." As it happened, M. Bloch paid no attention to us. He was occupied
in greeting Mme. Sazerat with a series of sweeping bows,
which were very favourably received. I was surprised at
this, for in the old days at Combray she had been indig-

my parents having young Bloch in the house, so
emitic was she then. But Dreyfusism, like a strong
of wind, had, a few days before this, wafted M. Bloch
her feet. My friend's father had found Mme. Sazerat
harming and was particularly gratified by the anti-semitism of the lady, which he regarded as a proof of the
sincerity of her faith and the soundness of her Dreyfusard
opinions, and also as enhancing the value of the call which
she had authorised him to pay her. He had not even been
offended when she had said to him stolidly: "M. Drumont
has the impudence to put the Revisionists in the same
bag as the Protestants and the Jews. A delightful promis-
cuity!" "Bernard," he had said with pride, on reaching
home, to M. Nissim Bernard, "you know, she has that
prejudice!" But M. Nissim Bernard had said nothing,
only raising his eyes to heaven in an angelic gaze. Saddened by the misfortunes of the Jews, remembering his
old friendships with Christians, grown mannered and
precious with increasing years, for reasons which the
reader will learn in due course, he had now the air of a
pre-Raphaelite ghost on to which hair had been incon-
gruously grafted, like threads in the heart of an opal.
"All this Dreyfus business," went on the Baron, still
clasping me by the arm, "has only one drawback. It de-
stroys society (I do not say polite society; society has long
ceased to deserve that laudatory epithet) by the influx of
Mr. and Mrs. Camels and Camelries and Camelyards,
astonishing creatures whom I find even in the houses of
my own cousins, because they belong to the Patrie Française, or the Anti-Jewish, or some such league, as if a
political opinion entitled one to any social qualification."
This frivolity in M. de Charlus brought out his family

398

likeness to the Duchesse de Guermantes. I rema...
him on the resemblance. As he appeared to think ...
did not know her, I reminded him of the evening at ...
Opera when he had seemed to be trying to avoid me. ...
assured me with such insistence that he had never even
seen me there that I should have begun to believe him, if
presently a trifling incident had not led me to think that
M. de Charlus, in his excessive pride perhaps, did not
care to be seen with me.

" Let us return to yourself," he said, " and my plans
for you. There exists among certain men, sir, a free-
masonry of which I cannot now say more than that it numbers in its ranks four of the reigning sovereigns of Europe.
Now, the courtiers of one of these are trying to cure him
of his fancy. That is a very serious matter, and may bring
us to war. Yes, sir, that is a fact. You remember the
story of the man who believed that he had the Princess
of China shut up in a bottle. It was a form of insanity.
He was cured of it. But as soon as he ceased to be mad
he became merely stupid. There are maladies which we
must not seek to cure because they alone protect us from
others that are more serious. A cousin of mine had
trouble with his stomach; he could not digest anything.
The most learned specialists on the stomach treated him,
with no effect. I took him to a certain doctor (another
highly interesting man, by the way, of whom I could tell
you a great deal). He guessed at once that the trouble was
nervousness; he persuaded his patient, ordered him to eat
whatever he liked quite boldly and assured him that his
digestion would stand it. But my cousin had nephritis
also. What the stomach can digest perfectly well the kidneys cease, after a time, to eliminate, and my cousin, in-

living to a good old age with an imaginary disease
stomach which obliged him to keep to a diet, died
rty with his stomach cured but his kidneys ruined.
en a very considerable advantage over people of your
ge, for all one knows, you will perhaps become what
some eminent man of the past might have been if a good
angel had revealed to him, in the midst of a humanity that
knew nothing of them, the secrets of steam and electricity.
Do not be foolish, do not refuse from discretion. Understand that, if I do you a great service, I expect my reward
from you to be no less great. It is many years now since
people in society ceased to interest me. I have but one
passion left, to seek to redeem the mistakes of my life by
conferring the benefit of my knowledge on a soul that is
still virgin and capable of being inflamed by virtue. I have
had great sorrows, sir, of which I may tell you perhaps
some day; I have lost my wife, who was the loveliest, the
noblest, the most perfect creature that one could dream
of seeing. I have young relatives who are not—I do not
say worthy, but who are not capable of accepting the moral
heritage of which I have been speaking. For all I know,
you may be he into whose hands it is to pass, he whose
life I shall be able to direct and to raise to so lofty a plane.
My own would gain in return. Perhaps in teaching you
the great secrets of diplomacy I might recover a taste
for them myself, and begin at last to do things of real
interest in which you would have an equal share. But
before I can tell I must see you often, very often, every
day."

I was thinking of taking advantage of this unexpected
kindness on M. de Charlus's part to ask him whether he
could not arrange for me to meet his sister-in-law when,

suddenly, I felt my arm violently jerked, as thoug.
electric shock. It was M. de Charlus who had hur
withdrawn his arm from mine. Although as he ta.
he had allowed his eyes to wander in all directions he h.
only just caught sight of M. d'Argencourt, who was com
ing towards us from a side street. On seeing us, M.
d'Argencourt appeared worried, cast at me a look of dis-
trust, almost that look intended for a creature of another
race than one's own with which Mme. de Guermantes had
quizzed Bloch, and tried to avoid us. But one would have
said that M. de Charlus was determined to shew him that
he was not at all anxious not to be seen by him, for he
called to him, simply to tell him something that was
of no importance. And fearing perhaps that M. d'Argencourt had not recognised me, M. de Charlus informed him
that I was a great friend of Mme. de Villeparisis, of
the Duchesse de Guermantes, of Robert de Saint-Loup,
and that he himself, Charlus, was an old friend of my
grandmother, and glad to be able to shew her grandson
a little of the affection that he felt for her. Nevertheless
I observed that M. d'Argencourt, albeit I had barely been
introduced to him at Mme. de Villeparisis's, and M. de
Charlus had now spoken to him at great length about my
family, was distinctly colder to me than he had been in
the afternoon; and for a long time he shewed the same
aloofness whenever we met. He watched me now with a
curiosity in which there was no sign of friendliness, and
seemed even to have to overcome an instinctive repul-
sion when, on leaving us, after a moment's hesitation, he
held out a hand to me which he at once withdrew.

" I am sorry about that," said M. de Charlus. " That
fellow Argencourt, well born but ill bred, more than feeble

...omat, an impossible husband, always running after ... like a person in a play, is one of those men who ...ncapable of understanding but perfectly capable of ...troying the things in life that are really great. I hope ...at our friendship will be one of them, if it is ever to be formed, and I hope also that you will honour me by keeping it—as I shall—well clear of the heels of any of those donkeys who, from idleness or clumsiness or deliberate wickedness trample upon what would seem to have been made to endure. Unfortunately, that is the mould in which most of the men one meets have been cast."

" The Duchesse de Guermantes seems to be very clever. We were talking this afternoon about the possibility of war. It appears that she is specially well informed on that subject."

"She is nothing of the sort," replied M. de Charlus tartly. "Women, and most men, for that matter, understand nothing of what I was going to tell you. My sister-in-law is a charming woman who imagines that we are still living in the days of Balzac's novels, when women had an influence on politics. Going to her house could at present have only a bad effect on you, as for that matter going anywhere. That was one of the very things I was just going to tell you when that fool interrupted me. The first sacrifice that you must make for me—I shall claim them from you in proportion to the gifts I bestow on you —is to give up going into society. It distressed me this afternoon to see you at that idiotic tea-party. You may remind me that I was there myself, but for me it was not a social gathering, it was simply a family visit. Later on, when you have established your position, if it amuses you to step down for a little into that sort of thing, it may,

perhaps, do no harm. And then, I need not point
invaluable I can be to you. The 'Open Sesame'
Guermantes house and any others that it is worth
throwing open the doors of to you, rests with me
shall be the judge, and intend to remain master of th
situation."

I thought I would take advantage of what M. de
Charlus had said about my call on Mme. de Villeparisis
to try to find out what position exactly she occupied in
society, but the question took another form on my lips
than I had intended, and I asked him instead what the
Villeparisis family was.

"That is absolutely as though you had asked me what
the Nobody family was," replied M. de Charlus. "My
aunt married, for love, a M. Thirion, who was extremely
rich, for that matter, and whose sisters had married sur-
prisingly well; and from that day onwards he called himself Marquis de Villeparisis. It did no harm to anyone,
at the most a little to himself, and very little! What his
reason was I cannot tell; I suppose he was actually a
'Monsieur de Villeparisis', a gentleman born at Villeparisis, which as you know is the name of a little place
outside Paris. My aunt tried to make out that there was
such a Marquisate in the family, she wanted to put things
on a proper footing; I can't tell you why. When one takes
a name to which one has no right it is better not to copy
the regular forms."

Mme. de Villeparisis being merely Mme. Thirion completed the fall which had begun in my estimation of her
when I had seen the composite nature of her party. I felt
it to be unfair that a woman whose title and name were
of quite recent origin should be able thus to impose upon

..poraries, with the prospect of similarly impos-
. posterity, by virtue of her friendships with royal
..ages. Now that she had become once again what I
..supposed her to be in my childhood, a person who had
..thing aristocratic about her, these distinguished kins-
..olk who gathered round her seemed to remain alien to
her. She did not cease to be charming to us all. I went
occasionally to see her and she sent me little presents from
time to time. But I had never any impression that she
belonged to the Faubourg Saint-Germain, and if I had
wanted any information about it she would have been one
of the last people to whom I should have applied.

"At present," went on M. de Charlus, "by going into
society, you will only damage your position, warp your
intellect and character. Also, you must be particularly
careful in choosing your friends. Keep mistresses, if your
family have no objection, that doesn't concern me, indeed
I can only advise it, you young rascal, young rascal who
will soon have to start shaving," he rallied me, passing his
fingers over my chin. "But the choice of your men friends
is more important. Eight out of ten young men are little
scoundrels, little wretches capable of doing you an injury
which you will never be able to repair. Wait, now, my
nephew Saint-Loup is quite a suitable companion for you,
at a pinch. As far as your future is concerned, he can be
of no possible use to you, but for that I am sufficient. And
really, when all's said and done, as a person to go about
with, at times when you have had enough of me, he does
not seem to present any serious drawback that I know of.
At any rate he is a man, not one of those effeminate
creatures one sees so many of nowadays, who look like little renters, and at any moment may bring their innocent

victims to the gallows." I did not know the me.
this slang word "renter"; anyone who had kno
would have been as greatly surprised by his use ⸱
as myself. People in society always like talking sla⸱
and people against whom certain things may be hintec
like to shew that they are not afraid to mention them.
A proof of innocence in their eyes. But they have lost
their sense of proportion, they are no longer capable of
realising the point at which a certain pleasantry will
become too technical, too shocking, will be a proof rather
of corruption than of simplicity. " He is not like the rest
of them; he has nice manners; he is really serious."

I could not help smiling at this epithet " serious ", to
which the intonation that M. de Charlus gave to it seemed
to impart the sense of "virtuous ", of " steady ", as one
says of a little shop-girl that she is " serious ". At this
moment a cab passed, zigzagging along the street; a young
cabman, who had deserted his box, was driving it from
inside, where he lay sprawling upon the cushions, apparently half drunk. M. de Charlus instantly stopped him.
The driver began to argue:

" Which way are you going? "

" Yours." This surprised me, for M. de Charlus had
already refused several cabs with similarly coloured lamps.

" Well, I don't want to get up on the box. D'you mind
if I stay down here? "

" No; but you must put down the hood. Well, think
over my proposal," said M. de Charlus, preparing to leave
me, " I give you a few days to consider my offer; write to
me. I repeat, I shall need to see you every day, and to
receive from you guarantees of loyalty, of discretion
which, for that matter, you do appear, I must say, to

But in the course of my life I have been so often …n by appearances that I never wish to trust them … Damn it, it's the least you can expect that before …ng up a treasure I should know into what hands it is …ing to pass. Very well, bear in mind what I'm offering you; you are like Hercules (though, unfortunately for yourself, you do not appear to me to have quite his muscular development) at the parting of the ways. Try not to have to regret all your life not having chosen the way that leads to virtue. Hallo!" he turned to the cabman, "haven't you put the hood down? I'll do it myself. I think, too, I'd better drive, seeing the state you appear to be in."

He jumped in beside the cabman, took the reins, and the horse trotted off.

As for myself, no sooner had I turned in at our gate than I found the pendant to the conversation which I had heard exchanged that afternoon between Bloch and M. de Norpois, but in another form, brief, inverted and cruel. This was a dispute between our butler, who believed in Dreyfus, and the Guermantes', who was an anti-Dreyfusard. The truths and counter-truths which came in conflict above ground, among the intellectuals of the rival Leagues, the Patrie Française and the Droits de l'Homme, were fast spreading downwards into the subsoil of popular opinion. M. Reinach was manipulating, by appeals to sentiment, people whom he had never seen, while for himself the Dreyfus case simply presented itself to his reason as an incontrovertible theory which he proved in the sequel by the most astonishing victory for rational policy (a victory against France, according to some) that the world has ever seen. In two years he replaced a Billot

by a Clemenceau Ministry, revolutionised public━━━
from top to bottom, took Picquart from his prisor.
stall him, ungrateful, in the Ministry of War. Perhap
rationalist manipulator of crowds was himself the pup,
of his ancestry. When we find that the systems of philo,
ophy which contain the most truths were dictated to their
authors, in the last analysis, by reasons of sentiment, how
are we to suppose that in a simple affair of politics like the
Dreyfus case reasons of this order may not, unknown to
the reasoner, have controlled his reason. Bloch believed
himself to have been led by a logical sequence to choose
Dreyfusism, yet he knew that his nose, skin and hair had
been imposed on him by his race. Doubtless the reason
enjoys more freedom; yet it obeys certain laws which it
has not prescribed for itself. The case of the Guermantes'
butler and our own was peculiar. The waves of the two
currents of Dreyfusism and anti-Dreyfusism which now
divided France from end to end were, on the whole, silent,
but the occasional echoes which they emitted were sincere.
When you heard anyone in the middle of a conversation
which was being deliberately kept off the Case announce
furtively some piece of political news, generally false, but
always with a hopefulness of its truth, you could induce
from the nature of his predictions where his heart lay.
Thus there came into conflict on certain points, on one
side a timid apostolate, on the other a righteous indignation. The two butlers whom I heard arguing as I came
in furnished an exception to the rule. Ours let it be understood that Dreyfus was guilty, the Guermantes' butler
that he was innocent. This was done not to conceal their
personal convictions, but from cunning, and in the keen-
ness of their rivalry. Our butler, being uncertain whether

..rial would be ordered, wished beforehand, in the
. failure, to deprive the Duke's butler of the joy
.ng a just cause vanquished. The Duke's butler
.ght that, in the event of a refusal, ours would be
.re indignant at the detention on the Devil's Isle of an
.nnocent man. The porter looked on. I had the impression
that it was not he who was the cause of dissension in the
Guermantes household.

I went upstairs, and found my grandmother not so well.
For some time past, without knowing exactly what was
wrong, she had been complaining of her health. It is in
moments of illness that we are compelled to recognise
that we live not alone but chained to a creature of a different kingdom, whole worlds apart, who has no knowledge of us and by whom it is impossible to make ourself
understood: our body. Say that we met a brigand by the
way; we might yet convince him by an appeal to his personal interest, if not to our own plight. But to ask pity
of our body is like discoursing before an octopus, for which
our words can have no more meaning than the sound of
the tides, and with which we should be appalled to find
ourself condemned to live. My grandmother's attacks
passed, often enough, unnoticed by the attention which she
kept always diverted to ourselves. When the pain was
severe, in the hope of curing it, she would try in vain to
understand what the trouble was. If the morbid phenomena of which her body was the theatre remained
obscure and beyond the reach of her mind, they were
clear and intelligible to certain creatures belonging to the
same natural kingdom as themselves, creatures to which
the human mind has learned gradually to have recourse
in order to understand what the body is saying to it, as

when a foreigner accosts us we try to find some
longing to his country who will act as interpreter.
can talk to our body, and tell us if its anger is seri
will soon be appeased. Cottard, whom we had called n.
see my grandmother, and who had infuriated us by aski
with a dry smile, the moment we told him that she was
ill: "Ill? You're sure it's not what they call a diplomatic illness?" tried to soothe his patient's restless-
ness by a milk diet. But incessant bowls of milk soup
gave her no relief, because my grandmother sprinkled
them liberally with salt (the toxic effects of which were as
yet, Widal not having made his discoveries, unknown).
For, medicine being a compendium of the successive and
contradictory mistakes of medical practitioners, when we
summon the wisest of them to our aid, the chances are
that we may be relying on a scientific truth the error of
which will be recognised in a few years' time. So that to
believe in medicine would be the height of folly, if not to
believe in it were not greater folly still, for from this mass
of errors there have emerged in the course of time many
truths. Cottard had told us to take her temperature. A
thermometer was fetched. Throughout almost all its
length it was clear of mercury. Scarcely could one make
out, crouching at the foot of the tube, in its little cell, the
silver salamander. It seemed dead. The glass reed was
slipped into my grandmother's mouth. We had no need
to leave it there for long; the little sorceress had not been
slow in casting her horoscope. We found her motionless,
perched half-way up her tower, and declining to move,
shewing us with precision the figure that we had asked of
her, a figure with which all the most careful examination
that my grandmother's mind could have devoted to her-

have been incapable of furnishing her; 101 For the first time we felt some anxiety. We shook —rmometer well, to erase the ominous line, as though —ere able thus to reduce the patient's fever simul- —eously with the figure shewn on the scale. Alas, it was —nly too clear that the little sibyl, unreasoning as she was, had not pronounced judgment arbitrarily, for the next day, scarcely had the thermometer been inserted between my grandmother's lips when almost at once, as though with a single bound, exulting in her certainty and in her intuition of a fact that to us was imperceptible, the little prophetess had come to a halt at the same point, in an implacable immobility, and pointed once again to that figure 101 with the tip of her gleaming wand. Nothing more did she tell us; in vain might we long, seek, pray, she was deaf to our entreaties; it seemed as though this were her final utter- ance, a warning and a menace. Then, in an attempt to con- strain her to modify her response, we had recourse to an- other creature of the same kingdom, but more potent, which is not content with questioning the body but can command it, a febrifuge of the same order as the modern aspirin, which had not then come into use. We had not shaken the thermometer down below 99.5, and hoped that it would not have to rise from there. We made my grand- mother swallow this drug and then replaced the ther- mometer in her mouth. Like an implacable warder to whom one presents a permit signed by a higher authority whose protecting influence one has sought, and who, find- ing it to be in order, replies: "Very well; I have nothing to say; if it's like that you may pass," this time the watcher in the tower did not move. But sullenly she seemed to be saying: "What use will that be to you? Since you are

friends with quinine, she may give me the or
go up, once, ten times, twenty times. And then
grow tired of telling me, I know her; get along wi.
This won't last for ever. And then you'll be a lot
off." Thereupon my grandmother felt the presence wit
her of a creature which knew the human body better tha
herself, the presence of a contemporary of the races that
have vanished from the earth, the presence of earth's first
inhabitant—long anterior to the creation of thinking man
—she felt that aeonial ally who was sounding her, a little
roughly even, in the head, the heart, the elbow; he found
out the weak places, organized everything for the prehistoric combat which began at once to be fought. In a
moment a trampled Python, the fever, was vanquished by
the potent chemical substance to which my grandmother,
across the series of kingdoms, reaching out beyond all
animal and vegetable life, would fain have been able to
give thanks. And she remained moved by this glimpse
which she had caught, through the mists of so many
centuries, of a climate anterior to the creation even of
plants. Meanwhile the thermometer, like a Weird Sister
momentarily vanquished by some more ancient god, held
motionless her silver spindle. Alas! other inferior
creatures which man has trained to the chase of the
mysterious quarry which he cannot pursue within the
pathless forest of himself, reported cruelly to us every
day a certain quantity of albumen, not large, but constant
enough for it also to appear to bear relation to some
persistent malady which we could not detect. Bergotte
had shocked that scrupulous instinct in me which made
me subordinate my intellect when he spoke to me of
Dr. du Boulbon as of a physician who would not bore

ld discover methods of treatment which, how-
ge they might appear, would adapt themselves
gularity of my mind. But ideas transform them-
n us, they overcome the resistance with which we
st meet them, and feed upon rich intellectual reserves
ch we did not know to have been prepared for them.
o, as happens whenever anything we have heard said
about some one whom we do not know has had the
faculty of awakening in us the idea of great talent, of a
sort of genius, in my inmost mind I gave Dr. du Boulbon
the benefit of that unlimited confidence which he inspires
in us who with an eye more penetrating than other men's
perceives the truth. I knew indeed that he was more of
a specialist in nervous diseases, the man to whom Charcot
before his death had predicted that he would reign supreme in neurology and psychiatry. "Ah! I don't know
about that. It's quite possible," put in Françoise, who
was in the room, and heard Charcot's name, as she heard
du Boulbon's, for the first time. But this in no way prevented her from saying "It's possible." Her "possibles",
her "perhapses", her "I don't knows" were peculiarly
irritating at such a moment. One wanted to say to her:
"Naturally you didn't know, since you haven't the faintest
idea of what we are talking about, how can you even say
whether it's possible or not; you know nothing about it.
Anyhow, you can't say now that you don't know what
Charcot said to du Boulbon. You do know because we
have just told you, and your 'perhapses' and 'possibles'
don't come in, because it's a fact."

In spite of this more special competence in cerebral and
nervous matters, as I knew that du Boulbon was a great
physician, a superior man, of a profound and inventive

intellect, I begged my mother to send for him,
hope that, by a clear perception of the malady, he
perhaps cure it, carried the day finally over the fea.
we had of (if we called in a specialist) alarming my gra
mother. What decided my mother was the fact that, e.
couraged unconsciously by Cottard, my grandmother no
longer went out of doors, and scarcely rose from her bed.
In vain might she answer us in the words of Mme. de
Sévigné's letter on Mme. de la Fayette: "Everyone said
she was mad not to wish to go out. I said to these persons,
so headstrong in their judgment: 'Mme. de la Fayette
is not mad!' and I stuck to that. It has taken her death
to prove that she was quite right not to go out." Du
Boulbon when he came decided against—if not Mme. de
Sévigné, whom we did not quote to him—my grandmother, at any rate. Instead of sounding her chest, fixing
on her steadily his wonderful eyes, in which there was
perhaps the illusion that he was making a profound
scrutiny of his patient, or the desire to give her that illusion, which seemed spontaneous but must be mechanically
produced, or else not to let her see that he was thinking
of something quite different, or simply to obtain the
mastery over her, he began talking about Bergotte.

"I should think so, indeed, he's magnificent, you are
quite right to admire him. But which of his books do you
prefer? Indeed! Well, perhaps that is the best after all.
In any case it is the best composed of his novels. Claire
is quite charming in it; of his male characters which
appeals to you most?"

I supposed at first that he was making her talk like this
about literature because he himself found medicine boring,
perhaps also to display his breadth of mind and even,

therapeutic aim, to restore confidence to his
to shew her that he was not alarmed, to take her
from the state of her health. But afterwards I
ed that, being distinguished particularly as an alienist
by his work on the brain, he had been seeking to as-
ertain by these questions whether my grandmother's
memory was in good order. As though reluctantly he
began to inquire about her past life, fixing a stern and
sombre eye on her. Then suddenly, as though catching
sight of the truth and determined to reach it at all costs,
with a preliminary rubbing of his hands, which he seemed
to have some difficulty in wiping dry of the final hesitations which he himself might feel and of all the objections
which we might have raised, looking down at my grandmother with a lucid eye, boldly and as though he were
at last upon solid ground, punctuating his words in a
quiet, impressive tone, every inflexion of which bore the
mark of intellect, he began. (His voice, for that matter,
throughout this visit remained what it naturally was,
caressing. And under his bushy brows his ironical eyes
were full of kindness.)

"You will be quite well, Madame, on the day—when it
comes, and it rests entirely with you whether it comes
to-day—on which you realise that there is nothing wrong
with you, and resume your ordinary life. You tell me that
you have not been taking your food, not going out?"

"But, sir, I have a temperature."

He laid a finger on her wrist.

"Not just now, at any rate. Besides, what an excuse!
Don't you know that we keep out in the open air and
overfeed tuberculous patients with temperatures of 102?"

"But I have a little albumen as well."

"You ought not to know anything about
have what I have had occasion to call 'mental an
We have all of us had, when we have not been ver
little albuminous phases which our doctor has done
best to make permanent by calling our attention to the
For one disorder that doctors cure with drugs (as I an
told that they do occasionally succeed in doing) they
produce a dozen others in healthy subjects by inoculating
them with that pathogenic agent a thousand times more
virulent than all the microbes in the world, the idea that
one is ill. A belief of that sort, which has a disturbing
effect on any temperament, acts with special force on
neurotic people. Tell them that a shut window is open
behind their back, they will begin to sneeze; make them
believe that you have put magnesia in their soup, they
will be seized with colic; that their coffee is stronger than
usual, they will not sleep a wink all night. Do you
imagine, Madame, that I needed to do any more than
look into your eyes, listen to the way in which you
express yourself, look, if I may say so, at this lady,
your daughter, and at your grandson, who takes so much
after you, to learn what was the matter with you?"
"Your grandmother might perhaps go and sit, if the
Doctor allows it, in some quiet path in the Champs-
Elysees, near that laurel shrubbery where you used to
play when you were little," said my mother to me, thus
indirectly consulting Dr. du Boulbon, her voice for that
reason assuming a tone of timid deference which it would
not have had if she had been addressing me alone. The
Doctor turned to my grandmother and, being apparently
as well-read in literature as in science, adjured her as
follows: "Go to the Champs-Elysées, Madame, to the

bery which your grandson loves. The laurel
nd health-giving. It purifies. After he had ex-
ed the serpent Python, it was with a bough of
in his hand that Apollo made his entry into Delphi.
ought thus to guard himself from the deadly germs
the venomous monster. So you see that the laurel is
he most ancient, the most venerable and, I will add—
what is of therapeutic as well as of prophylactic value—
the most beautiful of antiseptics."

Inasmuch as a great part of what doctors know is taught
them by the sick, they are easily led to believe that this
knowledge which patients exhibit is common to them all,
and they pride themselves on taking the patient of the
moment by surprise with some remark picked up at a
previous bedside. Thus it was with the superior smile
of a Parisian who, in conversation with a peasant, might
hope to surprise him by using suddenly a word of the
local dialect that Dr. du Boulbon said to my grandmother:
" Probably a windy night will make you sleep when the
strongest soporifics would have no effect." " On the contrary, Sir, when the wind blows I can never sleep at all."
But doctors are touchy people. " Ach! " muttered du
Boulbon, knitting his brows, as if some one had trodden
on his toe, or as if my grandmother's sleeplessness on
stormy nights were a personal insult to himself. He had
not, however, an undue opinion of himself, and since,
in his character as a " superior " person, he felt himself
bound not to put any faith in medicine, he quickly recovered his philosophic serenity.

My mother, in her passionate longing for reassurance
from Bergotte's friend, added in support of his verdict
that a first cousin of my grandmother, who suffered from

a nervous complaint, had lain for seven years
in her bedroom at Combray, without leaving her b
than once or twice a week.

"You see, Madame, I didn't know that, and y
could have told you."

"But, Sir, I am not in the least like her; on the con
trary, my doctor complains that he cannot get me to
stay in bed," said my grandmother, whether because she
was a little annoyed by the doctor's theories, or was
anxious to submit to him any objections that might be
raised to them, in the hope that he would refute these
and that, after he had gone, she would no longer find
any doubt lurking in her own mind as to the accuracy
of his encouraging diagnosis.

"Why, naturally, Madame, you cannot have all the
forms of—if you'll excuse my saying so—mania at once;
you have others, but not that particular one. Yesterday
I visited a home for neurasthenics. In the garden, I saw
a man standing on a seat, motionless as a fakir, his neck
bent in a position which must have been highly uncomfortable. On my asking him what he was doing there,
he replied, without turning his head, or moving a muscle:
'You see, Doctor, I am extremely rheumatic and catch
cold very easily; I have just been taking a lot of exercise,
and while I was getting hot, like a fool, my neck was
touching my flannels. If I move it away from my flannels
now before letting myself cool down, I am certain to get
a stiff neck, and possibly bronchitis.' Which he would, in
fact, have done. 'You're a fine specimen of neurasthenia,
that's what you are,' I told him. And do you know what
argument he advanced to prove that I was mistaken?
It was this; that while all the other patients in the place

ia for testing their weight, so much so that the
machine had to be padlocked so that they should
nd the whole day on it, he had to be lifted on to
.ily, so little did he care to be weighed. He prided
.self on not sharing the mania of the others without
.nking that he had also one of his own, and that it was
this which saved him from the other. You must not be
offended by the comparison, Madame, for the man who
dared not turn his neck for fear of catching a chill is the
greatest poet of our day. That poor maniac is the most
lofty intellect that I know. Submit to being called a
neurotic. You belong to that splendid and pitiable family
which is the salt of the earth. All the greatest things we
know have come to us from neurotics. It is they and they
only who have founded religions and created great works
of art. Never will the world be conscious of how much
it owes to them, nor above all of what they have suffered
in order to bestow their gifts on it. We enjoy fine music,
beautiful pictures, a thousand exquisite things, but we
do not know what they cost those who wrought them in
sleeplessness, tears, spasmodic laughter, rashes, asthma,
eplilepsy, a terror of death which is worse than any of
these, and which you perhaps have felt, Madame," he
added with a smile at my grandmother, " for confess now,
when I came into the room, you were not feeling very con-
fident. You thought that you were ill; dangerously ill,
perhaps. Heaven only knows what the disease was of
which you thought you had detected the symptoms. And
you were not mistaken; they were there. Neurosis has
an absolute genius for malingering. There is no illness
which it cannot counterfeit perfectly. It will produce life-
like imitations of the dilatations of dyspepsia, the sick-

nesses of pregnancy, the broken rhythm of th
the feverishness of the consumptive. If it is ca
deceiving the doctor, how should it fail to dece.
patient? No, no; you mustn't think I'm making fe
your sufferings. I should not undertake to heal th
unless I understood them thoroughly. And, well, they sa
there's no good confession unless it's mutual. I have told
you that without nervous trouble there can be no great
artist. What is more," he added, raising a solemn fore-
finger, "there can be no great scientist either. I will
go farther, and say that, unless he himself is subject to
nervous trouble, he is not, I won't say a good doctor, but
I do say the right doctor to treat nervous troubles. In
nervous pathology a doctor who doesn't say too many
foolish things is a patient half-cured, just as a critic is
a poet who has stopped writing verse and a policeman
a burglar who has retired from practice. I, Madame, I do
not, like you, fancy myself to be suffering from album-
inuria, I have not your nervous fear of food, nor of
fresh air, but I can never go to sleep without getting
out of bed at least twenty times to see if my door is shut.
And in that home where I found the poet yesterday who
would not move his neck, I had gone to secure a room,
for—this is between ourselves—I spend my holidays there
looking after myself when I have increased my own
trouble by wearing myself out in the attempt to cure
other people."

"But do you want me to take a cure like that, Sir?"
came in a frightened voice from my grandmother.

"It is not necessary, Madame. The symptoms which
you describe will vanish at my bidding. Besides, you have
with you a very efficient person whom I appoint as your

now onwards. That is your trouble itself,
activity of your nerves. Even if I knew how to
of that, I should take good care not to. All
do is to control it. I see on your table there one
ergotte's books. Cured of your neurosis you would
longer care for it. Well, I might feel it my duty to
substitute for the joys that it procures for you a nervous
stability which would be quite incapable of giving you
those joys. But those joys themselves are a strong remedy,
the strongest of all perhaps. No; I have nothing to say
against your nervous energy. All I ask is that it should
listen to me; I leave you in its charge. It must reverse
its engines. The force which it is now using to prevent
you from getting up, from taking sufficient food, let it
employ in making you eat, in making you read, in making
you go out, and in distracting you in every possible way.
You needn't tell me that you are fatigued. Fatigue is the
organic realisation of a preconceived idea. Begin by not
thinking it. And if ever you have a slight indisposition,
which is a thing that may happen to anyone, it will be just
as if you hadn't it, for your nervous energy will have
endowed you with what M. de Talleyrand, in an expression full of meaning, called 'imaginary health'. See, it
has begun to cure you already, you have been sitting up
in bed listening to me without once leaning back on your
pillows; your eye is bright, your complexion is good, I
have been talking to you for half an hour by the clock and
you have never noticed the time. Well, Madame, I shall
now bid you good-day."

When, after seeing Dr. du Boulbon to the door, I returned to the room in which my mother was by herself,
the oppression that had been weighing on me for the

last few weeks lifted, I felt that my mother w
to break out with a cry of joy and would see ι
I felt that inability to endure the suspense of the c.
moment at which a person is going to be overcome .
emotion in our presence, which in another category is
little like the thrill of fear that goes through one when
one knows that somebody is going to come in and startle
one by a door that is still closed; I tried to speak to
Mamma but my voice broke, and, bursting into tears, I
stayed for a long time, my head on her shoulder, crying,
tasting, accepting, relishing my grief, now that I knew
that it had departed from my life, as we like to exalt
ourselves by forming virtuous plans which circumstances
do not permit us to put into execution. Françoise annoyed
me by her refusal to share in our joy. She was quite overcome because there had just been a terrible scene between
the lovesick footman and the tale-bearing porter. It had
required the Duchess herself, in her unfailing benevolence,
to intervene, restore an apparent calm to the household
and forgive the footman. For she was a good mistress,
and that would have been the ideal " place " if only she
didn't listen to " stories ".

During the last few days people had begun to hear of
my grandmother's illness and to inquire for news of her.
Saint-Loup had written to me: " I do not wish to take
advantage of a time when your dear grandmother is
unwell to convey to you what is far more than mere
reproaches, on a matter with which she has no concern.
But I should not be speaking the truth were I to say to
you, even out of politeness, that I shall ever forget the
perfidy of your conduct, or that there can ever be any
forgiveness for so scoundrelly a betrayal." But some other

pposing that my grandmother was not seriously
may not even have known that she was ill at all),
ked me to meet them next day in the Champs-
ées, to go with them from there to pay a call together,
ling up with a dinner in the country, the thought of
which appealed to me. I had no longer any reason to forego
these two pleasures. When my grandmother had been
told that it was now imperative, if she was to obey Dr.
du Boulbon's orders, that she should go out as much as
possible, she had herself at once suggested the Champs-
Elysées. It would be easy for me to escort her there;
and, while she sat reading, to arrange with my friends
where I should meet them later; and I should still be in
time, if I made haste, to take the train with them to
Ville d'Avray. When the time came, my grandmother did
not want to go out; she felt tired. But my mother, acting
on du Boulbon's instructions, had the strength of mind
to be firm and to insist on obedience. She was almost
in tears at the thought that my grandmother was going
to relapse again into her nervous weakness, which she
might never be able to shake off. Never again would
there be such a fine, warm day for an outing. The sun
as it moved through the sky interspersed here and there
in the broken solidity of the balcony its unsubstantial
muslins, and gave to the freestone ledge a warm epidermis,
an indefinite halo of gold. As Françoise had not had time
to send a " tube " to her daughter, she left us immediately
after luncheon. She very kindly consented, however, to
call first at Jupien's, to get a stitch put in the cloak which
my grandmother was going to wear. Returning at that
moment from my morning walk I accompanied her into
the shop. " Is it your young master who brings you here,"

Jupien asked Françoise, "is it you who are br⌐
to see me, or is it some good wind and fortu⌐
bring you both?" For all his want of education, ⌐
respected the laws of grammar as instinctively as M⌐
Guermantes, in spite of every effort, broke them. W⌐
Françoise gone and the cloak mended, it was time foi
my grandmother to get ready. Having obstinately refused
to let Mamma stay in the room with her, she took, left
to herself, an endless time over her dressing, and now
that I knew her to be quite well, with that strange indifference which we feel towards our relatives so long as
they are alive, which makes us put everyone else before
them, I felt it to be very selfish of her to take so long,
to risk making me late when she knew that I had an
appointment with my friends and was dining at Ville
d'Avray. In my impatience I finally went downstairs
without waiting for her, after I had twice been told that
she was just ready. At last she joined me, without apol-
ogising to me, as she generally did, for having kept me
waiting, flushed and bothered like a person who has come
to a place in a hurry and has forgotten half her belong-
ings, just as I was reaching the half-opened glass door
which, without warming them with it in the least, let
in the liquid, throbbing, tepid air from the street (as
though the sluices of a reservoir had been opened) between the frigid walls of the passage.

"Oh, dear, if you're going to meet your friends I
ought to have put on another cloak. I look rather poverty-
stricken in this one."

I was startled to see her so flushed, and supposed that
having begun by making herself late she had had to hurry
over her dressing. When we left the cab at the end of

… Gabriel, in the Champs-Elysées, I saw my
…her, without a word to me, turn aside and make
… y to the little old pavilion with its green trellis,
… door of which I had once waited for Françoise. The
… ne park-keeper who had been standing there then was
…ill talking to Françoise's " Marquise " when, following
my grandmother who, doubtless because she was feeling
sick, had her hand in front of her mouth, I climbed the
steps of that little rustic theatre, erected there among the
gardens. At the entrance, as in those circus booths where
the clown, dressed for the ring and smothered in flour,
stands at the door and takes the money himself for the
seats, the " Marquise ", at the receipt of custom, was still
there in her place with her huge, uneven face smeared
with a coarse plaster and her little bonnet of red flowers and black lace surmounting her auburn wig. But I
do not suppose that she recognised me. The park-keeper,
abandoning his watch over the greenery, with the colour
of which his uniform had been designed to harmonise,
was talking to her, on a chair by her side.

" So you're still here? " he was saying. " You don't
think of retiring? "

" And what have I to retire for, Sir? Will you kindly
tell me where I shall be better off than here, where I
should live more at my ease, and with every comfort?
And then there's all the coming and going, plenty of
distraction; my little Paris, I call it; my customers keep
me in touch with everything that's going on. Just to
give you an example, there's one of them who went out
not more than five minutes ago; he's a magistrate, in
the very highest position there is. Very well, Sir," she
cried with ardour, as though prepared to maintain the

truth of this assertion by violence, should the
civic authority shew any sign of challenging its a
" for the last eight years, do you follow me, eve.
God has made, regularly on the stroke of three
been here, always polite, never saying one word lou.
than another, never making any mess; and he stay
half an hour and more to read his papers and do his
little jobs. There was one day he didn't come. I never
noticed it at the time, but that evening, all of a sudden
I said to myself: 'Why, that gentleman never came to-
day; perhaps he's dead!' And that gave me a regular
turn, you know, because, of course, I get quite fond of
people when they behave nicely. And so I was very
glad when I saw him come in again next day, and I
said to him : 'I hope nothing happened to you yesterday,
Sir ? ' And he told me that nothing had happened to him,
that it was his wife that had died, and it had given him
such a turn he hadn't been able to come. He had that
really sad look, you know, people have when they've
been married five-and-twenty years, and then the parting,
but he seemed pleased, all the same, to be back here.
You could see that all his little habits had been quite
upset. I did what I could to make him feel at home.
I said to him : 'You mustn't let go of things, Sir. Just
come here the same as before, it will be a little distraction
for you in your sorrow.' "

The " Marquise " resumed a gentler tone, for she had
observed that the guardian of groves and lawns was
listening to her complacently and with no thought of contradiction, keeping harmlessly in its scabbard a sword
which looked more like a horticultural implement or some
symbol of a garden-god.

sides," she went on, " I choose my customers,
everyone into my little parlours, as I call them.
esn't the place just look like a parlour with all
wers? Such friendly customers I have; there's al-
some one or other brings me a spray of nice lilac,
jessamine or roses; my favourite flowers, roses are."

The thought that we were perhaps despised by this
lady because we never brought any sprays of lilac or fine
roses to her bower made me redden, and in the hope of
making a bodily escape—or of being condemned only by
default—from an adverse judgment, I moved towards
the exit. But it is not always in this world the people who
brings us fine roses to whom we are most friendly, for the
" Marquise ", thinking that I was bored, turned to me:

" You wouldn't like me to open a little place for you?"

And, on my declining:

" No? You're sure you won't? " she persisted, smiling.
" Well, just as you please. You're welcome to it, but I
know quite well, not having to pay for a thing won't make
you want to do it if you don't want to."

At this moment a shabbily dressed woman hurried into
the place who seemed to be feeling precisely the want in
question. But she did not belong to the " Marquise's "
world, for the latter, with the ferocity of a snob, flung at
her:

" I've nothing disengaged, Ma'am."

" Will they be long? " asked the poor lady, reddening
beneath the yellow flowers in her hat.

" Well, Ma'am, if you'll take my advice, you'll try
somewhere else; you see, there are still these two gentlemen waiting, and I've only one closet; the others are out
of order."

"Not much money there," she explained whe[n]
had gone. "It's not the sort we want here, eithe[r]
not clean, don't treat the place with respect, it w[ould be]
your humble here that would have to spend the [best]
hour cleaning up after her ladyship. I'm not sorry to [see]
her penny."

Finally my grandmother emerged, and feeling that she
probably would not seek to atone by a lavish gratuity
for the indiscretion that she had shewn by remaining
so long inside, I beat a retreat, so as not to have to share
in the scorn which the "Marquise" would no doubt heap
on her, and began strolling along a path, but slowly, so
that my grandmother should not have to hurry to overtake me; as presently she did. I expected her to begin:
"I am afraid I've kept you waiting; I hope you'll still
be in time for your friends," but she did not utter a single
word, so much so that, feeling a little hurt, I was dis-
inclined to speak first; until looking up at her I noticed
that as she walked beside me she kept her face turned
the other way. I was afraid that her heart might be
troubling her again. I studied her more carefully and
was struck by the disjointedness of her gait. Her hat was
crooked, her cloak stained; she had the confused and
worried look, the flushed, slightly dazed face of a person
who has just been knocked down by a carriage or pulled
out of a ditch.

"I was afraid you were feeling sick, Grandmamma;
are you feeling better now?" I asked her.

Probably she thought that it would be impossible for
her, without alarming me, not to make some answer.

"I heard the whole of her conversation with the
keeper," she told me. "Could anything have been more

e Guermantes, or the Verdurins and their
? Heavens, what fine language she put it all
d she quoted, with deliberate application, this
e from her own special Marquise, Mme. de
né: "As I listened to them I thought that they were
paring for me the pleasures of a farewell."

Such was the speech that she made me, a speech into
which she had put all her critical delicacy, her love of
quotations, her memory of the classics, more thoroughly
even than she would naturally have done, and as though
to prove that she retained possession of all these faculties.
But I guessed rather than heard what she said, so in-
audible was the voice in which she muttered her sentences,
clenching her teeth more than could be accounted for by
the fear of being sick again.

"Come!" I said lightly, so as not to seem to be
taking her illness too seriously, "since your heart is
bothering you, shall we go home now? I don't want
to trundle a grandmother with indigestion about the
Champs-Elysées."

"I didn't like to suggest it, because of your friends,"
she replied. "Poor boy! But if you don't mind, I think
it would be wiser."

I was afraid of her noticing the strange way in which
she uttered these words. "Come!" I said to her sharply,
"you mustn't tire yourself talking; if your heart is bad,
it's silly; wait till we get home."

She smiled at me sorrowfully and gripped my hand.
She had realised that there was no need to hide from me
what I had at once guessed, that she had had a slight
stroke.